*With the fall of Coruscant and
a New Republic in turmoil,
a lost hero returns,
hoping to stem the tide of
sabotage and betrayal. . . .*

Other books by Walter Jon Williams

Novels:
AMBASSADOR OF PROGRESS
KNIGHT MOVES
HARDWIRED
VOICE OF THE WHIRLWIND
ANGEL STATION
ELEGY FOR ANGELS AND DOGS
DAYS OF ATONEMENT
ARISTOI
METROPOLITAN
CITY ON FIRE
THE RIFT

Divertimenti:
THE CROWN JEWELS
HOUSE OF SHARDS
ROCK OF AGES

Collections:
FACETS
FRANKENSTEINS AND FOREIGN DEVILS

Coming soon:
THE PRAXIS

STAR WARS

THE NEW JEDI ORDER

DESTINY'S WAY

WALTER JON WILLIAMS

arrow books

Published by Arrow Books in 2003

1 3 5 7 9 0 8 6 4 2

First published in the United Kingdom in 2002 by Century Books

Arrow Books
The Random House Group Limited
20 Vauxhall Bridge Road, London, SW1V 2SA

Random House Australia (Pty) Limited
20 Alfred Street, Milsons Point, Sydney,
New South Wales 2061, Australia

Random House New Zealand Limited
18 Poland Road, Glenfield
Auckland 10, New Zealand

Random House (Pty) Limited
Endulini, 5a Jubilee Road, Parktown 2193, South Africa

The Random House Group Limited Reg. No. 954009

www.starwars.com
www.starwarskids.com
www.randomhouse.co.uk

A CIP catalogue record for this book is available from the British Library
Papers used by Random House are natural, recyclable products made from
wood grown in sustainable forests. The manufacturing processes conform to
the environmental regulations of the country of origin

Printed and bound in Great Britain by
Bookmarque Ltd, Croydon, Surrey

ISBN 0 09 941047 8

For Kathleen Hedges

And with thanks to so many who helped: Daniel Abraham, Terry Boren, George R. R. Martin, Shelly Shapiro, Steve and Jan Stirling, Sue Rostoni, Sally Gwylan, Melinda Snodgrass, Terry England, Yvonne Coats, and Trent Zelazny. And special thanks to Spenser Ruppert for his encyclopedic knowledge of the *Star Wars* universe.

THE STAR WARS NOVELS TIMELINE

6.5-7.5 YEARS AFTER
STAR WARS: A New Hope

X-Wing:
Rogue Squadron
Wedge's Gamble
The Krytos Trap
The Bacta War
Wraith Squadron
Iron Fist
Solo Command

8 YEARS AFTER STAR WARS: A New Hope

The Courtship of Princess Leia
A Forest Apart
Tatooine Ghost

9 YEARS AFTER STAR WARS: A New Hope

The Thrawn Trilogy:
Heir to the Empire
Dark Force Rising
The Last Command

X-Wing: Isard's Revenge

11 YEARS AFTER STAR WARS: A New Hope

I, Jedi

The Jedi Academy Trilogy:
Jedi Search
Dark Apprentice
Champions of the Force

12-13 YEARS AFTER STAR WARS: A New Hope

Children of the Jedi
Darksaber
Planet of Twilight
X-Wing: Starfighters of Adumar

14 YEARS AFTER STAR WARS: A New Hope

The Crystal Star

16-17 YEARS AFTER STAR WARS: A New Hope

The Black Fleet Crisis Trilogy:
Before the Storm
Shield of Lies
Tyrant's Test

17 YEARS AFTER STAR WARS: A New Hope

18 YEARS AFTER STAR WARS: A New Hope

The Corellian Trilogy:
Ambush at Corellia
Assault at Selonia
Showdown at Centerpoint

19 YEARS AFTER STAR WARS: A New Hope

The Hand of Thrawn Duology:
Specter of the Past
Vision of the Future

22 YEARS AFTER STAR WARS: A New Hope

Junior Jedi Knights series

23-24 YEARS AFTER STAR WARS: A New Hope

Young Jedi Knights series

25-30 YEARS AFTER
STAR WARS: A New Hope

The New Jedi Order:
Vector Prime
Dark Tide I: Onslaught
Dark Tide II: Ruin
Agents of Chaos I: Hero's Trial
Agents of Chaos II: Jedi Eclipse
Balance Point
Recovery
Edge of Victory I: Conquest
Edge of Victory II: Rebirth
Star by Star
Dark Journey
Enemy Lines I: Rebel Dream
Enemy Lines II: Rebel Stand
Traitor
Destiny's Way
Ylesia
Force Heretic I: Remnant
Force Heretic II: Refugee
Force Heretic III: Reunion

UNKNOWN REGIONS
SSI-RÜUK STAR CLUSTER
BAKURA
ENDOR
BESPIN
HOTH
BORLEIAS
CORUSCANT
KOORNACHT CLUSTER
CORE WORLDS
DEEP CORE
FONDOR
INNER RIM
DURO
COLONIES
CORELLIAN TRADE SPINE
YAG'DHUL
TYNNA
EXPANSION REGION
RIMMA TRADE ROUTE
FALLEEN
RODIA
ANDO
NABOO
SULLUST
ELROOD SECTOR
DAGOBAH
KATHOL SECTOR
MINOS CLUSTER
CORELLIAN RUN

EMPIRE
BASTION
BELKADAN
HELSKA
TINGEL ARM
DUBRILLION
DANTOOINE
BIMMIEL
ORD BINIR
AGAMAR
DATHOMIR
CORPORATE SECTOR
YAVIN
ITHOR
MERIDIAN SECTOR
WAYLAND
MYRKR
OSSUS
OBROA-SKAI
TION CLUSTER
HAPES CLUSTER
CRON DRIFT
KASHYYYK
BIMMISAARI
KUBINDI
KESSEL
HUTT SPACE
YLESIA
NAL HUTTA
RIM
GAMORR

DRAMATIS PERSONAE

Admiral Ackbar; retired military officer (male Mon Calamari)
Nom Anor; executor (male Yuuzhan Vong)
Kyp Durron; Jedi Master (male human)
Jakan; high priest (male Yuuzhan Vong)
Traest Kre'fey; military officer (male Bothan)
Tsavong Lah; warmaster (male Yuuzhan Vong)
Lowbacca; Jedi Knight (male Wookiee)
Ayddar Nylykerka; director of intelligence (male Tammarian)
Cal Omas; politician (male Alderaanian human)
Onimi; Shamed One (male Yuuzhan Vong)
Danni Quee; scientist (female human)
Fyor Rodan; politician (male human)
Dif Scaur; director of intelligence (male human)
Supreme Overlord Shimrra (male Yuuzhan Vong)
Luke Skywalker; Jedi Master (male human)
Mara Jade Skywalker; Jedi Master (female human)
Han Solo; captain, *Millennium Falcon* (male human)
Jacen Solo; Jedi Knight (male human)
Jaina Solo; Jedi Knight (female human)
Princess Leia Organa Solo; diplomat (female human)
Sien Sovv; military officer (male Sullustan)
Tahiri Veila; Jedi Knight (human female)
Vergere (female Fosh)
Nen Yim; shaper (female Yuuzhan Vong)

They appeared without warning from beyond the edge of galactic space: a warrior race called the Yuuzhan Vong, armed with surprise, treachery, and a bizarre organic technology that proved a match—too often more than a match—for the New Republic and its allies. Even the Jedi, under the leadership of Luke Skywalker, found themselves thrown on the defensive, deprived of their greatest strength. For somehow, inexplicably, the Yuuzhan Vong seemed to be utterly devoid of the Force.

Despite an initial victory, the New Republic forces lost more than they won. Countless worlds were devastated, countless beings killed—among them the Wookiee Chewbacca, loyal friend and partner of Han Solo, and later Anakin Solo, Han and Leia's younger son. The only ray of light in the darkness was the birth of Luke and Mara's son, Ben Skywalker.

The New Republic unraveled a little more with each setback. Even the Jedi began to splinter under the strain, especially as the Yuuzhan Vong turned their attention to hunting down Jedi in particular. The fall of the capital world of Coruscant, and the capture of Jacen Solo sent hopes plummeting— and sent Jacen's twin sister Jaina spiraling downward into revenge and retribution.

Scattered after the fall of Coruscant, the panic-stricken surviving members of the New Republic Advisory Council struggled to save themselves, pausing only long enough to set up what was intended to be a mock defense on the planet Borleias—an attempt to buy time that fooled no one, least of all the Jedi. Under the command of Wedge Antilles and Luke Skywalker, the Borleias defense succeeded against all odds, a victory—if a small one—at last for the New Republic.

Meanwhile, the missing Jacen Solo was undergoing the education of a lifetime at the hands of Vergere, a fascinating creature whose loyalties were a mystery and whose powers were beyond compare. In doing so, he discovered the key both to sabotaging the efforts of the enemy to reshape Coruscant into the image of their legendary homeworld, Yuuzhan'tar, and to finding the Yuuzhan Vong in the Force. Now, at last, as the tattered New Republic works to build on its recent victory and readies itself to strike back at the Yuuzhan Vong, a changed Jacen is on his way home . . .

ONE

As she sat in the chair that was hers by right of death, she raised her eyes to the cold faraway stars. Checklists buzzed distantly in her mind and her hands moved over the controls, but her thoughts flew elsewhere, amid the chill infinitude. Searching . . .

Nothing.

Her gaze fell and there she saw, on the controls at the adjacent pilot's seat, her husband's hands. She drew comfort from the sight, from the sureness and power she knew was there, in those strong hands.

Her heart leapt. Something, somewhere in all those stars, had touched her.

She thought: *Jacen!*

Her husband's hands touched controls and the stars streamed away, turned to bleeding smears of light as if seen through beaten rain, and the distant touch vanished.

"Jacen," she said, and then, at her husband's startled look, at the surprise and pain in his brown eyes, "Jacen."

"And you're sure?" Han Solo said. "You're sure it was Jacen?"

"Yes. Reaching out to me. I felt him. It could have been no one else."

"And he's alive."

"Yes."

Leia Organa Solo could read him so well. She knew that

1

Han believed their son dead, but that he tried, for her sake, to pretend otherwise. She knew that, fierce with grief and with guilt for having withdrawn from his family, he would support her in anything now, even if he believed it was delusional. And she knew the strength it took for him to suppress his own pain and doubt.

She could read all that in him, in the flicker of his eye, the twitch of his cheek. She could read him, read the bravery and the uncertainty, and she loved him for both.

"It was Jacen," she said. She put as much confidence in her tone as she could, all her assurance. "He was reaching out to me through the Force. I felt him. He wanted to tell me he was alive and with friends." She reached over and took his hand. "There's no doubt, now. Not at all."

Han's fingers tightened on hers, and she sensed the struggle in him, desire for hope warring with his own bitter experience.

His brown eyes softened. "Yes," he said. "Of course. I believe you."

There was a hint of reserve there, of caution, but that was reflex, the result of a long and uncertain life that had taught him to believe nothing until he'd seen it with his own eyes.

Leia reached for him, embraced him awkwardly from the copilot's seat. His arms went around her. She felt the bristle of his cheek against hers, inhaled the scent of his body, his hair.

A bubble of happiness grew in her, burst into speech. "Yes, Han," she said. "Our son is alive. And so are we. Be joyful. Be at peace. Everything changes from now on."

The idyll lasted until Han and Leia walked hand in hand into the *Millennium Falcon*'s main hold. Through the touch, Leia felt the slight tension of Han's muscles as he came in sight of their guest—an Imperial commander in immaculate dress grays.

Han, Leia knew, had hoped that this mission would provide a chance for the two of them to be alone. Through the many months since the war with the Yuuzhan Vong had begun, they had either been apart or dealing with a bewildering succession of crises. Even though their current mission was no less urgent than the others, they would have treasured this time alone in hyperspace.

They had even left Leia's Noghri bodyguards behind. Neither of them had wanted any passengers at all, let alone an Imperial officer. Thus far Han had managed to be civil about it, but only just.

The commander rose politely to her feet. "An exceptionally smooth transition into hyperspace, Captain Solo," she said. "For a ship with such—such *heterogeneous* components, such a transition speaks well of the ship's captain and his skills."

"Thanks," Han said.

"The Myomar shields are superb, are they not?" she said. "One of our finer designs."

The problem with Commander Vana Dorja, Leia thought, was that she was simply too observant. She was a woman of about thirty, the daughter of the captain of a Star Destroyer, with bobbed dark hair tucked neatly into her uniform cap, and the bland, pleasant face of a professional diplomat. She had been on Coruscant during its fall, allegedly negotiating some kind of commercial treaty, purchasing Ulban droid brains for use in Imperial hydroponics farms. The negotiations were complicated by the fact that the droid brains in question could equally well be used for military purposes.

The negotiations regarding the brains' end-use certificates had gone nowhere in particular, but perhaps they had been intended to go nowhere. What Commander Dorja's extended stay on Coruscant had done was to make her a close observer in the Yuuzhan Vong assault that had resulted in the planet's fall.

Vana Dorja had gotten off Coruscant somehow—Leia

had no doubt that her escape had been planned long in advance—and she had then turned up at Mon Calamari, the new provisional capital, blandly asking for help in returning to Imperial space just at the moment at which Leia had been assigned a diplomatic mission to that selfsame Empire.

Of course it wasn't a coincidence. Dorja was clearly a spy operating under commercial cover. But what could Leia do? The New Republic might need the help of the Empire, and the Empire might be offended if its commercial representative were needlessly delayed in her return.

What Leia *could* do was establish some ground rules concerning where on the *Falcon* Commander Dorja could go, and where was strictly off limits. Dorja had agreed immediately to the restrictions, and agreed as well to be scanned for any technological or other secrets she might be smuggling out.

Nothing had turned up on the scan. Of course. If Vana Dorja was carrying any vital secrets to her masters in the Empire, she was carrying them locked in her all-too-inquisitive brain.

"Please sit down," Leia said.

"Your Highness is kind," Dorja said, and lowered her stocky body into a chair. Leia sat across the table from her, and observed the half-empty glass of juri juice set before the commander.

"Threepio is providing sufficient refreshment?" Leia asked.

"Yes. He is very efficient, though a trifle talkative."

Talkative? Leia thought. *What's Threepio been telling the woman?*

Blast it anyway. Dorja was all too skilled at creating these unsettling moments.

"Shall we dine?" Leia asked.

Dorja nodded, bland as always. "As Your Highness wishes." But then she proved useful in the galley, assisting Han and Leia as they transferred to plates the meal that had been cooking in the *Falcon*'s automatic ovens. As Han sat down with his plates, C-3PO contemplated the table.

"Sir," he said. "A Princess and former Chief of State takes precedence, of course, over both a captain and an Imperial commander. But a commander—forgive me—does not take precedence over a New Republic *general*, even one on the inactive list. General Solo, if you would be so kind as to sit above Commander Dorja?"

Han gave C-3PO a baleful look. "I like it fine where I am," he said. Which was, of course, as far away from the Imperial commander as the small table permitted.

C-3PO looked as distressed as it was possible for a droid with an immobile face to look. "But sir—the rules of precedence—"

"I like it where I am," Han said, more firmly.

"But sir—"

Leia slid into her accustomed role as Han's interpreter to the world. "We'll dine informally, Threepio," she told the droid.

C-3PO's tone allowed his disappointment to show. "Very well, Your Highness," he said.

Poor 3PO, Leia thought. Here he was designed for working out rules of protocol for state banquets involving dozens of species and hundreds of governments, interpreting and smoothing disputes, and instead she persisted in getting him into situations where he kept getting shot at. And now the galaxy was being invaded by beings who had marked for extermination every droid in existence—and they were *winning*. Whatever C-3PO had for nerves must be shot.

Lots of formal dinner parties when this is over, Leia decided. *Nice, soothing dinner parties, without assassins, quarrels, or lightsaber fights.*

"I thank you again for your offer of transit to the Empire," Dorja said later, after the soup course. "It was fortunate that you have business there."

"Very fortunate," Leia agreed.

"Your mission to the Empire must be critical," Dorja probed, "to take you from the government at such a crucial time."

"I'm doing what I do best."

"But you were Chief of State—surely you must be considering a return to power."

Leia shook her head. "I served my term."

"To voluntarily relinquish power—I confess I don't understand it." Dorja shook her head. "In the Empire, we are taught not to decline responsibility once it is given to us."

Leia sensed Han's head lifting as he prepared to speak. She knew him well enough to anticipate the sense of any remarks. *No,* he would say, *Imperial leaders generally stay in their seats of power until they're blasted out by laser cannons.* Before Han could speak, she phrased a more diplomatic answer.

"Wisdom is knowing when you've given all you can," she said, and turned her attention to her dinner, a fragrant breast of hibbas with a sauce of bofa fruit.

Dorja picked up her fork, held it over her plate. "But surely—with the government in chaos, and driven into exile—a strong hand is needed."

"We have constitutional means for choosing a new leader," Leia reassured. And thought, *Not that they're working so far, with Pwoe proclaiming himself Chief of State with the Senate deadlocked on Mon Calamari.*

"I wish you a smooth transition," Commander Dorja said. "Let's hope the hesitation and chaos with which the New Republic has met its current crisis was the fault of Borsk Fey'lya's government, and not symptomatic of the New Republic as a whole."

"I'll drink to that," Han proclaimed, and drained his glass.

"I can't help but wonder how the old Empire would have

handled the crisis," Dorja continued. "I hope you will forgive my partisan attitude, but it seems to me that the Emperor would have mobilized his entire armament at the first
threat, and dealt with the Yuuzhan Vong in an efficient and
expeditious manner, through the use of overwhelming force.
Certainly better than Borsk Fey'lya's policy—if I understood
it correctly *as* a policy—of negotiating with the invaders at
the same time as he was fighting them, sending signals of
weakness to a ruthless enemy who used negotiation only as
a cover for further conquests."

It was growing very hard, Leia thought, to maintain the
diplomatic smile on her face. "The Emperor," she said, "was
always alert to any threat to his power."

Leia sensed Han about to speak, and this time was too
late to stop his words.

"That's not what the Empire would have done, Commander," Han said. "What the Empire would have done
was build a supercolossal Yuuzhan Vong–killing battle machine. They would have called it the Nova Colossus or the
Galaxy Destructor or the Nostril of Palpatine or something
equally grandiose. They would have spent billions of credits, employed thousands of contractors and subcontractors,
and equipped it with the latest in death-dealing technology.
And you know what would have happened? *It wouldn't
have worked.* They'd forget to bolt down a metal plate over
an access hatch leading to the main reactors, or some other
mistake, and a hotshot enemy pilot would drop a bomb
down there and *blow the whole thing up.* Now *that's* what
the Empire would have done."

Leia, striving to contain her laughter, detected what might
have been amusement in Vana Dorja's brown eyes.

"Perhaps you're right," Dorja conceded.

"You're right I'm right, Commander," Han said, and
poured himself a glass of water.

His brief triumph was interrupted by a sudden shriek from

the *Falcon*'s hyperdrive units. The ship shuddered. Proximity alarms wailed.

Leia, her heart beating in synchrony to the blaring alarms, stared into Han's startled brown eyes. Han turned to Commander Dorja.

"Sorry to interrupt dinner just as it was getting interesting," he said, "but I'm afraid we've got to blow some bad guys into small pieces."

The first thing Han Solo did when he scrambled into the pilot's seat was to shut off the blaring alarms that were rattling his brain around inside his skull. Then he looked out the cockpit windows. The stars, he saw, had returned to their normal configuration—the *Millennium Falcon* had been yanked out of hyperspace. And Han had a good idea why, an idea that a glance at the sensor displays served only to confirm. He turned to Leia as she scrambled into the copilot's chair.

"Either a black hole has materialized in this sector, or we've hit a Yuuzhan Vong mine." A dovin basal to be precise, an organic gravitic-anomaly generator that the Yuuzhan Vong used for both propelling their vessels and warping space around them. The Yuuzhan Vong had been seeding dovin basal mines along New Republic trade routes in order to drag unsuspecting transports out of hyperspace and into an ambush. But their mining efforts hadn't extended this far along the Hydian Way, at least not until now.

And there, Han saw in the displays, were the ambushers. Two flights of six coralskippers each, one positioned on either side of the dovin basal in order to intercept any unsuspecting transport.

He reached for the controls, then hesitated, wondering if Leia should pilot while he ran for the turbolaser turret. No, he thought, he knew the *Millennium Falcon*, her capabilities, and her crotchets better than anyone, and good piloting was going to get them out of this trouble more than good shooting.

"I'd better fly this one," he said. "You take one of the quad lasers." Regretting, as he spoke, that he wouldn't get to blow things up, something always good for taking his mind off his troubles.

Leia bent to give him a quick kiss on the cheek. "Good luck, Slick," she whispered, then squeezed his shoulder and slid silently out of the cockpit.

"Good luck yourself," Han said. "And find out if our guest is qualified to take the other turret."

His eyes were already scanning the displays as he automatically donned the comlink headset that would allow him to communicate with Leia at the laser cannon. Coralskippers weren't hyperspace capable, so some larger craft had to have dropped them here. Was that ship still around, or had it moved on to lay another mine somewhere else?

It had gone, apparently. There was no sign of it on the displays.

The Yuuzhan Vong craft were just now beginning to react to his arrival—so much for the hope that the *Millennium Falcon*'s stealth capabilities would have kept her from being detected.

But *what*, he considered, had the enemy seen? A Corellian Engineering YT-1300 freighter, similar to hundreds of other small freighters they must have encountered. The Yuuzhan Vong wouldn't have seen the *Falcon*'s armament, her advanced shields, or the modifications to her sublight drives that could give even the swift coralskippers a run for their money.

So the *Millennium Falcon* should continue, as far as the Yuuzhan Vong were concerned, to look like an innocent freighter.

While he watched the Yuuzhan Vong maneuver, Han broadcast to the enemy a series of queries and demands for information of the sort that might come from a nervous civilian pilot. He conducted a series of basic maneuvers designed to keep the coralskippers at a distance, maneuvers as sluggish and hesitant as if he were a fat, nervous freighter loaded with cargo. The nearest flight of coralskippers set on a basic intercept course, not even bothering to deploy into military formation. The farthest flight, on the other side of the dovin basal mine, began a slow loop toward the *Falcon*, to support the others.

Now *that* was interesting. In a short while they would have the dovin basal singularity between themselves and the *Falcon*, with the mine's gravity-warping capabilities making it very difficult for them to see the *Falcon* or to detect any changes in her course.

"Captain Solo?" A voice on the comlink intruded on his thoughts. "This is Commander Dorja. I'm readying the weapons in the dorsal turret."

"Try not to blow off the sensor dish," Han told her.

He looked at the displays, saw the far-side squadron nearing eclipse behind the distorting gravity mine. His hands closed on the controls, and he altered course directly for the dovin basal just as he gave full power to the sublight drives.

The gravity mine was now between the *Millennium Falcon* and the far-side flight of coralskippers. The gravity warp surrounding the dovin basal would make it nearly impossible to detect the *Falcon*'s change of course.

"We have about three standard minutes to contact with the enemy," he said into the comlink headset. "Fire dead ahead, on my mark."

"Dead ahead?" came Dorja's bland voice. "How unorthodox . . . have you considered *maneuver*?"

"Don't second-guess the pilot!" Leia's voice snapped like a whip. "Keep this channel clear unless you have something of value to say!"

"Apologies," Dorja murmured.

Han bit back his own annoyance. He glanced at the empty copilot's chair—Chewbacca's place, now Leia's—and found himself wishing that he was in the second laser cockpit, with Chewbacca in the pilot's seat. But Chewie was gone, the first of the deaths that had struck him to the heart. Chewbacca dead, his younger son Anakin killed, his older son Jacen missing, presumed dead by everyone except Leia . . . Death had been haunting his footsteps, on the verge of claiming everyone around him.

That was why he hadn't accepted Waroo's offer to assume Chewbacca's life debt. He simply hadn't wanted to be responsible for the death of another friend.

But now Leia believed that Jacen was alive. This wasn't a vague hope based on a mother's desire to see her son again, as Han had earlier suspected, but a sending through the Force, a message aimed at Leia herself.

Han had no direct experience of the Force himself, but he knew he could trust Leia not to misread it. His son was alive.

So maybe Death wasn't following him so closely after all. Or maybe Han had just outrun him.

Stay alert, he told himself. *Stay strong. You may* not *have to die today.*

Cold determination filled him.

Make the Yuuzhan Vong pay instead, he thought.

He made a last scan of the displays. The near-side flight had turned to pursue, dividing into two V formations of three coralskippers each. They hadn't reacted very quickly to his abrupt change of course, so Han figured he wasn't dealing with a genius commander here, which was good.

It was impossible to see the far-side flight on the other side of the gravity-distorting mine, but he had a good read on their trajectory, and there hadn't been any reason for them to change it.

The dovin basal swept closer. The *Falcon*'s spars moaned as they felt the tug of its gravity.

"Ten seconds," Han told Leia and Dorja, and reached for the triggers to the concussion missile launchers.

Anticipation drew a metallic streak down his tongue. He felt a prickle of sweat on his scalp.

"Five." He triggered the first pair of concussion missiles, knowing that, unlike the laser cannon, they did not strike at the speed of light.

"Two." Han triggered another pair of missiles. The *Millennium Falcon*'s engines howled as they fought the pull of the dovin basal's gravity.

"Fire." The dovin basal swept past, and suddenly the display lit with the six approaching coralskippers. The combined power of the eight lasers fired straight at them.

The six coralskippers had also split into two Vs of three craft each, the formations on slightly diverging courses, but both formations were running into the *Falcon* and her armament at a combined velocity of better than 90 percent of the speed of light. None of them had shifted their dovin basals to warp space defensively ahead of them, and the pilots had only an instant to perceive the doom staring them in the face, and no time to react. The first formation ran right into the first pair of missiles and the turbolaser fire, and all three erupted in fire as their coral hulls shattered into fragments.

The second formation, diverging, was not so suitably placed. One coralskipper was hit by a missile and pinwheeled off into the darkness, trailing flame. Another ran into a burst of laser fire and exploded. The third raced on, looping around the gravity mine where Han's detectors could no longer see it.

Exultation sang through Han's heart. *Four kills, one probable.* Not a bad start at evening the odds.

The *Millennium Falcon* shuddered to the gravitic pull of

the dovin basal. Han frowned as he checked the sublight engine readouts. He had hoped to whip around the space mine and exit with enough velocity to escape the dovin basal's gravity and get into hyperspace before the other flight of coralskippers could overtake him. But the dovin basal was more powerful than he'd expected, or possibly the Yuuzhan Vong commander was actually *ordering* it to increase its gravitational attraction—there was a lot the Republic didn't know about how the Yuuzhan Vong equipment worked, so that was at least possible.

In any case, the *Falcon* hadn't picked up enough speed to be sure of a getaway. Which meant he had to think of something else brilliant to do.

The other flight of six coralskippers was following him into the gravity well of the dovin basal, intent on staying with him. The one intact survivor of the second flight was in the act of whipping around the dovin basal, and wouldn't enter into his calculations for the present.

Well, he thought, if it worked *once* . . .

"Hang on, ladies," he called on the comlink. "We're going around again!"

Savage pleasure filled him as he swung *Millennium Falcon* around for another dive toward the dovin basal. *Attack* my *galaxy, will you?* he thought.

They had doubtless seen the beginnings of his maneuver, so he altered his trajectory slightly to put the space mine directly between himself and the oncoming fighters. Then he altered his trajectory a second time, just to be safe. If the enemy commander had any sense, he'd be doing the same.

Both sides were now blind. The problem was that the Yuuzhan Vong were alert to his tactics. They wouldn't just run blindly toward him: they would have their dovin basal propulsor units shifted to repel any attack, and they'd come in shooting.

"Be alert, people," Han said. "We're not going to be so

lucky this time, and I can't tell precisely where your targets are going to be. So be ready for them to be anywhere, right?"

"Right," Leia said.

"Understood," Dorja said.

"Commander Dorja," Leia said. "You'll see that your four lasers are aimed so as to fire on slightly diverging paths."

"Yes."

"Don't readjust. There's a reason for it."

"I presumed so. I won't change the settings."

A pang of sorrow touched Han's heart. It was his son Anakin who had discovered that if he fired three shots into a Yuuzhan Vong vessel at slightly diverging courses, at least one shot would curve around the gravity-warping dovin basal shields and hit the target. The quad lasers had been set to accomplish this automatically, without Anakin's eye and fast reflexes.

Anakin, who died at Myrkr.

"Twenty seconds," Han said, to cover both his own rising tension and the grief that flooded him.

He triggered another pair of missiles at ten seconds, just in case he was lucky again and the enemy flight appeared right in front of him. And then, because he had no choice but to trust his luck, he fired another pair five seconds later.

You are not keeping me from seeing Jacen again, he told the enemy.

The next thing he knew plasma cannon projectiles of molten rock were cracking against the *Falcon*'s shields, and there was a blinding flash dead ahead as the first pair of concussion missiles found a target. Han's heart throbbed as coral debris pounded on the deflectors, bounded off like multicolored sparks. There was a flicker on the displays as another coralskipper flashed past at a converging speed somewhere close to that of light, too fast for Han's eye to track it.

If he hadn't blown up the first coralskipper, he might have actually collided with it and been vaporized along with the enemy.

Han tried to calm his startled nerves as he kept his eyes on the displays, searching for more enemy craft around and behind the dovin basal. In a moment he understood the enemy's tactic. The two Vs of three had split into three pairs and curved around the dovin basal on separate paths, in the apparent hope that at least one pair would be in a position to splash the *Falcon* as they flew past each other. It hadn't worked, but by sheer chance one of them had almost taken out the *Millennium Falcon* through ramming. What, Han wondered, were the odds on that?

The comm board began a rhythmic bleating, and Han shut it off. From the display he gathered that the *Falcon* had just lost her hyperspace comm antenna.

Oh well. They hadn't been planning to talk to anyone long distance, anyway.

Feeling cheered by the thought that he'd win the battle in jig time if he could go on killing at least one coralskipper with each pass, he prepared to swing the ship around and dive toward the dovin basal yet again. And then his displays lit up at the appearance of an enemy fighter, the one intact survivor from the flight of six he'd splashed with his opening salvo. It was curving toward him, its plasma cannons spitting out a stream of molten projectiles.

It was placed just so as to keep him from swinging around on the ideal trajectory for passing the dovin basal again. He suppressed the curses that were ringing around the inside of his skull and instead warned his two gunners.

"Enemy skip on the port side, ladies."

He maneuvered so as to put the target in the money lane, where the fields of fire of both sets of lasers overlapped, and he heard the quads begin to chunder. Coherent light flashed around the enemy craft, curving weirdly as the dovin basal's singularity-curved space to safeguard the target. Enemy fire spattered off the *Falcon*'s shields. Then flame sprayed from the coralskipper as one of the laser lances struck home. The craft seemed to stagger in its course. And then a second laser blast turned the coralskipper into a spray of flaming shards that shone briefly, like a falling firework, and was gone.

"Nice shooting, Commander!"

Leia's voice, complimenting Dorja on the kill. Han realized to his pleasure that Vana Dorja apparently *was* qualified on the quad lasers.

Six down, one damaged, five to go.

Han hauled the *Millennium Falcon* around for another pass at the dovin basal, but he knew that the last coralskipper had delayed his maneuver to the point where it might be the enemy pouncing on the *Falcon* this time, not the other way around.

A glance at the displays showed the five intact coralskippers had swept around again, with each two-skip unit—plus the singleton survivor of the third pair—on widely diverging courses. They would be sweeping past the dovin basal at different times, approaching from different angles. This meant that no matter what Han did, he wouldn't be able to place the gravity-distorting singularity between himself and all the enemy at once. Those who could see him could communicate his position to those who couldn't.

The advantage he'd made for himself was gone. Someone on the other side must have had a brainstorm.

But, Han realized, the fact that the enemy flights had separated meant he wouldn't have to fight more than two at a time. That was something he could use.

He looped around toward the dovin basal, letting its gravity draw him in.

"How are we doing, Han?" Leia called.

"Plenty left in the old bag of tricks!" Han called back.

But *which* trick? That was a puzzler, all right.

His mind sawed at the problem as he dived for the singularity. It was clear that the first pair of enemy skips would arrive at the singularity before he did, and the single fighter at about the same time as the *Falcon*, with the other pair arriving afterward. The only way he'd be able to repeat the head-on attack that had worked the first time was if he did it on the third group of Yuuzhan Vong, and that meant running the gauntlet of the three other coralskippers. If he attacked the first pair, the others would arc around the dovin basal and be on his tail fast.

The Yuuzhan Vong were prepared for any eventuality. Unless, of course, he simply didn't do what they expected. If he *didn't* dive into the dovin basal as their tactics clearly assumed . . .

Han cut power to the sublight engines and hit the braking thrusters. The *Millennium Falcon* slowed as if she'd hit a patch of mud.

"Skips crossing the bow port to starboard!" he called. A volley of plasma cannon projectiles preceded the lead pair of fighters that arced from behind the blind spot of the dovin basal, bright glowing projectiles that curved strangely in the mine's weird gravity well. The projectiles crossed the *Falcon*'s bows at a comfortable distance, followed an instant later by the fighters themselves, both moving too fast to alter their trajectory once they saw the *Falcon*'s position. Laser fire pulsed around them, but Han didn't see any hits. He was already pouring power to the sublight engines, letting the space mine's gravity well take the *Falcon* into its embrace.

He nearly missed his timing: the plasma cannon volley that preceded the single fighter's appearance from around the singularity almost clipped his tail. The fighter itself crossed his stern at a blistering pace. Han wrenched the controls and altered course, heading not toward the dovin basal, but away from it.

He was now counting on the fact that the enemy were communicating, but there was also an inevitable lag between their perception of the *Falcon*'s position, their transmission describing the position to comrades rendered blind on the far side of the dovin basal, and their comrades' ability to act on that knowledge. He had dived for the dovin basal until the first pair of fighters were committed to their attack, then braked: the fighters had crossed ahead of him. Then, once the single fighter had been told the *Falcon* had slowed and altered its own course to intercept, Han had accelerated, and the fighter passed astern.

That left the last two, who had been told that the *Millennium Falcon* had first slowed, then accelerated. If they appeared where Han thought they would, they were dead meat.

"Fighters crossing starboard to port: lay down interdicting fire dead ahead," Han ordered, sawing the *Falcon* around again, toward the singularity. It was easier to aim his ship at the enemy than to describe to his gunners where he thought the bad guys would appear.

His heart gave a leap as the two coralskippers arced into sight right where he thought they'd be, between the *Falcon* and the dovin basal, the two fighters flying wingtip to wingtip and preceded by a volley of molten projectiles that curved in the mine's hypergravity. The lasers laid down a blistering fire right in their path and caught both ships broadside. One flamed and broke up, and the other soared off into the night, trailing fire.

Seven down, two damaged! A nice total, and the day had hardly begun.

Adrenaline drew a grin across Han's face. He dived for the singularity again, not because he knew what he was going to do next but because he wanted to hide: the three remaining fighters were curving around and about to drop onto his tail. But this time he didn't use the dovin basal to slingshot himself around onto a new trajectory: instead he worked the controls to go into orbit around the singularity, the *Falcon*'s spars moaning from gravitational stress as she crabbed sideways through the dovin basal's gravity well.

Ahead, through space warped by gravity, he saw what might be an enemy fighter. "Open fire dead ahead!" he called again, and he saw laserfire streak outward, the bolts curving in the singularity's gravity like a fiery rainbow.

"Keep firing!" he urged, and brought the *Falcon*'s nose up just a touch. The curving laser blasts climbed up the fighter's tail and blew it to shreds.

There was wild cheering from the gun turrets: even the restrained Commander Dorja was yelling her head off. "Fire dead aft!" Han shouted over the noise as he fed power to the sublight engines: with the gravity well's distortion affecting his perceptions, he had no idea where the remaining enemy were, and he was afraid they were behind him, ready to wax his tail just as he'd waxed the single enemy fighter.

Relief poured through him as scans showed his precautions were unnecessary: they'd pulled away from the dovin basal on a completely different trajectory and were well out of range. Han held his course to see if the enemy had had enough—but no, they were coming around again, ready for more punishment.

And two more fighters were heading for him, the two he'd wounded, each coming in on its own trajectory.

Han rolled the *Millennium Falcon* around, heading for one of the two single fighters, figuring he could knock out one of the damaged craft before taking on the pair of uninjured craft.

And then proximity alarms blared, and Han's display lit up with twenty-four fighters coming out of hyperspace right on his tail.

Thwarted rage boiled through him. "We've got company!"

he shouted, and pounded the instrument panel with a fist. "I've gotta say this is *really unfair*—!" Then he recognized the new ships' configuration, and he punched on the inter-ship comm unit.

"Unknown freighter," came a voice on one of the New Republic channels, "alter course forty degrees to port!"

Han obeyed, and a section of four craft came roaring in right past his cockpit. His nerves gave a leap as he recognized the jagged silhouettes of Chiss clawcraft, Sienar TIE ball cockpits and engines matched to forward-jutting Chiss weapons pylons, the design the result of their fruitful collaboration with the Empire under the Chiss Grand Admiral Thrawn.

Once upon a time, Han thought, TIE fighters on his tail would have been a *bad* thing.

"Commander Dorja," Han said, "we've got some of your friends here." Another two sections of clawcraft came roaring past, followed by three sections of New Republic E-wings. Directly in front of the *Millennium Falcon* the formation came apart in a starburst, one section of four heading for each of the remaining coralskippers while two others remained in reserve.

Han hit the TRANSMIT button. "Thanks, you guys," he said, "but I was doing fine on my own."

"Unknown freighter, stand clear." The voice had a slightly pompous ring, and Han thought he recognized it. "We'll handle it from here."

"Whatever you say, sport," Han replied, and then watched as four fighters ganged up on each of the coralskippers. The enemy craft couldn't jump to hyperspace, and they couldn't flee the fighters because they had been chasing the *Millennium Falcon* at near lightspeed and couldn't alter course in time.

The newly arrived fighters took no chances, just professionally hunted down each of the coralskippers and blew it to smithereens, taking no casualties in return. Then the allied squadron turned on the dovin basal mine and very carefully destroyed it with a calculated barrage of torpedoes and laser bursts.

"Nice work, people," Han congratulated them.

"Please stay off this channel, sir," the fighter commander said, "unless you have an urgent message."

Han grinned. "Not so urgent, Colonel Fel," he said. "I'd just like to invite you to a meeting here aboard the *Millennium Falcon*, with Captain Solo, Princess Leia Organa Solo of the New Republic, and Commander Vana Dorja of the Imperial Navy."

There was a long, lonely silence on the comm.

"Yes, Captain Solo," Jagged Fel said. "We would be honored, I'm sure."

"Come right aboard," Han said. "We'll extend the docking arm."

And then, over the comlink, he called C-3PO and told the droid there would be guests for dinner.

TWO

Leia knew Jagged Fel fairly well. He was a decorated fighter pilot, the son of an Imperial baron who lived with the Chiss and who had on occasion aided the New Republic. Jag was a little stuffy, but not a bad sort once you got to know him. He had served with Jaina Solo in the defense of the Hapes Cluster, and later, as part of Jaina's Twin Suns Squadron, fought at Borleias; and the two had the same sort of complicated, antagonistic relationship that Leia had once shared with Han. Though Leia appreciated Jaina's having a friend who could take her out of her troubles, she rather hoped that Jaina would not resolve this skirmishing in the same way that Leia had resolved her feelings about Han: having an Imperial baron in the family would create far too many complications. Having Darth Vader for a father was bad enough.

Jag Fel came aboard in his vac suit. With his helmet under one arm, he gave Leia and Han a smart salute. "I'm sorry, sir," he told Han. "I didn't recognize *Falcon*'s profile."

"I wouldn't have made much of a smuggler if you knew my freighter from any other," Han said. "But I *was* offended that you didn't recognize my voice on the comm."

"I was calculating enemy trajectories." Stiffly. "Such things take one's full attention."

"Will you join us for dinner?" Leia asked.

"Perhaps I will take a bite or two. But I don't want to have a meal when my pilots are hungry."

C-3PO helped Jag remove his vac suit, revealing the red-piped black uniform of a Chiss fighter pilot. After Jag had been introduced to Vana Dorja, he joined the others at the table.

"Aren't you part of Twin Suns Squadron?" Han asked. "Isn't Jaina here?"

Jag explained that after Borleias, many new pilots had arrived fresh from the training schools, and a decision had been made to break up the old squadrons in order to build new squadrons around the experienced pilots. He and the Chiss had been pulled out of the Twin Suns Squadron in order to form a new squadron, and Kyp Durron had been pulled out as well, to re-form Kyp's Dozen.

Experienced pilots were at a premium. The military had apparently decided that for each unit to have *some* experienced pilots was preferable to throwing whole formations of rookie pilots at the enemy.

Jaina had been compensated for losing so many experienced pilots by a promotion. She was now Major Solo—her majority up until now had been a temporary, or "brevet," rank, but now it was real.

Leia didn't like that either. She knew that Jaina would now feel the necessity of proving she deserved her promotion, doing so no doubt at the risk of her life.

"What's your squadron doing here?" Han asked.

"The Yuuzhan Vong have been mining this section of the Hydian Way, pulling ambushes on freighters and refugee ships. We've been sent in to clear the enemy out of the area. Earlier today we destroyed the minelaying transport that had been dropping mines and coralskippers along this part of the Way, so any more skips that we find will have been stranded here for a while."

"I was hoping you'd get some rest and refit after Borleias."

"So was I."

For a moment both men looked weary. The fight had gone on for so many months, and so badly despite everything they had done. Both deserved a rest, but neither would get one, not unless it was the rest from which they would not return.

A twinge of anxiety prompted Leia's next question. "Have you seen Jaina?"

"No. My squadron was pulled away for this duty just after Borleias."

Jaina, Leia thought, deserved a rest no less than Jag and Han. Leia had wanted to force her daughter to take leave, and that was before the meat grinder that was Borleias, the rearguard action where the Yuuzhan Vong had been forced to pay for their victory in rivers of blood. But Jaina was, perhaps, too much like her mother, too committed to the cause of the New Republic, and the Jedi, ever to rest until some kind of victory was assured.

Wisdom is knowing when you've given all you can. Neither she nor her daughter had truly learned that lesson.

Jag turned inquiring eyes toward Leia. "And you, Highness?" Jag asked. "What are you doing here, so far away from the centers of power?"

"A diplomatic mission to the Empire," Leia said.

"You're alone? No escort?"

"There was no one with the authority to give us one, so we just went." No use explaining about her vain hopes of spending some time alone with Han, a combination vacation and second honeymoon, while they transited to Bastion and back.

"I assume you'll attempt to convince the Empire to make greater efforts against the Yuuzhan Vong," Jag said. His tone was insufferably superior. "A pity that the logic of the situation is so against you—it would really make more sense in the short term for the Empire to join the Vong."

Leia saw Vana Dorja's sudden, intent interest, and dreaded it. "Could you explain your reasoning, Colonel Fel?" Dorja asked.

Han, clearly furious, opened his mouth to interject a comment, but at a look from Leia said nothing.

"It's a question of what each side could offer the Empire," Jag said. "The Empire's a beaten shadow of its former self, strapped for resources. The New Republic is in no position to help the Empire, not when its own resources are being appropriated by the invaders. But think what the Yuuzhan Vong could offer the Empire—whole worlds! All the Empire would have to do is take them from the New Republic while the New Republic's forces are committed against the Vong. The Empire could double its size, taking its choice of worlds, and it would cost the Yuuzhan Vong nothing."

Vana Dorja's eyes narrowed with calculation. "That's a very interesting analysis, Colonel," she said.

Han finally couldn't contain himself any longer, and lodged his protest. "You forget what happens *next*," he said. "The Vong can't be trusted—they haven't kept their word yet! If the Vong let the Empire grow, it's because they're only fattening it for slaughter."

Jag rubbed the long scar on his forehead. "That's why I said *in the short term*, Captain Solo," he said. "In the long term, I don't believe the Empire would survive long in a galaxy dominated by the Yuuzhan Vong."

Vana Dorja's eyes glittered. "Could you explain, Colonel Fel?"

The superior tone was back in Jag's voice. "Leaving aside any issues of perfidy—and it's perfectly true that Yuuzhan Vong guarantees can't be trusted—there exist long-term issues of compatibility. The Vong and the Empire simply want different things. The Empire wants a return to the power and respect it once enjoyed. The Yuuzhan Vong want not only the complete domination of the galaxy, but an ideological and religious domination as well—they want their *way of life* to triumph. And while some aspects of Yuuzhan Vong life are compatible with the Empire—the discipline, the unquestioning obedience to authority—other areas are not. The Yuuzhan Vong are opposed to *all forms of technology.*"

He held up a hand. "And where is the Empire without its technology? The Empire has always relied on a technological solution to its problems. If it adopted Yuuzhan Vong biotechnology instead, it would concede whatever advantages it has, and make itself dependent on the Vong."

He shook his head. "And even an Empire doubled in size would be unable to resist the Yuuzhan Vong if—I should say *when*—the Vong move against them. The New Republic, if it somehow survived, would not come to the aid of an Empire that had aided its enemies. If the Empire allies with the Yuuzhan Vong, it will be isolated, ripe fruit for the Vong whenever they choose to pluck it. And even if the Yuuzhan Vong keep their promises and do not invade, the Empire will be overwhelmed quite peacefully in time—in a galaxy dominated by the Yuuzhan Vong, the Empire will have to become Vong-like in order to survive. The Yuuzhan Vong triumph either way."

Bravo! Leia thought in admiration. Jagged Fel's analysis had stated her own position succinctly.

Vana Dorja, listening, nodded but offered no opinion. Leia could only hope she would include Jag's analysis in her report.

Jag turned to Leia. "We're isolated here," he said. "I've heard very little information concerning what's happening elsewhere in the New Republic. Do you have any news I can give to my pilots?"

Leia took a deep breath. Only the sunny news, she thought: the Imperial spy was listening. "The Senate has established itself on Mon Calamari," she said. "They're in the process of reestablishing the regular processes of government and electing a Chief of State."

Amusement quirked a corner of Jag's mouth. "I thought Pwoe was Chief of State."

"Pwoe seems to be a minority of one at the moment." In the aftermath of the fall of Coruscant, Councilor Pwoe had declared himself in charge, and had begun issuing orders to the government and the military. He might have gotten away with it had the Borleias campaign gone differently— Pwoe had expected the defenders to buy time with their own annihilation, but instead Wedge Antilles and his scratch force had held out for much longer than expected, their example an inspiration to the remnants of the New Republic. The holodocumentary *Battle of Borleias*, by the historian Wolam Tser, was doing sellout business throughout the New Republic, and had shown the defenders of the planet as heroes battling against great odds. Wolam Tser's work had done a lot to change minds about the New Republic Defense Force and its capabilities.

When the Senate had finally reconvened on Mon Calamari, they'd remembered that it was they who had the right to elect the Chief of State, and they'd summoned Pwoe and his cohorts to join them. Even then Pwoe might have managed his election as the New Republic's leader, but instead he overplayed his hand: he insisted that the Senate leave Mon Calamari to join *him* at Kuat. The Senate refused, declared the office of Chief of State vacant, and sent out instructions that no organ of government should obey Pwoe's orders.

"Pwoe's been made unwelcome at Kuat," Leia said. "Even Niuk Niuv won't follow him any longer. He's left—for Sullust, I hear. I doubt he'll be welcome there, either."

Vana Dorja gave a slight shake of her head. "This is the sort of thing that can only happen when the chain of command is not clear," she said.

"It's clear enough," Han pointed out. "Pwoe chose to disregard it, is all. And now he's paying the penalty."

"In the Empire he would be shot," Dorja said.

Han gave a satisfied smile. "We're crueler than you are," he said to Dorja's surprise. "Instead of killing him, we're going to let him linger for years as an object of contempt and ridicule."

Jag, smiling also, rose from the table. "Duty calls, I'm afraid," he said. "We've got to destroy any remaining mines and coralskippers before the Yuuzhan Vong get a transport out to rescue them."

The others rose and said farewell to their visitor. Jag snapped out a salute. "Good luck, Captain. Your Highness." He hesitated. "Would you like an escort as long as your route takes you along the Hydian Way?"

"Thanks, but no," Han said. "We're not moving *along* the Way, we're *crossing* it. It's a coincidence that we're here at all."

"Very well, then." Jag picked up his helmet. "The best of luck on your journey. Good to meet you, Commander," he added, with a flick of his eyes toward Dorja.

"And you, Colonel."

"Good hunting," Leia said.

Jag smiled. "I think it will *be* good hunting," he said, and moved toward the air lock.

A few minutes later the twenty-four fighter craft flashed into hyperspace, and the crew of the *Millennium Falcon* continued alone to a meeting with their old enemies in the Empire.

THREE

"I have a few minutes only," Senator Fyor Rodan said. He sat—sank, rather—in an oversoft armchair while his aides bustled in and out of his hotel suite. All of them seemed to have comlinks permanently fixed to their mouths, and to be engaged in more than one conversation at the same time.

"I appreciate your taking the time to see me, Councilor," Luke Skywalker said. There was no place to sit—every chair and table was covered with holopads, datapads, storage units, and even piles of clothing. Luke stood before the Senator and made the best of the awkward situation.

"At least I have managed to get the Calamarian government to give the Senate a place to meet," Rodan said. "I was afraid we'd have to go on using hotel facilities." As he spoke, he punched numbers into a datapad, scowled at the result, and then punched the numbers again.

The Senate hadn't quite shrunk to the size where it could comfortably meet in a hotel suite, but it was certainly a much slimmer body than it had been just a few months previously. Many Senators had managed to find reasons not to be on the capital when the Yuuzhan Vong attacked. Others had been sent away to establish a reserve of political leaders, so that they wouldn't be caught all in one place. Yet others had commandeered military units in the middle of the action and fled. Still more had died in the fighting at Coruscant, been captured, or had gone missing.

And then of course there was Viqi Shesh, who had gone over to the enemy.

Fyor Rodan had done none of these things. He had remained at his post until the fall of Coruscant, then been evacuated by the military at the last moment. He'd joined the luckless Pwoe in his attempt to form a government, but then come to Mon Calamari when the Senate reconvened and summoned all Senators to their places.

His behavior had been both courageous and principled. He had won the admiration of many, and was now spoken of as a candidate to replace Borsk Fey'lya as Chief of State.

Unfortunately, Fyor Rodan was also a political opponent of Luke and the rest of the Jedi. Luke had asked for a meeting in the hope of swaying Rodan's position, or at least of understanding the man better.

Perhaps Rodan's animosity toward Luke and his friends dated from the time that an impatient Chewbacca hung him from a coat hook just to get him out of the way. There were also rumors that Rodan was connected in some way to smugglers—that he spoke against the Jedi because Kyp Durron had once taken action against his smuggler associates.

But those were rumors, not facts. Besides, if anyone was to be condemned for having friends who were smugglers, then Luke was damned a dozen times over . . .

"How may I help you, Skywalker?" Rodan asked. His eyes flicked briefly to Luke, then returned to the datapad.

"This morning," Luke said, "you were quoted on broadcast media as saying that the Jedi were an impediment to the resolution of the war."

"I should say that is self-evidently true," Rodan said. He kept his attention on the datapad screen as his fingers touched one button after another. "At times this war has been *about* the Jedi. The Yuuzhan Vong insist that you must all be handed over to them. That *is* an impediment to the war's resolution—unless of course we *do* hand you over."

"Would you do that?"

"If I thought that by doing so, I could save the lives of billions of the New Republic's citizens, I would certainly consider such an action." He frowned slightly. "But there are more serious impediments to peace now than the Jedi—such as the fact that the enemy are sitting in the ruins of our capital." His face hardened. "That and the fact that the Yuuzhan Vong will not stop until they have enslaved or converted every being in our galaxy. I personally will not support even an attempt at peace with the Yuuzhan Vong until such time as they evacuate Coruscant and the other worlds they have seized." His eyes flicked to Luke again. "Does that satisfy you that I'm not planning to sacrifice you and your cohorts, Skywalker?"

Though the man's words seemed reassuring, for some reason Luke didn't find them comforting. "I'm pleased to know that you're not in favor of peace at any price," Luke said.

Rodan's eyes returned to his datapad. "Of course I'm only a Senator and a member of the late Chief of State's Advisory Council," he said. "Once we have a new Chief of State, I will inevitably be forced to support policies with which I personally disagree. That's how our government works. So you should seek reassurances from our next Chief of State, not from myself."

"There is talk that you may *be* our next Chief of State."

For the first time, Rodan's fingers hesitated on the keyboard of the datapad. "I would say that such talk is premature," he said.

Luke wondered why the man was being so consistently rude. Normally a politician canvassing for support wouldn't close the door on someone who could potentially help him to power, but Rodan had always followed an anti-Jedi line even when there was no advantage to be gained, and that meant something else was going on. Perhaps the rumors about smuggling made more sense now.

Luke queried again. "Whom do you support for the post?"

Rodan's fingers grew busy once more. "One question after another," he said. "You sound like a political journalist. If you want to continue along this line, Skywalker, perhaps you could trouble yourself to acquire press credentials."

"I'm not planning to write any articles. I'm merely trying to understand the situation."

"Consult the Force," Rodan said. "That's what you people do, isn't it?"

Luke took a breath. This conversation was like a fencing bout, attack followed by parry as the two circled each other around a common center. And that center was . . . what?

Fyor Rodan's intentions toward the Jedi.

"Senator Rodan," Luke said. "May I ask what role you envision for the Jedi in this war?"

"Two words, Skywalker," Rodan said, his eyes never leaving the datapad. *"None whatsoever."*

Luke calmed the anger that rose at Rodan's deliberate rudeness, at his provocative answers. "The Jedi," he said, "are the guardians of the New Republic."

"Oh?" Rodan pursed his lips, glanced again at Luke. "I thought we had the New Republic Defense Force for that purpose."

"There was no military in the Old Republic," Luke said. "There were only the Jedi."

A half smile twitched on Rodan's face. "That proved unfortunate when Darth Vader turned up, didn't it?" he said. "And in any case, the handful of Jedi you command can scarcely do the work of the thousands of Jedi Knights of the Old Republic." Rodan's glance grew sharper. "Or *do* you command the Jedi? And if not you, who? And to whom is that commander responsible?"

"Each Jedi Knight is responsible to the Jedi Code. Never to act for personal power, but to seek justice and enlightenment." Luke wondered whether to remind Rodan that the councilor had opposed Luke's notion of refounding the Jedi Council in order to provide the Jedi with more direct guidance and authority in their actions. If the Jedi were disorganized, it was partly Rodan's doing, and it hardly seemed just for Rodan to complain about it.

"Noble words," Rodan said. "But what does it mean in practice? For justice, we have police and the courts—but the Jedi take it upon *themselves* to deliver justice, and are constantly interfering in police matters, often employing violence. For diplomacy, we have the highly skilled ambassadors and consuls of the Ministry of State—but Jedi, some of them mere children I might add, take it upon *themselves* to conduct high-level negotiations that frequently seem to end in conflict and war. And though we have a highly skilled military, the Jedi take it upon *themselves* to commandeer military resources, to supplant *our own officers* in command of military units, to make strategic military decisions."

Such as to hunt smugglers? Luke wondered. He considered bringing up the issue of smuggling, but decided against it—with Rodan in his present mood, Luke didn't want to remind him why he hated the Jedi in the first place.

"It's an amateurish performance," Rodan continued. "At worst the Jedi are a half-trained group of vigilantes. At best they simply make it all up as they go along, and the result is all too often disaster. I hardly think that the ability to do magic tricks is qualification for supplanting professional diplomats, judges, and military officers."

"The situation is critical," Luke said. "We're being invaded. The Jedi on the spot—"

"Should leave it to the professionals," Rodan said. "That's what we pay the professionals for."

Rodan turned to his datapad, called up information. "I have your record here, Skywalker. You joined Rebel Alliance forces as a starfighter pilot. Though you fought with distinction at Yavin Four and at Hoth, you shortly afterward left your unit, *taking with you the starfighter that didn't belong to you*, in order—" He paused to insert virtual quotation marks around his words. "—to conduct 'spiritual exercises' on some jungle planet. And you did all this without even asking permission of your commander.

"You afterward returned to the military, served bravely and with distinction, and rose to the rank of general. But you resigned your commission, *during wartime*, again to devote yourself to spiritual matters." Rodan shrugged. "Perhaps during the Rebellion such irregular practices were necessary, or at any rate tolerated. But now that we have a government, I fail to see why we should continue turning over state resources to a group of amateurs who are all too likely to follow their Master's example and abandon their posts whenever the mood—or the Force—takes them."

Luke stood very still. "I think you will find," he said, "that our 'spiritual exercises,' as you call them, strengthen us in our role as protectors of the New Republic."

"Possibly so," Rodan said. "It would be interesting to conduct a cost-benefit analysis to discover whether the Jedi are in fact worth the resources the government has devoted to you. But my point is this—" He looked up at Luke again from the depths of his oversoft chair, and his eyes were not soft at all. "You call yourselves protectors of the Republic; very well. But I have looked very carefully at the constitution of our government, and there is no Office of the Protectors of the Republic."

Rodan's expression turned quizzical. "What exactly *are* you, Skywalker? You aren't military—we *have* a military.

You aren't a diplomat—we *have* diplomats. You aren't a peace officer or a judge—we *have* those. So why exactly do we need you?"

"Jedi Knights," Luke said, "have been fighting the Yuuzhan Vong from the first day of this invasion—from the first *hour*. Many Jedi have been killed—some sacrificed to the enemy by their fellow citizens—but we continue our struggle on the New Republic's behalf. We are effective enough that the Yuuzhan Vong have singled us out for persecution—they are afraid of us."

"I don't question your bravery or your dedication," Rodan said. "But I do question your effectiveness. If your people want to fight the Yuuzhan Vong, why not join the Defense Force? Train with the other soldiers, accept promotion on the same basis as other soldiers, and *accept the same penalties for derogation of duty* as other soldiers. As it is, the Jedi expect special privileges, and the regular officers have every right to resent them."

"If you feel the Jedi are an undisciplined, uncontrolled force," Luke asked, "why do you oppose the re-formation of the Jedi Council?"

"Because the Jedi Council would form an elite group within the government. You *say* you do not seek power or personal gain—and I will take you at your word—but other Jedi have shown less admirable traits." His eyes flicked to Luke again, a chill, flinty gaze. "Your father, for one.

"If you want to fight the Yuuzhan Vong," Rodan continued, "advise your Jedi to join the military. Or any other branch of the government that appeals to their interests and skills. They can, of course, continue to practice their religion in private, as any other citizen, and not as a state-supported cult.

"No, Skywalker." Rodan settled deeply into his chair and returned his attention to his datapad. "Until you actually *join* this government you say that you defend, and join it on the same basis as any other citizen, then I have every intention of regarding you as I would any other lobbyist for any other interest group demanding special privileges for its members. Now"—his voice became abstracted—"I have many other appointments, Skywalker. I believe our interview is at an end."

Why is he behaving this way? Luke wondered. And then he left.

"He kept calling me 'Skywalker,'" Luke said. "Because I don't have a title—I'm not a Senator, I'm not a general any longer, I'm not an ambassador. He used the word like an insult."

"He could have called you 'Master.' Like I do sometimes." Mara Jade's voice was a smoky purr in his ear. Her arms slipped around Luke's waist from behind.

Luke smiled. "I don't think it would be the same as when you do it."

"It better not be . . . *Skywalker.*" Luke jumped as one of her hands gave his stomach a slap.

Luke had found Mara waiting for him as he returned to their rooms in the large hotel suite they shared with Han and Leia. He had been calm, even analytical, when he was speaking with Rodan, but when he related the substance of his interview to Mara, he found himself with less reason to maintain calm and objectivity, and the resentment that he hadn't actually felt in Rodan's presence now began to boil.

Mara, without comment, had begun to massage the growing tension out of his shoulders. The playful slap on his stomach had banished the rest of it. Luke smiled.

Luke turned and let his arms coil about his wife. "We've lost Coruscant," he said, "we're fighting the enemy every day, and the squabbling and fights for precedence never end. Rodan's not going to make it easy for us. He thinks the Jedi are claiming unjustified privileges and can evolve into a menace to the state." He hesitated. "And the problem is," he admitted, "I'm beginning to think that much of what he says might be true."

"Sounds like a depressing interview." She drew him closer, let her cheek rest on his shoulder as she directed a mischievous whisper to his ear. "Maybe I should cheer you up. Would you like me to call you 'Master' again?"

Luke couldn't help but laugh. With the successful delivery of their child, Mara had at last come out of the shadow of the terrible disease that had afflicted her for so long. For years she'd had to control herself precisely and ruthlessly in order to either fight the illness or keep it in remission. The birth of Ben had been a kind of internal signal that it was possible to feel joy again. To feel the least bit irresponsible. To be spontaneous and impulsive. To laugh, to play, to take delight in life—despite the seemingly endless war that raged around them.

And since Ben had been sent for his own safety to the Maw, Mara's principal plaything had become Luke.

"Say what you like," Luke said, "if the mood strikes."

"Oh, it strikes. It definitely strikes."

"Well," Luke said. "Let it strike, then."

Some time later, Luke turned to Mara and said, "So how was *your* day?"

"Thirsty. I need a glass of water."

Luke reluctantly allowed her to slip out of his embrace and into the kitchen.

Mon Calamari had been swarmed by refugees from worlds conquered or threatened by the Yuuzhan Vong, and housing in the great floating cities was expensive, particularly for those who insisted on breathing only air.

Mara brushed her red-gold hair back from her freckled shoulders and took a long drink. She put the glass down, turned to Luke, and sighed. "It was work, but I think Triebakk and I finally convinced Cal Omas that he needs to be our next Chief of State."

"Congratulations to both of you," Luke said. In the past few weeks he'd grown accustomed to the way their lives, and their conversation, veered sharply from the political to the personal and back again.

Cal Omas had fought with the Rebel Alliance, and had shown himself sympathetic to the Jedi. Certainly, from the Jedi point of view, he was a better candidate for Chief of State than Fyor Rodan.

"Fyor Rodan wants the job, too," he said. "The possibility was the only thing that got a reaction out of him."

"There are two more candidates. Senator Cola Quis announced his intention to run this morning, after you left."

Luke searched his memory. "I never heard of him."

"A Twi'lek from Ryloth. Serves on the Commerce Council. I don't think he stands much of a chance, but maybe he thinks he can forge an unbeatable lead if he starts now."

"And the fourth?"

"Ta'laam Ranth of the Justice Council. He's known to be canvassing for support."

"Can he win?"

"Triebakk thinks he isn't *trying* to win. Ranth is trying to build a bloc of supporters in order to play a decisive role in the outcome. At the last second he can swing his bloc to another candidate in return for favors."

Luke shook his head. "At least there are four Senators left who think the job is worth having. That means they think they've a future in the New Republic yet."

Or a future in looting the New Republic before it goes down. The dark thought intruded before Luke could quite prevent it.

Carefully, he pushed the thought away, and chose a different tack.

"The question is," he said, "how much do we involve ourselves in this election?"

"As Jedi? Or as private citizens?"

Luke smiled. "That's a separate question."

Mara considered this. "Would it benefit Cal to be known as the Jedi's choice?"

Luke sighed. "Well, *that* question's answered."

Mara was surprised. "You think it's that bad?"

"I think somebody's got to be blamed for the fall of Coruscant."

"Borsk Fey'lya seems a fair choice. He was Chief of State, and he made a lot of mistakes."

"Fey'lya was martyred during the battle. He died a hero. It's going to be politically impossible to assign him blame."

Mara nodded slowly. "So you think it's the Jedi who are going to be assigned responsibility."

"I think we should take care that it's *not*. The question is how." He reached for Mara's water glass and took a sip. "If we're seen as interfering in the selection of the Chief of State, then we'll start hearing complaints of 'Jedi interference' and 'Jedi power grab' and 'secret Jedi cabal'—from Fyor Rodan, if no one else."

"So we act as private citizens."

"And we don't do anything Cal Omas doesn't want us to do. He's the professional. He knows just how far to push, and where."

He's the professional. Luke smiled at the irony. Rodan had wanted him to follow the professionals' advice, and here he was doing it.

Mara smiled. "So—let's assume we win, and we get a government that will work with the Jedi . . ."

"That's a lot of assumptions."

"What becomes of the Insiders?"

Luke paused. During the Battle of Borleias he and Mara, together with Han and Leia and Wedge Antilles and some others, had formed the conspiracy that was the Insiders, a group intended to form a Rebel Alliance *within* the New Republic, dedicated to fighting the war with the Yuuzhan Vong.

"We don't go public with the Insiders under *any* conditions," Luke said. "We don't tell Cal, even if he wins. The Insiders are our reserve, the people we know we can trust. It remains our secret."

And then suddenly, he thought, *Jacen!*

The water glass fell from his fingers and shattered on the floor. Mara stared at him.

Luke didn't notice. A strange bliss had fallen on him.

Now everything changes, he thought.

"It's the turning point." The words fell from his lips without volition. And even as he spoke, he came to the realization that he didn't know the place, amid all the great stars of the universe, from whence the words had come.

FOUR

Jaina Solo sat alone at the controls of her ship, the tendrils of the alien hood fixed to her face. Her attention was focused on the ship's displays, where she expected her quarry to appear.

Her quarry was Shimrra, Supreme Overlord of the Yuuzhan Vong.

Kill this one, she hoped, and the Yuuzhan Vong invaders might fall like a house of cards.

Word had flashed from New Republic Intelligence only three standard days earlier that the Supreme Overlord was expected at the library world of Obroa-skai. Obroa-skai had been conquered, and the contents of the library were now being translated into the Yuuzhan Vong language. Yuuzhan Vong priests had been placed in charge of the library; there were Yuuzhan Vong soldiers on the ground to protect their interests. Yuuzhan Vong ships were common in the system, and the planet was home to a yammosk that would coordinate any alien pilots in the area.

If anyone consulted the library any longer, it was the enemy. Possibly Shimrra himself was coming to view a critical piece of information that had just been translated. Obroa-skai had become an enemy asset.

And if Jaina had her way, it would become an enemy graveyard.

So Jaina hovered here, with the bulk of the gas giant

Obroa-held masking her from any detectors on the library planet, and waited to spring her trap.

Just this one last effort, she thought, *and maybe it's all over.* If Shimrra were killed, the Yuuzhan Vong might collapse. And even if the enemy didn't fall apart, Shimrra's death would serve as revenge for the fall of Coruscant, and give the New Republic a much-needed breathing space.

Jaina badly wanted an end to the war. She had been on the front lines literally since the first day. Then she had been joyful, confident, certain of her abilities, of the power of the Force and the order of the universe. Since then the war had taught her much. It had taught her doubt, terror, anxiety, fear, and anger. She had learned the limits to the Force, and to Force mastery. The war had shown her the darkness that lay within her, and how easy it had been for the darkness to overcome her, to drive her to fury, vengeance, and slaughter.

Most of all, the war had taught her sorrow. Sorrow for her lost brothers Jacen and Anakin, for Chewbacca, for her wingmate Anni Capstan, for the Hapan Queen Mother Teneniel Djo, for all the warriors who had died fighting alongside her, for the Jedi lost to the Yuuzhan Vong's relentless program of extermination, for the billions of nameless refugees who had been caught in the conflict and destroyed, or dispossessed of all they had owned or known.

She had learned her own fragility. She had been blinded in battle and learned the frustration of the invalid. She had been captured by the enemy. She had learned how easy it was for her to die, and how easily the universe would permit such a thing.

Jaina had learned too much, and in too short a time. She needed a rest in order to try to understand it all, to reconcile herself to her new knowledge and to her new reality.

But there was no time to rest. Her work was too critical, her expertise too necessary. She would have to win the war first, and then work out what it all meant.

If, of course, the war didn't kill her first.

There was a howl from Lowbacca on her comlink.

"The Vong have been late before, Streak." *Though not often enough,* she thought.

[You don't suppose that New Republic Intelligence has once again drop-kicked their brains and sent us out here for nothing?]

"That wouldn't surprise me."

[In which case we can return to base, take a nice long rest, no?]

"That *would* surprise me."

"*Huuuh.*"

"But if New Republic Intelligence is *right*," Jaina said, more to herself than to her lieutenant, "then this is *it*. This is like the destruction of the second Death Star, with the Emperor on it."

"*Hrr.*" [Then let the Supreme Overlord *come*!]

Even as Lowbacca growled his impatience, Jaina sensed a distant trembling through her connection with the alien frigate, a shudder like a groundquake in the ether, her ship's dovin basals responding to the gravity surge that marked the arrival of a great many ships from hyperspace.

"Lowie," she said, "I think you just got your wish."

She had not learned to love the captured Yuuzhan Vong frigate as she had her other ships. Jaina had learned her ships through her hands, by tearing them apart and putting them back together: she had learned to love every component, every servo, every power cable, every rivet. The captured ship, on the other hand, *couldn't* be taken apart, not without killing it: it was a single organic whole and had to be approached as such. The interface through the cognition hood was difficult, the organic ship systems were complex and frustrating, the dovin basals used for propulsion and defense were as baffling as they were effective. Her other craft had been fighter craft: agile, fast, and responsive. The Yuuzhan Vong frigate *Trickster* was huge, and though it was fast, maneuvering it was like maneuvering a city block. Changing course seemed to take forever. And there was no way to dodge or evade enemy fire: she just had to hope that the ship's defenses were strong enough to take the hits and survive.

But if she couldn't love the frigate, she had learned to respect it. She respected its toughness, the wholeness of its design, its ability to repair itself, its stubborn refusal to die even when it had been shot to pieces in combat against its own kind. In fighting around Hapes, the ship had been wounded almost to the death, but somehow, with the care of the Hapan scientists who were studying Yuuzhan Vong life-forms, it had survived and repaired much of the damage, though not all. Yet despite the fact that some of the ship's damage was beyond repair, despite the torn yorik coral and the dovin basals that had died, it was still as willing as ever to risk itself at Jaina's behest.

Jaina named it *Trickster*. The name proclaimed her a manifestation of Yun-Harla, the Cloaked One, the Yuuzhan Vong Trickster goddess. As such the name was a slap in the face to Yuuzhan Vong religious orthodoxy. Though the guise had proved useful—at both Hapes and Borleias, it had given her a clear tactical advantage—it also only added to the considerable number of enemy who wanted very badly to kill her.

A thought at which she could only shrug. So what else was new?

"Let's go, Lowie."

Lowbacca, through his alien cognition hood, ordered *Trickster* to accelerate, sweeping out from behind the Obroa-held gas giant and into view of any enemy detectors. Directed gravitational energy began to throb from the dovin basals built into the frigate, and even though some of the dovin basals had been killed at Hapes, the huge living craft began a ferocious, smooth acceleration that any New Republic vessel would be hard put to equal.

Jaina followed this call with a coded message sent through the New Republic subspace communicator that Lowbacca had implanted in the frigate. *Target arrived. Let's start the party.*

It was only then that *Trickster*'s sensors got a full reading on the fleet that had just arrived in the Obroa-skai system.

Jaina felt the hairs on the back of her neck prickle as she looked at the display. Eight frigates the size of her own. Two huge transport craft. More coralskippers and picket ships than she could count.

And one enormous ovoid vessel, glowing in the displays like a burning, unwinking eye. Not as big as a worldship, but larger than anything else in the Obroa-skai system other than planets and moons.

The personal command ship of Supreme Overlord Shimrra, Jaina thought. Oh yes. New Republic Intelligence was right.

Another wave of gravity pulsed over the ship. These were the commands of the yammosk, the Yuuzhan Vong war coordinator that executed the will of the enemy commander. Lowbacca allowed *Trickster* to obey the yammosk's commands to alter course for the enemy, but slowly, as if the frigate were damaged, or unable clearly to understand its instructions.

The yammosk no doubt verified that the frigate *was* damaged, a fact that would make its lack of communication with the fleet more convincing.

And then the party started. Dropping out of hyperspace, as if they'd been following *Trickster*, came the forces of the New Republic.

Nine flights of fighters. Four Corellian gunships. Three

Kuat Systems *Republic*-class cruisers. A refurbished *Lancer*-class frigate captured from the Empire during the Rebellion. And two MC80B Mon Calamari cruisers, both wildly different in appearance but possessing a world-shattering complement of turbolasers, ion cannons, and their own ten squadrons of fighters, all of which now came boiling like swarms of stinging insects from their scalloped hulls. All under the command of General Keyan Farlander, the Agamarian hero of the Rebellion, and all appearing just behind Jaina, with the Obroa-held gas giant only partially masking their appearance.

This, Jaina thought exultantly, is a *real battle*.

And they were following her plan. *Hers.* For a moment her own fierce joy overcame all doubt, and she basked in the glorious sensation of power. *Shimrra, you better watch out.*

The New Republic forces had been hovering just four light-hours, waiting for Jaina's signal to make the smallest possible hyperspace jump into the Obroa-skai system. They appeared slightly out of range of *Trickster*, as if they'd misjudged their return to normal space. It should look to Supreme Overlord Shimrra like a perfect chance to ambush the ambushers.

More commands came from the yammosk, too many and too complex for Jaina to even attempt to decode. Through the weird perceptions gained through her hood, she saw the enemy fleet deploying, the heavy ships rolling ponderously into position behind darting swarms of coralskippers that flashed like schools of fish against the blackness of space, all moving with the simultaneity and impossible precision gained from coordination with the yammosk's controlling intelligence.

But they were doing what Jaina had hoped they would do. Perhaps encouraged by their modest advantage in firepower, they were maneuvering to engage the New Republic forces.

Jaina had feared that if the New Republic fleet had simply leapt into the system and attacked, the Yuuzhan Vong would have clumped up around Shimrra's command ship, and the New Republic forces would never have been able to get to the enemy leader. But instead the damaged *Trickster*'s leaping first into the system made it seem as if the New Republic, not the Yuuzhan Vong, had been surprised, that they had jumped into the system in pursuit of a wounded frigate and found instead a task force.

The Yuuzhan Vong war psychology was based on attack, on the calculated ferocity of an all-out offensive. Jaina had hoped to trigger that psychology, and she had succeeded.

For the moment there was nothing for her to do but follow the yammosk's orders. She leaned back in the huge command chair that had been configured for an armored Yuuzhan Vong warrior and tried to relax her muscles, control her breathing. She let Force-awareness, always on the edge of her perceptions, flood her mind with its focused clarity.

She felt Lowbacca's nearby presence, under the hood that gave him command of the frigate's navigation. Her other lieutenant, Tesar Sebatyne, had his efficient predator's mind focused on controlling the frigate's weapons systems. Farther afield Jaina sensed the grim, reliable Corran Horn leading Rogue Squadron, and Kyp Durron flying at the head of his re-formed Dozen. Kyp's reflex, on sensing her through the Force, was to project concern, and she made a point of sending him warm reassurance. Since Jaina's involvement with Jag Fel, Kyp had been a nurturing presence, almost parental, and neither he nor Jaina quite knew how to reconcile his new persona with his earlier smoldering identity as the angry young man of the Jedi.

Then, lastly, Jaina sensed a less familiar presence, the Anx Jedi Madurrin, who served on the bridge of the Mon

Cal cruiser *Mon Adapyne*, ready to use her Force link with the other Jedi to aid the New Republic.

Other friends, she knew, would soon be engaging the enemy, friends who weren't Jedi and whom she couldn't feel through the Force. Friends in Blackmoon Squadron and Saber Squadron, not to mention the hypersecret Wraiths, flying snoopships that could outrun anything in the enemy inventory.

Jaina basked for a moment in the pleasure of those she had trained with, served with, those who had shared her triumphs as well as her despair . . . At Myrkr she had learned the power of the Force-meld that could come when a number of Jedi united their minds and thoughts, becoming stronger than if each stood alone, and for a long moment she rejoiced in their unity.

Jacen! she thought, his presence a song in her mind, and then she fought her way clear of Force-awareness and of the sudden surges of contradictory emotion that streamed through her.

A Wookiee howl came into her comlink.

"I don't know what that was about!" She hesitated. "I must have lost it for a second. Sorry."

Lowbacca grunted his reassurance.

"I opened to the Force, and I must have opened to—to something else as well."

Tentatively, Jaina reached out again to the Force, and felt nothing but the warm concern of her friends.

Everything's fine, she tried to send to them.

But she couldn't help but echo Lowbacca's question. *What* was *that* about? What had she opened to, that caused the flood of memories and emotions connected with her dead twin?

Distantly she perceived the orders of the enemy yammosk, saw the Yuuzhan Vong fleet instantly carry them out. There was no hesitation in the enemy, no sense of indecision or fear. *Wish we could say that about ourselves,* Jaina thought.

Her own mind was gnawing at her situation, trying to deduce enemy intentions from their deployments. The plan for the upcoming battle had been largely hers, and it was based on several assumptions, none of which Jaina could be sure still applied.

She could no longer have complete confidence in the assumption that the Yuuzhan Vong hadn't realized that *Trickster* was no longer one of their own ships. She'd already used the frigate for deception, and it was perfectly possible that they would be wise to her by now.

Part of her plan was also based on the use of decoy dovin basals that could attach to enemy ships and identify them as enemies to their own side. This had been a spectacular success in the Hapes Cluster and in the Battle of Borleias, but sooner or later the Yuuzhan Vong would learn to ignore or counter the false signals.

The most crucial element of the plan were the yammosk jammers developed by Danni Quee. These would override the signals of the Yuuzhan Vong war coordinator, preventing the eerie, single-minded, instantaneous maneuvering that had been the hallmark of enemy victories.

If the Yuuzhan Vong had worked out a way to counter the jammers, then Jaina was leading a New Republic fleet to certain destruction, with Supreme Overlord Shimrra as a highly interested spectator in yet another glorious triumph for the Vong . . .

Let it all work just one more time.

Both fleets were maneuvering now. They were no longer hurtling directly toward one another on opposing tracks: both had altered course in order to avoid the Obroa-held gas giant and to approach at a far more acute angle that would allow wide fields of fire to the capital ships' broadside guns. Among the enemy was a swarm of coralskippers that seemed dedicated to guarding the presumed flagship of Overlord Shimrra, which itself hovered somewhat behind the action, screened by other fleet elements. And the flagship itself guarded the large transports, which took station on its far side.

And between the fleets, Jaina's frigate—apparently ignored by both sides—fled across the gap, heading toward the presumed safety of the Yuuzhan Vong squadrons.

More orders came to *Trickster* courtesy of the enemy yammosk.

[We're being ordered to take station astern of the enemy flag,] Lowbacca said.

"Well," Jaina judged, "*that's* about perfect."

[Shall I comply?]

"Yes. But act naturally—you know, slow and clumsy."

Lowbacca answered with a snarl, but Jaina could hear the laughter in it.

Jaina relaxed again into the Force, integrating the picture she received through the alien cognition hood. Both sides were nearing the point of no return, the point at which missiles and fighters would start swarming across the gap between the squadrons.

Jaina watched the ships move across space, tried to gauge the movement.

Now, she sent through the Force. She felt Madurrin receive the order, relay it verbally to others on the flagship.

On receipt of the signal, a device on one of Wraith Squadron's snoopships began pulsing out gravity waves that interfered directly with the signals of the enemy yammosk.

And then, when the enemy war coordinator was no longer able to communicate with the elements of its fleet, the New Republic fleet undertook one more maneuver. Each fleet element altered course to drive directly for the largest enemy ship, Shimrra's personal vessel.

Shimrra was now the sole target of more than one hundred New Republic craft. If the Yuuzhan Vong yammosk was jammed, the enemy would not be able to coordinate a response in time, and because of the proximity of Obroa-held's gravity field, the enemy couldn't escape into hyperspace.

Jaina sat, trapped in what seemed an eternal moment of suspense, while she waited to see if the jammers worked, if the enemy responded. She could dimly perceive the jammer through her connection to the dovin basals of *Trickster*, the rhythm of its transmissions overriding the sendings of the enemy yammosk.

And then she felt another rhythm intrude on the first, and saw the enemy ships respond, swinging in a unified response to the New Republic's maneuver, every single ship in the enemy armada altering course at the same instant.

No! Jaina thought, horrified. *It can't be!*

The jammer had failed—or rather it had worked for only a few moments, producing a hesitation in the enemy countermaneuver.

At least the enemy maneuver had been delayed. Their position was no longer ideal.

Despair flooded over Jaina. *Get out of here,* she thought through the Force-meld. *Get away from Obroa-held and into hyperspace now!* It wasn't actual words she sent, but a frantic tumble of images and impulses and emotions that reflected her own anxiety.

No. Corran Horn's strong presence flooded Jaina's Force-awareness. His answer was a powerful cocktail of feelings, impulses, words, and fierce reason. *Think!*

Jaina was frantic beyond thought. Her frigate was sweeping directly toward the enemy, and one enemy squadron, led by two frigates her own size, had altered course so as to pass right by her—headed not for *Trickster*, she hoped, but for an element of the New Republic fleet.

Missile tracks began to fly through her displays. Again, none aimed at her.

Madurrin's presence floated into the Force-meld, alerting the others that Farlander was going to try another maneuver at the last second.

Jaina ordered her frigate to scatter weapons as the enemy squadron approached. As if they were shadow bombs, she used the Force to shove them toward the Yuuzhan Vong warships, but these *weren't* shadow bombs, nor would they cause damage to the enemy—at least not directly. Each contained a dovin basal that, when attached to an enemy vessel and triggered, would identify the ship carrying it as an enemy of the Yuuzhan Vong. In the past she had used these devices to cause the enemy to fire on one another, but now she had no confidence in the tactic: if the Yuuzhan Vong had worked out how to counter the yammosk jammer, it wasn't very many steps from there to being able to counter every weapon in Jaina's arsenal.

The enemy squadron flashed past, several of the decoy dovin basals attaching to each ship. Jaina felt a surge in the Force as the order was given for the New Republic fleet's last-second maneuver. She held her breath as Farlander's squadrons turned and accelerated, an attempt to cross the bows of the oncoming Yuuzhan Vong squadrons, shifting their target back from Shimrra's flagship to the enemy fleet elements. And then Jaina's despair deepened as she felt, through her connection with *Trickster*'s dovin basals, another series of commands raining out from the distant yammosk. The enemy ships all turned, once again, to counter Keyan Farlander's maneuver.

The Yuuzhan Vong hadn't even been *delayed* this time. They had responded to the maneuver the instant they detected it.

Jaina's blood ran cold. The yammosk jammers had been countered. The single greatest contribution to the war, the keystone of Jaina's plan for winning the battle—and it was *useless*.

Out of pure despair she triggered the dovin basal decoys she had fired at the enemy craft. Despite her impulsiveness the timing was perfect: the decoys switched on just as the enemy craft opened their main attack on the New Republic squadron. All the missiles and bolts that would otherwise have poured into the New Republic ships were fired instead at the two frigates and a few other smaller craft, which in their turn furiously fired at each other. Jaina watched as the elements of the Yuuzhan Vong squadron began maneuvering against each other with the same uncanny precision they had always shown under the guidance of a yammosk.

Yuuzhan Vong pilots and gunners were shrouded by the living hood that fed them information, and they knew only what the hood told them. When it told them a ship was enemy, they fired at it.

"It worked," Jaina said.

[Of course,] Lowbacca answered.

But why? The question floated to Jaina from Corran Horn. *Think. Something's . . . going on.*

Fire spattered the flanks of the two enemy frigates as projectiles and missiles struck home. Their dovin basal shields had been aimed to repel the attacks of the New Republic squadron, not their own fire, and they were taking heavy damage. And then, once the enemy were fully engaged with one another, New Republic concussion missiles and bolts from New Republic laser cannons arrived, followed by Kyp's Dozen and two other flights of starfighters. Smaller enemy ships were vaporized. The two frigates staggered to repeated hits. Muffled by her hood, Jaina gave a cheer. Through the Force she could feel Corran, Kyp, and Madurrin as they fought together, bringing separate elements of the fleet into a synchronization similar to that granted to the Yuuzhan Vong by their yammosk.

But they flew only three ships, and led only three elements of the fleet, two of them fighter squadrons. The rest of the New Republic fleet was forced to communicate through more conventional means. And only one of the five enemy squadrons was in trouble, the squadron that Jaina had seeded with decoy basals. The rest were engaged with New Republic forces in a far more standard give-and-take, with the Yuuzhan Vong still maneuvering with the eerie simultaneity given them by their war coordinator.

The New Republic forces were presumably firing more decoy dovin basals at the enemy, but the missiles would have to get through in order to have any effect, and so far none had.

Contrary to what intuition might suggest, fighter combat generally grew *less* deadly, not more, as greater numbers of fighters were involved. When fights were large and confusing, pilots spent more time watching their tails than hunting the enemy. The brains of the pilots simply couldn't keep track of all the craft maneuvering against them.

But that wasn't the case with the Yuuzhan Vong war coordinator. The yammosk kept track of every craft in the sky and ordered those in jeopardy to maneuver while others were guided to rescue their comrades. The New Republic starfighter pilots, brave and well trained though they might be, were simply outclassed by a dedicated intelligence that could process all the data from a large battle at once.

Jaina's heart lifted when first one, then another enemy frigate blew to bits, both betrayed by the decoy dovin basals she'd fired at them. But otherwise the Yuuzhan Vong were doing well. Flames poured from one of the Corellian gunships, and the vessel was staggering out of formation, out of control, its sublight drives slagged. One of the *Republic*-class cruisers was taking a lot of hits. And around every formation winked swarms of little fireflies, starfighters and coralskippers dying in battle, their lives flaring away in brief, silent fire.

Only Jaina, who had flown unmolested clear through the

enemy fleet, was in a position to observe it all, and despair. The enemy yammosk gave the Yuuzhan Vong too great an advantage. She could sense Corran and Kyp as they battled against an enemy whose maneuvers were simply without flaw.

Think! Jaina echoed Corran Horn's command. She led the only crew not engaged with the enemy; she was the only person with *time* to think. Why was the yammosk working even though it was jammed? Why was the jammer not working while the decoy basals were functioning perfectly, even though they were both based on the same principles?

Through *Trickster's* dovin basals, she could distantly sense the commands of the enemy yammosk, the gravity-wave instructions that commanded the Yuuzhan Vong formations. But she could also hear the regular beats of the jammer, the jammer that should be overriding the enemy signal.

What was going on?

Think! She answered her question with a command.

She submerged her awareness into the complex signals, tried to sense the pattern. The rhythms of the densely coded messages patterned through her mind, too fast for her to follow. There were *two* distinct patterns, she found, not one overlaid atop the other—the jammer and the yammosk seemed almost not to have anything to do with each other. What was the problem?

And then, beneath the jammer, Jaina began sensing something else, another pattern.

Her awareness slowed, tried to tune out the relentless beats of the jammer. *There* . . . Surprise sang along her nerves. What she detected seemed to be the signals of another yammosk.

Two yammosks?

The truth came in a sudden flash. Supreme Overlord Shimrra had brought his own war coordinator to the battle, probably on his flagship. But there was a second yammosk in the system, one seeded by the invaders on Obroa-skai, the yammosk that New Republic Intelligence had known about all along.

Whatever yammosk was first in command had been jammed by the Wraiths. But then the second yammosk, operating on a different part of the gravity-wave spectrum, had stepped in to take control.

For a moment Jaina's hands twitched in her command gloves, on the verge of ordering the jammer in *Trickster* to commence operations, but then she hesitated. If the enemy detected the origin of the jamming, then they'd know *Trickster* was a decoy vessel. Instead she yanked off her cognition hood and reached for the comm.

"Twin Suns Leader to Wraith Leader. There's a second yammosk! You'll have to tune another jammer to it."

Face Loran's tone failed to reveal whatever surprise he might be feeling. "This is Wraith Leader. Message understood, Major."

There was a slight delay before Jaina detected the second jammer begin its hammering beat, and another few seconds before it found the correct signal and began jamming it. Anxiously Jaina scanned the battle scene laid out behind her.

It was working. The eerie synchrony of the enemy ships was breaking up. Coralskippers hesitated in their movements, waiting for instructions in all the deadly chaos, and the New Republic craft took instant advantage.

Momentum was with the New Republic now. They were *used* to operating with less-than-perfect communications and coordination, but the Yuuzhan Vong pilots were bewildered once deprived of the commands of the yammosk.

Got one! Kyp's triumph floated through the Force.

Get another, Corran Horn sent—had *time* to send, now that he was no longer so hard-pressed. Jaina could have wept with relief.

She relaxed into the Force again. She couldn't affect the

battle directly, but she could help her friends, could send strength, love, and support through their Force-link. She sensed their growing strength, their growing triumph. Coralskippers blazed in front of their guns.

Through the combined Force awareness and the knowledge gained through *Trickster*'s sensors, she watched the progress of the battle. When the two enemy frigates had destroyed each other, the capital ships fighting them had found themselves free and had moved to assist a second New Republic squadron, sandwiching a Yuuzhan Vong squadron between them. Elsewhere, another of the enemy's frigates had been hit with one of the decoy dovin basals, and was being pounded by another Yuuzhan Vong frigate and swarms of coralskippers under the impression that it was an enemy. The tide had definitely turned, and Jaina quietly exulted.

My plan. It was working after all.

[Jaina.] Lowbacca's voice.

"Yes?"

[I thought you'd like to know I've just laid *Trickster* right astern of the enemy flagship.]

Jaina snapped alert and pulled the alien cognition hood over her head. At once she detected the rounded aft section of Shimrra's ship dead ahead, studded with plasma cannon barrels, launch tubes, and rounded fairings that doubtless held *something*, probably dovin basals used for propulsion or defense.

And they ordered *us to come here!* she thought in delight.

"Right," she said, this time through the comlink that connected her to everyone in her squadron. "I want every cannon and projectile tube on that ship's stern targeted. And those fairings, too, whatever's in them."

Acknowledgments crackled over the comlink, and Jaina busied herself in following her own orders. Most of her squadron members were dispersed over the frigate, hooded and gloved as she was, in charge of weapons or defense stations. Though she could command the ship with fewer than twelve crew, the efficiency was greater if there were more sentients onstation.

And her rookie pilots—exactly half of her squadron of twelve—were a lot safer here than piloting their starfighters against an experienced enemy.

All stations reported readiness. Jaina's gloved hands hovered in the air. Through the Force, she sent the message that they were ready to open fire on the flagship.

After a moment came General Farlander's reply, relayed through Madurrin. *Carry on*.

Carry on. Right.

"All weapons ready? *Open fire!*"

Trickster's bow blazed as a host of missiles and projectiles sped for the undefended enemy stern. Fire blossomed over the dark silhouette of the enemy ship, patterns of pinpoint flares marking dozens of hits. Jaina made certain that amid the volley were two of her decoy dovin basal missiles—one primary, one reserve—and as soon as the first volley was over, she triggered the primary, informing every Yuuzhan Vong in the area that their own flagship was now an enemy.

This encouraged the sixty nearby coralskippers to do their bit, plunging toward their flagship, fire raking along its flanks. The small craft probably couldn't do very critical damage to anything as huge as their target, but every little bit helped.

There was a pause between the first volley and the second only because the gunners were checking their targets and retargeting those that hadn't been destroyed. And then *Trickster*'s bow blazed again, and this time the blaze didn't stop.

Jaina was going to keep firing until every gun barrel and every missile tube on her ship was empty.

The flagship was surprisingly slow to respond. Dovin

basal energy was directed aft, sucking incoming projectiles into their black-hole singularities, but the dovin basals were seemingly unable to cover all the stern, so some of the attacking volley struck home anyway, and other bolts from the *Trickster* arced through dovin basal–warped space over the stern of the enemy ship, only to plunge down somewhere amidships.

After Jaina's first strike the enemy simply had no weapons remaining that fired dead aft, so missiles were fired out of the broadside batteries. These had to loop toward *Trickster* on a long arc, however, which made them easy to spot, and *Trickster*'s own dovin basals warped space to pick them off.

"We're in their shadow!" Jaina cried, and kept firing.

Through her Force-awareness, she sensed Kyp's satisfaction as he nailed a pair of coralskippers, Corran's grim pleasure in leading his flight onto the tails of a group of enemy skips, and Madurrin's awe as two more enemy frigates were destroyed.

The stern of the enemy flagship was *glowing* now, an eerie orange-red as repeated impacts broiled the target.

Jaina kept firing.

"The enemy's breaking off, Twin Leader." The flagship's voice came over her comm.

"Good news, flag."

"Not so good for you. They're pulling back to help their leader."

That meant four enemy frigates would soon be engaging her. No, *three* enemy frigates—she saw one break up as it tried to maneuver away from the fight.

"Better call on the—"

"Already taken care of, Twin Leader."

Already taken care of. Through her dovin basals Jaina felt the surge of gravity waves as two more squadrons of starships entered realspace.

Two Battle Dragons, three *Nova*-class battle cruisers,

and accompanying fighters, all courtesy of the Hapan Navy, and led in person by Jaina's former classmate, Queen Mother Tenel Ka, ruler of the sixty-three inhabited planets of the Hapes Consortium.

Greetings! Tenel Ka sent. Her strong personality flooded Jaina's Force awareness. The presence of a single additional Jedi had greatly increased the power of the Force-meld.

Welcome to Obroa-skai, Majesty, Jaina tried to send. *We've saved the flagship for you.* She couldn't tell whether such a complex thought got through, but she could sense that Tenel Ka understood at least the substance of it.

The Hapan fleet, like the New Republic ships, had been hovering only a few light-hours from Obroa-skai, ready for the call. Previous Hapan experience in fighting alongside the New Republic, at Fondor, had been nothing short of a catastrophe, and Tenel Ka had taken a political risk in bringing her ships here at all. Both Jaina and General Farlander wanted to be careful in using their ally, and so it had been agreed that the Hapans were to be used either to complete a victory or, if necessary, to cover a withdrawal.

What the Hapans managed instead was to complete a massacre. Hapan tactics had always consisted of a direct charge that launched a massed energy wall, all weapons blasting at once at a single target, a tactic that proved ideal for this situation. The Battle Dragons, on their way to the flagship, first took out the enemy transports, their concentrated wall of fire shattering the ships to fragments.

Jaina watched in awe as the three battle cruisers, acting as one, dashed at the enemy flagship in a single pass, their batteries blazing. Much of the fire got through, and Jaina saw towering explosions and geysers of debris erupt from the enemy hull.

Hapan energy weapons had once taken a notoriously long time to recharge, but after Fondor the New Republic had given the Hapans quick-charge turbolasers, so the battle cruisers stayed in the fight and kept hammering, now joined by the Battle Dragons. The flagship quaked to impacts, flame pouring from gaping holes in its sides.

At this point the rest of the Yuuzhan Vong apparently conceded their flagship lost, abandoned the battle, and fled in all directions with allied squadrons in pursuit. Jaina was surprised—she'd assumed they'd defend their Supreme Commander to the last warrior.

One alien frigate, surrounded by enemies, jumped into hyperspace too soon and was dragged back into realspace by Obroa-held's gravity. The inertia-damping dovin basals failed at the shock, and every individual on the ship was flung into the nearest bulkhead at nearly six-tenths speed of light. The result was a superheated plasma that ruptured the enemy hull as it blasted outward. Another frigate was blown to shreds by New Republic cruisers. Of the capital ships, only one frigate escaped into hyperspace, along with however many of the coralskippers it had managed to recover.

The Hapan ships blew up the flagship on their next pass. The starfighters began to hunt down the stranded coralskippers.

All that remained was for the surviving allied capital ships to move to Obroa-skai, destroy the planet's yammosk with a well-placed shot, and then plaster any Yuuzhan Vong barracks or installations until they glowed, taking care not to harm what remained of the library.

Jaina watched the end game play itself, her mind ringing with awe. *It worked.* Her plan. *It worked.*

She had just killed Shimrra, Supreme Overlord of the Yuuzhan Vong. If she hadn't just won the war, she might have provided its decisive moment.

A Wookiee howl came over the comlink.

"Yes!" Tesar said. "Congratulations!"

Cheers and congratulations erupted over the comlink.

Jaina's squadron, the comrades she'd led into danger, cheering her success. An unaccustomed joy filled Jaina.

"Thank you," she babbled. "Thank you all."

More congratulations came through her Force-awareness. And then, from the flagship, "Stand by. The general's sending a message."

Keyan Farlander's voice, when it came over the comm, sounded bemused.

"I've just received a subspace communication from Intelligence advising me not to make the attack, or to break off if I've begun," he said.

Jaina laughed. In the heady triumph of the victory, New Republic Intelligence seemed even more behind the times than usual.

"I don't suppose they mentioned why?" Jaina responded.

"Well," Farlander said, "it seems there's a problem. It looks as if Supreme Overlord Shimrra wasn't in the flagship after all."

FIVE

"Can you tell me what's going on here?"

General Keyan Farlander stood on the bridge of *Mon Adapyne*, bent in conference with one of his captains, a spike-headed Elomin named Kartha. He turned briefly toward Jaina, a grim expression on his face, and said, "Just a minute, Jaina. This is important."

Jaina had a hard time imagining anything more important than whether or not Supreme Overlord Shimrra had just been turned into a chunk of charred space debris, but she bit back her reply and crossed the bridge to where Madurrin waited. The Anx Jedi stood more than four meters tall, with a thick tail that balanced her massive body and pointed head. She had volunteered for the war against the Yuuzhan Vong but could hardly be crammed into the cockpit of a starfighter; the bridge of *Mon Adapyne* was far better suited to her.

"What happened?" Jaina demanded. "What's going on?"

"I don't know any more than you do." Madurrin sent reassurance to Jaina through the Force. "It's all right. We did extremely well. We *won*. We took the offensive and we won—for the first time."

Jaina took a breath and tried to calm her outraged nerves. "Thanks. But what about Shimrra?"

"You saved a lot of lives today," Madurrin reminded her. "You saved us when you realized the Yuuzhan Vong were using a second yammosk." She inclined her long, pointed head toward the Elomin officer speaking to Farlander. "You saved Kartha's life, for one. He was captain of the *Pulsar*."

"Was?" *Pulsar* was one of the Corellian gunships. Was that the one she'd seen out of control?

"*Pulsar*'s completely disabled. We'll have to scuttle her. The general's making arrangements for bringing off the crew and getting medical attention to the wounded."

The wounded . . . Jaina had been so completely focused on combat that she had forgotten about the price of the battle. The bloody toll of even a victorious fight.

She straightened. She didn't want to think about the dead and wounded now. Her service had to be to the living, and her focus on victory.

"The kill ratios were very much in our favor," Jaina said.

"Yes," Madurrin said. "They were."

Jaina scanned the bridge as she waited for Kartha and Farlander to conclude their conference. Though there were many different species aboard the cruiser, from the human Keyan Farlander on down, the bridge crew was made up entirely of Mon Cals. The brilliant display monitors, with their strange distortions, were configured for Mon Calamari eyes, and the chairs and instrument panels were adapted to their amphibious physiology. The bridge architecture, with its shell-like, scalloped design, suggested a peaceful subaquatic grotto. So different, Jaina thought, from the hard, geometric shapes of starfighter controls, let alone the strange, melting organic patterns of her captured Yuuzhan Vong frigate.

Other captains entered while Farlander spoke with Kartha. Last of all came Queen Mother Tenel Ka, sweeping onto the bridge with her female Hapan captains echeloned behind her, and dressed in a magnificent sky-blue admiral's uniform covered with gold insignia and braid, her red-brown hair tied back by a glittering royal diadem.

Jaina looked at her old classmate in surprise. She was more used to seeing Tenel's lithe, muscular body clad in the reptile-skin tunic of a Dathomirian Witch-warrior. This sleek look was something new.

The ruler of sixty-three planets clearly outranked a Jedi Knight, because General Farlander broke off his conference with Captain Kartha, approached Tenel Ka, and gave a bow.

"Your Majesty," he said, "your fleet's arrival was well timed."

"The timing was yours," Tenel replied. She turned her gray eyes to Kartha. "And the casualties, too."

"Hapes has taken many casualties on behalf of the New Republic," Farlander said. "We hoped to spare you more."

"You've spared us political embarrassment as well." Tenel Ka gave Farlander a frank look. "We can present this to our people as a nearly bloodless victory," she continued. "This will aid our alliance. Fact. We are profoundly grateful."

That was the royal we, Jaina thought. Tenel Ka was fitting with surprising ease into her new role as queen.

"We should return to the Hapes Cluster before our loyal subjects learn we're not, as we claimed, on a routine fleet exercise," Tenel went on. "But first, I'd like to know—*was that Shimrra we killed or not?*"

The *I* had been a slip, Jaina thought, indicating just how much Tenel had invested in the answer.

Farlander quirked an eyebrow. "I think I can guess how New Republic Intelligence made the mistake," he said. "They know that Supreme Overlord Shimrra is moving from the Rim to his new capital of Coruscant. They received a report that a Yuuzhan Vong big shot commanding a fleet was due in the Obroa-skai system to consult the library. They put two and two together and came up with seventeen." He shrugged. "Resistance units on the ground on Obroa-skai just confirmed that the enemy commander was someone named Supreme Commander Komm Karsh."

"Supreme Commander." Tenel's look was thoughtful. "A rank second only to warmaster. Still a notable victory."

"Yes, Majesty," General Farlander said. There was relief in his eyes. "I'm relieved as well. I put this operation together in the absence of any instructions from my superiors—" His eyes flicked to Jaina. "—and at the urging of one of my officers. Who—even if she *is* a goddess—is still rather junior."

Tenel Ka gave Jaina an appraising look.

"Goddess?" she said.

"You can call me 'Great One,' " Jaina said. "Most people do."

Partly as a propaganda exercise, and partly because it suited the role she had played in the war so far, the New Republic military had gone out of its way to behave toward Jaina as if she were an emanation of the Yuuzhan Vong Trickster goddess, Yun-Harla. They hoped to take advantage of Yuuzhan Vong superstition about twins, or to outrage the orthodox and drive them into an ill-judged frenzy.

Jaina couldn't say whether this was working or not, but she had found the goddess routine amusing . . . for at least the first ten minutes. After that it had become a drudgery.

Tenel Ka's words were thoughtful. "Does a mere mortal queen dare to hug a goddess?"

"You have our permission," Jaina said.

Tenel crossed the deck between them and embraced Jaina with her single arm, hard enough so that Jaina's breath went out of her.

General Farlander tactfully cleared his throat.

"Majesty, Great One, I'd like to proceed with the conference if we may," he said. "Komm Karsh may have called for reinforcements before his death, and I'd like to get out of this system while I'm ahead."

"Sensible," Tenel Ka said.

Tenel bade farewell to Madurrin, and then she and the captains retired to the cruiser's conference room, a seashell-shaped room with subdued, shimmering blue lighting that presented the illusion of being underwater. The room's central table was a gleaming work of art, subtly curved, gleaming like mother-of-pearl beneath the hushed lights.

Tenel Ka, walking with easy dignity, took her place before the seat of honor. At her nod, everyone took their seats.

The captains first presented damage and casualty reports—Jaina was pleased to report that her unit had suffered no losses, and her ship only minor harm—and then there was discussion of what to do with *Far Thunder*, a *Republic*-class cruiser that had suffered significant damage, including damage to its hyperspace drives. Farlander was inclined to abandon and scuttle the ship, but *Far Thunder*'s Captain Hannser argued forcefully that he could repair his ship given time, and Farlander finally gave his assent. *Far Thunder* would be evacuated except for command, drive, and damage control crews, then make a microjump out of the Obroa-skai system under escort by the *Lancer*-class frigate. A tender would be sent with the necessary spare parts to rendezvous with *Far Thunder*, and—with any luck—preserve the Kuat Systems cruiser for future encounters with the Yuuzhan Vong.

"We'll hope to see you at Kashyyyk," Farlander told Hannser.

"Kashyyyk?" Tenel Ka was surprised. "Why Kashyyyk?"

"We're shifting our base there, Majesty," Farlander said. "We want to be able to defend that section of the Mid Rim yet still be close enough to offer you assistance at Hapes if you should come again under attack."

Tenel nodded. "Your long-term plans?"

Farlander looked uncertain. "The fact is that we've received no instructions from headquarters since the fall of Borleias. I'm making everything up as I'm going along."

Tenel frowned. "Who is your immediate superior?"

"Admiral Traest Kre'fey. But he is a relative of Borsk

Fey'lya, and was compelled to return to Bothawui for the period of official mourning."

Jaina lifted one eyebrow but otherwise remained silent. She couldn't bring herself to mourn the late Chief of State, but she supposed *someone* had to.

Keyan Farlander clasped his hands and leaned forward across the conference table. "Please understand, Majesty," he said. "I hope that we may once more operate together against our common enemy. I will cooperate with you to the utmost of my power, and if the Hapes Cluster is again attacked, I hope you will feel free to call for my assistance. But I can't speak for my superiors, and I may be superceded at any time."

"Understood," Tenel said.

Uncertainty dogged them all, Jaina thought. She had hoped, with a strike at the enemy leader, to bring things into focus. But her target had been a phantom, and even though a victory had been won, it was hard to say, in the fog of doubt, just what even such a victory really meant.

SIX

Jacen rose gently from the embrace of the Force like a man rising slowly and reluctantly from the warmth and buoyancy of a mineral spring. He paused before rising fully to the mundane world and basked for a moment in the luxurious, shining unity of all living things, and then, like a garment, he donned his ego—put himself into himself, as it were—and he opened his eyes.

"You were successful?" Vergere asked.

The strange being's feathery whiskers floated in an alien breeze, a wind heavy with warmth and the thick spoor of organics. They had escaped Coruscant in a Yuuzhan Vong coral craft, a vessel with a resinous interior that looked like half-melted ice cream and ventilation that smelled like old socks.

"I think I found them," Jacen said. "I touched my mother, and I know she recognized me. But we were cut off suddenly— I don't know why. And I think I may have reached my uncle— my Master—Luke. And I touched my sister, briefly." He frowned as the harmonious sensation brought by his connection with the Force was disturbed by the unsettling memory. "But she was involved in a confrontation—a battle, I think, with the Yuuzhan Vong. I broke the connection before I could turn into a fatal distraction for her."

Anxiety for Jaina gnawed at his mind. "Maybe I shouldn't

have. Maybe I should have stayed with her, tried to send her calm and strength."

"You made the choice, and it was uncoerced," Vergere said. "For you to question such a choice is not simply useless, but harmful. Such doubts will chain the mind to an endless circle of pointless speculation and self-recrimination. You should prepare yourself to live with the consequences of your decisions, whatever they may be."

"It's different when the consequences are going to happen to your sister," Jacen said.

The diminutive Vergere hunkered down, the knobs of her reverse-articulated knees rising strangely behind her. "The rise or fall of a civilization can depend on the decision made in a fragment of a second. There are many seconds in a day. How many seconds can you regret? How many choices?"

"Only the bad ones," Jacen said.

"And if you don't know immediately whether the decision was good or bad? What if you don't find out the answer for fifty years?"

Jacen looked at her. "Fifty years," he said. "I'm not even twenty. I can't imagine fifty years."

Her tilted eyes shimmered like waves over cold, deep water. There was unconquerable sadness in her voice. "Fifty years ago, young Jedi, I made a decision," she said. "The consequences of that decision echo down the years until today. And I still do not know whether the decision I made was the right one."

"What decision was that?" Jacen asked.

"The decision that brought about this war." Vergere's feathers rippled. "I am responsible, you see, for all the fighting, all the suffering, all the death. All because of a decision I made fifty years ago, on Zonama Sekot."

SEVEN

Zonama Sekot! (cried Vergere.) The Green Land. Taller than the tallest tree are the boras, with balloon-shaped leaves in rainbow colors, and limbs with iron tips that call down the lightning. Deep valleys from which the morning mist rises in waves like ocean rollers breaking on the shore. A northern hemisphere of sun and bright green, and a southern hemisphere hidden in a perpetual cloud that forever cloaks its mysteries.

Zonama Sekot! Where mobile seeds attach themselves to living clients in their eagerness to be shaped. Where airships bob gently amid the mountain peaks. Where the vines and creepers carve out terraces over which the bright blossoms spill like living waterfalls. Black-haired Ferroan colonists who live among the generous life in a kind of symbiosis. Dwellings where the walls, the roof, even the furniture is alive. Factory valleys where boras seeds are forged into living ships, the fastest ever to fly between the stars.

Zonama Sekot! Where the air itself intoxicates. Where transforming lightning ignites life rather than destroys it. A world covered with a benevolent organism in the form of its own vegetation. An entire world that sings with billions of voices a great and continual hymn to the Force.

I had become so besotted with the place that I had almost forgotten my mission. How hard it is to concentrate when the harmonies of Zonama Sekot sing in your ears! How blissful is sleep when an entire world shares with you its dreams!

But I knew that I must remain alert. Even before my arrival I sensed that a great terror lurked nearby. The Jedi Council had learned of an intrusion of a strange enemy and sent me to find them, and also, if I could, to locate the fabled Zonama Sekot. I found the second before I found the first, but from the behavior of the Ferroan natives I guessed that the intruders were near: the Ferroans were too nervous, too reticent. Zonama Sekot was overripe with secrets and about to explode.

I had come, I told the natives, to buy a ship—and this was true, for the Jedi Council wished to know of the living ships that were bred in this distant world, and were willing to pay for the knowledge. I surrendered my ingots of aurodium in payment, and I went through their ritual. I was chosen by three seed-partners, spiky creatures who clung to my garment and sang to me of the great ship they would become once transformed by the lightning and the fire. This caused a sensation—no one had been chosen by three before. The seed-partners were intrigued by my connection to the Force.

So for two nights the seed-partners clung to me, and I lived in a joyous trance that I shared with them, their dream of becoming. When I had my living ship, I planned to fly it in a search for intruders.

And then came the first strike of the Far Outsiders.

Those whose worlds have been subdued by the Yuuzhan Vong will recognize the pattern. It has been seen at Belkadan, at Sernpidal, at Tynna, Duro, Nar Shaddaa. At first there is an invasion of a hostile life-form, a living wind of change that sweeps across the world like a consuming plague, scores of native species dying as the invading life takes its hold. Suddenly entire regions become friendly to the Yuuzhan Vong, hostile to the world's own native life.

So it became with Zonama Sekot. The Far Outsiders—

the Yuuzhan Vong—seeded the southern hemisphere with their own devouring forms of life. Two complete ecosystems engaged in pitched battle. The beautiful, towering boras died, writhing in their death agonies as they called the lightning to blast the alien parasites that devoured their flesh.

Through the Force I felt the planet shudder. From my dwelling near the factory valley, I saw the boras tossing their leaves and limbs in horror at the battle that was being lost in the other hemisphere. The Ferroans ran about in confusion and growing panic. Even the clouds reacted, flying through the sky in fright and terror. The forging of my ship was postponed as the entire planet mobilized to deal with the emergency.

At this point I revealed myself as Jedi. The reaction of the Ferroans was strangely ambivalent—not hostile, precisely, but warier than I expected. I later learned that they had been taught a version of Jedi doctrine, though far from an orthodox one. They were believers in the Potentium, the doctrine that the Force is light only and that evil and the dark side are a kind of illusion. They were afraid I had come to persecute them for heresy. By the time I appeased their fears, the ecological onslaught had grown to embrace much of the southern hemisphere.

I was brought to meet their leader, their Magister—by that time his mountain palace was besieged by the world-plague. Here, in a symbiosis with the planet that was his home, he directed his world's defenses. And he succeeded! The living world of Zonama Sekot possesses more resources than the Yuuzhan Vong had imagined. In the war of ecosystems, Zonama Sekot began to push the enemy back. The invading organisms began to die.

It was then that the Yuuzhan Vong attacked with conventional forces. Frigates bombarded the world from orbit; coralskippers descended into the atmosphere to bomb and strafe.

But Zonama Sekot again had hidden resources, fighters and other planetary defenses, and the Yuuzhan Vong were driven off. This was not, you see, an invasion such as the one you know, but merely a reconnaissance in force, the Yuuzhan Vong scouting our defenses.

I tried to protect the Magister, but in the end I failed him. A Yuuzhan Vong squadron attacked his palace, and that brave, inventive man was killed. His belief that evil was an illusion did not save him.

But scarcely did I have a chance to mourn the greatness of the man. His death brought forth a miracle! I felt, stirring in the living Force, a powerful Presence—a great mind un-coiling and feeling its power for the first time. A new being caught in the first, astonishing moment of self-awareness.

That being was Zonama Sekot! For three generations the Magisters, with their unconventional doctrine of the Force, had communed with the living world that they believed was their mythical Potentium, their all-benevolent Force. Un-knowing, they had taught the harmony that was Zonama Sekot to realize itself as an individual. What had been an egoless perfection now became a self-conscious, self-aware being, with all the confusion and uncertainty of a new, fragile creature dropped suddenly into a hostile universe.

I needed to give the planet time. I offered to negotiate with the enemy on its behalf, in the hope of either turning away the attack or delaying the next assault. Sekot assumed the personality of its dead Magister and communicated to the Yuuzhan Vong its wish to parley. The Yuuzhan Vong consented, feeling that they might gain through intimida-tion what they had failed to gain through violence.

The Ferroans gave me a shuttle and a brave pilot, and I went to speak to the Far Outsiders. They were led by Supreme Commander Zho Krazhmir—he died in his sleep years ago, you would not have heard of him.

Imagine the scene. The air lock dilating like a living membrane. The air that reeked of organics. The chamber with its curves and half-melted resinous walls. The mass of Yuu-zhan Vong, the commander with his staff, his priests, his in-tendant. In armor, bearing weapons. All in an angry group, a crowd massed to intimidate. A group designed by Zho Krazhmir to shock an envoy into submission.

I did not face them quite alone. My seed-partners, the embryos of my future ship, were with me, clinging to the robes that I had worn since the ceremony.

But you can imagine what truly shocked me. All I had seen to that point was nothing compared to the realization, as I summoned the Force to my assistance, that I had brought the Force into a place that was alien to the Force itself.

I could not touch them with the Force. They were blank— they were *worse* than blank, they were an abyss into which the Force could drain forever, drain until it was all gone, until all existence, all life, had drained away . . .

At first I thought that they were all Force masters; that they had devised ways of shielding themselves from me. But as I tried again and again to pierce their defenses, I realized what the Yuuzhan Vong truly were.

A sacrilege. Everything a Jedi knows is based on the belief—on the absolute, unquestioned *knowledge*—that all life is a part of the Force, that the Force is life. But here were beings whose very existence denied this sacred truth. From the depths of my heart I hated them all, I wished them blotted out. A rage rose in me, an anger so complete that I almost attacked them then and there in the hope that I could obliterate them all from the face of the universe. Never had I been so close to surrendering to darkness.

My anger was not the only anger in that room. The Supreme Commander was furious because his attack had failed and he had lost face before his intendant. The priests were angry because I had flown to them in a machine they considered a blasphemy. The intendants were outraged because of the loss of scarce matériel, which they would have to justify to their own superiors. The Far Outsiders were eons away from their home, and Zonama Sekot had damaged their ability to survive here.

But one creature there was not angry. The mascot of the priestess Falung, a feathery birdlike thing, only semi-intelligent, long-legged, and orange-yellow.

That being was the key. For I could touch it with the Force! I could feel its mind, benign, witless as a child, too mindless to feel the anger that surged about it.

And it was discovering that creature that caused my rage to ebb. Perhaps the realization that the Far Outsiders kept pets made me realize they were not so far removed from ourselves. I realized that within hours I had just encountered the two extremes of the Force. Zonama Sekot was a living embodiment of the Force, of its harmony and potential. The Far Outsiders, on the other hand, were creatures completely outside the Force, whom the Force could not touch. One was a contradiction of the other!

I wondered if it were possible for me to bring these two forces into balance.

But first I had to deal with the rage of the Yuuzhan Vong. Such was their fury that it was possible that these mad beings would obliterate me on the spot, parley or no parley.

Again the priestess's mascot was the key. Using the Force to influence its simple mind, I coaxed it forward. At my urging it warbled. It crooned. It fell upon me as if I were a long-lost cousin, and put around me its many-jointed wings.

The Yuuzhan Vong stared.

We danced together, the mascot and I. In unison we stamped and thumped and caroled. The Yuuzhan Vong, I saw, had forgotten to be angry. They began to be amused. Some even swayed back and forth, if only slightly, to the tempo of our dance.

And then I made them stare. With a push of my mind, I sent the alien mascot into the air. Singing, it spiraled toward the Yuuzhan Vong and orbited the commander. Singing, I joined it. The two of us continued our dance, sailing in a stately spiral about Supreme Commander Zho Krazhmir. The Yuuzhan Vong stared in utter wonder.

The Far Outsiders were capable of anger, of violence, of amusement, of awe. Were they then so very different from us? Was their very existence a blasphemy? I needed to know.

Before their wonder began to fade, I brought the dance to an end. Zho Krazhmir grew suspicious. He demanded to know what trick I had just played.

No trick, I replied. What you have seen is the power of Zonama Sekot.

I told them I was not from Zonama Sekot; that I was a teacher who had come to the planet in order to learn of its wonders. I described what I could of the world, that it was a glory, covered with a single great organism that formed a single intelligent mind.

Then the Supreme Commander grew excited.

I did not know then that the Yuuzhan Vong, in their own way, revere life. Not as a Jedi reveres life, cherishing each individual as a component of the Force that is both life and greater than life, but in their own perverse way, the reverence for life mixed with their own ideas of pain and death. The Yuuzhan Vong revere life in the abstract but sacrifice their own lives without thought. Their veneration of life is as extreme as their other beliefs, so extreme that they believe nonliving things—droids, starships, even simple machines—are a blasphemy and an insult to Yun-Yuuzhan, their Creator.

The Supreme Commander had been tasked to locate habitable worlds for the increasing and increasingly discontented inhabitants of the rapidly deteriorating Yuuzhan Vong worldships. To find a living world was beyond his wildest dreams.

Then the intendant pointed out that the Yuuzhan Vong lacked the resources to launch another strike. If the Supreme Commander attacked and was defeated, then the Yuuzhan Vong would be without sufficient means to return to the great worldships that moved between the galaxies. If they conquered the planet but took losses, they would be stuck on the planet without the resources to defend it.

The Supreme Commander reluctantly submitted. He would return to the worldship convoy and inform the Supreme Overlord of his discovery. He gave the order to withdraw.

It was then that I had to make my decision. I had bought at least a temporary peace for Zonama Sekot, but the mystery of the origin and nature of the Far Outsiders had yet to be resolved. They were clearly a menace to the galaxy, to the Jedi, and perhaps to the Force itself. Yet they did not seem beyond understanding, and reacted in many ways as other sentients do. These beings were so extraordinary that my mind was dizzied with their strangeness.

Though I could now return to Zonama Sekot with much of my mission accomplished, I knew I could not leave the Yuuzhan Vong before I had answered my many questions. I approached the priestess Falung and asked whether I might stay on the ship with my "cousin"—by this I meant her pet—and she conceded. Perhaps Falung would be kind enough to instruct me on her doctrine. In return, I would tell her as much as she wished to know of our own galaxy.

The priestess agreed, and without reference to the Supreme Commander. I saw that she was powerful enough in her own right to make these decisions.

So I was committed to remain. I returned briefly to my shuttle, and contacted the spirit of Sekot, who was still assuming the form of the planet's dead Magister. I told the planet that it was safe for now, but that it should prepare for another, stronger assault in the future.

And then—and this was very hard—I had to bid farewell to my seed-partners. They had dreamed with me of the great ship that would flash between the stars like the lightning that the boras drew from the skies, but this was not to be. I told the seed-partners that they had to return to the planet. I told them that a Jedi would be coming to Zonama—for I was certain that Jedi would follow in my footsteps when I did not return—and that they must hold themselves in readiness. I impressed upon them a message that was to be delivered to that Jedi, saying that an invading force was poised to overrun the galaxy, that the Force was useless in fighting these creatures.

If a Jedi came, I know not. If the message was delivered, I cannot tell. I did what seemed best, but in this I may have failed somehow.

Following this came the hardest task of all. I destroyed my lightsaber, the outward symbol of everything to which I had dedicated myself. I knew that the Yuuzhan Vong would not permit me to retain anything of a technological nature. My comlink and my few other metal objects I gave to the shuttle pilot who had brought me.

And so I bade farewell to everything I had known. I returned to the Yuuzhan Vong and the priestess Falung, and Zho Krazhmir's forces returned to that limitless space between the stars where the Yuuzhan Vong worldships traveled.

From time to time, the Yuuzhan Vong asked to see me dance with the priestess's mascot. The mascot and I danced, and flew—but we flew less and less, the farther we traveled from Zonama Sekot. When we left the galaxy, I told Falung that we were at such a distance that the power of Sekot could no longer reach us, and from that point on we no longer danced.

I did not want the Yuuzhan Vong to know that it was *my* power, not Sekot's, that had created the aerial dance. I did not want the Yuuzhan Vong even to consider the possibility that I had any power of my own.

For his action in discovering Zonama Sekot, Supreme Commander Zho Krazhmir was granted a new leg implant as a reward. He did not make a good recovery, and was dead in a few years.

Falung, priestess of Yun-Harla, instructed me in the religion of the Yuuzhan Vong and in particular the mythology of Yun-Harla herself.

Yun-Harla the Trickster is never visible. Her body is made of borrowed parts, and cloaked in borrowed skin. Over the borrowed skin are garments designed to deceive and deflect. Yun-Harla herself is never seen. Only her spirit is to be found working in the world, laying traps and deceiving the unwary.

As Yun-Harla is, so I became. I became cloaked, as it were, in borrowed garments, in my assumed identity as a simple teacher eager to learn the True Way. My weapons were those I could borrow or adapt from my opponents, those and my own cunning. My Force abilities I learned to keep hidden, even from telepathic creatures such as yammosks. I meditated upon Yun-Harla every day—every day for fifty years.

I turned my true self completely inward. It required little effort to maintain my identity as the familiar of Falung the priestess, in part because the Yuuzhan Vong expect so little from a familiar. But in my mind I built my home. There, I could consider the matter of the Yuuzhan Vong, and contemplate the Force. In my mind I learned true freedom.

In my conversations with Falung I tried to suggest the key Jedi principle of the unity of life, and somewhat to my surprise she agreed with me. All life, she explained, was a part of Yun-Yuuzhan, who created it through his own sacrifice, tearing himself into bits and flinging himself through the universe to spawn all existence. Though the reverence for life was real, it was not possible to separate it from the Yuu-zhan Vong obsession with pain and death.

Others than Falung questioned me, but not about philo-sophical matters—as far as they were concerned we were all infidels, and our beliefs were of no possible interest. The in-formation that truly interested them was of a military and political nature.

I agonized over what I would tell them. Should I tell them the Republic was unprepared, in the hope that the Yuuzhan Vong would attack prematurely, carelessly, and with over-confidence? Or should I suggest that the Republic's defenses were invincible, and force the Yuuzhan Vong to make elabo-rate, thorough preparations that I hoped other Jedi, fol-lowing in my footsteps and warned by my message, would detect?

In the end I dared not lie to them. I knew not what other sources of information were available to them. But I could feign ignorance—I had assured them I was a simple teacher, no authority on the defenses of the Republic.

I was not in a position to influence the Yuuzhan Vong for good or ill. Falung died, and I became the property of her junior, Elan, who was not in a position to affect policy.

And so the war began, and it began the way it did because of the decisions I made fifty years ago, at Zonama Sekot. Because I danced in the air, and proclaimed my power the power of a world.

Was I wrong to do so? Right? And if it was wrong, should I have spent the last fifty years in sadness and recrimination, fearing to act in the event that I made another mistake?

I chose. I acted. And then I resolved to face the conse-quences. Tell me then, young Jedi—was I wrong?

EIGHT

Jacen heard Vergere's story in silence as he squatted on his heels on the resinous floor of the coral ship. He did not answer her question, but instead asked a question of his own.

"Where is Zonama Sekot? I've never heard of a living planet."

Vergere shrugged her narrow shoulders. "It left," she said simply.

Jacen stared at her.

"I felt Sekot's good-bye. I had saved it once, but I sensed it was under a new threat. The planet had hyperdrive engines—it was capable of going into hyperspace. So it fled."

Jacen blinked. "Where did it go?"

"I remind you that I have been away for a number of years. I will not venture to guess."

Jacen rubbed his chin. "One hears stories of planets that move. But usually in the same tapcafs, and from the same people, who tell you of the Cursed Palace of Zabba Two, or old Admiral Fa'rey's ghost ship that plies the Daragon Trail."

Vergere gave a sniff. "I do not venture into tapcafs. I would not hear such stories."

Jacen gave a quiet smile. "No. You venture into more dangerous places than bars."

Vergere's crest feathers rippled. "You did not answer my question. Did I do wrong on Zonama Sekot? Or did I not?"

"What I think," Jacen said, "is that I'm still worried about my sister." He knew perfectly well that Vergere had told her story at this moment partly in order to distract him from his anxiety over Jaina.

Vergere made a sound somewhere between a snort and a sneeze. She straightened her legs and reared to her full height of slightly over a meter. "You haven't been paying attention!"

"I have. I'm still thinking about it. But I'm also still concerned about Jaina."

Vergere made the noise again. Jacen's thoughts returned to the mystery of the vanished planet.

"I've never heard of Zonama Sekot by that name. And if your warning ever reached the Jedi Council, I haven't heard of it—but then it's not likely I would have. We haven't had a Jedi Council in more than a generation."

"What became of it, then?" Vergere paced back and forth before Jacen, the patchy feathers on her frame fluffing and then smoothing again. "Perhaps you can tell me what has happened to the Republic in my absence. Tell me why the thousands of Jedi Knights I expected to contact on my return no longer exist, why there are only a few score half-trained young Jedi in their place, and what all of this has to do with this Sith Lord you mentioned on Coruscant, this Vader, your grandfather, whom I remember as that turbulent little Padawan, Anakin Skywalker."

Crouching, Jacen watched Vergere's agitated pacing. He shook his head and gave a laugh. "Well," he said, "you'd better sit down again, because this is a very long story."

This time Vergere sat in silence while Jacen spoke. When he was done with his bare narrative, she asked questions, and Jacen replied as completely as he could. At the end, they were both silent for a long, long moment.

Finally Jacen broke the silence. "May I worry about Jaina now?"

"No, you may not."

"Why not?"

Vergere straightened and approached the coral ship's little control station. "Best to worry for ourselves," she said. "We're about to fall out of hyperspace. When we arrive in realspace, we'll be near a well-defended world of the New Republic, guarded by fighters very jumpy after the fall of Coruscant. We are in a Yuuzhan Vong vessel, with no means of contacting these trigger-happy defenders, and we have no defenses and no weapons."

Jacen looked at her. "What do you suggest we do?"

Vergere's feathery crest gave a little flutter. "Foolish question," she said. "Naturally, we trust the Force."

NINE

Surrounded by rainbows, the great shadow descended in majesty from the sky. Like the wings of a butterfly just emerged from its cocoon, enormous wings slowly unfolded from the great craft. Rainbow colors pulsed and swam.

"Do-ro'ik vong pratte!" The roar came from ten thousand throats. The perfect rectangular formation of warriors, in their vonduun crab armor, raised their amphistaffs and roared their battle cry as the shadow of the craft passed over them.

"Taan Yun-forqana zhoi!" Ten thousand priests, in red cloaks emblazoned with the symbol of Yun-Yuuzhan, crossed their arms in salute and roared their devotion as the vessel's shadow enveloped them.

"Fy'y Roog! Fy'y Roog!" Ten thousand members of the shaper class, dressed in stainless white, howled their pride, fear, and obedience as the belly of the great craft passed over them.

Beyond the three giant formations of priests, warriors, and shapers, massed workers cried nothing, but simply flung themselves onto their faces, groveling in submission to the great shadow as it passed before the sun.

Shamed Ones, mutilated and crippled and barred from the ceremony, hid in their barracks or workhouses and shivered in fear.

The smallest group, the twelve hundred members of the

intendant class, stood motionless in three long lines in front of the three larger formations of Yuuzhan Vong, each member in his long green cloak. They did not shout, but stood in perfectly disciplined silence, arms crossed over their chests, as the massive craft moved silently overhead.

If we *had* a battle cry, thought Nom Anor from the second rank, it would probably be *Have you triple-checked this order with your superiors?* For it was the intendants who administered the new empire of the Yuuzhan Vong, and tried to balance the competing claims for resources among the other castes. A task that grew harder, it seemed, even as victory followed victory and more resources became available.

For years now, since before the time he had poisoned Imperial Interim Ruling Council members in the cause of Xandel Carivus, Nom Anor had been living among the enemy as a spy and saboteur. In the service of the Yuuzhan Vong, he had spun his treachery and left a trail of bodies across half the galaxy.

It had almost been enough to forget that the normal job of an intendant was a bureaucratic one.

Rainbows spiraled off the craft's great unfolded wings, dovin basals with their space-warping capabilities tuned to the spectrum of light. The great shadow hovered over the massive cradle that had been built for it, then slowly, majestically, descended.

Another great cry roared up from the triumphant multitude as the huge craft settled into its cradle like a monarch slowly sitting on his throne. Dazzling, spinning rainbows reached into the heavens, cast brilliant light onto the plaza where the Yuuzhan Vong masses waited. Beneath the ship, hidden from view, the living craft and the living cradle joined, linking power and communications and resource systems so that the craft now drew its nourishment from the planet, and the Supreme Overlord was in direct contact with the World Brain, the dhuryam that controlled the re-making of Yuuzhan'tar, formerly known as Coruscant, capital of both the New and Old Republics.

The Supreme Overlord's craft, ship and palace in one, was now joined with its cradle, just as the spaceborn Yuuzhan Vong had settled onto the conquered worlds that their gods had promised them. The craft would remain here permanently, its rainbow-edged wings outstretched over this world the Yuuzhan Vong had conquered. The conquered world would be altered from the bedrock up to re-create the legendary homeworld of the Yuuzhan Vong, lost long ago in another galaxy.

At the moment the shout went up, Nom Anor began to feel an itching at the base of his toes. He resisted the impulse to bend and scratch, or to scrape one boot over the other. The Yuuzhan Vong did not regard bodily discomfort as significant. Only those who had most successfully embraced pain and mutilation were promoted to the highest degrees. Surely an itch could be overcome.

As if to dispute this claim, the itch increased its fury. Nom Anor found that it was all he could do to keep his mind on the ceremony, on the ritual steps and obeisances that prepared the way for the appearance of the Supreme Overlord.

He panted with the effort to ignore the itch. He alternately stretched and clenched his toes inside his boots, hoping the effort might relieve his torment. It didn't.

Another roar went up from the crowd. Through his single, rainbow-dazzled eye, Nom Anor saw two figures on the summit of the great building.

Shimrra's personal quarters arched up above the plaza like a head on the end of a long neck. At the apex was a circular walkway surrounded by a rail that glittered like mother-of-pearl in the artificial rainbows. Standing amid the brilliance was Supreme Overlord Shimrra, unquestioned leader of the Yuuzhan Vong, sanctioned by the gods to bring all these new worlds under his heel. Nom Anor's eye was so dazzled by rainbows that he could see nothing of Shimrra but a silhouette—a *giant* silhouette, towering over the bent, ungainly figure next to him. Onimi, apparently, a member of the Shamed Ones whom the Supreme Overlord had adopted as his familiar.

As Shimrra's loyal subjects bellowed their triumph, several mon duuls waddled out from the shadow of the building. Giant, placid beings weighing four metric tons or more, the creatures had been implanted with specialized, dedicated villips by the shapers who had crafted them, villips that enabled them to receive communications from a master villip employed by the Supreme Overlord. Each mon duul, on receiving a message, could then broadcast it to others in its vicinity through the use of a giant two-meter tympanum of skin that stretched over its belly.

The mon duuls spread out over the plaza, then sat back on their haunches, their tympani directed toward the formations of Yuuzhan Vong. Nom Anor could hear joints cracking as the nearest of the massive creatures settled itself into an upright posture.

The Supreme Overlord's voice, amplified by the tympani in the mon duuls, echoed and reechoed over the plaza, and for a moment Nom Anor forgot his aggravating itch.

"Yuuzhan Vong, conquerors, blessed of the gods!" Shimrra roared. *"We have come to the turning point!"*

Luke found out the next afternoon why Fyor Rodan had behaved in such an extraordinary way at their meeting. Rodan hadn't been having a conversation; he'd been rehearsing a speech.

"He laid it all out before the Senate this morning," Cal Omas said. "His whole program—the Jedi shouldn't be a privileged group within the state, we should stop spending money on Jedi concerns, a new Jedi Council would be a threat . . ."

"Jedi should just get jobs like every other working stiff," Mara added. Cal laughed.

"How was the speech received?" Luke asked.

Cal Omas clasped his lanky arms behind his head. "I imagine it went down well with the working stiffs. As for the Senators, some agreed, some didn't, some saw it only in political terms. Since Fyor made no motion, just stood up in the Senate and gave his speech and made sure there were plenty of reporters there to cover it, there wasn't a head count one way or another."

"So why did he make the speech at all?"

Triebakk, the Wookiee who served with both Omas and Rodan on the Advisory Council, gave a long series of roars, all translated by the elderly protocol droid that Cal used for a secretary. "He spoke in order to make the Jedi an issue in the upcoming election. Now that he has made his speech, Cal and the other candidates are forced to respond."

"Whether they want to or not," Luke said.

"Precisely," Cal said. "Fyor's started up a tune, and the rest of us will have to dance to it."

Cal Omas's apartment was cramped and underwater, though built with the usual Mon Calamari attention to elegant design, which made it seem larger than it actually was. A transparent wall looked out onto the floodlit inverted cityscape of Heurkea Floating City, showing Mon Cals and Quarren swimming past or jetting by in their vehicles. Unfortunately, the transparent wall sweated heavily, the air was dank and tasted of brine, the carpet was soggy, and the small sofa that Luke and Mara shared gave off a distinct smell of mildew. There was no security. Cal's protocol droid was beginning to show rust stains. Still, Cal's place was better than most refugees' quarters, and a testimony to his character—he had refused to pull rank and demand better quarters for himself.

Such were the circumstances of the man whom Luke hoped would be the next Chief of State of the New Republic. Even Fyor Rodan's cramped, overflowing hotel suite was more impressive than this.

"I made a response to Fyor's speech," Cal went on. "I said that anyone who had fought alongside the Jedi in the war against Palpatine would never believe that they were a threat to the rest of us, and that it was unfortunate that Rodan lacked the experience."

Triebakk gave a howl of appreciation.

"Clever," Mara said. "Good to point out that while you were fighting for the freedom of the galaxy, Rodan was off selling protocol droids to Lurrians, or whatever."

"That didn't end it, though," Cal said. "CZ-Twelve-R here," nodding at his protocol droid, "has been swamped with messages from reporters wanting to know the details of my 'Jedi program.' "

"And of course," Luke said, "we don't know what that is yet."

"I'm afraid not." Cal leaned his long body forward in his chair and looked at Luke. "I'd like to reestablish the Jedi Council, of course, but I don't know if it's a good idea to say so."

"When all else fails," Mara advised, "fall back on the truth."

Cal Omas gave a look of mock horror. "No! I'm a politician! I can't tell the truth!"

"Seriously, Cal," Mara said, "what *can* you say?"

Cal Omas hesitated.

"Suppose," Luke offered, "you say that you will bring the Jedi firmly under the control of the government. You don't have to specify how."

"I'll have to give *some* details," Cal said. "Otherwise it'll seem as if I don't really have a plan at all, and that would be uncomfortably close to the truth, which"—with an amused glance at Mara—"as a politician I absolutely cannot speak."

He frowned. "Luke, can you tell me how the Jedi Council was set up in the past? If we know how it used to work, maybe we can make it work again."

"The Jedi Council was a dozen or so respected Masters," Luke said, "who oversaw the other Jedi and their training, and who reported to the Supreme Chancellor. If the Chancellor saw a problem that required Jedi abilities, he would inform the Council, who would send Jedi to deal with it. Usually not many, because it was well known that behind the first Jedi were a few thousand more. And I imagine that information went both ways—that the Jedi themselves would alert the Supreme Chancellor if their own network of contacts pointed to a problem somewhere."

"A few thousand Jedi," Cal mused, "to cover an entire galaxy."

Mara gave a smug smile. "We're *good*," she said.

"But there are somewhat less than a few thousand of you now," Cal said. "Which is why we now have a military and a diplomatic service and so on. So how do I counter Fyor's contention that you're redundant?"

"Well," Mara said, "what happens if you need a diplomat who can also practice philosophy, fight with a lightsaber, and levitate small objects? Who else are you going to call but us?"

Triebakk gave a snarl of amusement. Luke felt a kind of bliss sing through his heart at the fact that Mara could joke again, and he put an affectionate arm around her, after which he decided to ignore the scent of mildew that rose from the pillows.

"Mara has a point," he said. "We provide a specialized service—all-arounders, if you like."

"The Council of All-Arounders." Cal Omas sighed. "I don't think we're getting anywhere."

"Not the Council of All-Arounders," Luke said. "The Chief of State's Special Investigative Service. Your eyes, ears, and sword arm throughout the galaxy. When you need more muscle than a diplomat, and less than a battle cruiser, you send us."

Cal's eyes brightened. "I think you're getting somewhere," he said. "But there are still problems with that scenario. Either they're going to say that you're secretly controlling me and I'm your puppet, or they're going to claim you're a bunch of superpowered clandestine agents whom I'm going to use to subvert the constitution. Probably Fyor will manage to say both things at once." He sighed. "Unfortunately, we're stuck with a constitutional, representative, multibranched government, heavily scrutinized by a self-interested media. We're inefficient, divided, and prey to conflicting and contradictory interests—even, and perhaps especially, in moments of crisis."

Triebakk gave a low moan.

Luke gave Triebakk a sharp look. "No," he said. "Never even think of sympathizing with Palpatine."

Triebakk conceded with a graceful bow of his shaggy head.

But even as he spoke to Triebakk, Cal's words seemed to echo for a long moment in Luke's mind. *Constitutional, representative, multibranched . . .* As opposed to what? he wondered. *Elite, clandestine, autocratic, threat to the constitution.*

The old Jedi had personified the rule of order and the will of the state. But they were also secretive, and removed from the people and their representatives. Their link to the outside was through the Supreme Chancellor, and once a malevolent figure like Palpatine became Chancellor, with his disciple among the Jedi, the Jedi were cut off by the secret enemy, isolated, and destroyed.

The Jedi should never be so isolated again.

He became aware that the others were staring at him.

"Another message from the beyond?" Mara asked.

Luke smiled. "No. At least I don't think so."

"What, then?"

"I think I've worked out how to reestablish the Jedi Council in a way that will disarm Fyor Rodan."

Cal leaned forward. "Tell," he said.

"I had a nagging feeling when I was listening to Fyor Rodan yesterday," Luke began. "The nagging feeling I had," he continued, "was that Rodan was *right*, in a way. We *are* doing the jobs that other people are being paid to do. We *are* asking the government for privileges, and we're asking a great deal of people to believe that we ask in all humility and mean no harm—yet all they have to do is remember Darth Vader, and they'll suspect the contrary."

"And your solution?" Cal looked deeply intrigued.

"Suppose the council isn't composed entirely of Jedi," Luke said. "We can have one member from each of the government branches that might feel threatened by us. Say we have a Senator chosen by the Senate. Someone from the Defense Force. Another representative from the Ministry of State, and another from the Justice Council to make certain we stay within the law. Rodan would have a hard time convincing people that *all* those representatives were Jedi puppets. Especially if the Chief of State himself was on the council as well."

"The Chief of State or his ambassador," Cal said. "The Chief of State is a busy person."

"Conceded."

Cal frowned as he considered the matter. "You've just given me quite a list. That's five non-Jedi on the Jedi Council."

"Six," Luke corrected, on second thought. "We'd also need someone from the Intelligence division."

"And how many Jedi?" Cal asked. "If we make the council too large, we'll start having the same problems as the Senate—it'll be too big to be effective."

"Six Jedi," Luke said. "That will bring the government representatives into balance with the Jedi."

Cal's long face grew abstract as he considered the implications of the new idea. "That's giving up a lot of the traditional Jedi power," he said.

"It's power we've already lost," Luke said. "We lost it when the old Jedi fell."

Cal's eyes focused, searching Luke's face. "You're sure? You're sure that you're comfortable departing this far from Jedi tradition?"

Luke felt an utter certainty in his answer. "On Ithor, I surrendered the guardianship of the Jedi tradition. I'm content with the idea."

Triebakk gave a triumphant roar.

"And you'd be welcome as the first Senatorial representative," Luke replied. "But the Senate would still have to vote on your nomination."

"And there would have to be security and background checks and so on." Cal continued to think out loud.

Triebakk snarled a reference to the late Viqi Shesh.

"I—" Luke began. And then he felt a touch on his mind, and again he thought, *Jacen!*

Jacen's presence sang in his head.

"I think we've got another brainstorm here," Mara said. Her voice seemed to be coming from a distant place, somewhere outside the universe.

"I thought I had sent you to your death," Luke said. Dimly he was aware of the shock and sudden concern of the others in the room as they reacted to the words he'd spoken out loud—but not to them.

It was Jacen all right—Luke recognized the ingenuousness, the dry earnestness. But Jacen wasn't all that Luke sensed. Hovering remotely in the Force, Luke perceived another presence, one who seemed entirely unfamiliar.

"Is someone else there?" Luke asked.

Vergere. It wasn't a name that floated to him, but a thought, an image, a *presence*.

Luke took a breath at this direct, surprising confirmation. He had never met the alien personally, but he'd been briefed about her, and had also heard from Han about the defection she'd once staged from the Yuuzhan Vong, along with her redefection in the opposite direction.

He had every reason to be suspicious of Vergere. But on the other hand, Vergere, through her tears, had healed Mara of the disease that had threatened her life. It was Vergere who was responsible for Mara returning from the serious, focused, almost grim person she had become to the laughing, spontaneous woman she had once been, and now was again.

What Luke hadn't known was that Vergere was strong in the Force. He could feel her power, restrained at the moment but perfectly genuine. And it was strangely cloaked—even though they were in telepathic contact, Luke could detect nothing of Vergere's personality or purpose. That bespoke training—Vergere was no mere Force-sensitive with a talent for telepathy; she had been carefully educated.

But where had she received such training? Not at his Jedi academy. And that left a number of dark alternatives—Palpatine, Vader, the Shadow Academy. But why would a Dark Jedi bring Jacen to Luke?

More impressions came from Jacen. A Yuuzhan Vong craft, with its organic scent and resinous walls. Alarm. New Republic ships moving in swarms.

Luke broke contact and turned to his three friends, all of whom were gazing at him with deep concern.

"The short version," he prefaced. "Jacen Solo just contacted me through the Force. He's in the Mon Cal system in a Yuuzhan Vong escape pod, and we've got to stop the military from blowing him up."

Cal's response was immediate. He turned to his protocol droid and said, "Call Fleet Command—priority urgent and immediate. Place another urgent and immediate call to Supreme Commander Sien Sovv."

"Yes, Councilor," the droid said.

Cal turned back to Luke. "Don't worry," he said. "We'll get him back."

But Luke was already reaching into the Force, his mind stretching out into the great void beyond. Alongside him he felt the spirit of his wife, her strength supporting his, striving through the darkness of space for his lost apprentice.

TEN

Nom Anor forgot his itch as he filed into the Hall of Confluence behind his superior, High Prefect Yoog Skell. The hall was magnificent, broad at the four palpating doors by which high-ranking members of the four ruling castes entered, then narrowing as it approached the far end. The room was a trompe l'oeil, designed so that all eyes were drawn toward an artificial vanishing point, at which point was the seat of the Supreme Overlord.

The walls were chitin marbled black and white; pillars of white bone supported the roof, and coral spread pale lace over the arches of the ceiling. Though the planes of the room were flat, the dovin basals that provided the room's artificial gravity were tweaked slightly so as to provide the sense of walking uphill as one approached the Supreme Overlord; it felt as if he sat at a summit, and all others toiled upward toward him.

At the focus of all eyes was the largest Yuuzhan Vong that Nom Anor had ever seen, a giant even among the most massive warriors. Shimrra sat in silence on a bloodred throne of yorik coral that thrust spines and spikes from its central mass, as if warding an enemy from the Overlord's presence. His ceremonial robes were somber, black and gray—the gray was leather, the carefully preserved flesh of Steng, who in the distant past had lost the Cremlevian War to Yo'gand, the first Supreme Overlord of the Yuuzhan Vong. Shimrra's massive head was so covered with scars, slashes, tattoos, and the marks of branding that he could barely be said to have a face at all, just a torn collection of barely healed wounds. But fierce, discerning intelligence could be seen behind the glowing mqaaq'it implants in his eye sockets, which shifted through the spectrum as he watched the dignitaries enter.

Crouched at the feet of Shimrra was a lanky figure dressed in rags that hung in shreds on his flabby skin, his lip curled back over his teeth to show one yellow fang. His skull was misshapen, with one lobe swollen. Shimrra's familiar, Onimi.

The dignitaries plodded—"uphill"—toward Shimrra and took their places, each of the four castes equidistant from the throne. Shimrra loomed over them, and for once this was not a trick of the gravity—the Supreme Overlord was *enormous*. All prostrated themselves, and then in mighty voice chanted their salutation.

"*Ai' tanna Shimrra khotte Yun'o!*" Long life to Shimrra, beloved of the gods!

A deep rumble came from the throne. Nom Anor could barely see Shimrra's lips move as he spoke.

"Let the Great Council be seated."

The leading members rose to their feet and took their seats, which had been adjusted so as to compensate for the room's peculiar gravity.

Nom Anor rose and then remained on his feet. He did not rate a chair in the Supreme Overlord's presence.

Standing across the room Nom Anor saw the priest Harrar, with whom he had shared several serious misjudgments.

Harrar gave no sign of knowing him. *Good,* Nom Anor thought. Let all that be forgotten.

He shifted on his feet, propping himself against the gravity that made him lean to his right. The movement triggered the itching again, and Nom Anor clenched his teeth against the blaze of sensation. The itching had spread across his belly and under one armpit, and it felt as if half his skin were aflame. His fingers twitched with the urge to scratch, and he forced them straight.

The Shamed One, Onimi, rose to his feet. *"Great lords all,"* he began,

> "—whose plans profound
> Have put our feet on solid ground.
> I hope you will not think it crime
> If for this day I speak in rhyme."

Onimi paused for an answer, mismatched eyes scanning the crowd. As if anyone would object. Shimrra's status as Supreme Overlord was unquestioned, and a reflection of his power was that he had actually adopted a Shamed One as his familiar, a grotesque, twisted being who had been rejected by the gods. Shimrra permitted his familiar extraordinary liberties, and to all appearances enjoyed the creature's grotesque capers as well as the discomfort they caused among onlookers.

After the pause, Onimi raised his arms and performed a lurching pirouette, spinning to display the rags he wore.

> "Permit me to recite an ode
> To raiment new, this latest mode.
> For like my lord, I glory in
> My garments made of foemen's skin."

Surprise flashed through Nom Anor as he realized that Onimi's rags were the remnants of New Republic uniforms taken from those who had fallen at Coruscant.

There were intakes of breath around the chamber as others realized this as well.

Onimi capered on, shambling near High Priest Jakan,

who hissed and drew back so that none of the whirling rags could contaminate him. Shamed Ones had been rejected by the gods themselves, damned to all the contempt and hatred they surely deserved.

"*Enough.*" The single word came from Shimrra, and was sufficient for Onimi to fall silent, a glimmer of fear in his eyes.

"Back to your place, creature," Shimrra growled. "Our meeting will be long enough without having to endure your capers."

The Overlord's familiar cringed in apology, then dragged himself back to the throne and dropped like a sack of bones at his master's feet. Shimrra's head turned left and right, viewing all the delegates in turn.

Then he turned his massive body toward Tsavong Lah. "I should like to discuss the prosecution of the war. What do you have to say, Warmaster?"

Tsavong Lah's hand formed a fist, which he brought down with a crash on the arm of his chair. "I have but one word to say, and that word is *Victory*!" His delegation growled in agreement. "The enemy capital is ours," the warmaster continued, "and you have taken formal possession of it! We followed the capture of Yuuzhan'tar with our victory at Borleias! Supreme Commander Nas Choka's fleet does well in Hutt space. With the exception of the unfortunate Komm Karsh, our forces have been victorious everywhere."

Onimi, at the overlord's feet, gave a little giggle that echoed strangely in the room's cavernous spaces.

The warmaster bared his teeth. Shimrra gave a rumble of warning to Onimi at his impudence, and then his gaze settled on Tsavong Lah.

"Onimi may spawn wretched doggerel," he said, "but he has a point. Your attempt to capture Jaina Solo at Hapes was a complete failure."

Having no choice but to acknowledge his defeat, Tsavong Lah bowed his head. "I confess it."

"And the casualties we took for the capture of Yuuzhan'tar were enormous. The first two waves were wiped out, and the third wave, though victorious, was decimated. After that, Borleias was a very expensive victory—more, in my judgment, than the planet was worth. Your own father died. Plus Komm Karsh's defeat was expensive in both lives and matériel. I am not as lenient as my predecessor."

A fanatic gleam entered Tsavong Lah's eyes. "We would give these lives again, and more!" he said. "Life is less than nothing! What is a warrior's life compared to the glory of the Yuuzhan Vong?"

Shimrra's answer was sharp. "I do not dispute your warriors' glory, or their willingness to die! That is not what is at issue."

"I beg the Supreme Overlord's pardon," Tsavong Lah said. "I did not understand—"

"Do not assume that I am a fool!" Shimrra barked. He pointed at Tsavong Lah. "You have won your victories by sending your troops over a rampart of our own dead! How do you intend to replace these casualties?"

Nom Anor gloated at the sight of Shimrra taking the warmaster to task for his failings. He and Tsavong Lah had butted heads often enough, and it did his heart good to see the warrior taken down a few steps in front of his rivals.

"My lord—I—" The warmaster was at a loss. "I have fulfilled all our primary objectives—I have given you the capital—"

"We may *grow* more warships, but warriors must be *bred*," Shimrra said. "It will take a generation or more before our formations stand again at full strength, and we now have many worlds to defend."

"I will give you more victories!" Tsavong Lah cried. "The

infidels are routed! If I follow up our victories, they will break!"

The warmaster was interrupted by yet another giggle from Onimi. "The warmaster is not listening! He needs a new pair of ears—or perhaps instead the organ that lies between them."

A hiss of fury escaped his throat as Tsavong Lah glowered at Onimi.

"Silence." Again the word came from Shimrra. Though the Overlord's tone was soft, the room's admirable acoustics made the word sing in the air. A hush followed, though Tsavong Lah seemed visibly to be choking on his words as he again bowed before his superior.

The Supreme Overlord spoke on. "You ask to follow the enemy. I have read our strength reports. We do not have sufficient forces both to maintain the offensive and to hold what we have already taken."

"My Lord." Tsavong Lah kept his head bowed. "With all respect—we pursue a broken foe. We may expect nothing but a glorious slaughter that adds great glory to your name."

Shimrra's voice was icy. "The enemy that wiped out Komm Karsh was hardly *broken*. And may I remind the warmaster that Komm Karsh's fleet was our sole strategic reserve? From this point, moving any warrior to strengthen one force will weaken another."

Tsavong Lah had no answer. His eyes stayed fixed on the ground.

"Our forces will break off offensive operations for the present," Shimrra said. "We may resume the offensive once we conclude a reorganization that brings more warriors into the field."

"As the Supreme One wishes." Tsavong Lah's voice was a barely audible hiss.

"I wish it." Shimrra's glowing gaze rose from the warmaster and swept over the room. "Many of our warriors are tied down in garrison and pacification duties far from the front. I wish to liberate them for combat against the infidels." His eyes sought out the delegation of shapers, who had until this point remained silent.

"I require you to create more warriors," he said.

Ch'Gang Hool, master of Domain Hool, a shaper clan, responded quickly. "The Supreme Overlord refers to surge-coral implants?"

"Yes. Captives will be given implants enabling them to receive the commands of a yammosk. They will then be placed under the command of warriors." Shimrra turned again to Tsavong Lah. "Thus will you have larger forces to bring against the infidels."

"I am grateful, God-Chosen."

Nom Anor couldn't help but observe that gratitude did not seem foremost in the warmaster's mind.

"If the warriors are not *wasted*," Shimrra said pointedly, "these measures should serve to correct the problem for the short term. In order to make up our losses in the long term, I command the following:

"All warriors will now be ordered to breed at the age of sixteen, if they have not already. If no mate chooses a given warrior, his or her commander will award a suitable mate from the warriors available. Afterward, awards and incentives will be devised to reward those who produce children."

Tsavong Lah bowed again. "It shall be as you wish, Supreme One."

"*Nothing* shall be as I wish if we continue to lose battles," Shimrra reminded. "The enemy have developed new tactics that enable them to gain victories. I command a full report."

Tsavong Lah at last raised his head. "The infidels have discovered a way to use a . . . machine to override the signal sent to our units by the yammosks. Our units are thus forced to operate on their own, without strategic guidance."

"And the remedy?" Shimrra's question was prompt.

The warmaster hesitated. "We have not developed one as yet, Supreme One. We are—we have discussed the problem—" He hesitated again. "The fact is, Supreme One, that this development is unprecedented in our history, and—"

"You are baffled," Shimrra said.

Again the warmaster bowed. Nom Anor felt a surge of gloating pleasure.

"I confess it," Tsavong Lah said. "My life in payment."

Shimrra turned again to the shapers. "Has the shaper caste any suggestions?"

This time Ch'Gang Hool's answer was not as swift as before. "We could attempt to create yammosks that could function despite these evil machines' influence. But it would be more useful if we had a better understanding of the technical dimensions of the problem. Have any of these—" He hesitated even to speak the foul word. "—these *machines* been captured?"

"No," Tsavong Lah said. "We do not capture machines, we destroy them."

"And they have another *type* of new machine, do they not?" the Supreme Overlord asked. "One that causes our vessels to fire on one another?"

"It is the cause of much misfortune," Tsavong Lah said. "The infidels have developed machines that adhere to our ships, like grutchins to a foe, and broadcast a signal identifying them as an enemy. Our own loyal ships, perceiving an enemy, then open fire." His expression grew wooden. "The enemy insults us by placing on these machines the device of Yun-Harla, the Trickster."

"They insult not us, but the gods!" shouted the high priest, Jakan. "Blasphemers! Infidels! Let us capture those responsible, and their agony shall be undying!"

The Supreme Overlord gestured toward the priest. "Not

now, Lord Priest." Jakan fell silent. Shimrra leaned toward Tsavong Lah. "These deceptive devices are able to penetrate our ships' defenses?"

"No more than any other missile. But the infidels have also used treachery and surprise. They have captured one of our frigates. This vessel maintains a pretense of being friendly until such time as it launches missiles against us that turn our vessels against each other. The captured frigate then escapes in the confusion."

Shimrra was silent for a long moment. Then he said, "You have been fooled *how many times* by this trickery?"

"Once, Supreme One. At Hapes, the first time the tactic was used. And Komm Karsh was tricked fatally at Obroa-skai, but he was encountering the tactic for the first time."

"The solution seems elementary. You will develop recognition signals for friendly frigates. If any frigate fails to make the correct signal, all elements in the fleet should be instructed to regard it as an enemy."

"I have already begun to implement this reform," the warmaster said.

"Let it be your greatest priority," Shimrra said. "We must restore the superiority of our forces."

"It shall be done, Supreme One."

Shimrra turned to Yoog Skell. "Let the high prefect inform us of the disposition, strength, and intentions of the infidels."

Yoog Skell bowed to the Supreme Overlord and presented a digest of the latest information procured from sources within the New Republic. Unfortunately, the digest was not as complete as once it would have been: several of the most useful Yuuzhan Vong agents among the enemy had been killed or neutralized. The late Senator Viqi Shesh was particularly missed.

The enemy government, Yoog Skell reported, had moved to Mon Calamari in the Outer Rim, though it was not clear whether it would remain there. The government had not as yet chosen a new head, though a human named Fyor Rodan was a possible candidate. There was also a Quarren named Pwoe who had declared himself Chief of State shortly after Coruscant, but it appeared that fewer and fewer of the New Republic were willing to follow his orders.

The New Republic military appeared to be in a state of disarray since the fall of their capital. They had undertaken no coordinated operations since Borleias, and showed no sign of doing so.

Delegates from several worlds had come to the Yuuzhan Vong offering surrender or neutrality. It was difficult in the current conditions to determine whether or not their credentials were genuine, so it wasn't often clear whether they had been sent officially or not.

Leaders of the Peace Brigade, infidels who were collaborating with the Yuuzhan Vong, had established their capital on Ylesia. They had the beginnings of their own fleet, though their equipment was drawn from a variety of sources and was hardly uniform. Yuuzhan Vong cadres were doing their best to train them.

While Yoog Skell made his report, Nom Anor tried his best to remain rigidly calm. The itch had turned his skin to fire. Desperately he willed himself to be still.

He noticed, as he stood in silence behind his chief, that Yoog Skell's hand was surreptitiously scratching his leg under cover of his desk. So Yoog Skell had the itch as well, and the stress of his report had made him surrender to the weakness of scratching.

Nom Anor wished *he* dared surrender to such a weakness.

After Yoog Skell's report, there was a moment of silence before Shimrra responded. "This 'Fyor Rodan,' " he said. "This 'Cal Omas.' Is it known whether they will favor submission or war?"

"Supreme One, I will defer in this matter to my junior

colleague Nom Anor," Yoog Skell said. "He is a specialist on the subject of the infidels, having lived among them for many years."

Shimrra's baleful rainbow gaze lifted to Nom Anor, and again Nom Anor felt the chill of fear. He could feel Shimrra's *presence*, the gods-given power he possessed, and it sat on Nom Anor's heart like a great weight.

At least he forgot all about his itch.

"Supreme One," he began, and was thankful he hadn't stammered, "according to the analysis provided by our agent Viqi Shesh, Fyor Rodan was a supporter of Borsk Fey'lya, though he occasionally showed signs of independence. His only consistent position was on the matter of the Jedi, whom he always opposed. As far as we know, he hasn't expressed an opinion on the matter of peace or war. Neither has Cal Omas—who has, however, consistently supported the Jedi."

Nom Anor wished, as the word left his lips, that he hadn't mentioned the Jedi, which might remind the Supreme One of too many mistakes that Nom Anor had committed in the field. But Shimrra, to the intendant's relief, pursued a different tack.

"This Fey'lya punished Rodan and Omas for their independence?"

"Not as far as I know, Supreme One."

"Fey'lya was a weak creature," Shimrra mused. "He scarcely deserved the honorable death we gave him."

"Supreme One," Nom Anor said, "the citizens of the New Republic lack a proper understanding of hierarchies and the duties due to one's superior. They believe that a certain amount of independence of mind is permissible. Borsk Fey'lya's attitude was not unusual among their leaders."

Shimrra absorbed this, then nodded. "One of our great missions, then, shall be to teach these creatures the proper meaning of submission."

Nom Anor bowed. "Undoubtedly, Supreme One."

"I wish this Cal Omas killed. Have your agents carry out an assassination."

Nom Anor hesitated. "Few of my agents are in place on Mon Calamari," he said. "We—"

Shimrra's eyes glittered dangerously. Nom Anor crossed his arms obediently. "It shall be as you desire, Supreme One."

The Supreme Overlord's next question was so soft-spoken that it caught Nom Anor by surprise. "We shall teach the New Republic the glory of the gods. And what shall we teach the *Jeedai*? More importantly, what have they taught *us*?"

At the mention of the Jedi, fear paralyzed Nom Anor's tongue, but after a brief internal struggle he managed to wrench a satisfactory answer from his half-numbed mind.

"We shall teach them how to increase the glory of the Yuuzhan Vong through their extermination! And what they have taught us is that their treachery is boundless, and must be answered with death and blood."

He heard a growl of agreement from the warriors, and also from members of the intendant delegation.

Shimrra, however, was silent. Nom Anor felt the Overlord's eyes on him, and felt again the *presence* of Shimrra's mind pressing on his own. It was as if his very thoughts had become transparent, completely exposed to the Overlord's inquiring mind. Again fear shimmered up Nom Anor's spine.

"And whose fault," Shimrra asked in a voice all the more ominous for its quiet tone, "was the fiasco in the Well of the World Brain?"

Nom Anor fought his way to the surface through a current of blind panic. "My Lord," he said, "though I am not blameless, I beg you to remember that I operated under the authority of Warmaster Tsavong Lah."

The warmaster stood tall, not deigning to respond.

Nom Anor battled terror as he realized the others were

perfectly willing to sacrifice him. "We all underestimated the treachery of the Jedi, Supreme One," he said. "We were misled by the creature Vergere—I no more or less than others."

Shimrra fixed Nom Anor again with his baleful look. "Thousands witnessed this disaster," he said. "One of the *Jeedai*, they were told, had been converted through the Embrace of Pain to the True Path, and would willingly sacrifice one of his peers in the Well, and offer his death to the gods. And instead what do they see? The great doors slammed in their faces as our tame *Jeedai* escaped, while the supposed sacrificial victim held off an army with the special *Jeedai* weapon that was supposed to have been taken from him."

"The World Brain was endangered!" Ch'gang Hool cried. "The *Jeedai* could have destroyed our last dhuryam, just as he destroyed all the others!"

"This catastrophe has led to heresy!" spoke the priest, Jakan. "Thousands were led to doubt the wisdom of their superiors and the reality of the gods!"

Shimrra's eyes once again settled on Nom Anor. "Heresy. Doubt. Danger to the dhuryam on which all our plans for our new homeworld depend. Proof of the heroism of the *Jeedai* fighting in our own capital, before the eyes of thousands. And, Executor, you will have us believe that this was entirely the workings of one little avian, this Vergere?"

Nom Anor's vision began to darken. He felt as if his soul were being squeezed by a ruthless velvet hand. He gasped in air and tried to speak in his defense.

"Supreme One," he managed, "none of us trusted her completely. All her meetings with the captive Jedi were monitored. Nothing seditious passed between them. Her explanations for her behavior were plausible. She proved her loyalty more than once—she led Jacen Solo into captivity on three separate occasions. When the Jedi was tortured, his physical responses were monitored, and truly indicated that he was learning the Embrace of Pain—he was accepting the pain as if he were Yuuzhan Vong! When he announced his willingness to proclaim the True Doctrine and sacrifice the other Jedi whom he himself had captured, no one doubted him."

"And the importance of the twin sacrifice?" Shimrra inquired. "The idea that this Jacen Solo should not be killed immediately, but held until he could be sacrificed along with his sister? Whose notion was that?"

"Vergere's," Nom Anor said. He felt the *presence* of the Supreme Overlord begin to squeeze his mind again, blotting out his thoughts. He could see only Shimrra's ruthless, glowing eyes. It is like the Embrace of Pain, he thought, mental torture at the hands of a yammosk. Through the horrible pressure he held to one word. "Vergere!" he cried. "Vergere! It was all Vergere!"

"Supreme One," another voice said. Through the blur of oppression and terror, Nom Anor recognized the priest Harrar. Another betrayer, he thought, another one come to crush me with some burden of blame.

"I was present, Supreme One," Harrar said. "The idea of the twin sacrifice was partly my own, partly Khalee Lah's, partly Vergere's. I confess that I was duped. The truth is that Vergere fooled us because none of her actions seemed capable of a treacherous interpretation. Why did she lead Jacen Solo into captivity not once, but thrice? She had numerous opportunities to help him escape, but did not do so. Why did she participate in his torture? Why did she manipulate him—or *seem* to manipulate him—on our behalf?

"I have concluded," Harrar finished, "that if Vergere is not loyal to us, neither is she loyal to the infidels."

Nom Anor sobbed for breath as the mental pressure was released. Through his dimmed eye he could make out Harrar standing in the delegation of High Priest Jakan. The high priest did not seem pleased to hear his subordinate's confession—thus far the college of priests had escaped any blame for the catastrophe, and now Harrar was likely to bring unwelcome attention to his caste.

Nom Anor's blood sang with gratitude for Harrar. The priest had saved him.

The warmaster, on the other hand, looked at Nom Anor as if he were on the verge of throttling him.

While Nom Anor struggled to recover his presence of mind, Shimrra interrogated Harrar and the warmaster. In the end, the Supreme Overlord leaned back on his throne, disappearing into its spiky interior.

"Interesting," he said. "For fifty years this Vergere has lived among us, and none of us knew her true nature. For fifty years she studied us, and learned our ways, and was able to plan her treachery." He leaned forward and turned to Jakan. "Priest!" he said. "Is this creature not the true incarnation of Yun-Harla the Trickster?"

Outrage quivered in the priest's jowls, but when he spoke his voice was firm. "Never!" he said. "Say rather that Vergere is the embodiment of evil!"

"Is she a *Jeedai*?" someone queried.

"She can't be," Harrar said. "The *Jeedai* derive their abilities from something called the 'Force,' and their use of it can be detected by a yammosk. If Vergere were *Jeedai*, she would have been unmasked."

Shimrra's deep voice was reflective. "*Jeedai* or not, I wonder about her. Isn't such a deception, over such a long period, a kind of masterpiece?" He looked down at his creature, Onimi. "Is she not worthy of admiration, to deceive so many for so long?" he asked, and gave Onimi a kick. Onimi, startled, looked up and began to warble.

"Out of the World-Well, and into thin air,
That devious trickster, the traitor Vergere."

And then, with a fawning glance at his master, Onimi added slyly:

> "But some little pets are more suitably loyal,
> I'll still be your friend, and share your throne royal."

Shimrra burst into laughter at this, and shoved Onimi with his foot, pushing him another step lower. "You may share my throne from *there*, Onimi!" he said.

Onimi shaded his eyes with a hand and peered out at the assembled delegations. "I still have a better view of things than any of *these*, Supreme One," he noted, thankfully forgetting to speak in rhyme.

"That wouldn't be hard," Shimrra said, almost as an aside.

Uneasy laughter rolled around the great chamber. Nom Anor, still dizzied from his interrogation, sensed the anxiety and fear that lay beneath the laughter. Would the Supreme Overlord choose another one to humiliate?

Shimrra faced his audience. "The lesson of all this is simple," he said. "Let all follow my example, and permit no pet to inhabit a position of trust."

The delegates chorused agreement. Nom Anor couldn't help but think, however, that Onimi was trusted at least to the extent of being permitted to attend meetings where important matters were discussed. If Onimi were a spy, he could give his secret masters much useful information.

But if Onimi were a spy, surely Shimrra, through his powerful presence that saw into souls, would discover the fact?

But Vergere, too, should have been discovered, should she not?

"High Priest," Shimrra said, turning his head toward Jakan. "My apologies for delaying this vital discussion until now. I wished us all to give it our full attention. Please bring to everyone's attention this matter of heresy."

The better to make his presentation, Jakan rose to his feet, his formal robes brushing the floor. His daughter, the priestess Elan, had adopted the treacherous Vergere as a pet, and then died on a mission to assassinate the Jedi. The loss of his daughter had hardened Jakan in his religious orthodoxy, and hardened him in his determination to implement the will of the gods.

"I, too, bring word of infiltration," he said. He gave a ponderous pause, his head turning left to right to view each delegation in turn. As the priest's eyes crossed with his, Nom Anor felt a thrill of fear. Was the high priest about to accuse someone here?

"Not by dangerous spies," Jakan went on at last, "but by dangerous *ideas*. Priests from as far away as Dubrillion have reported that they have discovered unauthorized, clandestine meetings among the lower orders—meetings that claim to be religious ceremonies. Meetings in private quarters or empty countryside. Meetings where our own True Way is denied, and where treasonous, heretical concepts are spread to the people."

Again the priest paused solemnly, as if to emphasize the gravity of his words. Shimrra spoke into the silence.

"Heresy is nothing new. Why is this of such great import? What sort of people take part in these ceremonies?"

"*Shamed Ones,*" Jakan said in a fierce whisper, as if the words themselves were obscene. "Shamed Ones, and workers. Precisely those castes needing the greatest guidance in matters of belief. Sometimes"—again his voice dropped into a dramatic whisper—"workers and Shamed Ones are found at the heretical ceremonies *together*."

Nom Anor's single eye was drawn irresistibly to the Shamed One Onimi, condemned by the gods through the failure of his implants. For once Onimi seemed inclined to remain silent, though his lanky body half reclined in a pose of insolence. His upper lip was again curled to reveal one long, yellow tooth.

"And the nature of these heretical ceremonies?" Shimrra prodded.

"They venerate the *Jeedai*," Jakan said, and this time there was a murmur of outrage and surprise from the crowd. "The power of the *Jeedai* has brought into question that the gods favor the Yuuzhan Vong. They believe that Yun-Harla and Yun-Yammka are aligned with the twins Jaina and Jacen Solo. And some of the heretics, here on Yuuzhan'tar, have in the last weeks begun to revere a being they call the *Ganner*. Ganner, of course, was the name of the *Jeedai* who gave his life at the battle of the World-Well."

Shimrra fingered his chin. "Where do the lower orders acquire these heresies?"

"The contamination was probably begun by slaves from the New Republic who labor alongside the workers and Shamed Ones," Jakan explained. "Slaves who admired the *Jeedai* and their philosophy."

Jakan clenched his fist and shook it. "At the moment the heretics are not organized, they have no real leaders, and their doctrine is a jumble of contradictory ideas. Stop them *now*—root them out, before they grow into a force that weakens us from within!"

Again the priest offered a dramatic moment of silence, and then he turned and bowed toward Shimrra. "Such is my report, Supreme One."

Nom Anor heard a sigh from his own superior, Yoog Skell, but he was unable to work out what the sigh meant. The itching was a tormenting blast that seared Nom Anor's flesh.

"Have you any *specific* recommendations concerning this crisis?" the Supreme Overlord inquired. "*Kill the heretics* is final, but lacks detail."

Jakan bowed again. "Supreme One, my recommendations would demand absolute segregation of the slaves from our own people so as to prevent the spread of inappropriate ideas. Public sacrifice of the heretics. Rewards for those who renounce their false paths and turn in their fellows."

Yoog Skell sighed again, more loudly this time, more wearily. "Supreme One," he said, "while I am certainly no friend to heresy, I must beg for less drastic methods. We are engaged in a war that may continue for klekkets or even longer. The combined labors of workers and Shamed Ones and slaves are necessary to advance our objectives. We have settlements to grow, food crops to raise in half-wrecked ecosystems, ships and weapons and other vital items to ripen and harvest, and Yuuzhan'tar itself to transform from a machine-poisoned, artificial landscape into our perfect ancestral paradise."

Jakan bowed toward Yoog Skell. "Our paradise can scarcely be perfect if it contains heresy."

"I concede the high priest's point," Yoog Skell said. "But an inquiry into all our workers would be disruptive. Segregation of the workers from the slaves is impossible at this stage—they are all engaged in vital work. Going amid them with bribes aimed at getting them to turn on one another—imagine the disruption! Imagine the situation if the workers start accusing overseers in the hope of seeing them brought down! Imagine how many false accusations we should have to weed out from the true!"

"That would be the task of the priests," Jakan said. "Your own people need not concern themselves."

"But if the workers should accuse warriors? Or shapers? Or even loyal priests?"

Nom Anor realized that Yoog Skell was pointing out to the shapers and warriors that Jakan's plan put them at risk as well as the workers, whom no one cared about.

Yoog Skell spoke on. "Besides, who cares what the Shamed Ones think? The gods hate them anyway. And whose fault is it that the workers lapse into heresy? Haven't the priests *already* failed in their duty?"

Jakan, bloated with injured dignity, was about to make a furious rebuttal when Shimrra held up a hand for silence. All eyes respectfully turned to him—all except that of Nom Anor, who was blind to everything but a sudden blaze of his own itching torment. The itch was *spreading*. Now his back was on fire, where he couldn't scratch even if he wanted to!

"The gods have placed me upon this throne as their instrument," Shimrra said, "and I agree with the high priest that heresy may not be tolerated."

A satisfied look inflated Jakan's face, a satisfaction that died away at the Overlord's next words. "But the high prefect has a worthy point. When we are at war, it is foolish to disorder one's own forces. I don't want disruption among the workers at such a time, particularly since the workers are uneducated and may have adopted these beliefs without knowing their dangerous nature. Therefore—"

He turned to the high priest. "Priest Jakan, I direct that the priests inform the people of the danger of this heresy. Tell them from *me*, from their Supreme Overlord, that the *Jeedai* are not emanations of the gods. Tell them that such beliefs are unsound and forbidden. Those workers who are properly obedient to their superiors will then know to avoid any such contamination in the future."

"And"—the priest bowed—"if they persist in their error?"

"You may kill any heretics you come across, as publicly as you like," Shimrra said. "But I wish no large-scale investigation of the masses of workers, no rewards for accusations. When we win the war"—he nodded at Jakan—"then we may have a more thorough inquiry. But for the present, I want the Yuuzhan Vong focused on defeating our enemies, not interrogating each other."

Jakan's face had fallen, but he bowed and acceded with grace. "It shall be as you wish, Supreme One."

"You may return to your seat, High Priest Jakan."

With great dignity, the priest returned to his desk. Behind him, Onimi sneered and scratched himself again.

Fury raged in Nom Anor as he watched the misshapen figure scratch. How he would love to have those fingers beneath his boot!

An agreeable expression crossed Shimrra's face. "The Shamed One reminds me," he said, "that I should ask the shapers how their work progresses? How goes the world-shaping of Yuuzhan'tar?"

"Supreme One," Ch'Gang Hool said, "it goes well."

"This news is pleasing," Shimrra said. "May we inquire of the master whether there have been any problems?"

A look of caution crossed the master shaper's face. He spoke quickly. "Some difficulties are inevitable, Supreme One. We are dealing with an alien environment that we have largely destroyed, and some of the native life-forms—microscopic ones, mostly—are proving persistent. Perhaps," he admitted, "some of you have experienced some . . . minor discomforts . . . as the result of a fungal infection. We are attempting to, ah—"

"And the *nature* of this minor discomfort?" the Supreme Overlord asked sweetly.

Ch'Gang Hool hesitated. "Ah—itching, Supreme One—persistent itching."

Nom Anor's nerves flamed at the very mention of the word *itch*. Anger began to simmer in his blood.

Ch'Gang Hool gave what was probably intended to be a confident growl. "A mere itch, Supreme One. Nothing that any member of the higher castes cannot overcome with the discipline demonstrated in the course of earning rank and honor."

"And you are, of course, a disciplined member of the highest caste," Shimrra said.

Ch'Gang Hool rose to his feet, lordly in his ceremonial robes. "I have earned that distinction, Supreme One."

Shimrra jumped to his feet, both fists smashing the arms of his throne, and roared at the top of his lungs. *"Then why have I watched your surreptitious scratching through this whole meeting?"*

Ch'Gang Hool froze. In the sudden ominous silence Onimi jumped to his feet, rags of uniforms swirling around him, and scratched himself with abandon. Then he sat down with a broad grin on his face.

The Supreme Overlord pointed one long-clawed, implanted finger at the master shaper. "The worldshaping of our new homeworld is being botched. Do you think I don't know that this plague has spread among our entire population here? Even *I* was infected within hours of landing on Yuuzhan'tar!"

Anger erupted in Nom Anor's mind. This wasn't just about his own personal torture by this demonic itch. What was this whole war *about*, if not to re-create the perfection of the long-lost homeworld? What a catastrophe it would be if the worldshaping failed!

"Supreme One," Ch'Gang Hool said, "this complete reconstruction of an entire ecosystem is a complex matter, and though perfect success is within reach, it may take longer than our earlier estimates—"

Shimrra gave a scornful laugh. "It's not simply the fungus, though, is it, master shaper? Do you think I haven't heard of the grashals intended for worker barracks that melted down into a mass of undifferentiated protein? Or the crop of villips that grew imprinted on some local animal, and could only transmit the beast's screech of a mating call? The blorash jelly that attempted to devour the shapers who tended it?"

"Supreme One, I—" Ch'Gang Hool attempted again to protest, then sagged in defeat. "I confess the fault," he said.

"Death!" someone roared in Nom Anor's ear.

The Supreme Overlord himself growled his rage. "The worldshaping shall be placed in more competent hands than yours," he said, and then he turned to the group of warriors behind Tsavong Lah. "Commander! Subalterns! Take this imposter of a master shaper and carry him from this chamber. Execute him as soon as you get him out of our sight! Make him pay for his incompetence!"

ELEVEN

Dif Scaur, the head of New Republic Intelligence, was alone in his office when his secure comm chimed. This was a comm unit that was used for one purpose only, and he tried to control the sudden lurch of his heart as he reached for the comm with one long, pale hand.

The display brightened, and he saw the caller. The caller with flame-colored eyes.

"Yes?" Scaur said. Anticipation hummed in his nerves.

"The experiment was a success."

Scaur took a breath. "Very well," he said.

"I believe I can now guarantee the success of the project."

Scaur gave a single, deliberate nod. "Then I will make the necessary arrangements."

"We will need a larger facility. And we will also need the silence of certain individuals."

"That has already been arranged." Scaur hesitated. "We should meet in person."

"Very well." The caller seemed satisfied. "I will await your arrival."

Transmission ceased. Scaur reached out a hand to turn off the comm unit, and when he drew it back in, he realized it was trembling.

Now everything has changed, he thought. Now *I* am the Slayer.

* * *

The shipyards of Mon Calamari glittered in the light of its sun, structures as graceful and strong as the ships they produced. Luke could see three cruisers partially completed, each in the MC80 class, each different in appearance from the others. Half a dozen smaller craft were also in various stages of completion. One always wished the Mon Cals would develop a sense of urgency, at least in wartime, but their desire to customize and perfect each vessel never abated, and each was lovingly crafted and beautified and refined until it became both a work of art and the deadliest force in the New Republic arsenal.

Beneath a transparent dome, Luke and Mara stood on a graceful mezzanine thrust out over the main concourse of the Fleet Command annex. Both gazed upward at the glittering silver shipyards afloat over the brilliant blue of the planet, both set off by the depthless velvet night of space and its spray of stars. The scene, the emptiness and beauty and the blue jewel of life set within it, settled around Luke like a cloak, a vision of peace and perfection. "It's the turning point," he said.

Mara gave him a quizzical look. "Do you know what made you say that yesterday?" she asked.

After that strange moment, when he'd been touched by something that reminded him of Jacen, he'd gone into deep meditation and a Force trance in the hope of regaining the fleeting contact, but he'd been unable to find the answers to any of his questions.

Now that he'd made contact with Jacen a second time, he had begun to suspect he knew what had spoken to him.

"It may have come from the Force itself," he said.

Distant stars reflected in her jade-colored eyes as Mara considered this. "The Force can offer us a view of what is to come," she said. "But usually it's . . . a bit less spontaneous."

"I'm more sure than ever that Jacen has a special destiny." He turned to Mara and squeezed her hand.

Mara's eyes widened. "Do you think Jacen himself knows his destiny?"

"I don't know. And I don't know if he would accept it if he did—he's always questioned his purpose as a Jedi, and even the meaning of the Force. I can't imagine him *not* questioning any fate that lay in store for him." His thoughts darkened, and he looked at Mara soberly. "And a special destiny is not always something joyous, or easy to bear. My father had a special destiny, and see where it took him."

Mara's look turned grave. "We must help him," she said.

"If he'll let us. He hasn't always been cooperative that way."

Luke raised his head to gaze out the great dome, and to the dome of star-spangled blackness beyond, where Jacen's coral craft, caught in the tractor beams of one of the fleet's MC80A cruisers, was being carried to a nearby docking bay. Though the craft itself was too distant for Luke to see it, Luke thought he saw the Mon Cal cruiser, a distant wink of light swooping gracefully toward the annex.

"Hey!" called a loud voice from the concourse below. "It's Senator Sneakaway! And Senator Scramblefree!" This was followed by booming laughter, and then. "Yes! *You!* I'm talking to *you!*"

Wordlessly Luke and Mara drifted to the mezzanine rail and looked down onto the concourse. Below, the tallest Phindian Luke had ever seen, her long arms thrusting out of the sleeves of her Defense Force uniform, lunged toward a human and a Sullustan who had just emerged from a consular ship docked at the annex. Luke recognized both the newcomers as members of the Senate.

The Phindian stepped into the path of the two Senators, then reeled. Luke realized that the Phindian was drunk; she had probably just stormed out of the officers' club beneath the mezzanine.

The Phindian thrust out her tiny little chin. "Do you know

how many friends I lost at Coruscant?" she asked. "Do you?"

The two Senators remained silent, their lips pressed closely together. They tried moving around the Phindian, but her long, long arms blocked their way.

"Ten thousand?" the Phindian boomed, extending one finger from a delicate-looking fist. "Twenty thousand? Thirty thousand comrades lost?" Two more fingers thrust out. "F-forty?" The Phindian tried to hold out a fourth finger, but then seemed a little late to realize there were only three fingers on her hand.

"We all lost friends on Coruscant," the human Senator said grimly, and tried to push one of the Phindian's enveloping arms out of his way. The Phindian blocked him again. Her yellow eyes tried to focus on his face.

"Too bad you didn't think about your friends when you ran away, Senator Sneakaway!" she said. "Too bad that when you commandeered *Alamania*, you left your friends to die!"

Luke felt Mara's hand on his arm. "Should we intervene?" she asked in a low voice.

"Not unless it turns violent," Luke said. "And I don't think it's going to." He glanced directly below the mezzanine rail at a group of officers who were quietly watching the confrontation from the officers' club. "Look there."

Mara turned her gaze to the group of officers. "They're not intervening, either."

"No," Luke said significantly. "They're not."

"Please stand aside, Captain," the Sullustan Senator said to the Phindian. "We have important business here on Mon Calamari."

"Important business!" the Phindian said. "Is that anything like the *important business* that required you to order Green Squadron to escort you and your shuttle into hyperspace? Green Squadron, which was covering my *Pride of*

Honor? My poor *Pride*, which got hammered by the Yuuzhan Vong and suffered two hundred and forty-one dead? My poor *Pride*, which barely made it to Mon Calamari and is going to have to be scrapped, because it simply isn't worth the expense it would take to patch it back together? What business was so important that it was worth two hundred and forty-one lives, Senator Scramblefree?" One spindly hand prodded the Sullustan in the chest. "Eh?" the Phindian asked. "Senator Flyaway? Senator Cowardheart? Senator Curdleguts? Eh?"

"Take care, Captain," the human Senator said. "You're endangering your commission."

"You've already taken away my ship!" the Phindian said. "You've already killed half my crew! You've already cost us the capital!" She hooted with laughter. "Do you think I care about my *commission*? Do you think there's anything you could do to me that's worse than what you've already done? Do you think I care about the *solemn oath* I swore to protect craven little bootlickers like you? Do you think *any* of us care?"

The Phindian waved one long arm in the direction of the officers on the threshold of the club. The two Senators turned and saw the solemn group who watched this confrontation in silence.

The Senators stared. The officers stared back. And for the first time, the Senators seemed nervous.

The Phindian still stood with her long arm extended, pointing to the officers' club, and the human ducked beneath it and walked briskly for the exit. When the drunken Phindian swung around after the human, the Sullustan dodged around her and scuttled after his human colleague.

But even if her arms were longer than her legs, the Phindian was fast in pursuit. She caught the two and draped her arms around their shoulders as if they were old friends.

"Tell you what," the Phindian said. "There's nothing you

can do *to* me, but there's something you can do *for* me. There's a fleet appropriations bill coming up in the new session—it will be in *your* committee, Senator Decamp—and you're going to vote *for* it. Because if you *don't*, we won't be able to go on protecting cowards and thieves and politicians from the Yuuzhan Vong, will we? And besides, if you don't *give* us the money—" The Senators stopped dead in their tracks as the Phindian caught their heads in her elbow joints, half strangling them. Her yellow eyes glittered. "If you don't *give* us the money," the Phindian said drunkenly, importantly, "we'll *take* it. After all, we've got the guns, and we already *know* how brave you are around guns, don't we?"

She released her two captives, and the Senators hastened for the exit. The Phindian raised her tiny chin and called after them. "One more thing, Senators! Don't ever expect to run from the enemy on a fleet ship ever again! Because if you ever try to commandeer one more fleet vessel, we're going to pack you into an escape pod and fire you straight at the Yuuzhan Vong. And *that's* a solemn oath, and we've all sworn it!"

The Senators were gone. The Phindian stared after them for a moment, her long arms dangling past her knees, then wheeled and returned to her friends.

The group of officers burst into applause. There were cheers. They put their arms around the Phindian and half carried her into the club for a celebration.

Luke and Mara stood on the mezzanine in the sudden weighty silence and thought about what they had just seen.

"Natural high spirits?" Mara suggested.

"You know that's not what it was."

"Mutiny?"

"Not mutiny. Not *yet*." Luke looked at the blank doors through which the two Senators had fled. "But it's close. The military haven't had anything but defeats in this war, and they know it's not their fault. They know the leadership has been corrupt and stupid and cowardly and inept. They know that Coruscant might have fallen because of politicians like those two." He paused as he heard a muffled cheer from the officers below. "I'd feel better," he said, "if one of those cheering weren't wearing the insignia of a fleet commander."

"Me, too," Mara said. She gave a nervous glance over her shoulder. "We'd better get a government the fleet can respect, and soon. If the military break free of the civilian government and start grabbing resources at blasterpoint, they're no more than pirates."

"Extremely well-armed pirates," Luke added.

It's the turning point, he reminded himself. And hoped it wasn't turning the wrong way.

He glanced overhead again, out the great dome, and this time he could see Jacen's coral craft with the naked eye, suspended by tractor beams below the great scalloped hull of the MC80A cruiser. The alien origin of the pod was clear: the coral hull and its bulbous organic form were unlike anything else in the sky. The graceful Mon Cal structures, with their fluid curves, *imitated* nature; but the Yuuzhan Vong pod *was* nature, and extragalactic nature at that.

Doors slid open behind Luke, and a file of soldiers trotted onto the mezzanine, all armed and armored for combat, their faces masked to keep out alien poisons. They were followed by a combat droid that brandished half a dozen weapons on the ends of its brazen arms.

The military was clearly taking no chances with a Yuuzhan Vong pod docking in vital New Republic space. Not only was an armed escort meeting the vessel, but the vessel was being docked not to Fleet Command, but to its annex, which could be completely sealed off from the headquarters itself and, if necessary, jettisoned into space by firing explosive bolts.

The young officer commanding the soldiers approached Luke and Mara and saluted.

"Masters Skywalker," he said to both of them. "Admiral Sovv's compliments, and after Jacen Solo and his companion are brought on board, he would be honored if you would all join him for refreshment."

Poor Sien Sovv, Luke thought. As Supreme Commander of the Defense Force, he'd been held responsible for the multiple catastrophes that had befallen the military. Last Luke had heard, Sovv had been wandering Mon Calamari trying to find someone to submit his resignation to—but without a Chief of State, no one was in a position to take it.

"I would be delighted to see the admiral," Luke answered, "provided, of course, that my nephew doesn't require medical attention."

"Of course, sir. Understood."

Luke and Mara followed the soldiers to the docking port. The soldiers took positions left and right of the hatch, and the droid directly in front of it, multiple weaponry directed forward. Luke looked at Mara. She was focused inward, her eyes half closed.

"I don't sense anything wrong," Mara said.

"I don't, either."

Without a word, Luke and Mara stepped between the battle droid and the docking bay hatch. Luke felt his nape hairs prickle at the thought of all that firepower directed at his back.

"Sir—" the officer began.

Luke made a gentle gesture. "We'll be fine, Lieutenant," he said.

"You'll be fine. Yes, sir."

There was a gentle tremor as tractor beams brought the pod to the hatch, and a hiss as the lock pressurized. Then lights blinked on the inner hatch and it swung open. Jacen stood in the open hatch.

He was dressed in a kind of colorless poncho, clearly of Yuuzhan Vong origin, tied at the waist with what looked like a vine. He had lost weight, and his ropy muscles flexed plainly under pale, sickly skin that didn't seem to hold an ounce of fat. Scars, healed but still vivid, striped his bare arms and legs.

It was Jacen's face, however, that showed the most change. Beneath an untrimmed mane of hair and a short, equally scruffy beard was a sharp, chiseled face, any remains of baby fat burned away, with brown eyes that showed an adult, restless, penetrating intelligence.

When Jacen had left for Myrkr, he had been on the cusp of adulthood. It was clear that whatever else he may have left there, his boyhood was gone.

The relentless eyes turned toward Luke and Mara and blossomed at once with warmth and recognition. Luke felt his heart surge with joy. He and Mara each took an involuntary step forward, and Jacen sped from the hatch, and his arms swept out to embrace them both. Laughter burst from all three at the joyous reunion.

Tears stung Luke's eyes. *The turning point,* he thought. *Yes. From this point, we turn from sorrow toward joy.*

"My boy!" The words spilled from Luke. "My boy!"

It was Mara who broke the embrace. She took a half step back, her hand gently placed on Jacen's chest as if to touch the heart of him. "You've been injured."

"Yes." The word was simple, accepting. Whatever had happened to him, Jacen seemed at peace with it.

"Are you all right?" Mara continued. "Do you need a healer?"

"No, I'm fine. Vergere healed me."

It was then that Mara and Luke turned to Jacen's companion. The piebald little alien had taken a few steps into the station, and was looking at the ranks of armed soldiers with what seemed to be both skepticism and humor.

"I owe Vergere thanks of my own, it seems," Mara said.

Vergere turned her wide, slanting eyes toward Mara. "My tears served you?" she asked.

"Yes. I'm cured, apparently."

"Many years ago, Nom Anor poisoned you with a coomb spore. Did you know that?" Vergere's words were precise, a little fussy.

"Yes, I know." She hesitated. "But—healing *tears*? How did you—how is it done?"

Vergere's feathery whiskers rippled in what may have been a slight smile. "It is a long story. Perhaps someday I will tell you."

Luke faced Jacen again and found the young man grinning at him. Luke grinned back. And then an idea struck him.

"We've got to tell your parents you're alive," he said. "And your sister."

Jacen's grin faded slightly. "Yes. I tried to contact them through the Force. But—yes—they should have official word, as well."

"Sir." It was the lieutenant commanding the military detachment. "Master Skywalker, I have to take possession of the escape pod. If you'll wait for a few minutes on the mezzanine, I'll escort you to the communications center where you can send your message, and then on to Admiral Sovv."

"Certainly," Luke said. An irresistible urge to grin struck him again, and he ruffled Jacen's hair with his hand.

With the young man between them, their arms around Jacen's shoulders and waist, Luke and Mara walked past the battle droid to the mezzanine rail. Vergere followed in silence.

Below, travelers moved back and forth from docking ports, all too busy to look up and see the strange reunion taking place on the balcony above them.

"Welcome back," Luke said. "Welcome back, young Jedi."

"I'm not the only one you should welcome back," Jacen said, with a nod toward Vergere.

Luke turned to Vergere. "Welcome, of course," he said politely. "But I don't know where you're *from*, so I can't be sure whether you're *back* or not."

"That is a paradox without an easy answer," Vergere said.

Jacen laughed. "That's true. Haven't you guessed?" And when Luke and Mara turned to him, Jacen laughed again.

"Vergere is a Jedi. A Jedi of the Old Republic. She's been living among the Yuuzhan Vong for more than fifty years."

Luke stared at Vergere in astonishment.

"And you're still *alive*?" Mara blurted.

Vergere looked down at herself, and patted herself as if demonstrating her own existence. "Apparently so, young Masters," she said.

"*How*—" Mara began. How had she lived among the Yuuzhan Vong without having her Jedi powers unmasked by a yammosk?

"Another long story," Vergere said, "perhaps for another time."

"You keep your secrets, Vergere," Luke observed.

"I didn't survive by offering my secrets to anyone who might be interested," Vergere said. "My secrets shall remain mine alone, unless I see a reason to set them free." She didn't speak defiantly, but in a matter-of-fact tone, as if describing the color of the carpet.

"We don't want to pump you for information unnecessarily," Luke said, "but I do hope we'll be able to talk sooner or later."

Vergere's feathers ruffled a bit, then smoothed. Perhaps it was her version of a shrug. "We may speak, certainly. But please recall what I told you earlier—I am not a partisan of your New Republic."

"What *does* hold your allegiance?" Luke asked.

"The Jedi Code. And what you would call the 'Old' Republic."

"There *is* no Old Republic." Luke tried to speak gently.

"But there is." Her eyes lifted to his, and he felt a shimmer of Vergere's power and conviction, like a vibration in his bones.

"As long as I draw breath," she said, "the Old Republic lives."

There was a moment of silence, and then Luke spoke. "Long may it live, Vergere," he said.

Vergere bobbed her head. "I thank you, young Master." And then she fell silent and turned to look out over the concourse, her eyes sweeping left and right, gazing at the busy people and droids moving swiftly about their business, the ships, the cargo moving back and forth.

It was a world, Luke thought, that Vergere had abandoned fifty years ago. She had lived among a people immeasurably strange, and Luke wondered how alien Vergere's own native galaxy seemed to her now, with its many races, its bustle, and its humming, clicking, chattering machines.

Sadness sifted through Luke's veins. He had welcomed Jacen back to his home, but no such welcome was possible for Vergere—everything she had known was gone.

The reunion did not end with the reappearance of Jacen.

When Luke and his party were brought into Admiral Sovv's suite, Luke found that Sovv wasn't alone. Sitting on the long curved cream-colored sofa behind their Sullustan host were two familiar figures posed like a painterly study in white, a white-uniformed Mon Calamari and a white-haired human.

"Admiral Ackbar! Winter!"

The joy of reunion with his old friends died, however, as he saw Ackbar struggle to rise from the sofa, and he had to force the smile to remain on his face.

Ackbar leaned heavily on Winter's arm as he stood. The amphibian's shiny pink skin had turned grayish and dull. When he spoke, his words were lisped out of a slack mouth that gasped for air.

"Master Skywalker. Friends. I regret to say that living out of water is a burden for me these days."

"Please don't stand, then," Luke said.

He went to Ackbar's side, and with Winter's help eased the admiral again onto the sofa. "Have you been ill?" he asked the admiral, but his eyes went to Winter.

The white-haired woman looked at Luke and gave a brief nod, a quiet confirmation.

"Ill?" Ackbar said. "Not exactly. What I am is *old*." He gave a sigh from his slack lips. "Perhaps Fey'lya was right when he refused to let me return to the service."

"More likely he remembered the times you'd humiliated him in Council," Mara said.

Winter approached Jacen and wrapped him in a long, thorough, and powerful embrace. "Welcome back, Jacen," she said simply. Winter had looked after the Solo children through much of the early days of the New Republic, when Han and Leia had been driven by the war from one end of the galaxy to the other, and over the years she had probably spent as much time with Jacen as his mother had.

"Have you heard from Tycho?" Luke asked. While Winter's husband, Tycho Celchu, was away with the military, Winter had returned to Ackbar's side as his aide and companion, serving him as loyally as she'd once served Leia.

"He's helping Wedge Antilles organize the defense of Kuat and the establishment of resistance cells. And he's well."

"I'm glad to hear it."

Ackbar lifted his large head toward Mara. "I understand that I should offer congratulations. Did you receive my gift?"

"We did, thank you. The toy holoprojector will do wonders for Ben's vision and coordination."

"The child is well?"

"Ben's fine." A shadow crossed Mara's face. "He's been sent to safety for as long as we're in danger, which may be a while."

"The Solos did the same thing with their children," Winter reminded them. She sent an affectionate look toward Jacen. "They turned out all right."

"Will you all please make yourselves comfortable?" Sien Sovv said in his nasal voice. "Shall I send for refreshment?"

Luke turned to Sovv and felt mild embarrassment at having ignored the Supreme Commander of the New Republic Defense Force for so long. "I beg your pardon, Admiral," he said. "I should—"

The Sullustan made a dismissive gesture. "Since I asked you here to meet old friends, I can hardly object if you let them take precedence over me." His black plate eyes turned to Admiral Ackbar. "For that matter, I wish the admiral would take precedence over me during this war."

He wasn't alone in that wish, Luke knew. It couldn't have been easy for Sien Sovv to be the successor to a legend like Ackbar, and Sovv's modesty and hard work were hardly the sort of gifts to fill the void left by Ackbar's genius and charisma. Sovv might have done better if his term had been blessed by peace, since his administrative talents were genuine and he could have kept the service running at high efficiency, but he'd been unlucky in being forced to fight the wrong war against an enemy for whom the New Republic had been completely unprepared.

Unlucky. It was the worst thing you could say about a military commander. Soldiers trusted a commander's luck much more than they trusted a commander's intelligence.

"I do not believe," Sovv said gently, "that I have met all your party?"

Luke apologized again, and introduced Jacen and Vergere. Sovv complimented them both on their survival skills.

"And young Solo," he added. "I am pleased to report that your sister is not only well, but has taken part in a major victory at Obroa-skai."

Apparently comfortable with his ragged, half-clothed appearance, Jacen had perched on a chair near Vergere. Honest relief broke across his face at the news.

"I was worried," he said. "I sensed she was in a—a situation."

"An entire Yuuzhan Vong fleet was attacked by our fleet combined with a squadron of Hapans. General Farlander was quite explicit in his praise of Jaina. It appears she was responsible for much of the operational plan."

Jacen listened to Sien Sovv with interest, then responded cautiously. "Jaina planned this offensive?" he asked.

"Not all the details, of course, but yes, the attack was her inspiration. Two Yuuzhan Vong troopships were destroyed, with tens of thousands of warriors. Our first completely successful offensive battle."

Jacen nodded. "A good plan, then." His lips smiled, but there was no smile in his eyes.

A light began pulsing on Sovv's comm unit, and he put a small listener to his ear for a private message.

"Your pardon," he said, "but I alerted Fleet Intelligence once I understood that Jacen and a—a defector were on their way. They would like to debrief the both of you." His plate eyes turned to Jacen. "If you're physically strong enough, of course."

Luke couldn't help but notice that Vergere, unlike Jacen, was not being given a choice.

"I'm willing." Jacen rose from his chair, then turned to his avian companion. "Vergere?"

"Certainly." The feathered Jedi wore the same wry, skeptical expression she had worn when she'd first stepped out of the air lock and seen the soldiers with weapons at the ready.

"I suppose this will go on for a while," Jacen said to Luke. "Since I don't know where I'll be staying, may I have your comm code?"

Luke assured Jacen that he was welcome to stay with him and Mara, and gave Jacen his code. Then, turning to Vergere, he repeated the offer.

"Vergere may be detained a little longer than Jacen, unfortunately," Sovv said, which only increased the cynical look in Vergere's eye.

Vergere padded ahead of Jacen as the two made their way out. Through the briefly open door Luke caught a glimpse of Ayddar Nylykerka, the Tammarian director of Fleet Intelligence, at the head of a group of guards; and then the door closed. He turned to Sien Sovv.

"You're taking every precaution," he said.

"Yuuzhan Vong use of defectors and infiltrators is very effective," the Sullustan said. "Before I free her to go where she wishes, I want to make sure that Vergere is what she claims to be."

"I know what she claims to be," Luke said. "I just wonder how she can be expected to prove it."

TWELVE

"Now remember," Leia said, "*we* call it the Remnant, but to these people it's still the Empire."

"An Empire without an Emperor," Han commented.

She patted his hand. "For which we may be thankful, my dear." She sighed as a darker thought intruded. "And the New Republic is something of a remnant these days, as well."

The *Millennium Falcon* had finally completed its long, dangerous crossing of enemy-dominated space to the Imperial capital of Bastion. A squadron of Imperial Star Destroyers flew escort close alongside, their long, wide hulls almost walling off the stars. Their destination wasn't the planet at all but a Super Star Destroyer that stretched a full four kilometers left and right from the docking port, and which carried a crew larger than the population of cities. In the docking bay, a military escort met Leia, officers quivering at the salute. Behind them was a military band that drummed and thumped them the fifty or so meters to their shuttle, a deluxe *Lambda*-class vehicle that featured a passenger compartment with fixtures of solid gold and a soft-spoken military aide who offered drinks and refreshments to fortify Leia and Han for the ten-standard-minute trip to the world's surface.

"The Empire hasn't changed its style much," Han said. He tugged at the collar of his general's uniform. Leia had made him wear full dress on the theory that Imperials were conditioned to defer automatically to anyone wearing a uniform with sufficient badges of rank. Leia herself had chosen for the occasion a gown that was as uniformlike as possible, with a high collar and a double row of jeweled buttons down the front.

"Did you notice when Vana Dorja left us?" Leia asked.

Han gave a startled look over one shoulder. The only person to share the compartment with them was the aide, who had perched on a chair a tactful distance away, far enough to permit them to speak in lowered voices without being overheard.

"No," Han answered.

"I'll lay you a wager that Grand Admiral Pellaeon is listening to her report right now," Leia said.

"I don't take sucker bets."

The *Lambda*-class shuttle dropped close to the planet's surface and sailed low down a long avenue, past formations of thousands of stormtroopers and uniformed fleet personnel, all bracing into a salute as the shuttle drifted past. The late-afternoon sun stretched the soldiers' long shadows across the pavement, producing the illusion that each ranked formation was followed by a dark legion of ghosts.

"Quite a welcome," Han said.

"They're trying to show us what valuable allies they'd make. Troops galore, a Super Star Destroyer, precious metals plating the furniture . . ."

"And what do they expect us to give them in return for all this?"

Leia gave her husband a significant look. "They'll tell us, I'm sure."

The shuttle began to float upward as it approached Imperial Headquarters, a stupendous monolith of polished black marble, gleaming bronze, and dark reflective windows, with shield generators and turbolaser installations perched on a series of stepped-back ledges from which emerged a final, slim pinnacle that stretched upward to a bright crystalline starburst at the very top. It was as if a giant black fist had raised a single finger to indicate that the galaxy could have only one law, one government, and one absolute ruler.

It was toward the starburst that the shuttle rose. It lined up on one of the long crystal rays of the starburst, then brought its docking arm to its tip and hovered there effortlessly on its repulsorlifts.

The aide rose from his seat and stepped to the hatch. "I hope you enjoyed your flight," he said, and at a touch of his fingers the hatch hissed open. The crystal ray, fragile-seeming from the ground, was actually a quite sturdy docking arm, transparent crystal supported by a strong silver-alloy skeleton.

Leia thanked the aide, straightened her shoulders, and marched down the tube, with Han one pace behind and off her right shoulder. After about sixty meters the docking arm ended in a large glittering room roofed with faceted crystal. To Leia's surprise she realized it was an arboretum, filled with thousands of bright exotic blossoms spilling out of their neat rows. Their fragrance perfumed the air. The setting sun set their petals aflame.

As if in deliberate contrast to the brilliant color that rose in profusion behind him, Gilad Pellaeon dressed in the plain white uniform of an Imperial Grand Admiral. He had put on ten kilos since Leia had last seen him, and his hair and bristling mustaches were white. But alert intelligence still shone in his dark eyes, and his pace was brisk and his clasp firm as he walked to the docking port to take Leia's hand.

"Princess." Pellaeon gave her a courtly bow.

"Supreme Commander."

Pellaeon greeted Han as well, but did not bow over his hand. He stepped back and turned again to Leia.

"I received an urgent message for you from New Republic Fleet Command," he said. "They failed to contact you and wished me to relay the message to you."

Leia took an involuntary step back as her heart gave a lurch. *Jaina!* During the Borleias campaign Leia had seen for herself the relentless way Jaina was driving herself, both against the Yuuzhan Vong and against the darkness that threatened to claim her soul. Jaina was far too young to cope with the constant tragedy and loss that had been hers since the beginning of the war, her friends and comrades killed in action, her teachers lost, her brother Anakin killed before her eyes, and Jacen gone to . . . to wherever Jacen had gone. In response Jaina had grown hard, but to grow hard was also to risk growing brittle. Jaina had been riding with death sharing her cockpit for far too long, and it was only her ferocious willpower that was keeping her from toppling over the brink.

Her willpower, which must one day fail, along with her luck. Which *had* failed. Leia knew it.

Han's strong hands caught Leia's shoulders and buoyed her up.

A smile drew itself across Pellaeon's face. "Good news, Princess!" he said. "Your son Jacen has escaped the Yuuzhan Vong. He's arrived at Mon Calamari in good health."

Leia felt her knees weaken, and willed herself to remain upright. Without Han's support she might not have succeeded. Whatever minor doubts she might have had about Jacen's survival had been erased days ago when she'd received his Force message, but still she should have known an official transmission would follow.

It wasn't about Jaina after all. It wasn't about more death, more sorrow, more grief.

"Yes!" Han hissed in her ear. "Did you hear that, Leia? Jacen's alive!"

His arms wrapped her from behind, and she felt the ferocious joy of his embrace. Dizzily she realized that he hadn't

entirely believed her last assurance about Jacen's survival.
He loved her, and so had consciously *decided* to believe her,
an act of will, but still a part of him doubted, and that part
wanted official word.

With effort Leia summoned speech.

"Thank you, Supreme Commander," she said. "You've—"

Still wrapping Leia in his arms, Han gave an unrestrained
whoop of pleasure that nearly deafened her.

"You've made us very happy," she finished, more under-
stated than she would have liked.

"If you would like to use our channels to send your son a
message, you are welcome," Pellaeon offered.

"Certainly. Thank you."

Han's message—WAY TO GO, SPROUT!—was composed
quickly enough, but Leia's was more measured and took
longer.

"Once again, Jacen," she dictated into Admiral Pellaeon's
comm, "you have answered a mother's prayers."

"An elegant sentiment," Pellaeon judged. A wry smile
formed beneath his white mustache. "Jacen seems to have
inherited his parents' gift for escaping capture."

"As well as our gift for getting captured in the first
place," Han said.

Pellaeon gestured toward the garden and its profusion of
bright blossoms. "Shall I show you my garden?" he asked.
"We can speak privately about your embassy."

Leia hesitated. "Won't I need to speak to others as well?"

"The Empire is not run by committee, Princess," Pellaeon
reminded. "If I find that the Moff Council needs to know
the substance of your message, then I'll be the one who tells
them."

Pellaeon drew Leia and Han along the rows of blossoms,
pointing with obvious pride to his hybrid native orchids, to
rainbow-colored fungi from Bakura, to lofty yellow Py-
dyrian blossoms that so strangely resembled the moon's

tall, aloof sentients. Contentment rose in Leia at the sight and scent of the flowers, at Pellaeon's pleasure in them.

"I had no idea you were a gardener, Admiral," Leia said.

"Every ruler should have a garden," Pellaeon said. "It's always useful to draw lessons from nature."

"True." Leia cupped a vast pink blossom and lifted it to her face, inhaled its scent.

"From a garden one learns to cull the weak and unfit," Pellaeon continued, "and to encourage the strong and vigorous." He held up his thumb and forefinger. "An inferior bud soon feels the strength of my pinch!"

Leia sighed and straightened, letting the blossom fall from her fingers. She supposed it was too much to hope that she could stay for long on Bastion without being reminded what the Empire was really about.

Han gave Pellaeon's pinching hand an appraising look. "And you make your plants grow in rows," he said.

"Each receives its proper allotment of space and sunlight, and no more," Pellaeon said. "That's fair, don't you think?"

"But plants *don't* naturally grow in rows," Han pointed out. "This is only possible—" He gave a deliberate glance at the glass arboretum overhead. "—in a highly artificial environment."

Bravo! Leia thought at her husband. *I swear I'll make a diplomat of you yet!*

Pellaeon gave a judicious smile. "You prefer the state of nature, then? I think you will find that in a state of nature, the weak are culled in a far more merciless fashion than you find here."

Leia took her husband's arm. "Let's say that I prefer a balance," she said. "There should be enough nature so that the plants can thrive by following *their* natures, if you see what I mean."

"That notion of balance is derived from Jedi philosophy, if I'm not mistaken," Pellaeon said. "But such hybrid beauty as you see here"—he indicated the blossom Leia had just cupped in her hands—"is not a matter of balance, or nature, but a contest of wills. The will of the gardener, and the will of the plant he must coerce into surrendering her treasure."

Leia dropped Han's arm and sighed again. "I see we're doomed to talk about politics," she said.

Pellaeon gave her one of his courtly bows. "I fear so, Princess."

"The New Republic," Leia said, "would like to request that the Empire furnish us its maps of routes through the Deep Core."

"Those," Pellaeon said, "are among our most closely held secrets."

During the Rebellion, the Empire had held out for years in the galaxy's Deep Core. The Imperials' knowledge of the narrow, twisting paths among the closely packed star masses was unmatched; though the Rebels had finally cleared their enemies out of the Core, it had been grinding work, and probably a good many of the Empire's routes lay undiscovered.

"There are no more Imperial bases in the Deep Core," Leia said, "so the information has no value to you. On the other hand, you're aware of how useful such bases would be to the New Republic now that Coruscant is gone. And," she added, seeing the skeptical look on Pellaeon's face, "you know that the longer we tie up the Yuuzhan Vong in mopping-up operations around the Deep Core, the less likely they are to look at Bastion as their next conquest."

"I have no fear for the safety of my capital," Pellaeon said.

Then you haven't been paying attention, Leia thought. But she knew that Pellaeon didn't mean this in all truth; it was probably just one of those things that Supreme Commanders of totalitarian regimes were expected to say.

"Once," Leia said, "I had no fear for the safety of Coruscant."

Which wasn't exactly true, either.

"Perhaps you would like some refreshment," Pellaeon said. He took Leia's arm and escorted her down the row of blossoms that seemed to get more extravagant and colorful the farther they traveled. Han followed, pretending interest in the flowers.

"I hope you can offer me something in exchange for this information," he said. "The Moff Council won't want these secrets given up."

Leia smiled. "Didn't you just say that you'd tell them what you wanted them to know?"

"I will. But unfortunately," he added, "their busy little minds are capable of drawing their own conclusions, and it would be useful for them to know that something of equal value was given in exchange."

Leia had anticipated this. Offer, counteroffer, outright payment, blackmail—all the arsenal of politics. "The New Republic would be pleased to offer in exchange everything we know about the Yuuzhan Vong. Weapons, tactics, communications, internal organization, the whole package."

"Communications?" Pellaeon pounced on the word. "You've discovered that secret?"

"We have," Leia said. *Thank you, Danni Quee.*

"Obsolete Core routes in exchange for the greatest secret of the Yuuzhan Vong," Pellaeon mused. "I predict no trouble with the Moff Council."

Leia was pleased to hear this, but if necessary she had been perfectly prepared to give the information to Pellaeon free of charge. As far as she was concerned, anything that weakened the Yuuzhan Vong relative to everyone else was a positive good.

They came to the end of the row of plants, and Leia discovered a circular space surrounded by the trunks of Gamorrean coolsap trees, with their dense canopy providing an arbor overhead. Beneath the foliage a grand buffet had been laid out on a hollow, circular table, a long array of silver chafing dishes along with great bowls of salads, fruit, and a selection of desserts and pastry. One entire table was covered with a glittering selection of choice liquors. In the center of the circle was a crystal-topped table set for three, the plates arranged around a bouquet of the most exquisite blossoms the arboretum had to offer.

"Please forgive the informality and help yourselves," Pellaeon said.

Han eyed the banquet skeptically. "We're sharing this meal with *which* regiment?" he asked.

Pellaeon smiled beneath his white mustache. "Our previous meetings really hadn't given me an idea of your tastes. So I ordered a little of everything."

"Must be *good* to be on top of the food chain," Han commented.

Leia thanked Pellaeon and thought, *Now I know how you gained those extra ten kilos.*

Leia and Pellaeon talked through the meal, but of matters of no importance. Talking of matters of no importance was an important political skill. Later, over cups of naris-bud tea, Leia resumed.

"After you've had the opportunity to review the information we've gathered on the Yuuzhan Vong," she began, "I hope the Empire will accept our offer of alliance against the enemy."

Pellaeon raised his white eyebrows. "I expected you to raise the matter earlier," he said.

"Dinner first," Leia said. "War later."

Pellaeon laughed. "Very civilized."

"The main forces of the Yuuzhan Vong are facing the New Republic now," Leia said. "You could cut their supply line from the Rim with very little effort."

Pellaeon gave her a dubious look. "I can present your offer to the Moff Council," he said, "but I know what they'd say."

"Yes?"

"They would ask how the Empire would benefit from this action."

"Surely the Empire would benefit by helping to rid the galaxy of a menace like the Yuuzhan Vong."

Pellaeon considered this, then shook his head. "I would rather not go to the Moff Council with this offer," he said. "They won't approve it."

Jag Fel's voice whispered in Leia's memory. *It would really make more sense in the short term for the Empire to join the Vong* . . . Leia found a muscle behind one knee trembling, and she stilled it. "Why not?" she asked.

"Because, quite frankly, the New Republic is losing its war," Pellaeon said. "Your forces are undisciplined, your government is in disarray, your capital is lost, and your Chief of State was tortured to death in his own office. Why should the Empire join such a debacle?"

Leia silently cursed Vana Dorja and the report Pellaeon had doubtless heard before this meeting.

But maybe that wasn't fair, she thought; Pellaeon didn't need Vana Dorja for this.

"If we join with you now, you'll only drag us down with you," Pellaeon continued. He hesitated. "That's what the Moff Council would say."

That's what you *say*, Leia translated.

"Now, if you start to win some real victories," Pellaeon went on, "then the Moffs' position would be altered. But you'd have to convince us you're not dragging us into a disaster." His dark eyes looked quite solemnly into hers. "And that, Princess, is the truth."

"Well," Leia said, "that's that."

Something shifted in Pellaeon's face. "On the other hand,"

he said, "if you could offer something to the Moff Council. Something concrete . . ."

"Such as?" Leia queried.

"The Moff Council is impressed by *real* things," Pellaeon said. "*Solid* things. For instance, if the Empire could retain any worlds we took from the Yuuzhan Vong, it would impress the Moffs considerably. *Not,*" he added, at the protest in Leia's face, "any worlds that still have your population on them. Only those the Yuuzhan Vong have remade for themselves." He nodded confidingly. "I think the Moff Council is most impressed by *worlds*, Princess."

The Empire could double its size, taking its choice of worlds, and it would cost the Yuuzhan Vong nothing . . . Again Jag's voice whispered in Leia's mind.

Leia managed to seize control of her whirling thoughts. "I— I have no authority to make such a concession," she said. "And in any case, there are millions of refugees who want their worlds back."

"They would be welcome in the Empire," Pellaeon said. "I think we could support them better than could your own overstrained resources."

Then you can prune and cull to your heart's content. Leia saw the cynical remark in Han's brown eyes, but fortunately Han didn't speak it out loud.

"As I said," Leia managed, "I have no authority to make such a concession."

"But you will take my words back to your government?"

Leia nodded. "Certainly."

If we have a government when I get back, she thought.

It wasn't until long after Shimrra had dismissed them all that Nom Anor thought to question what had happened, and then it was Yoog Skell who spoke the words that made him stop and think. The delegation had walked in procession to the Damutek of the Intendants and broken up, and Nom Anor's path lay alongside that of his master, walking along the coiled corridors of the damutek, breathing in the healthy organic stench of the building as young intendants dodged respectfully to the side.

"So," Yoog Skell said, "you have seen the power of the Supreme Overlord."

"Indeed, High Prefect."

"You felt his mind on yours, I know, when he interrogated you."

Nom Anor recoiled inwardly at the memory of the mental pressure that had squeezed him dry. "Yes," he said.

"Never think to lie to the Supreme One. He will know."

"Never," Nom Anor agreed. "I'll never think it."

Yoog Skell gave him a sidelong glance. "Did you feel the Supreme One again when he incited us against Ch'Gang Hool?"

Nom Anor almost stumbled as he walked alongside his leader. "High Prefect?" he said.

"Oh yes," Yoog Skell said, "unless you think it's normal for high-caste Yuuzhan Vong to scream and rant and drool in that way."

The breath went out of Nom Anor in a long, awed hiss. The Supreme Overlord had *created* that? Turned his closest subordinates into a mob of murderous fiends rejoicing at the fall of one of their number?

"Oh yes," Yoog Skell said, "the gods have given him that power, among others." His voice turned reflective. "Not that Ch'Gang Hool is such a loss. His ambitions always exceeded his talents. I remember an Escalatier Ceremony that he performed for one of my most talented advisers, young Fal Tivvik. A fairly basic procedure, I recall, but—as our high priest would say—'the gods discovered a flaw' in the poor girl, and she joined the Shamed Ones. I have myself always wondered whether the flaw might instead have been in Ch'Gang Hool."

Nom Anor gave his superior a sharp glance—the high prefect's words flirted with heresy. But Yoog Skell was in a reflective mood, and he continued.

"Perhaps you remember Fazak Tsun, another of Ch'Gang Hool's unfortunates," he said. He paused as he came before the door to his chamber, and turned to face Nom Anor. He dropped a heavy hand on his subordinate's shoulder.

"You have made mistakes, Executor," he said, "and now you see what happens when too many mistakes come to the attention of the Supreme Overlord."

"Yes, High Prefect." Nom Anor's mind ran so fast he could almost hear the wheels spinning. "How do you suggest I avoid Ch'Gang Hool's fate?"

"Don't make any more mistakes," Yoog Skell said blandly. The door behind him quivered open, and he stepped through it.

"And my particular advice, Executor," Yoog Skell added, "is that whatever you do, don't give the Supreme Overlord an itch, particularly one he can't scratch in public."

The door shimmered shut behind him and left Nom Anor alone in the corridor. He was thinking hard.

The stars streamed aft, and Han sat back in the pilot's seat and gave Leia a grim smile. "Well," he said. "That's that. Next stop, Mon Calamari."

The day after their meeting in the arboretum, Leia and Han had returned Grand Admiral Pellaeon's hospitality by having him to dinner on board the *Millennium Falcon*. Pellaeon and Leia exchanged disks: he had given her the charts of the Deep Core hyperspace routes, and she gave him everything the New Republic knew about the Yuuzhan Vong. Then formal toasts had begun, with Leia toasting the Empire—it had been getting easier with repetition—then

Pellaeon toasting the New Republic, and, very kindly, the success and survival of Jacen Solo.

Then Pellaeon had presented Han with a new hyperspace comm antenna to replace the one shot off in the fight with the Yuuzhan Vong. If there were any more bulletins about Jacen or any other friends or family, Han and Leia would be able to receive them without Pellaeon acting as a relay.

Han eased himself out of the pilot's seat. "I want to get that antenna installed at our next jump point," he said, "and get your message and a copy of that Deep Core map off to the capital. And I'm going to send a copy of the map to Wedge Antilles, too, just in case no one in the capital knows what to do with it."

"Good idea." An idea struck Leia. "I wonder if Pellaeon's antenna has been tampered with. Maybe anything we send will be transmitted to Imperial Headquarters."

"It won't matter," Han said. "The Empire already *has* the information they gave us."

"True."

"I'll replace the antenna again, with one of our own, when we get back to Mon Calamari."

Leia followed Han to the galley. He looked at her. "So were those Core charts worth this trip?"

"Yes. We can keep fighters in the Core for years, raiding the Yuuzhan Vong."

"Even though the Empire isn't about to attack."

"Not without preconditions, anyway."

Han looked grim. "He had a lot of nerve asking for our planets," he said.

"They're not *our* planets anymore, which I suppose was his point. But I think that was just a test. If I'd agreed to his idea, it would have told him how desperate we are."

Han's tone turned thoughtful. "Would that have brought him into the war, or scared him off?"

"Good question." Leia considered the matter. "I think

I've come to the conclusion that we don't want the Empire in this war."

Han was startled. "You sure? All those Star Destroyers? Those troops?"

"That's right," Leia said. "Pellaeon said he'd join us if we started winning victories. But once we start winning, *we don't need the Empire any longer*. What Pellaeon really wants are concessions ahead of time, and then to be at the peace table when it's over. He wants a peace that serves the Empire's interests."

Han began slicing up charbote root. "And here I was starting to think that Pellaeon was a good guy."

Leia made an equivocal motion of her hand. "I'm not saying he isn't, at least by Imperial standards. But he's a head of state, and he has to look out for that state's benefit. He didn't persuade the Empire to end the war with the New Republic on the grounds that it was the *moral* thing to do, he did it by persuading the Moffs that it was in the Empire's *best interests*. Right now the Remnant has barely recovered from the last war—why should Pellaeon get into another life-and-death struggle unless it's to his advantage?"

"I guess," Han said.

"Not *too* much charbote root, Han," Leia said.

"I'm a Corellian. I *like* charbote root." But he stopped cutting, and instead gathered the root slices and dropped them into the saucepan. Then he turned to her.

"Do you know," he said. "I'm not sure I need any food right now."

"Really?" She frowned down at the stove. "Normally you're ravenous at this time of day."

"What I just remembered," Han said, "is that we had hoped to be alone together on this voyage. And that now that Grand Admirals and Imperial spies are off the ship, we *are* alone."

"Oh." She blinked at him. "Oh my." The look in his eyes made her skin flush with warmth.

He took her in his arms. "I think we deserve a little time together," he said, "don't you?"

THIRTEEN

"Pray to the Pardoner Yun-Shuno," the Shamed One said. "Pray that her promises will soon be fulfilled. Pray that the *Jeedai* soon liberate us from those who oppress us with terror and violence."

"So we pray!" the tiny group echoed. Some of them, even as they chanted the response, did not cease from scratching at the fungus that tormented them. Beneath the sound of the ceremony was the constant whisper of fingers against inflamed skin.

"So we pray!" Nom Anor echoed the words with the others. Wearing an ooglith masquer that disguised him as a common worker, he had infiltrated the tiny heretical sect. This was his second meeting.

Infiltration was one of his skills, and he had fooled more suspicious folk than these fools.

But no more, he thought as he scratched idly at one leg. *These people are doomed.*

There were fewer than a dozen in the little group, which met in the shadowy lower levels of a minor office of the intendants, a place normally empty at night. The group was led by a Shamed One, a former member of the intendant caste whose arm implant had gone spectacularly wrong, and still dripped a trail of slime wherever he went. Even workers should have had better taste than to listen to anything said by this pitiful creature.

It was plain curiosity that had driven Nom Anor to infiltrate the sect. Was this group such a mighty threat to orthodoxy as High Priest Jakan had said? Was the message of redemption by Jedi so powerful that it constituted a danger to the Yuuzhan Vong and all they stood for?

When the meeting was over, Nom Anor made his way out of the structure through a door used only by workers.

The night of Yuuzhan'tar was cool and refreshingly free of the scent of the Shamed Ones' rotting flesh. A night breeze soothed Nom Anor's flaming skin. Phosphorescent lichen shone on bits of undigested rubble, relics of the planet's old civilization that were gradually being broken down into more useful, basic elements. By the phosphorescent light Nom Anor wandered away from the center of the new Yuuzhan Vong city into an area of wreckage and half-dissolved rubble that had not yet been cleared for settlement. He wanted to be free of distraction so that he could think.

The workers' heresy was an incoherent muddle, he thought. And yet, if the heretics had a leader, a prophet—no, a Prophet—someone who knew how to adapt this doctrine into a weapon, then they would become something to reckon with.

Obedience, yes, but not obedience to the ruling castes; obedience to the Prophet. Outward passivity and humility to those they considered their oppressors, but inside the keenest resentment and hatred, and an arrogance that demanded a galaxy. Someone—yes, someone like Nom Anor who had spread a religious doctrine on Rhommamool that had caused the inhabitants to destroy themselves in an interplanetary war—someone like Nom Anor could make out of these heretics something very dangerous. All that was necessary was to create a tipping point, a point at which the arrogance and hatred could be brought to overwhelm passivity and caution, and then the heretics would become an army.

Yes, it was lucky these heretics were being suppressed.

Scratching himself on the elbows, Nom Anor turned back toward the city, and in the sky saw the spiraling rainbows created by the dovin basals on the great hovering palace that housed Shimrra. *Now* there *is power*, he thought. *But what rainbows have these heretics cast?*

He walked back toward the settled area, and to his surprise found himself walking along a clearly defined road. He hadn't realized that the shapers had grown roads out this far.

And then he saw something coming toward him along the road, a riding quednak with someone astride it. Nom Anor stepped to the side of the road, and—in his character as a simple worker—bowed in servitude with his arms crossed. It was only as the scaled, six-legged creature thumped by that Nom Anor thought he recognized the silhouette of the rider.

Onimi. That bulbous, misshapen head was unmistakable.

What was the Supreme Overlord's familiar doing here, so far from the palace and any of the centers of government?

Nom Anor thought for a long moment as the beast thudded into the distance, and then followed.

Kashyyyk was a brilliant green crescent in the glittering darkness of space, and around it Jaina could see the silver gleam of the New Republic capital ships that had turned the planet into one of the New Republic's forward bases.

She was in command of *Trickster*, tensed under the cognition hood in case enemy were present as they jumped out of hyperspace. Instead a message of jubilant welcome came from the elements of the New Republic fleet that had remained behind at their new base, and she and the rest of the fleet had stood down from their alert.

Lowbacca growled cheerfully.

"I'd love to join your family on Kashyyyk," Jaina said.

"A furlough in the green trees would be ideal." Just what she needed to ease the tension she felt in her shoulders and arms, the dirge of grief and sorrow that played in her mind, the sadness that flooded her heart.

Lights flashed on the comm system that Lowbacca had jacked into the Yuuzhan Vong ship, and the unit tweedled. [Message from the flagship,] Lowie said.

"What does the general want?" Jaina wondered.

[It's not Farlander,] the Wookiee said. [The message is from Admiral Kre'fey. He wants you and General Farlander to report on board *Ralroost*—"at your earliest convenience," he says.]

And now we pay for our success, Jaina thought.

"O great warrior, is this the damutek of the noble intendant Hooley Krekk?"

Tattoos on the warrior's face creased as she scowled at Nom Anor. She waved her amphistaff in the direction of the city.

"You are not permitted here! Get your miserable carcass back to your barracks!"

Nom Anor, still in his worker guise, bobbed in feigned humility. "With all respect, O Commander, if this is the damutek of Hooley Krekk, then I *am* permitted here."

The warrior was not appeased by Nom Anor's casually promoting her two degrees. "This is *not* the damutek of Hooley Krekk! Now begone!"

It was not the damutek of Hooley Krekk, whom Nom Anor had just invented on the spot, but it *was* the heavily guarded damutek to which the Shamed One Onimi had traveled, a fact proven by Onimi's riding beast seen standing before the building and quietly licking a fungus-covered rock. The damutek was a large, bulbous, three-lobed structure that radiated a faint pinkish light. There was at least a platoon of warriors either on guard or camped in the vicinity, so whatever the function of the building might be, it was of some importance.

And standing in the entrance to the damutek, a pair of Yuuzhan Vong were in conversation, their distinctive living headdresses marking them as shapers.

"Oh, woe! Oh, misery! Oh, unhappiness!" Slapping himself on the head repeatedly, Nom Anor pranced about in a little circle.

This was enough to attract two more warriors, one of them a subaltern, unusually short, with stringy hair.

"What is the meaning of this?" the subaltern demanded. The warrior explained, and the subaltern turned to Nom Anor.

"There is no Hooley Krekk here! Now get back to where you belong!"

"But I belong at the damutek of Hooley Krekk!" Nom Anor wailed. "I was given very explicit directions—left at the Square of Hierarchy, then south to the Boulevard of the Crushing of the Infidels, then right at the Temple of the Modeler, then on down the long road to the end." He began slapping himself again. "Oh woe! My supervisor will punish me!"

"*I'll* punish you if you don't get out of here!" the subaltern said. He cocked his amphistaff over his shoulder.

Nom Anor fell on his face and groveled before the others. "May I beg the officer's pardon? May I ask where I went wrong?"

"*You* went wrong when you were born," one of the warriors joked, and the other laughed.

"Where *is* this damutek?" Nom Anor asked. "What is the name of this place, so that I can explain to my master Hooley Krekk how I came to be here?"

"This damutek is for shapers only!" the subaltern said. His amphistaff slashed down like a whip, and fire burned along Nom Anor's back. "Now clear out before they stick *you* in their blasted cortex!"

Nom Anor scuttled away sideways like a great crustacean, then rose to his feet and scurried down the road. Inwardly, despite the pain that flamed down his back, he gave a smile of satisfaction. *Warriors are so predictable,* he thought.

Cortex was a shaper term for some kind of shaping protocol or technique, which meant that this was a shaper project secret enough to move some distance out of the capital, where its business could go on unobserved, and important enough to station warriors as its permanent guard. The two shapers seen in the entrance only confirmed this.

And Onimi was a part of it somehow.

Nom Anor stumbled on a fault in the road, and at the jar fresh pain shot along his back. That warrior hadn't held back when he'd slashed down with the amphistaff. Nom Anor's teeth ground as he thought of the arrogant little pipsqueak with a weapon longer than he was, and he cast an angry glance over his shoulder at the sawed-off subaltern with his two warriors. *I'll remember this,* he thought.

And then he thought of the heretics at their meeting, the anger and hatred that they couldn't acknowledge even to themselves, and he thought: *Yes. This is how it starts.*

Jaina combed her hair and changed out of her coveralls to walking-out dress, which was as smart as she could get for the admiral, since her full-dress uniform hadn't caught up to her as she'd moved through her last several postings. Walking-out dress, however, was still sufficiently formal that she felt uncomfortable, and kept tugging at her collar as she sat with Farlander in the shuttle that carried her to the admiral's Bothan Assault Cruiser.

One of Kre'fey's Bothan aides met Jaina and Farlander at

the lock, and escorted them to the admiral's suite. The cruiser's air had a spicy alien scent.

When they reached Kre'fey's quarters, they were kept waiting a quarter of an hour by a secretary until they were called in to meet the admiral. Kre'fey was alone in a formal briefing room, standing at the head of a long, empty table. Farlander and Jaina approached the admiral and saluted.

"General Farlander and Major Solo reporting as ordered, Admiral."

Kre'fey's milk-white fur rippled as he returned the salute. "You have your report?"

"Yes, sir." Farlander handed the admiral a disk.

Kre'fey dropped it in a reader and glanced at the information. "One capital ship lost, another disabled," he said. "Nearly a hundred starfighters lost, with only forty percent of the crews rescued—all in an unauthorized action to chase an enemy Supreme Commander who wasn't even there, and following an operational plan devised by a junior lieutenant."

"Yes, sir," Farlander admitted.

"And a stunning victory," Kre'fey continued, still reading. "Seven enemy capital ships destroyed, a pair of transports holding thousands of warriors, and a Supreme Commander killed along with his flagship." His eyes lifted first to Jaina, then to Farlander.

"My warmest congratulations to the both of you," he said. "I wish my other subordinates demonstrated this kind of initiative." He shook Farlander's hand. "Brilliant work! I will put you both in for commendations."

Jaina flushed at the warmth of the admiral's response. She felt the tension in her wire-strung muscles ease. "Thank you, sir," she murmured, and then was surprised to see Kre'fey step before her, then pause for a long moment with his gold-flecked violet eyes fixed on her.

"I wished to see you in comparative privacy in order that I might give you some news of your family." Jaina stared at him in rising horror and felt herself brace for it, her parents dead or captured, or perhaps little Ben Skywalker ambushed in the Maw and killed.

"Your brother Jacen has escaped the enemy and has arrived safely on Mon Calamari," Kre'fey said. "When you have a chance to catch up with your personal messages, no doubt you'll hear the story in more detail."

Jaina stared at Kre'fey in cold astonishment. "Are you sure, sir?" she said. "I saw him, and the Yuuzhan Vong—I was *there*—"

"Of course it's true," Kre'fey said. "Your brother's been on the holonews—he's very much alive."

Jaina could only gape at him. *Why didn't I know?* It had been Jaina who had insisted on the reality of Jacen's death in the face of her mother's belief in his survival. *Why didn't he reach me through our twin bond?* she demanded of herself. And then an answer came to her.

Because I cut him off. She had been driven into a near-mad frenzy by Anakin's death and Jacen's capture; she had embraced the dark and turned her life to vengeance. She had cut off all contact with those she loved. Including Jacen, who must have needed her dreadfully.

She pictured Jacen calling to her over and over, and receiving no answer. *He must have thought* I *was dead.* What kind of despair had she brought him?

She tasted bitter failure on her tongue.

"Would you like to sit down, Jaina?" Farlander's voice floated toward her from beyond the shadowy wall that cloaked her mind.

"Yes," she answered. "If I may."

She groped her way to a chair, and as she lowered herself into it, she managed to remember the niceties. She looked up at Traest Kre'fey. "Thank you, Admiral," she said. "I appreciate your telling me this way."

"It was the least I could do for our new hero," Kre'fey

said as he took the seat at the head of the table. "You and General Farlander have given us a great victory, and I would like you to give me an informal briefing now, before I arrange a full staff conference tomorrow."

"Very good, sir," Farlander said. Even as he answered Kre'fey, his concerned eyes still rested on Jaina.

"Your tactics involving the Jedi?" Kre'fey asked. "Creating a kind of meld? Were they successful?"

"They worked, but we had too few units with Jedi in them," Jaina said. "We need more Jedi in order to make it really useful. And even then it doesn't always work." Her thoughts darkened as she remembered Myrkr. "If the Jedi aren't in agreement among themselves, the meld can fall apart."

Kre'fey brushed aside all doubt. "I'll put in a request for as many Jedi pilots as they can send us. Who knows what the high command will make of it?"

"Who knows?" Jaina repeated. The New Republic had never quite decided what to do with Jedi in this war, but then the honors were even—the Jedi hadn't been quite sure what to do with themselves.

"I'd like to share some other news," Kre'fey said. "I've just returned from Bothawui, where the mourning for my cousin Borsk Fey'lya has now ended. While I was there, I managed to meet with a good many important Bothans, and I'm pleased to report that I achieved some success."

"That's very good, sir," Farlander said.

"As you may know, intrigue is common among Bothans," Kre'fey said. "The periods when we are united as a species are rare, and usually occur only when we are facing a common danger, as we did during the Empire. But now, as a result of Chief of State Fey'lya's death, the Bothan Council has decided to declare that the highest state of war now exists between Bothawui and the Yuuzhan Vong."

Something in Kre'fey's phrasing caused Jaina to look up.

"*Highest* state of war?" she repeated. "But you're at war already, aren't you?"

Kre'fey looked solemn. "We've been in what you could describe as an 'ordinary' state of war," he said. "The highest state of war—it is called ar'krai—was not declared even in the days of Palpatine. Ar'krai has been declared only twice in our past, and was declared only when our survival as a species seemed to be at stake. It means that we will declare total war against our enemy, and not cease until he has been completely destroyed."

"You've . . . destroyed species?" General Farlander asked.

"In the distant past," Kre'fey said. "We did not cease our ar'krai until our enemies were destroyed to the last individual, their names written out of the histories, and their planets reduced to dust floating on the stellar wind." He placed his hands on the tabletop, his white fur reflecting perfectly in its dark polished surface. "So shall we do with the Yuuzhan Vong," he said. "They shall become dust, or we shall become dust ourselves."

Jaina looked at Kre'fey's determined face, and a chill ran up her spine at the quiet certainty that lay behind his words.

Nen Yim couldn't quite suppress a shudder as she reached toward the Shamed One, if only to hand him a bladder-flask. Nor could she suppress her alarm as he opened the flask immediately and began splashing the balm on his misshapen body. The tendrils on her headdress waved in agitation.

"This is for the Supreme Overlord!" she said.

"I'll save enough for Shimrra," Onimi said.

"There must be enough for, for the other shapers," Nen Yim said. "They must be able to create tons of—"

"I know, master heretic shaper," Onimi said. "I'll leave enough for the shapers."

He slathered the pale green lotion over his grayish, inflamed flesh and sighed. "It works," he said.

"Of course it works!" Nen Yim snapped. Even if Onimi was her only conduit to the Supreme Overlord, his impudence was often more than she could bear.

Onimi seemed oblivious to the shaper's loathing. "Think of all the hours of labor you've saved us," he said. "All that scratching."

The balm had certainly saved Nen Yim's own sanity. Since she had returned from Tsavong Lah's command to work on Yuuzhan'tar directly under Shimrra, she had been one of the worst affected of the itching plague's victims. She had barely been able to focus her mind to the point that she could puzzle out an antidote.

She and Onimi faced each other in a room screened off by membranous partitions that pulsed with bright oxygenated blood. Phosphorescent lichen filled the air with a reddish light that was useful when dealing with photosensitive tissues. The tang of the lotion contrasted with the organic odors that normally filled the air, the coppery scent of blood or the loamy scent of undifferentiated protoplasm, the tissue on which Nen Yim performed her grafts, forced mutations, and other experiments.

Performed her *heresy*. The eighth cortex was known to the Yuuzhan Vong as the ultimate grade of shaper knowledge, the most refined and perfect of the procedures given by the gods in ancient times, known only to the Supreme Overlord and the few master shapers with whom he shared the knowledge.

Only the handful who had seen the eighth cortex knew that it was a fraud. It was, in fact, practically empty. It contained only a few advanced techniques, most of which Shimrra had already given to his people.

Yuuzhan Vong knowledge had reached its end. And so Shimrra had found Nen Yim, a shaper already convicted of the heresy of not merely repeating the procedures given the Yuuzhan Vong in ancient times, but actually seeking new knowledge. It was now the task of Nen Yim and her adepts to *create* the eighth cortex, to provide the new knowledge and new procedures that would enable the Yuuzhan Vong to win the war and exist successfully in their new homeland.

Nen Yim had first call on any Yuuzhan Vong resources. Her research took first priority in any dispute, even over urgent war aims. Her team was housed in its own damutek, isolated and guarded. Her only visitor was Onimi, her direct conduit to the Supreme Overlord.

But the guards, she knew, were not simply to prevent an enemy from interfering—they were to prevent Nen Yim and her own people from escaping to contaminate other Yuuzhan Vong with their heretical ideas. The Yuuzhan Vong chosen for the eighth cortex project were insulated from the rest of their own race.

Insulated like a plague.

Nen Yim more than half suspected that after the project's completion, after the eighth cortex was filled with a thousand and one useful shaping protocols, she and her coworkers and Onimi would be quietly liquidated, and all record of their existence erased.

But should that happen, Nen Yim was prepared to accept it. She had accepted death more than once in her life already. All life, after all, was preparation for death, and once the eighth cortex was filled she would have contributed her whole life's adventure to the defeat of the infidels, and the greatness of her people.

Onimi finished applying the lotion and straightened to the full height of his gangling limbs. "This cure is limited, I understand?"

"Yes. It will kill any infection on contact, but you can always be reinfected."

Onimi's unsettling eyes, one lower than the other, focused on her. "And we *will* be reinfected, yes?"

"I'm afraid so. The spore is everywhere."

"Can the World Brain be instructed to produce an organism that will kill the spore? Some kind of virus or bacterium that can devour the plague?"

Nen Yim hesitated. "I fear," she dared to say, "that the World Brain may be the problem."

The room's ruddy light shone eerily on Onimi's eyes, now suddenly alert. His tilted slash of a mouth twitched. "How can this be, master shaper?" he asked.

"I have examined the organism that causes the itching plague most carefully. Though further examination would be necessary to confirm this, I believe that the spore and the fungus it causes are of Yuuzhan Vong origin, not native to Yuuzhan'tar."

A hiss escaped Onimi's lips. "Ch'Gang Hool. That imbecile! He has contaminated the World Brain!" He paused for a moment's thought. "Can you instruct the World Brain to cease production of the spore?"

"Perhaps. I'd have to put aside my other work."

"Don't, then. A new clan has been put in charge of the worldshaping project and the World Brain—let the work be theirs." His expression grew thoughtful. "The gods can speak to Shimrra on the matter, and he can then advise the new shapers."

Distaste flooded Nen Yim. She might be a heretic, but even she had more respect for the gods than to claim her knowledge was of divine origin.

"The Supreme Overlord wants you to concentrate on the yammosk project," Onimi went on. "We must develop a war coordinator that is free from the infidels' attempts to manipulate the gravity spectrum. To this end, the Supreme Overlord has granted you absolution in advance for investigating any of the enemy's machines and weapons."

Nen Yim feigned surprise. "If we knew how the infidels were producing the interference," she said, "the work would be easier."

"It is known that the infidels have gravity-manipulation devices called 'repulsorlifts.' Not as flexible or as useful as our dovin basals, but perhaps operating on the same principles. They might have modified these to interfere with the yammosks."

Nen Yim considered. "Would it be possible to bring me one of these repulsorlifts?"

Onimi gave a mirthless smile. "I shall have one delivered, along with a translation of its specifications."

"Please see they are protected from our metal-destroying bacteria."

"Yes. Of course." His lopsided eyes glimmered. "Shimrra prays daily for a solution to this problem. May I say the gods will provide an answer soon?"

"The gods should first provide a repulsorlift."

Onimi gave a bow and a cross-armed salute, but his head was tilted at an ironic angle. "May your efforts prosper, master shaper," he said.

"And yours, Onimi."

The deformed figure made his way out of the chamber. Nen Yim watched him leave, her lips twitching with distaste.

"Whatever they may be, creature," she repeated, "whatever they may be."

FOURTEEN

Cal Omas announced his "Jedi plan," and his official candidacy, at midmorning before an army of holojournalists, in the lobby of the building that the Mon Calamari had donated for the Senate's use. Luke stood quietly behind Cal amid a group of friends and supporters, not wanting to attract attention, but when Cal called for questions, at least half were directed to Luke, and Cal finally called Luke to his side.

"Are you and the Jedi supporting Councilor Omas's candidacy?" he was asked.

"I hope to be able to work with any Chief of State," Luke said, "but I'm supporting Councilor Omas's plan for restoring the Jedi Council."

The holojournalist was skeptical. "So you're saying you could work with Fyor Rodan if he wins the election?"

"I will work with Councilor Rodan if he will work with me." Luke smiled. "My impression, though, is that he'd rather not."

Laughter trickled lightly through the crowd.

"Rodan says the Jedi Council is your means of seizing power," someone else called.

Cal stepped to the front. "May I answer that one?" he said. "Let me point out that if Luke Skywalker was after power, he wouldn't have needed to work with politicians like me or Fyor Rodan. He wouldn't have needed to destroy the Death Star, or fight Emperor Palpatine hand to hand, or help his sister found the New Republic. All Master Skywalker would have needed to do would have been to join his father, Darth Vader, at the right hand of the Emperor, and in that case his power would be unlimited, and you and I and everyone here would either be dead or enslaved."

Cal scowled at the crowd, and there was a touch of anger in his voice. "This isn't some little jumped-up lobbyist or politician we're talking about, this is *Luke Skywalker*. There isn't a single person in the New Republic who doesn't owe him a profound debt of gratitude. So if anyone suggests that Luke Skywalker is involved in some kind of shabby power play, I'd suggest that person not only can't read history, but is incapable of reading human character."

There was actually applause at that, and not just from Cal's supporters.

"I'd like to thank you for your words on my behalf," Luke said later, after the meeting had broken up.

Cal grinned. "Did you like the hint of anger? I thought I judged that pretty well."

Luke was surprised. "You were faking that?"

"Oh no, it was real enough," Cal said. "I just let it show enough to get the top spot in tonight's holonews." He rubbed his chin. "The question is, did I let it show *enough*."

Luke left Cal Omas pondering this and other political questions and shuttled up to the New Republic Fleet Command annex, where Vergere was still undergoing interrogation. Jacen had been released after a few hours' debriefing, but the fleet showed every inclination to keep Vergere indefinitely.

Luke didn't necessarily think that was a bad thing.

"She's given us reams of material," said Intelligence Director Nylykerka. "It'll take us hundreds of hours to process it all. None of it contradicts what we already know—but then, if she were a bogus defector controlled by the enemy, it wouldn't, would it?" Nylykerka seemed amused. "She's also eaten about twice her weight—I've never seen such an appetite."

"If you had to eat Yuuzhan Vong cooking for fifty years, you'd be hungry for our food, too." Luke asked the Tammarian if he could speak to Vergere himself, and Nylykerka was agreeable. "Any information you can get out of her . . ." he said with a wave of his hand.

He found Vergere in her cell, squatting on a stool and watching a holo transmission from the planet—a news program that featured Luke and Cal Omas. ". . . incapable of reading human character," Cal was saying. Vergere waved the holo to silence as Luke entered.

"In my time," she said, "a Jedi Master would not have intervened so with the Senate and an election."

"In your time," Luke said, "it wouldn't have been necessary."

Vergere accepted this with a graceful bob of her unlikely head. Luke gathered up his robe and sat cross-legged on the chair before her.

He calmed himself. He was trying not to dislike Vergere, though he had very, very good reason to.

Out with it, he thought.

"I've spoken to Jacen about his captivity," he said.

"Your apprentice bore it well," Vergere said. "You are to be congratulated."

Anger swirled in Luke's heart. Exhaling a deliberate slow breath, he banished it.

"Perhaps Jacen didn't have to bear it at all," he said. "He said that you led him into captivity no less than three times."

Vergere's head bobbed. "I did," she confirmed.

"He was tortured," Luke said. "Tortured to the point of death. And *you led him to it.* You could have escaped with him earlier than you did."

"Yes."

"Why?" he asked.

Vergere held herself still, as if listening intently to a voice that Luke couldn't hear. "It was necessary that your apprentice learn certain lessons," she said.

"Lessons in betrayal?" Luke tried to keep the anger out of his voice. "Torture? Helplessness? Slavery? Degradation? Pain?"

"Those, naturally," Vergere said blandly. "But chiefly he had to be brought to the edge of despair, and then over it." Her tilted eyes gave Luke an intense, searching gaze. "You taught him well, but it was necessary for him to forget every lesson you gave him, by showing that none of the gifts you gave him could help him."

"*Necessary?*" Luke's outrage finally broke through his reserve. "Necessary for what? Or for who?"

Vergere tilted her head and looked at him. "Necessary for my plans, of course," she said.

"*Who gave you—*" Luke suppressed his anger. "Who gave you the right?"

"A right that is *given* is as useless as a virtue that is *given*," Vergere said. "Rights are *used*, or they have no value, just as virtues must be *performed*. I *took* the right to lie to your apprentice, to betray him, to torment him and enslave him." Her piebald feathers fluffed, then smoothed again: a shrug. "I also take upon myself the consequences. If you, as his Master, wish to punish me, so be it."

"Was there a point to this?" Luke gazed at her. "Other than exercising your rights, I mean?"

Vergere nodded. "Of course, young Master," she said. "Jacen Solo had to be bereft of friends, of relatives, of teachers and knowledge and the Force and everything that could help him. He had to be reduced to *nothing*—or rather, to himself only. And then he had to *act*—to act *purely out of himself*, out of his own inner being. In that state of complete disinterest, everything else having failed him, he had no choice but to be himself, to choose and to act."

Her voice turned thoughtful. "I regret the means, of course, but I used what I had at hand. The same inner state could have been reached more gently, given time and opportunity, but neither were at hand. I tricked the Yuuzhan Vong into preserving his life and inflicting the Embrace of Pain. I made the Yuuzhan Vong my instrument." She gave a little dry cough, or perhaps it was a laugh. "Perhaps that was my greatest accomplishment."

Vergere's words resonated in Luke's mind, and as he followed their reasoning he found his anger abating, if only by virtue of his abstraction. "And the point of *this*?" he asked.

The slanted eyes closed and Vergere's body relaxed, as if she were entering meditation. "Surely you know the answer, young Master, if you know Jacen Solo at all."

"Humor me," Luke said. "Spell it out."

The avian's eyes remained closed. Her voice seemed to come from far away. "Once, or so the story that Jacen told me suggests, you had your own props similarly knocked away. Deprived of help, of hope, of weapons, blasted by the Emperor's Force lightning—what did you have then? You had only your self. You were made to choose between the Emperor's path and your own."

"I had no choice," Luke said.

"Exactly. You had no choice, and even with annihilation staring you in the face, you chose to remain true to yourself." A hint of satisfaction entered Vergere's tone. "Likewise, it was necessary to reduce Jacen to himself, in order that, with every other door closed to him, he might embrace his destiny."

Destiny. For the second time in two days the word rose in connection with Jacen. And deep in his bones, in complete inner certainty, Luke knew that Vergere was right, that somewhere in the complex weavings of fate, Jacen had a special place.

The previous evening, over dinner in the small apartment, Luke and Mara had asked Jacen about his experience at the hands of the Yuuzhan Vong. At first Jacen had been reluctant to speak at all, saying it was a large subject; but after the first few questions he spoke matter-of-factly of his imprisonment, the way Vergere had repeatedly betrayed him into the hands of the enemy after somehow taking away his connection to the Force. Mara and Luke had glanced at each other in growing horror.

But Jacen had shown no resentment of Vergere; in fact, he had spoken of her with profound respect and admiration. Luke hadn't understood this until later that evening, when he and Mara were alone, and Mara quietly reminded him how hostages sometimes grew strangely attached to their captors. Sometimes captives even grew to love their warders, particularly if the warder was skilled enough in manipulating people. Vergere—old and experienced and serving her own agenda—had been able to manipulate young Jacen's growing psyche.

And so Luke, angry, certain he knew what had happened, had traveled to Vergere's cell to confront her with her actions. But somehow it hadn't quite come out the way he'd anticipated.

"And what do you know of Jacen's destiny?" Luke asked.

Vergere pondered a moment before answering. "I believe that Jacen is intimately connected with the fate of the Yuuzhan Vong," she answered.

Of all things, Luke had not expected that. "He can destroy them?" he asked.

"Destroy them. Save them. Transform them." The tilted eyes opened, gazed expressionlessly into Luke's. "Perhaps all three."

"Can he open them to the Force?" Luke asked.

"I don't know if that's possible."

Luke felt bitterness poison his heart. "Then the Yuuzhan Vong will remain . . . outside."

Vergere's head tilted. "That bothers you?"

Luke blinked. "Yes. Of course. The Force is life. All life is the Force. But the Yuuzhan Vong are outside the Force. So are they outside life as well?"

"What do you think?"

"I think it was easier dealing with enemies from the dark side." Luke looked narrowly at Vergere. "I also think you're very good at interrogation. This conversation started with *me* asking the questions."

"If you didn't want me to ask questions," Vergere said, "you should have explained that at the beginning." Her piebald body stirred on her stool. "I've been answering question after question ever since I arrived, and I'm tired of it. So if you insist that the only questions in this room must come from you, then I decline to answer them."

"Very well." Luke rose to his feet. Her head craned after him on its odd little neck.

"But I will ask one more question before you leave," she said. "You may answer it or not, as you like."

"Ask," Luke said.

Her eyes blinked slowly. "If the Force is life," she said, "and the Yuuzhan Vong are alive, and you cannot see them in the Force—then is the problem with the Yuuzhan Vong, or is it with your perceptions?"

Luke, choosing not to answer, nodded politely and left.

"Tricky, isn't she?" Ayddar Nylykerka asked a few moments later.

"You heard?" Luke asked.

"Of course. Everything in that room is recorded." The Tammarian inclined his head. "What do you suggest we do with her?"

"Hold her here," Luke said, "and keep asking her questions."

Nylykerka smiled. "Just what I planned, Master Skywalker."

Mon Calamari, goggle eyes gleaming in the floodlights, swam easily past Cal Omas's window. The scent of mildew in the room was greater than ever. Mara looked up as Luke entered.

"Vergere?" she said.

"It's complicated," Luke said. "I'll explain later." He looked at Cal Omas, who was sharing a hasty meal with Mara. "What news from the Senate?"

Cal swallowed the mouthful he'd been chewing, and said, "The Senate had a vote this afternoon. I got twenty-eight percent."

"And Rodan?"

"Thirty-five."

"And Cola Quis got ten percent," Mara added, "and Ta'laam Ranth eighteen. Pwoe got three votes total—though he sent a message saying that the vote was illegal and that he was still Chief of State. The rest of the votes were abstentions, or scattered among half a dozen others."

Luke and Mara had decided that, of the two of them, Mara would be the one who would work more openly with Cal and his campaign. Luke had other business, with Jacen and Vergere and the Jedi, and Mara could move more openly among the politicians and lobbyists than he could.

Luke joined the others at the table, and Cal amiably pushed a bowl of giju stew in his direction. "Where's Triebakk?" Luke asked.

"Talking to Cola Quis," Cal said. "By now it must be clear to Cola that he can't win, so we need to find out what it would take for him to drop out of the race and endorse me."

"I'm sure Rodan's asking him the same thing," Mara said.

"And then we ask the same thing of Ta'laam Ranth," Cal continued, "though I don't suppose Ta'laam is ready to answer yet. He'll want a few more floor votes first, just to show what a valuable ally he could be."

"What's he likely to want?"

"A place on the Advisory Council, certainly," Cal said. "Plus he'll want places in the government for his friends—he's always been very serious about controlling patronage."

Luke finished his bite of stew and spoke. "In order to control patronage, there has to be a government for him to control patronage *in*. If the government falls apart in the meantime . . ."

Cal shrugged. "Ta'laam wants what he wants. If we start giving him speeches about patriotism and duty, he'll think we're trying to put something over on him. He's the sort who thinks that patronage is the whole *point* of government."

"In that case," Luke said, sighing, "you may as well point out that if the war goes on, his people will gain access to a lot of military contracts."

Cal grinned. "We'll make a politician of you yet."

"I hope not," Luke said.

Cal reached across the table for a datapad. "It's Fyor's supporters that worry me." He tapped the display. "I've been looking at the people who voted for him, and if I were to make a mental list of the members of the Senate who would want a truce with the Yuuzhan Vong, or even a surrender, I'd find quite a number of them among Fyor's supporters."

"Senator Sneakaway," Luke said, with a significant look at Mara. "Senator Scramblefree."

Cal frowned at the datapad. "I count at least a dozen Senators who either ran away from Coruscant during the fighting or found reason to flee before the fighting started. And some of them are influential."

"Rodan told me that he didn't trust the Yuuzhan Vong to keep a truce," Luke said.

"He repeated it publicly, this afternoon," Mara said.

"But can he hold out against his own supporters?" Cal said. "When the people he depends on for his position tell him they want peace with the Yuuzhan Vong, how can he resist?"

"I don't understand," Mara said. "Rodan was brave during the fight, maybe even heroic. How can he associate with these people?"

"Some people don't question the folks who give them what they want," Cal said, and then his long face creased in a sly smile. "I haven't exactly made my own supporters fill out a questionnaire, either."

Luke finished his stew. "We need a government soon," he said. "And one the military can respect. Because the military won't hold still for a surrender or a truce. And then we'll have a military government that won't hold any legitimacy other than what they acquire at blasterpoint."

Cal looked serious. "Mara told me what you saw this afternoon. I agree we need a government soon. A parliamentary system like ours is inefficient in certain ways, but it's what we're stuck with."

"The question is," Mara said, "does the military understand that?"

It was a question to which none of them had the answer.

Luke and Mara found Jacen in the suite when they returned. Jacen sat on the floor in a meditation pose, and Luke could feel the Force surrounding him, swirling in great eddies through the boy's body, cleansing, healing, strengthening, and restoring. Jacen's eyes opened as soon as Luke and Mara stepped into the apartment, and he smiled.

"The Intelligence people are done with me, for the present," Jacen said. "I think they'll be a while with Vergere, though."

"I spoke with her myself," Luke said.

Jacen's smile broadened. "What did you think?"

"I think she's not simple."

Mara had scowled at Jacen's pleased reaction to the mention of Vergere, but she put the frown away and sat next to Jacen. "I have to wonder about her loyalties," she said.

"They're not simple, either," Jacen said. "She's very harsh sometimes."

Mara's mouth twisted, and Luke knew why, because his own insides were queasing at the thought of torture. He swallowed back a bitter surge of stomach acid and dropped cross-legged to the floor in front of Jacen.

Jacen looked at him. "I'm still your apprentice, Master Skywalker," he said. "Do you have any assignments for me?"

Harsh, Luke thought. Whatever he was going to be, he wasn't going to be Vergere. He smiled. "A very difficult assignment, Jacen," he said. "You're to take a vacation."

Jacen was surprised. "What *kind* of vacation?" he asked.

Luke almost laughed. "Whatever kind you like," he said. "You've been through a lot, and I want you to take the time to think about it. Many of your friends are here—I want you to reconnect with them. Meditate, as you were doing. Try to discern what it is that the Force wants for you, if anything, and whether it's what you want for yourself."

Jacen tilted his head in curiosity. "You'd give me that option?"

"You of all people," Luke said, "should know that you've *always* had that option." He looked into Jacen's solemn eyes. "I want you to get *beyond* what I want for you, beyond what Vergere wants, beyond *any* of us. I want you alone with the Force. A dialogue, with just the two of you, alone."

"*Harsh,*" Mara said. Luke could feel her muscles tense. "Days and days of torture. *Harsh.*"

They were alone in bed, lying nested like spoons, Mara in the curve of Luke's body. Jacen was presumably asleep in the next room, and they conversed in low tones so as not to be overheard.

"She claims she had good reasons for what she did," Luke said. "And they sounded plausible, if—well—*harsh.*"

Mara looked thoughtful. "She helped heal me with her tears."

"Perhaps a gesture of compassion, perhaps a coldhearted calculation to pave her way to a defection—or should I say a *re-re*-defection, to our side."

"She tortured Jacen, but she brought him back."

"And she collaborated in the deaths of hundreds of billions of citizens of the New Republic," Luke said. "The reasons she gives are, perhaps, adequate. Or perhaps she is simply a being with absolutely no conscience and an agenda of her own."

Mara's eyes turned hard. "We've got to get Jacen out from under her influence."

"That's why I told Jacen to take time off and to reconnect with his friends," Luke said. "I can't order him not to feel a connection to Vergere, but I *can* tell him to connect to all the parts of his life that *aren't* Vergere."

Mara nodded. "Good idea."

"Whatever may have happened to Jacen while he was gone, he's more mature than he was. More balanced. And more centered than ever in the Force."

Mara bit her lip. "I agree. Not everything that happened to him was negative."

"After Jacen's gotten his bearings back, I'll send him on a

mission. After he's had a chance to think and regain his balance, he'll need to reconnect with his job."

"Yes." She hesitated. "That may be hard, but it's necessary."

"I spoke this morning of Jacen's having a special destiny," Luke said. "Vergere thinks he has one as well."

Mara looked at him over her shoulder. "Maybe you'd better tell me what she said."

FIFTEEN

Because he needed to know, he returned.

He needed to know whether or not he was doomed, and along with him the revived Jedi Order he had created.

Vergere peered up at Luke from her perch on the stool. "Come to ask more questions?" she inquired. "I should warn you I've already spent my day answering questions from Fleet Intelligence, and I'm tired of it."

"I'll trade you," Luke said. "One of my questions for one of yours."

Her whiskers rippled. "You didn't answer my last. If you can't detect the Yuuzhan Vong in the Force, is the fault with the Yuuzhan Vong or with your perceptions?"

Luke settled onto the chair opposite Vergere. "You left out a third possibility. The fault may be in the Force."

Vergere's feathery crest rose in surprise. "Is this your answer?"

"No. I don't *have* an answer," Luke admitted. He looked at Vergere. "Do you?"

Vergere smoothed her crest with one hand. "Is that your first question?"

"It is."

Vergere paused for a long moment, as if mentally rehearsing an answer. "Before I can answer, I need to know whether Jacen told you what happened to me on Zonama Sekot."

"He did," Luke said.

"So you know that I chose to accompany the Yuuzhan Vong in order to discover their true nature."

"You spent fifty years with them. And so if anyone should have an answer to the question of whether the Yuuzhan Vong are outside the Force, it should be you."

"Yes." There was a long pause while Luke waited for Vergere to continue. Then she said, "That was your answer."

Luke smiled. "The answer to my first question is 'yes.' "

"Correct."

"And I'll have to ask another question if I want further information."

"Also correct."

"Isn't this a little bit childish?"

Her feathers fluffed, then smoothed. "It's your game, not mine. And I believe it's my turn."

He shrugged. "Go ahead."

She fixed him with her tilted eyes. "If the Yuuzhan Vong are completely outside the Force, what does that imply for the Jedi and our beliefs?"

Luke hesitated. This wasn't just a question, this was the Question of Questions, the issue he had been wrestling since the invasion began. When he spoke, he spoke carefully.

"It implies that our knowledge of the Force is in error, or incomplete. Or it implies that the Vong are . . . an aberration. A profanation of the Force. A thing that should not be." He hesitated again, but the implacable logic of his train of thought forced him to continue. "To life we owe our compassion and our duty. But I must wonder what we owe to something completely outside our definition of life, to something that is a kind of living death. I must wonder if we owe them anything but a *real* death?"

"You shrink from this thought." It was a statement, not a question.

"Any being of conscience must," Luke said. He could feel

tension in his clenched jaw muscles. "But still it is my duty to the Jedi not to fear where this leads." He centered himself, and tried to send the tension into the far distance. "My turn," he said.

Vergere nodded. "Proceed."

He took a breath, and forced himself to ask the question that he suspected would doom him. "*Are* the Yuuzhan Vong outside the Force?"

"I have only what amounts to an opinion."

"But it's the opinion of a Jedi Knight, experienced in the Force, who has spent fifty years among the Yuuzhan Vong."

"Yes. And my opinion is this: *by definition* the Force is all life, and all life is the Force. So therefore the Yuuzhan Vong, who are living beings, are within the Force, even though we can't see them there."

Luke felt months-long tension draining from his limbs, and a heavy stone fly weightless from his heart.

"Thank you," he murmured.

She looked at him and spoke with quiet intensity. "You owe to the Yuuzhan Vong the same measure of compassion you owe to all life. No war of extermination is justified. You will not have to eradicate this profanation from the heart of existence."

Luke bowed his head. "Thank you," he repeated.

"Why were you afraid of my answer?"

"Because if the enemy were not life, if they did not deserve compassion, then leading a war against them would have furnished a means of letting the dark side enter not only myself, but all the Jedi I have trained as well."

"My understanding of your position, then, is that such traits as anger and aggression are to be avoided, because they may lead to domination of the mind and spirit by the dark side of the Force."

Luke looked at her. "Was that your second question?"

"Young Master," Vergere said, "it was phrased very carefully so as *not* to be a question. I was merely attempting a clarification of your position."

Luke smiled. "Yes, your understanding is correct."

"Then my next question is this: do you believe that nature would have given us traits such as anger and aggression if they were not useful?"

"Useful for *what*?" Luke countered. "They are useful to the dark side. What use does a Jedi have for anger and aggression? The Jedi Code is specific: we act not from passion, but from serenity."

Vergere settled onto her stool. "I understand now," she said. "Our difference concerns where this serenity originates. You believe serenity is an absence of passion, but I believe it is a consequence of knowledge, and self-knowledge most of all."

"If passion is not opposed to serenity," Luke said, "why are they paired in the Jedi Code?"

"Because the *consequences* of these two states of mind are opposed to one another. An unchecked passion produces actions that are hasty, ill considered, and often destructive. Serenity, on the other hand, may well result in no action at all—and when it does, serenity produces actions that proceed from knowledge and deliberation, if not from wisdom." Her wide mouth suggested a smile. "My turn."

"I haven't asked my question yet."

"I beg your pardon, but you asked a question about the Jedi Code. I answered."

Luke sighed. "Very well. Though it seems to me that I'm conceding a great deal."

"On the contrary. You are acting from serene self-knowledge."

Luke laughed. "If you insist."

"I do." Vergere stroked her delicate whiskers and considered her next question. "It was my observation that on your last visit, you were angry with me. You believed that I had deliberately harmed your apprentice—which was accurate—though your anger was moderated somewhat when I explained my motivations."

"That's true," Luke admitted.

"Now my question is, was that anger dark? Was it an evil passion that possessed you, such that the dark side might have taken you as a consequence?"

Luke chose his thoughts carefully. "It *could* have been. If I had used that anger to strike out at you, or harm you, particularly through the Force, then it would have been a dark passion."

"Young Master, it is my contention that the anger you experienced was natural and useful. I caused *deliberate harm*—pain and anguish and suffering, over a period of weeks—to a young man for whom you had accepted responsibility and for whom you felt a measure of love. *Naturally* you felt anger. *Naturally* you wanted to break my thin little neck. It is absolutely natural, when you discover that a person has inflicted deliberate pain on a helpless victim, to feel angry with that person. It is equally as natural an emotion as to feel compassion for the victim."

Vergere fell silent, and Luke let the silence build.

After a moment, Vergere bobbed her head. "Very well, young Master. You are correct when you said that if you had entered my cell and struck out at me with the Force, that such an action would have been dark. But you didn't. Instead your anger prompted you to speak to me and find out the reasons for my actions. To that extent, your anger was not only natural but *useful*. It led to understanding on both our parts."

She paused. "I'm about to ask a rhetorical question. You need not answer."

"Thank you for the warning."

"My rhetorical question is: *why wasn't your anger dark?*

And my answer is: *because you understood it*. You understood the cause of the emotion, and therefore it did not seize power over you."

Luke thought for a moment. "It is your contention, then," he said, "that to understand an emotion is to prevent its being dark."

"Unreasoning passion is the province of darkness," Vergere said. "But an understood emotion is not unreasoning. That is why the route to mastery is through self-knowledge." Her tilted eyes widened. "It's not possible to suppress all emotion, nor is it desirable. An emotionless person is no more than a machine. But to understand the origin and nature of one's feelings, that *is* possible."

"When Darth Vader and the Emperor held me prisoner," Luke said, "they kept urging me to surrender to my anger."

"Your anger was a natural response to your captivity, and they wished to make use of it. They wished to fan your anger into a burning rage that would allow the darkness to enter. But *any* unreasoning passion would do. When anger becomes rage, fear becomes terror, love becomes obsession, self-esteem becomes vainglory, then a natural and useful emotion becomes an unreasoning compulsion and the darkness is."

"I let the dark side take me," Luke said. "I cut off my father's hand."

"Ahhh." Vergere nodded. "Now I understand much."

"When my rage took control, I felt invincible. I felt complete. I felt free."

Vergere nodded again. "When you are in the grip of an irresistible compulsion, it is then that you feel most like yourself. But in reality it was *you* who were passive then. You let the feeling control you."

"My turn for a question," Luke said, and at that point a comm unit chimed.

"Master Skywalker." Nylykerka's voice. "A fleet has just arrived out of hyperspace, and they wish to contact you."

Vergere blinked at him. "Next time," she said.

Luke rose. "Next time," he said.

Outside, Nylykerka met him with a bow. "Sixteen ships just arrived, mostly freighters or modified freighters, but including a Star Destroyer, *Errant Venture*. There are messages to you from Captain Karrde, and also from Lando Calrissian, who commands one of the ships."

"Thank you."

Nylykerka walked with him to the nearest comm unit. "I'm running out of questions to ask her," the Tammarian said. "And I'm running out of reasons to hold her."

"Keep her until I can talk to her one more time," Luke said. "I'm still not convinced that she's benign."

The Tammarian's air sac pulsed meditatively. "Then why would she rescue Jacen?"

"To gain access to the Jedi, perhaps so she can destroy us."

Air whistled from Nylykerka's sac. "No wonder you want her held."

The problem, Luke thought, was that if Vergere was as powerful as he thought, she wouldn't be in Nylykerka's cell any longer than she wanted to be there.

Luke stepped aboard *Wild Karrde* to a salute from a double row of skull-headed, glowing-eyed droids with massive physiques and sloping foreheads. The ship smelled of machine oil. Luke returned the salute and marched down the line to be embraced by Lando Calrissian and to have his hand pumped by Talon Karrde.

"I see your droid factory is thriving," Luke told Lando.

"Everything you see," Lando said with a grin, "is for sale to the government for a very reasonable price."

Luke frowned at his friend's flippant remark. "That strongly depends on whether we *get* a government," he said.

Karrde looked serious and tugged his small goatee. "You'd better tell us about that," he said.

Karrde took Luke to his cabin, and Luke told Lando and Karrde of the latest developments in the Senate. "There have always been rumors about Fyor Rodan," he said finally. "Rumors that he's connected with smuggling operations on the Rim. If either of you know any of the details, perhaps you can help us . . ."

"Discredit Rodan by associating him with *us*," Karrde said, and laughed.

"No offense," Luke said.

"None taken," Karrde said. "But I'm afraid I can't help you. It's not Fyor Rodan who's the smuggler, it's his older brother Tormak."

"Tormak Rodan used to fly out of Nar Shaddaa for Jabba the Hutt," Lando said. "After Jabba had his, ah, accident, Tormak went independent and set up on the Rim."

"He and his brother *hate* each other," Karrde added. "Tormak was into anything shady, and little brother Fyor grew up as straitlaced as they come, probably in reaction to how big brother Tormak behaved. If Fyor's sensitive on the subject of smuggling, I guess that's why. Still," he added, stroking his goatee. "I think Lando and I can help your candidate along."

Alarm tingled along Luke's nerves. "How?" he asked.

Karrde gave a private little smile. "It's best you don't know."

"I don't want Cal Omas discredited," Luke said quickly. "If you get caught in something shady, no one will believe that Cal wasn't behind it."

Lando put a reassuring hand on Luke's arm. "Not getting caught at something shady is our specialty."

"There's always a first time."

"Luke," Lando said, "we're just businessmen. We're trying to get government contracts. We have a perfectly legitimate reason for talking to anyone who could help us."

"And we have sixteen ships full of supplies that we're donating to the refugees on Mon Calamari," Karrde added. "All courtesy of the Smugglers' Alliance. So we're going to be *very, very popular* for a while, and politicians will want to be seen with us."

"I'm not sure I like what I'm hearing," Luke said.

"Then we'll change the subject," Karrde said smoothly. He opened a locker and took out a metal container, which he thumped down onto the table and opened. "Like it?"

Luke saw a boxy, wheeled droid, and gave a little shiver of distaste. "It looks like a mouse droid," he said. Millions of mouse droids were in existence, chittering and squeaking and running their obscure errands beneath the feet of annoyed citizens. Why anyone had chosen to model a droid on disease-carrying vermin was beyond him.

"It's a mouse droid chassis," Lando said. "We get them cheap—people practically pay us to take them away. But this mouse droid now contains the sensor unit of one of our Yuuzhan Vong Hunter droids."

"Ah," Luke said, understanding.

"The Yuuzhan Vong Hunter units are better at sensing Yuuzhan Vong than they are at sensing humans," Karrde said. "But they *are* aggressive, and, well—"

"Murderous," Lando said.

Karrde gave him a sharp look. "*Conspicuous* was the word I was looking for." He tapped the mouse droid. "One of our YVH-M units can sniff out Yuuzhan Vong infiltrators and, unlike one of our Hunters, won't be tempted to immediately blow him to smithereens. Instead, it can be programmed to follow the infiltrator, record his movements, and take note of anyone that the infiltrator talks to."

"Who ever notices a mouse droid?" Lando said. "Most people do their best to *avoid* noticing them."

"Our next model will feature a small repulsorlift. *Flying* Yuuzhan Vong Hunters—just think about it!"

Luke had been making some quiet calculations while the others were involved with their sales pitch. "I don't think you should talk about your YVH-M models to just anybody," he said. "We want these to be a surprise, especially to the Yuuzhan Vong."

Lando smiled and nodded. "Can you suggest who we *should* talk to?"

"Dif Scaur and Ayddar Nylykerka, for two."

"The head of New Republic Intelligence, and his military equivalent. That's very good."

Luke reached out and gave the smooth plastic surface of the mouse droid a pat. "I have a feeling," he said, "this little critter is going to be very, very useful."

Trickster was parked in orbit around Kashyyyk, and a group of Wookiee technicians descended on it, supervised by Lowbacca. Quarters for the Twin Suns Squadron and docking bay space for their X-wings had been found on the old Rendili Dreadnaught *Starsider,* which had been converted to a tender and supply depot for other ships. Jaina found her new cabin and threw herself down on a mattress that still smelled of the previous occupant's unwashed body.

The first thing she checked were the holomessages that had piled up waiting for her while she'd been on the Obroa-skai mission.

Yes. There was a holomessage from Jacen. Her fingers trembled as she pressed the buttons that would play the recording.

"Hi," Jacen said. "I'm back from the dead." And he looked it—he was ten or twelve kilos underweight, and the long hair and scraggly beard gave him the appearance of a hermit just rescued from a long period of fasting in the desert.

He briefly explained that he'd been held prisoner by the

Yuuzhan Vong, and rescued by a Jedi named Vergere, a Jedi of the Old Republic.

"I'm sorry I didn't try to contact you through our twin bond," he said. "You were in my thoughts the whole time. But I knew that the Yuuzhan Vong *wanted* you to try to rescue me—they were ready for it. They wanted to sacrifice us both in a special ceremony. So my greatest chance of staying alive was to keep you as far away from me as possible.

"They tell me you've played a big part in a victory." His brown eyes gazed mildly out of the holo. "I hope that means you've been all right while I've been away. It must have been bad enough knowing that Anakin was dead without thinking that I was gone as well." He hesitated. "I know you're too sensible to get into anything really hurtful, but I hope you're well, and I hope we'll be able to talk soon. Tell Lowie and everyone hi. Take care. I love you."

The holographic image fizzled out. Jaina's thoughts whirled. It seemed she was forgiven for not trying to contact Jacen through the twin bond they shared, but on the other hand Jacen seemed to have sensed, or perhaps heard about, her mad, angry brush with the dark side, her surrender to the fury that was her legacy through the blood of Vader.

What could she tell Jacen? It had been bad enough confessing her actions to her mother.

The next message was from Jagged Fel, reporting that he'd encountered her mother and father on the Hydian Way, and that Leia had told him Jacen had escaped the Yuuzhan Vong.

Did everyone know before I did? she thought.

"I've missed you," Jag said. "I wish I was with you. I wish I could see your reaction when you find out that Jacen is alive. I want to kiss you in celebration."

Even though she wanted to bask in misery at this moment, Jag's words brightened her spirit. The memory of his arms around her, and the phantom taste of his lips on hers, whispered like a warm summer wind through her memory.

She really couldn't, she thought. Being in love at a time like this was madness. Not when death reached out to her at every moment, when another person to love meant only another person to mourn when the time came.

But Jacen had come back . . . perhaps that meant that things had changed.

Her mind whirled. But one thing was clear: soon death would come for her.

The fewer people to mourn then, the better.

Jaina found Kyp Durron in the pilots' mess, chewing without enthusiasm on a reconstituted, freeze-dried iagoin steak that may have been in a storage locker since the days of Empress Teta. "Great One," he said, looking up, "please exercise your godly powers and summon real food. We're orbiting six hundred kilometers above the greenest planet in the New Republic, and the mess can't seem to find any fresh vegetables." He paused, then looked at her in surprise. "What's wrong, Sticks?"

"Jacen's alive," she said. "He's on Mon Calamari with Uncle Luke and Mara."

Kyp's expression cleared. "Wonderful!" he said. "Get yourself a plate of rehydrated salthia bean paste, and we'll have a feast and celebrate!"

Jaina sat heavily on the seat opposite him. "What do I tell him I've been up to since he was captured?" she asked.

Comprehension dawned. "I see," Kyp said. "Well." He looked down at his plate and pushed the iagoin away with distaste, then looked at Jaina again. "You may as well tell him the truth."

"There's more to it than that," Jaina said. "During his capture he made no attempt to contact me through the Force, for fear that I'd try to rescue him and run into a trap.

So what do I tell him—that because he didn't contact me I ran amok? What's that going to do to *him*?"

Kyp listened carefully and nodded. "I understand your concern," he said, "but I think Jacen can take care of himself. He always has. And besides, Anakin's death had as much to do with your going to the dark as Jacen's capture did."

"Maybe so. But it's hard to know how he's going to take things. What if it sends him into another spiral of—of whatever it was that paralyzed him in the first place?"

"You saw the hologram," Kyp said. "Did he *look* paralyzed?"

Jaina found herself smiling. "No. He looked like he'd been through a lot, but—he looked all right. And he was right enough to be concerned about me."

Kyp nodded at her solemnly. "Then I think—when you see him—you'll know what to say."

Jaina looked at her hands. "I hope so."

Kyp grinned. "Is there anything *else* that's going to keep you from celebrating?"

Jaina smiled, but sobered quickly. "Admiral Kre'fey," she said. "He and the Bothans have gone mad—they've all decided they're going to wipe out the Yuuzhan Vong to the last germ cell. So now we have a commander who's bent on destroying a whole species." She looked at him. "Is that an invitation to the dark side, or what?"

Kyp was impressed. "Even *I* never went that far," he said. He leaned across the table toward Jaina. "I think that the dark side can only take command when you're feeling certain emotions," he said. "In my case it was anger. In yours it was the desire for vengeance."

"On behalf of a brother who turned out not to be dead," Jaina added bitterly.

"As well as the one who was. Yes. That was wrong, and

we're agreed on that. But I think we should try to make several distinctions here."

"All right," Jaina said, though she felt cautious at the idea of too many shadings and distinctions between light and dark.

"There's aggression for its own sake. Which is bad."

"Yes."

"There's defensive war, fighting against invaders on behalf of your own worlds or people or government. Which, if not necessarily *good*, is at least justified."

Jaina nodded. "I'm following you."

"And then there's a counterattack in an otherwise defensive war. Which was Obroa-skai."

"And it's what?" Jaina asked. "Good? Bad? Justified?"

"Justified," Kyp said. "I've been thinking hard about this, and I think justified." Then he saw Jaina's dubious look, and said, "Let me give you an analogy."

"All right."

"Say you have a friend who has something valuable, like a ring. And a thief attacks your friend and steals the ring, and for some reason you can't prevent it."

"I'm following you."

"And later, you meet the thief, and you see the thief wearing the ring. So is it aggression to bring the thief to justice, and return the ring to its rightful owner?"

"So you're saying," Jaina said, "that the thief is like the Yuuzhan Vong, who have been stealing our worlds, and that it's not aggression to want our worlds back and the Yuuzhan Vong out of our hair?"

"I'm not saying that there isn't a degree of aggression. But I'm saying it's justified."

"But if your aggression lets in the dark?"

"Then it's *not* justified," Kyp said. He sighed. "Look. You can go after the thief because you're angry at him and you want to give him a good pounding, or you can go after the thief because you want to see justice done. There's a difference. Anger is dark, but the love of justice is light."

"And perfect justice is impossible," Jaina countered.

"Perfect justice isn't the issue. You're setting too high a standard. We haven't sworn oaths to be perfect." He considered for a moment. "Look, it's like when Luke was fighting Darth Vader, and the Emperor stood by urging him to strike out of anger. Fighting Darth Vader *wasn't the wrong thing to do!* But fighting him out of anger *was*."

Jaina looked at him for a long while. "No offense, Kyp, but I wish it was Uncle Luke who was making this argument, not the greatest living expert on the dark side of the Force."

Kyp looked at her soberly. "So do I, Jaina. So do I."

When Winter opened the door, there was a slight hiss of changing pressure. She saw Luke, Mara, and Jacen, and stepped away from the door to let them inside.

"Please. Come in."

Admiral Ackbar's apartment was deep below sea level in Heurkea Floating City, and was filled with the scent of the ocean. The rooms were rounded and dimly lit, and echoed to the music of falling water. There were deep seawater pools in every room, connected by submerged tunnels or by channels spanned by small arched bridges. The walls and ceilings shimmered with golden light reflected by the waves, and the floors were tiled in colors that reflected the moods of the sea, green, blue, turquoise, and aquamarine.

The door hissed shut behind them.

Winter wore a long white gown and a necklace of sea-green jade. She greeted Luke and Mara with an embrace, and kissed Jacen on each cheek.

"How is the admiral?" Luke asked. He pitched his voice low in the hope that these artificial caverns wouldn't amplify his voice and carry it through the house.

"His body is failing him," Winter said. Her calm voice was matter-of-fact, but Luke could see the lines of sadness radiating from the corners of her eyes.

"Can anything be done?" Mara asked.

"As he told you the other day, there's no single thing wrong," Winter said. "The real problem is age, and the way he drove himself during the Rebellion. He wasn't young even then, you know."

"I suppose not," Luke said. "It never occurred to me to wonder how old he was. He seemed as young as—as he needed to be, I guess."

"You'll find his mind is as supple as ever," Winter said. "He can still work for ten hours at a stretch if he takes care of his body."

"Work?" Mara asked. "At what?"

"I'll let Ackbar tell you that." Luke, Mara, and Jacen followed the tall, white-haired woman over a small bridge and across stepping-stones—actually the tops of tall pillars—set in a quiet pool. They came to a comfortable drawing room with a central pool set amid comfortable furniture. There Ackbar waited, bobbing in the pool. He waved one huge hand.

"Luke!" he called. "Mara! Young Jacen! Welcome to my home!" His voice showed no sign of the slurred diction it had shown in Admiral Sovv's office, and boomed out as vigorously as if he were shouting orders on the bridge of his flagship.

"Thank you, sir," Luke said.

"Please seat yourselves. Forgive me for not joining you— I'm much more comfortable these days if I stay in water."

"Your home is lovely," Mara said.

"It suits me," Ackbar said simply.

Winter efficiently served refreshments while Ackbar and his guests chatted. Then Ackbar floated toward Jacen, and looked up at him with his goggle eyes.

"Can you tell me of the Yuuzhan Vong, young Jacen?"

"I'm willing," Jacen said. "But it's a large topic."

"You're the only person I know who has any exposure to them. Tell me what you can."

Jacen spoke for a long time, of the Yuuzhan Vong and their castes, their leadership, their religion, the way they interacted with each other and their captives. He touched on his own experience only lightly. Luke was surprised and impressed that Jacen, in pain and in slavery and alone, had observed his captors so acutely, and was able to organize his material so well.

Winter listened in silence, and after a while sat on the edge of the pool, pulled up her gown, and dangled her legs in the water. Ackbar floated next to her, and she rested an affectionate hand on his sloping glabrous shoulder.

Luke watched them and thought of the many tragedies contained in Winter's mind. The white-haired woman possessed a holographic memory that recorded her entire life in perfect detail but would not permit her to forget. The grief she must have felt at the destruction of her home world of Alderaan, with her family and friends, was as fresh in her mind now as it had been twenty-seven years ago. The battles of the Rebellion, the struggles against Furgan and Joruus C'baoth, the kidnapping of the infant Anakin Solo . . . Winter could relive all these with the same intensity with which she'd first experienced them. Likewise, the years she had spent with Jacen when he was a child were as vivid as her experience of the adult Jacen himself, sitting near her.

Winter's mind *was* a hologram, Luke realized: it contained a complete template of her life. Birth, death, joy, tragedy, violence, triumph, despair. Seen that way, it wasn't surprising that she'd joined Ackbar in his retirement: perhaps her mind contained more than enough severe experience by now, and she needed tranquil memories to place alongside those that were not in the least tranquil.

But now, as Ackbar declined, Winter was going to acquire even more long, sad memories that she would never be able to forget.

Ackbar listened to Jacen's story, and then he and Winter asked a series of questions. Finally Ackbar sighed, and settled peacefully in the water.

"Very good," he said. "I know how to beat them now."

Luke looked at the admiral in surprise. "So that's what you've been working on."

"Oh yes." Ackbar looked up at Winter and gave her knee a pat. "With Winter as my memory and my invaluable assistant, I've been working very hard on a strategic plan for the war, and now Jacen has confirmed my ideas of the Yuuzhan Vong character. I think victory is now conceivable."

"Are you planning to come out of retirement?" Luke asked.

Ackbar gave a burbling sigh. "I don't know if that's possible. Admiral Sovv is willing to take my counsel on this matter—but will anyone listen to poor Admiral Sovv?"

"They'll listen to *you*," Luke said. "I can't imagine anyone not listening."

"Borsk Fey'lya wouldn't listen," Ackbar said. "And Borsk Fey'lya had many friends." He shook his huge head. "I truly miss Mon Mothma. We understood one another—our skills were so entirely complementary. She and I were a perfect team, she the great orator and politician, and I her sword. She was able to see the traps that I was blind to, and I saw the dangers that she could not see. Her wisdom saw the Rebellion to its conclusion and created the New Republic. And with my fleets I helped bring about the defeat of the Empire." Again he shook his head. "She spoiled me!" he said. "She understood my methods, and I understood hers. Since her passing, I've had to deal with others who were not so understanding, and I lacked the skill for it—I had never needed it before." He sighed, and for the first time he slurred his words, as he had the other day. "Mon Mothma. Perhaps I shouldn't have outlived her."

Winter looked at Ackbar in concern. "Never say that."

"No," Luke said. "You still have much to contribute. Your plan will prove that."

Ackbar sighed again. "But who will see this plan? It requires not only the cooperation of the military, but of the highest levels of government. And our government *has* no highest levels."

Ackbar was obviously tired, and the visitors didn't stay long after that. As Winter saw them out, she paused and put a hand on Jacen's shoulder. "I was so sorry to hear about Anakin," she said.

Jacen nodded slowly. "He was always grateful to you," he said. "He knew how you fought for him on Anoth." His two hands took Winter's between them. "If it weren't for you, he wouldn't have had the last fourteen years of his life. And it's not just Anakin who was grateful for that, it's Jaina and I and everyone who knew him." He kissed Winter's hand, and let it fall.

Mara and Luke embraced Winter, and left the apartment. Perhaps, Luke thought, Winter's holographic memory was not always a cause for sorrow. She would remember Anakin as an infant, as a growing boy, and those brilliant, undying memories might well be brighter than the more distant knowledge of his death.

Somewhere at least memories of Anakin were preserved perfectly, Anakin as he was, alive and vital, unscarred by the tragedy that was his end.

Luke took great comfort in the thought.

SIXTEEN

In the end Jaina decided to put aside any other considerations, and concentrate once again on being a good leader to the Twin Suns Squadron. Half her squadron had no combat experience beyond operating battle stations on *Trickster*, and that was hardly their normal line of work. They were starfighter pilots, and Jaina knew too well that even experienced pilots had a very short life expectancy when going up against the Yuuzhan Vong. She planned an ambitious training schedule, putting the pilots in their cockpits almost every day, battling against formations of A-wings, whose speed and combat characteristics most resembled the Yuuzhan Vong coralskippers. On the days when the squadrons weren't in their X-wings, they would do classroom work on tactical theory and practice.

Jaina's ambitious schedule fell apart on the second day. Twin Suns Squadron was practicing hyperlight maneuvers, pursuing a squadron of A-wings under Colonel Ijix Harona. Harona and his Scimitar Squadron made repeated short hyperspace jumps while Twin Suns Squadron tried to both follow them through hyperspace and end their jumps in an advantageous tactical position relative to their quarry. The two squadrons were evenly matched: both were composed half of experienced pilots and half of rookies.

The two squadrons had completed their second pursuit—

a modest success, Jaina thought—when a distress signal flashed across their hyperspace comm units.

"This is New Republic cruiser *Far Thunder*. We and the frigate *Whip Hand* are under attack by approximately sixty enemy coralskippers. Our hyperdrive engines are disabled. Coordinates follow. We request assistance from all nearby New Republic forces. I repeat . . ."

Jaina's blood ran chill. *Far Thunder* was the cruiser that had been disabled at Obroa-skai, and had been left under escort by the ex-Imperial *Lancer*-class frigate *Whip Hand*. Most of *Far Thunder*'s personnel had been evacuated, and there weren't enough remaining to make up a fighting crew. Jaina thumbed the intership comm and signaled Major Harona.

"Scimitar One, did you copy the distress message?"

"I copy, Twin One." Harona's voice was slightly distracted. "Ask them for details. I'm going to query Fleet Command."

"Understood, Scimitar One." Jaina triggered the hyperspace comm. "*Far Thunder,* this is Twin Suns Squadron. Can you give me an idea of your situation?"

"Major Solo?" A new voice came on-line, and Jaina recognized *Far Thunder*'s Captain Hannser. "We have only damage control and bridge crew aboard. We've slaved the weapon systems to droid brains, but it's not as effective as a real fighting crew. We've lost our tender. We've lost a lot of our shields and we're getting hammered. *Whip Hand* is holding her own but is too hard-pressed to protect us." Jaina heard quiet despair in the voice. "I just want to buy some time to evacuate my crew and scuttle the ship. That's all I ask."

Her heart went out to him. Hannser had argued so forcefully against Farlander, who had wanted to scuttle the cruiser, and finally won his point . . . only to come to this.

"Understood, *Far Thunder*," Jaina said. "Stand by."

She switched to intership comm. "Scimitar One, *Far Thunder* reports—"

"I heard," Harona said shortly, and then added, "Fleet Command is concerned that it's an ambush."

"The messages aren't faked," Jaina said. "I recognize the captain's voice."

"Stand by, Twin One." Jaina waited a long moment while Harona signaled headquarters. Then his voice returned. "Fleet Command has left the decision to me," Harona reported. "If we don't go, they'll order *Whip Hand* to save herself and abandon the fight."

Jaina bit her lip. It would take a considerable effort for coralskippers to destroy even a disabled capital ship, but they could do it in time. The two reinforcing squadrons would go a long way toward evening the odds, but half the starfighter pilots were rookies who couldn't be expected to hold their own against the Yuuzhan Vong, and the experienced pilots would be distracted by having to look after them.

Plus, the Yuuzhan Vong themselves may have sent for reinforcements.

She thought of shields falling, the hull being breached, death and slow-marching obliteration as *Far Thunder* was destroyed piece by piece, compartment by compartment.

Jaina thumbed her comm button. "I'd risk it, Colonel," she said. "If it's too hairy, we can jump out."

There was a long silence before Harona's voice returned. "Agreed, Twin One," he said. "We'll use the A-wing slash, so that puts you in the lead."

"Understood, Scimitar One." Jaina spoke through clenched teeth—Harona's plan would commit Jaina's squadron first, and keep his own A-wings out of the battle until after the fight got nasty.

Not that Harona's plan didn't make sense. The A-wings were little more than a pair of giant Novaldex engines with weapons and a pilot strapped on—they couldn't take punishment like an X-wing, and were best at hit-and-run fighting.

"Stand by to receive jump coordinates. Prepare to jump on my mark."

"I copy, Scimitar One."

Jaina switched to the channel she used for communication with her squadron. "We have received a distress call from two capital ships under attack," she said. "We're going in to help them. *This is no drill.*" She paused a moment to let that sink in. "I want wingmates to stick close to their leaders. You are *not* to go off on a Vong hunt on your own. Each flight is to form single file with two kilometers between ships. Twin Five, I want your flight twenty kilometers astern of my flight and to right." Lowie howled an acknowledgment. "Twin Nine, your flight will fly cover twenty kilometers astern of Twin Five."

"Acknowledged," Tesar said.

She wanted her squadron in single file because it was easier for the rookies to keep up. They had all been assigned as wingmates to more experienced pilots, so all they had to do was follow the ship ahead of them and shoot at any enemy that got in the way. If the wingmates themselves got bounced, they'd have a veteran pilot behind them who might be able to keep their tails from being waxed.

Jaina watched the displays as her squadron settled into the assigned formation. Not a whole lot of bumping and weaving, which was good.

"We won't know the full picture until we get in," she said, "so be prepared to maneuver the second we get into realspace. Any questions?"

No questions. Everyone in her squadron, she thought, was either very smart or very stupid. Jaina knew which way she wanted to bet.

"Extend your foils. Arm and test weapons *now*."

Laser bolts flew past Jaina's cockpit as weapons were

tested. At least her rookies hadn't blown her tail off, which under these conditions had to count as a success.

Her navigational computer lit as Ijix Harona fed her coordinates. "Jump on the colonel's mark," Jaina said, and switched to the "all ships" frequency to hear Harona's voice.

"On my mark," he repeated. "Five. Four. Three. Two. Mark."

The starlight streamed away around the cockpit, and Twin Suns Squadron was on its way.

It was a twenty-minute hyperspace jump, which gave Jaina far too much time to think about what was going to happen. Plans and contingencies swarmed through her mind. Most of them ended with the New Republic forces getting splattered.

She thought of plasma cannon projectiles shredding her rookies. Or Lowbacca. Or herself. She knew that if the war went on, it was only a matter of time before it happened. Sooner or later the death lottery would call her number, just as it had called so many others.

With an act of resolute will she banished the dead from her mind. She had to think of ways to survive, not brood on the long list of the lost. Her mental armor slatted into place around her. She would concentrate only on the outcome, on a successful resolution of the fight.

It was not until her nav computer gave her the two-minute warning that she thought to call on the Force. She had been neglecting her daily Force exercises and meditations, and not just because she was busy. Opening to the Force meant opening to the totality of life, and that included the emotions she was denying herself—grief, terror, panic, horror. It meant being vulnerable, and she couldn't afford vulnerability right now. She had to keep focused on the outcome, and anything that didn't lead directly to the survival of her squadron was irrelevant.

Nevertheless she called on the Force, calling only on its strength to refresh her, its vigor to keep her mind alert. She knew she could do that, for short periods at least, and not be distracted by all the other things to which the Force connected.

Distantly, in her Force awareness, she could sense Low-bacca and Tesar, and they sent her a burst of fierce warrior joy. She absorbed it, felt its keen anticipation of the coming combat, and tried to use it to give herself strength. She wished she had other Jedi here, Jedi who could form the linked Force-meld they had called into being at Obroa-skai, but she and Lowie and Tesar were the only three present, and three really weren't enough.

The X-wing nav computer gave its chiming warning, and suddenly the stars hurled themselves against the black backdrop of space and stuck there. Jaina scanned her displays and saw at once the two New Republic capital ships, big vessels surrounded by swarms of swift-flying gnats. Energies flashed on the displays: it was clear that the two big ships were still fighting. Far in the distance, standing off, were a pair of tender analogues, unarmed coral craft that had brought the coralskippers to the battle.

They were in deep space. No suns, no planets, no moons, no asteroids, no comets.

"Twin Squadron," she ordered, "alter course sixty degrees to left, in succession. Once you hit my mark, accelerate to ninety-five percent maximum thrust. This is Twin One, turning *now*."

The controls responded smoothly in her hands as she swung the ship on its new trajectory and punched the engine controls. Behind her each X-wing followed in turn, the line of ships, almost fifty kilometers long, turning toward the fight. Tesar and Lowbacca were a distant, reinforcing presence in the Force.

Ijix Harona and his A-wings stayed behind, but Harona's ships had enough acceleration, Jaina knew, to catch her any time he wanted.

"This is Twin Suns Squadron and Scimitar Squadron," Jaina told *Far Thunder* and *Whip Hand*. "Where do you want us?"

Whip Hand replied first. "We're holding our own," Jaina was told. "Your priority is to help *Far Thunder*."

"Copy that, *Whip Hand*." *Whip Hand* was a *Lancer*-class frigate, developed by the Empire to guard convoys against attacks by Rebel starfighters. It was a ship dedicated to battling swarms of small craft, and was ideal for holding off groups of coralskippers. If *Far Thunder* hadn't suffered so much damage and evacuated so many of its crew, the two of them together could have done more than hold their own, but as it was, *Whip Hand* was severely handicapped by having to guard its crippled consort.

Jaina studied the displays and realized to her relief that the enemy were not moving with the eerie synchrony that meant a yammosk guided their attacks. That was good, because she didn't have any of her yammosk-jamming devices with her—there had been no point in taking one on what was supposed to be a training flight.

The relationships of the two big ships, she saw, were interesting. They were flying abreast, with *Whip Hand* making big rolls around the cruiser to wherever the threat seemed greatest. At the moment, *Whip Hand* was rolling toward Jaina and her approaching squadron, almost eclipsing her view of the damaged cruiser.

"*Whip Hand*," Jaina transmitted, "can you roll another fifteen degrees and then hold your position relative to *Far Thunder*? I might be able to do you some good."

There was a moment's hesitation. "Very good, Twin

One." *Whip Hand* ponderously rolled into place, completely eclipsing *Far Thunder*.

"Heads up, people," Jaina told her squadron. "We're going to strip off some of the furball around *Whip Hand* before we get tangled up in *Far Thunder*'s trouble. Pair leaders, pick your own targets. Wingmates, stick to your leaders—remember, you're just there to keep their tails clear. Once you're clear of the skips around *Whip Hand*, look for *me* and hang on to my tail if you can, because things are going to get hairy fast. If you have any questions, talk now."

No questions. She'd made her instructions very clear for the rookies—just follow the guy in front. The veterans, on the other hand, probably understood what she was up to.

Whip Hand was getting very close. The enemy coralskippers had been fully committed to their attack runs and were only now beginning to react to Jaina's presence. Too late. Jaina picked one coralskipper that was only now finishing a run on *Whip Hand*'s aft engine assembly. The skip was arcing in preparation for turning and making another run, and its dovin basal shield was probably deployed aft in order to keep the frigate's defensive fire from climbing up its tail.

Perfect. Jaina was closing so fast, the target probably didn't even know she was within ten kilometers.

It was a deflection shot, but Jaina's reflexes synched perfectly with the controls of her X-wing, and she turned the nose just slightly into the enemy's turn and quadded the laser cannon. The coralskipper shattered into fragments as the X-wing whipped past. Then the big frigate, surrounded by streams of coherent light from its turbolasers, flashed beneath the belly of Jaina's fighter.

"Rolling to right, Twin Two." Jaina wanted to roll in order to clear her tail of any enemy who might be bouncing her, but she didn't want to lose her rookie wingmate as she shook the enemy free.

"I copy, Twin One."

On her displays Jaina could see her wingmate matching her maneuver. Twin Two was a female Duro named Vale, who had thus far shown herself a reasonably capable pilot for someone just out of flight school.

Jaina looked ahead and saw *Far Thunder* in bad shape. Parts of the big cruiser were shattered, other areas were blackened as if by flame. But at least two-thirds of her turbolasers were still pumping out fire at the forty or so coralskippers that hovered around her, and defensive missiles were still being launched. Space around the cruiser was filled with brilliant fire.

Again Jaina chose a target, the hindmost of a flight of four coralskippers that had just made a run on *Far Thunder*'s bridge. She lifted the X-wing's nose, matched trajectories, and blew the skip apart with the second shot. Then she pulled the stick hard, her fire climbing to the second coralskipper, and watched flame erupt from its stony hull as her laser bolts stitched its surface.

The remaining two skips dodged left and right, and Jaina was unable to follow. In seconds she had left *Far Thunder* far behind and began to pull on the stick in order to loop around and make a second pass. Suddenly laser bolts were slashing past her cockpit. Something crashed on her aftermost shields.

"Skip on your tail, Major!" Vale's shriek dinned in her ears, and Jaina's heart jolted against her ribs.

"Breaking left!" Jaina said, and yanked the controls. The laser bolts slid off to the right, and she caught a glimpse of a coralskipper as it flashed past, bright projectiles still flaming from its plasma cannons. She doubled back onto the coralskipper and launched a missile at it, but its dovin basal sucked the missile into oblivion and the coralskipper shot away, accelerating fast.

"Thanks, Twin Two," Jaina said. Her heart was still hammering, and she could only hope that Vale's frantic laser barrage had frightened the enemy pilot as much as it had terrified her.

She spent the next few frantic seconds sorting out her command, getting Twin Suns Squadron organized after its fighting pass and in a position to make another run at the enemy. Seven coralskippers had been killed, with no casualties among the X-wings, but the Yuuzhan Vong were ready for them now, two battle group–sized formations having separated themselves from the main body, ready to bounce the X-wings when they next approached.

"Lowie, you follow me," Jaina said. "Tesar, your job is to fly cover and keep those guys off our tails."

"I copy," Tesar said.

"The A-wings should help you," Jaina said. *We hope.*

She aimed her flight for the furball surrounding *Far Thunder* and punched the throttles. An attacker's chief advantage was speed: once she had to slow down in order to maneuver against the enemy, she'd be easy meat for those two battle groups hovering out of the action, waiting for just such an opportunity.

So, if she could help it, she wouldn't slow down. The A-wings weren't the only starfighters that could make a slashing attack.

The problem was those two battle groups hovering on either side of *Far Thunder*, just waiting for her to do exactly what she was doing.

"Rolling to left," she announced. That would put *Far Thunder* between her squadron and one of the enemy battle groups, which would mean that the enemy would have to run the cruiser's gauntlet of fire before it could reach her. Maybe it wouldn't try. She could only hope.

"Leaders, choose your targets," Jaina said. "Wingmates stick close." She already had a coralskipper picked out, one just beginning its pass on *Far Thunder*. She followed it into its run, lined it up, fired lasers . . . only to see the bright bolts of light curl and shift blue and vanish beneath the event horizon of the dovin basal. She fired again, to the same result.

And then one of *Far Thunder*'s turbolasers punched right through the craft like a knife thrust through a bar of soap, turning it to bright rainbow fragments that spattered on Jaina's shields. The skip's dovin basal hadn't been able to guard against Jaina and the cruiser both.

She breathed thanks to whatever droid brain had fired the lucky shot, then rolled away from *Far Thunder* and punched the throttle to escape the danger zone.

"Twin Leader, you're being bounced!" Tesar's voice. "Watch your six!"

"Rolling left," Jaina said again. That would put her in the overlapping fields of fire from both *Far Thunder* and *Whip Hand*, which she hoped might intimidate the Vong. Her cockpit brightened to streams of turbolaser fire, the blue and red and green light strobing on her control switches and dials.

Then plasma cannon projectiles flamed past her extended right foils, and she jerked her X-wing left again, then rolled back onto the tail of the skip as it raced past. She could see the dovin basal singularity deployed aft, but she lined up the target anyway. Why not? Shooting at it might keep it honest.

"Skip on my six!" Vale's frantic voice jolted Jaina's heart again. *"I'm breaking right!"* Behind Vale's words she could hear the slam of plasma cannon projectiles on the X-wing's shields.

Jaina abandoned her quarry and broke left, then right, an S curve that she hoped would let her line up on the coralskipper that was hunting Vale. It flashed across her sights and she fired, but the deflection shot missed. Cursing, Jaina hauled the X-wing after the enemy.

"I've lost shields!" The enemy's dovin basal had jumped forward and eaten Vale's shields. At least that meant the singularity wasn't deployed aft.

"Twin Two, break left!" Vale overreacted to Jaina's command, hauling the stick around so hard that her maneuvering thrusters killed her own speed and made her craft a perfect target, but the skip swam across Jaina's nose and she launched a missile. The enemy craft shattered like an egg, and for a moment Jaina mistook the buffeting on her shields for debris until a bright scarlet plasma cannon projectile slammed her canopy like a giant hammer ringing a bell. She rolled her ship to right but the cannon rounds followed, slamming her again and again.

"Vale, your six is clear!" she shouted. "But I've got a skip on my tail! I'm breaking to right!"

Her astromech droid R2-B3 gave a squeal of chittering anger as a dovin basal overloaded one of her rear shields. She spun the ship in a wild corkscrew spiral as plasma rounds blazed past her cockpit.

Jaina licked sweat from her upper lip. *"Vale, get me out of this!"* First *Far Thunder*, then *Whip Hand* whirled through her vision.

"I can't find you, Major!" her wingmate wailed. One of the enemy rounds darted through the broken shield and took off a chunk of Jaina's upper left foil. She led the enemy pilot on a mad dance through the void, but the skip hung on, its plasma cannons hammering.

"Breaking left!" Jaina called, and hoped *someone* was in a position to hear and act on the knowledge. Turbolaser fire from *Whip Hand* traced surreal patterns across her vision. She could feel sweat beneath her arms and across her forehead, and felt her shoulders tense as if awaiting the shot that would blow her away.

"Twin One, roll right!" Tesar's voice. Jaina heard the command through the Force before she heard Tesar's words, and she yanked the X-wing around. Laserfire streamed past her canopy, and then actinic light flared off her cockpit instruments as the pursuing coralskipper was blown to fragments.

"Thanks, Twin Nine." Jaina blinked sweat from her eyes. Tesar's third flight had done exactly what Jaina had intended them to do: hang out of the fight until one of the hovering enemy squadrons bounced Jaina, and then bounce the attackers.

It wasn't over, though, by a long shot. Jaina's squadron was still tangled up with a swarm of coralskippers, and they were all moving very fast. By now they had overshot the cruiser and frigate, and were engaged in a fighter-to-fighter duel outside the zone of the capital ships' protective fire. They were all on their own, and the numbers were fairly even.

A burning X-wing crossed Jaina's path, and she felt a steel fist clamp on her insides and twist. The two skips that had flamed the X-wing flashed past too quickly for her to get a shot at them.

"Twin Two, get on my tail!" The lost aft shield was preying on Jaina's mind, and she very much wanted Vale behind her helping to cover the gap.

"*I still can't find you, Twin Leader!*" Vale's bewildered cry nearly shattered Jaina's eardrums.

"Never mind," Jaina said. "Just stay alive. I'll find *you.*" Jaina pushed her Force-sense outward, tried to locate Vale in all the confusion.

"Twin Ten and I will stick with you, Jaina," Tesar said.

"Thanks again." And then she had to dodge a Yuuzhan Vong missile that was trying to find the hole in her shields. She yelled at her astromech droid to get the shield up again and took a snap shot—and missed—at a coralskipper that flashed past. She found Vale in her heads-up display and chased her down just in time to shoot a coralskipper off her wingmate's tail. "Right behind you, Twin Two," Jaina said as the burning coralskipper flamed off into the darkness.

"Oh thank you!" Vale's exclamation was heartfelt.

"Twin Nine," Jaina told Tesar. "Vale and I both have damaged shields aft. Can you stick with us?"

"Affirmative."

There followed several minutes of burning, tearing, confused combat that alternated with bewildered moments in which Jaina couldn't seem to find anyone to shoot at. She took shots at several coralskippers and launched a pair of missiles but had no idea whether she'd succeeded in hitting anything. And then she heard Lowie's roaring cry.

More coralskippers were arriving—at least ten of them!

This was the second enemy battle group that had been hovering out of the combat, waiting to jump Jaina when she made her attack. Thanks to her maneuvering, they'd been forced to fight their way past the capital ships in order to reach Jaina and had lost a pair of skips in doing so, but now they had arrived. Now the odds against Twin Suns Squadron turned fatal.

Jaina's next few moments were frantic with evasive action as she danced and weaved and fled across the face of the void. In the course of her frantic maneuvers she lost track of Vale, Tesar, and Twin Ten; she lost a sense of everything except her own terror. Through the Force she could only sense desperation and terror, and she closed down her extended Force-sense, not wanting the other pilots' emotions to distract her. She saw an X-wing explode in a shower of orange light, and she fired at skips that crossed her path without knowing whether she hit them or not. The intership comm filled with shouts, warning, and screams of frustration, fear, and anger. Jaina was nearly blind with the sweat that poured into her eyes. Finally she'd had enough. This was a fight that it was impossible to win.

"Twin Suns Squadron!" she shouted. "Prepare for hyperflight—return to origin! On my mark!"

"Return to origin" called for a hyperspace leap to the jump point previous to this one, meaning the place in empty space where Jaina had first heard *Far Thunder*'s distress call. There was no problem jumping from here—they were in deep space, where every point was a jump point.

"Negative, Twin Leader!" came a voice. "Negative! Do not jump!"

Only now Jaina remembered Ijix Harona and his flight of A-wings.

"*Where are you?*" she demanded. She pulled her X-wing hard to the right to evade the bright fire of a plasma cannon. Another cannon jolted her front shields as a coralskipper tried a deflection shot.

Colonel Harona's voice was maddeningly calm. "We're right here."

And suddenly the dark night of space lit with the fires of burning coralskippers.

Seven enemy craft were destroyed in two seconds as Harona's twelve A-wings punched through Jaina's fight. Jaina's squadron had become so entangled with the enemy that both she and the coralskippers had slowed in order to maneuver, leaving the Yuuzhan Vong easy, sluggish targets for the A-wings' blazing storm of fire.

Jaina gave a shriek of relief and joy. "Cancel that hyperspace jump!" she called. "We're back in business!"

There was more desperate fighting for Jaina while Harona and his A-wings turned for another pass, but this time the odds were more even. She splashed one enemy, and scared another off the tail of one of her rookie pilots. Then Harona and the A-wings came slashing through again. The Yuuzhan Vong this time were more prepared and the A-wings nailed only four, but that tilted the odds more decisively in Jaina's favor, and now it was the enemy desperately evading across space while the X-wings pursued.

Before the A-wings could make a third pass, the Yuuzhan Vong broke contact and ran, heading for the tender analogues that had carried them here. Not just those engaged with Jaina, but all the rest as well, all those harassing *Far Thunder*.

"Good work, Twin Suns," Harona congratulated. "A fine day."

A fine day for you, Jaina thought. Her jumpsuit was soaked with sweat, and the air in her cockpit fairly smoked with the tang of adrenaline.

"Form your squadron astern of *Far Thunder*," Harona ordered.

Jaina's squadron had lost three craft and two pilots, both rookies. Jaina had barely had time to learn the names of the two pilots before the war tore away their lives. Her own wingmate Vale had survived. The rookie pilot who had succeeded in ejecting from his damaged craft was picked up by one of *Far Thunder*'s shuttles that carried its evacuating crew to *Whip Hand*.

Once the crippled cruiser was evacuated, *Whip Hand* maneuvered to within point-blank range of *Far Thunder* and opened fire. The unresisting cruiser blew to bits in a furious explosion, leaving nothing behind for the Yuuzhan Vong. Jaina pictured the unlucky Captain Hannser on the bridge of *Whip Hand* as he watched the destruction of the ship for which he had fought so hard.

Jaina knew just how he felt.

The Yuuzhan Vong had lost a couple of dozen coralskippers in exchange for the destruction of a *Republic*-class cruiser. Even though they'd fled the battle, the Yuuzhan Vong had every reason to call it a victory.

The two starfighter squadrons formed on *Whip Hand*

and leapt together into hyperspace, heading for Kashyyyk. Once there, Jaina knew, Twin Suns Squadron would bind its wounds, acquire two new replacements, and set out on its ambitious training schedule—until, of course, they were again called upon to face the Yuuzhan Vong, and the roll of death's dice in the void.

SEVENTEEN

Nom Anor left the temple square in a thoughtful mood. The temple's head priest, standing before the altar, had just delivered the message that High Priest Jakan had written on the subject of heresy, a message that all priests were ordered to repeat to all Yuuzhan Vong over the course of the next few days: Reverence of the Jedi was explicitly condemned.

The congregation had been attentive—much more attentive than they would have a few days earlier, before the shapers had produced the antifungal balm that had relieved their itching.

Nom Anor, his skin no longer aflame, had listened to the message with approval, at least until the message ended and the crowd began to disperse. It was then that he realized that the priests' message had been, perhaps, a little *too* detailed.

What Jakan had done, the executor suddenly realized, was to explain to any potential heretics exactly how to behave. The little band of heretics that Nom Anor had infiltrated possessed a confused, inchoate doctrine, the elements of which they barely understood. But now it had all been explained to them. They had now been told that heretics believed that the Solo twins were emanations of the gods; that the power of the Jedi was a threat to the gods. Jakan had just defined heretical doctrine for the heretics themselves!

If Nom Anor should ever attend another meeting of the

heretical congregation, he suspected they would have a much better idea of what they were doing.

Nom Anor rose from his thoughtful trance and discovered that he was leaving the temple alongside a young shaper, one who had—judging from the freshness of the scars—only recently acquired the shaper's specialized hand. Nom Anor remembered the guarded damutek on the fringes of the new city, the one where he'd observed Onimi, and he approached the shaper.

"Pardon me, friend shaper," Nom Anor said. "I wonder if I may have a moment of your time."

"Honored thir?" the shaper said in surprise. He had knocked out several of his own teeth and replaced them with some kind of coral implants, presumably ones that aided him in his shaping duties. Nom Anor didn't really want to know what shaper protocol required modified *teeth*, and he regretted the young shaper's lisp extremely.

"My name is Hooley Krekk, from the Damutek of the Intendants," Nom Anor said. "We're from the Emergency Resources department, and we've recently received a requisition from the office of—well, I shouldn't give the name, save to say that he's a master shaper. Unfortunately the requisition is couched in rather technical language, and neither I nor my superior quite understand the purpose of the requisition. He *says* it is important work to do with the war, but we can't quite understand what the Shaper Lord intends to do, and my superior is unwilling to release the resources until it can be made clearer."

Nom Anor now had the shaper's full attention. *Yes,* Nom Anor thought at him, *this is all about making* your *caste richer.*

"How may I athitht you, thir?" the shaper asked.

"The requisition has to do with supplies necessary in order to 'fulfill the directives' of—" He feigned hesitation. "—of something called a 'cortex,' I believe."

"A cortecth is a body of shaper knowledge," the helpful shaper lisped. "Each cortecth wath delivered in the Before-Time by the godth themselvth to the Thupreme Overlord or to mathter shaperth."

"I see," the intendant said. "And how many cortexes are there, exactly?"

"Eight."

"The eighth would be the highest, then?"

"Yeth, Lord Intendant. The eighth cortecth is the thupreme body of knowledge of the shaper'th art. Motht of it wath delivered by the godth to the Dread One Shimrra himthelf, and he hath not yet theen fit to deliver the knowledge even to mathter shaperth."

Nom Anor felt a chill run up his spine. *We're doomed,* he thought. Who would have thought that extinction would be heralded by such an absurd, lisping voice?

He barely managed to stammer out his thanks to the shaper, and quickly tore himself away in order to contemplate in private what he had just learned. He knew how governments worked—how else could he subvert them?—and that knowledge enabled him to draw conclusions from a sprinkling of facts.

The eighth cortex, the supreme knowledge possessed only by Shimrra and the gods, *did not exist*. The cortex project, headquartered just beyond the city and guarded by a corps of warriors, was intended to *create* the knowledge, which Shimrra would then deliver to his people.

The Yuuzhan Vong were in a war of indefinite length, and they had run out of the knowledge that would enable them to win it. If the New Republic continued to learn and innovate while the eighth cortex of the Yuuzhan Vong remained empty, then the Yuuzhan Vong were finished. Doomed. About to be wiped from history.

His mind whirled. Nom Anor put a hand against a wall in order to steady himself. *And if the gods,* he thought in terror, *have not delivered the knowledge to Shimrra, then Shimrra is a fraud, and so are the gods.*

Nom Anor wanted to laugh and shriek and wail all at the same time. The greatest pillars of faith, obedience, and hierarchy, the pillars that held up the great edifice that was the Yuuzhan Vong, were nothing but a swindle. Nom Anor had always suspected this—but he had never expected to have it proved!

Others were staring at him, he realized. He managed to pull himself upright and put one foot in front of the other as he marched to his office.

The Yuuzhan Vong needed to win the war fast, he thought. Before the lack of an eighth cortex could make a difference. Nom Anor would demand more information from his agents and would sift their reports with the greatest care and diligence. He would find the enemy weaknesses and devise ways to take advantage of them. He would help the Yuuzhan Vong hammer the enemy until the enemy surrendered, or was no more.

And he would also try to work out a way to use the knowledge for his own advantage. Because he was, after all, Nom Anor.

A holo blared in the small room, and tiny three-dimensional figures swung their fists: heroes fighting evil in the days of the Sith.

"You've returned," Vergere said.

"I have," Luke said. "And I brought you something."

He offered a package of sweets, candies made from a Mon Calamari seaweed drizzled with a sauce of jewel-fruit.

"*Welcome, young Master!*" Vergere cried, and took the package.

"I'm afraid you won't find a file or a concealed vibroblade," Luke said.

Vergere, chewing candy with an expression of bliss, did

not immediately reply. When she managed to speak, she said, "My debriefers seem to have run out of questions. This means that they're busy cataloging all my answers so they can ask the questions all again, and try to catch me in contradiction." There was a trace of amusement in her tone. "If I contradict myself, they prove I'm a spy because I can't keep my story straight; whereas if I *don't* contradict myself, they prove I'm a spy because I'm too well briefed."

Luke laughed to himself, imagining Ayddar Nylykerka cursing as he heard this. He had just shown Luke the transcripts of Vergere's interviews, all annotated for the reinterrogation; he'd now learned that Vergere had anticipated his every move.

Vergere waved off the holo as Luke settled onto his chair. "There's this comfort at least," she said, "the holos are as witless as I remember."

"That must be a consolation."

She peered at him. "You've come to ask a question."

"You owe me an answer from last time."

Vergere settled comfortably onto her stool and popped another candy into her mouth. "Begin, then," she mumbled.

"How did you prevent the Yuuzhan Vong from finding out about your abilities? We know that yammosks can detect Force-users."

"It is easier to demonstrate than to explain." She faced him directly. "Please attack me through the Force."

He looked at her in surprise. "Attack you how?"

"Mentally." Her whiskers rippled. "If it helps, you may use a component of that anger you first brought to this room. I'll trust that you're a gentleman and won't make it lethal."

Give in to your anger. The Emperor's seductive voice echoed in his mind. Was Vergere trying to provoke him to anger, bring him to the dark side?

If so, that attempt was doomed. He had withstood Vader

and Palpatine when he was barely more than a boy; now that he was a Jedi Master in the prime of life he would hardly fall victim to such a trick.

Luke turned his chair to face her and crossed his legs. The Force welled into his mind like water rising in an artesian spring. Force awareness expanded in all directions: he was aware of Ayddar Nylykerka outside the room, the two techs who monitored the equipment, a prisoner in another cell, others who worked in an office just above them. He could sense the glow of their lives in the Force, hear the throb of their hearts, and time their whispering breaths. He knew that one of the techs was concentrating on a technical problem, and that his friend was daydreaming of her fiancé, who had four arms and bright blue fur and who sent her flowers and reams of bad poetry . . .

But what Luke could not detect was Vergere. She seemed to have vanished completely from his Force-awareness, even though he could plainly see her sitting on her stool across from him.

He refined his awareness and finally detected her, a kind of fitful uncertain presence, her life force a faint cool phosphorescence compared to the bright candle flames of the others.

Luke tried to refine his sense of Vergere to a greater degree, but she was remarkably evasive: she kept sliding away from his perceptions, like a slippery melon seed squeezed between the fingers. The difficulty of keeping Vergere in focus produced in Luke a sense of frustration, which he used deliberately to fuel an attack at the elusive target, a fast snakelike strike configured as a command simply to remain still. The mental bolt fired but failed to find its target.

He built a strike more deliberately, drawing more of the Force to power the attack, not a jab this time but a battering ram. REVEAL YOURSELF, he commanded, and launched the strike. Again Vergere eluded him.

His frustration rose, and he used it to power another fast strike, like a reflex backhand blow. Nothing.

Luke began to vary his attacks between massive, deliberate cannonades and swift, intuitive reflex strikes, hoping that one or the other would catch Vergere by surprise. Nothing worked.

Vergere continued to sit on her stool, her reverse-articulated knees poking up above her head like knobby horns, her eyes gazing mildly into Luke's. *I can see where she is,* Luke realized. He didn't have to search for her in the Force.

So he built a Force wall around her, an iron box to keep her mind from slipping away, and he made up the walls of the box with the command REVEAL YOURSELF. After this he shrank the box, forced it smaller around Vergere's small body, molding it until it fit her form exactly, a prison to contain her spirit. And then he called more of the Force to him, building a vast mental cannonball that would obliterate anything in its path, again with the command REVEAL YOURSELF, and he aimed the cannonball at the tiny figure that he'd trapped inside the iron box.

REVEAL YOURSELF, he commanded again, and he launched the cannonball.

He knew it entered the box. He knew Vergere's spirit was trapped there, boxed in, unable to move. But somehow the tiny target eluded him and the cannonball slid away on a curving trajectory, through the wall, into the next cell, and Luke was suddenly and startlingly aware of the prisoner there, who jumped from his cot and screamed, *"Yes! I confess! I stole the captain's shoes while he was drunk!"*

Revealing himself.

Luke laughed and let the Force-awareness ebb to its normal level. "I'm going to get tired if I keep this up," he said.

"That last one almost worked," Vergere said from around a piece of candy.

"I hope you can teach this technique," Luke said.

"There is more than one technique involved. I managed to evade that last strike with a kind of mental parry, as in fencing. You know how a thrust can be parried not by opposing it, but by redirecting it slightly so that it misses its goal?"

"Of course."

"I did something similar. I added just enough mental energy to your strike to cause it to divert. The timing was very difficult to judge, and there was no small measure of luck involved in my success."

"And your other techniques?"

"Do you know the definition of a master of defense?"

"Tell me."

"A master of defense is *one who is never in the place that is attacked*. One can move the attack, as I just did with my parry, but one can also simply *not be there*."

"Not so simply," Luke murmured.

"I call it *making myself small*. I narrow my focus bit by bit until it becomes, well, microscopic. Tiny. My mind and Force-awareness I shrank to an infinitesimal size. An enemy has the same chance of finding me as his chance of finding one molecule amid billions of others."

"Your tears," Luke said. "That's how you make your tears."

"Very good, young Master," Vergere said. "Yes. In that state I can rearrange molecules, take them apart, and build new ones bit by bit. I use my tears because they are convenient, but I can accomplish the same thing with other material."

"I know a Jedi healer, Cilghal, who would delight in this technique."

"I'll try to teach her, if you and she are willing. If I'm ever permitted to leave this place."

"You can teach without leaving this room," Luke reminded her.

A sly smile drifted across Vergere's face. "I can—but will I?"

Vergere gave one of her wheezing laughs, and popped a candy into her wide mouth.

"If the military releases you from here," Luke said, "will you aid us in the fight against the Yuuzhan Vong?"

Vergere rolled the sticky candy into her cheek as she spoke. "Insofar as it coincides with my goals, I will. Though I am much more a teacher than a warrior, and I believe my greatest objective is to help Jacen to his destiny." Her eyes narrowed. "I understand that he is your apprentice, not mine, and that you may have other intentions for him."

"I'm glad that you appreciate that." Luke had no clear idea whether he wanted to let Vergere near Jacen ever again.

"I think I have much to teach him."

"I don't want him to become dependent on you," Luke hedged.

"Nor do I."

There was a moment of silence. Then Vergere said, "Correct me if I'm wrong in my understanding. But Jacen gives me to understand that you've put restrictions on the Jedi during the course of this war, forbidding aggressive actions."

"I've tried to do so," Luke said, and then laughed. "My success has been modest."

"But my understanding is that you, yourself, undertook offensive warfare against the forces of the late Emperor. For instance, you were part of a party that attacked the first Death Star. You led the destruction of the criminal organization of the Hutt called Jabba. You accepted military rank and participated in numerous offensive actions against the forces of the Empire and other enemies. You didn't confine yourself to spying missions and aiding refugees."

"All true."

"So my question is, *what has changed*?"

Luke paused and considered how best to marshal his arguments. "The Yuuzhan Vong are a different enemy, for one thing," he began. "Our special talents are ineffective against them. And—as I expressed yesterday—I didn't know what we owed a species so far outside life as we knew it."

Vergere nodded her understanding. "You have heard my opinion that the Yuuzhan Vong are not outside the Force. I wonder if this has changed anything."

Luke hesitated. "I don't think so. The Jedi Code is clear in its statements against aggression. I know much more about the dark side than I did when I was twenty. I know how easily the dark can enter, how the dark can infiltrate the heart even when it's most certain of its own actions, and I know that many of my students aren't ready to face it."

"You cut off your father's hand."

"Yes."

"You want to prevent your students from making the same mistakes that you have made."

"Of course."

A disdainful look crossed Vergere's face. "That is egotism speaking."

Resentment prickled along Luke's nerves. "You don't know my students. You don't know how impulsive and reckless they are. Don't judge them all by Jacen." He hesitated. "Kyp Durron killed *millions*."

"And this was your responsibility."

Again Luke hesitated. "The situation was complex. I was paralyzed, and Kyp was under the control of—"

"You mean to say that it was *not* your responsibility," Vergere interrupted, her tone harsh.

"I could have been more aware of the situation," Luke insisted. "There's so much I could have done—"

"So it *is* your responsibility." Interrupting again.

"The next time it will be!" Luke insisted. "The *next* time one of my students is swept away on a dark whirlwind and catastrophe results, it *will* be my fault!"

Vergere's feathery crest rose. She smoothed it with her fingers. "Of course it would not be your fault," she said. "You are a Jedi Master, not a nursemaid!"

"I trained them," Luke said. "If their training fails—"

"When you cut off your father's hand, was it the fault of your teachers?" Vergere demanded. "Did Yoda fail to instruct you what dark passion could do?"

"No, I—" Frustration throbbed in Luke's heart. "That's different. I—"

"I," Vergere mocked. "I, I, I. Upon you lies the spiritual health of yourself and all those whom you taught. Is that not ego speaking?"

Luke looked at her as realization struck. "You're trying to make me angry," he said.

"Yes," she said simply. "Did I succeed?"

"You did." Luke found his anger easing as he realized that Vergere had been manipulating him—though it didn't fade entirely, it still hummed, subdued, in his nerves.

"I preyed upon your weakness," Vergere said. "I preyed upon your lack of self-knowledge, your uncertainty about where your responsibility lies for the behavior of those who have been your students." Her piebald feathers rippled. "Was your anger dark?"

"It was getting there," Luke said.

"So where was the darkness? In me, in you, or in the Force?"

"I think you've been asking too many questions."

Vergere sat back on her haunches. "I wondered when you were going to notice. If you have a question, ask it."

"You've been saying that dark passions are caused by lack of self-knowledge. But Emperor Palpatine was dark, and I can hardly imagine that he lacked self-knowledge. He seemed perfectly comfortable within his evil. How do you reconcile this with your theory?"

Vergere paused, assembling her argument. "Darkness *enters* through the dark passions," she said finally. "But sometimes it remains through *invitation*. Palpatine, knowing himself thoroughly, may simply have decided to become dark, or to let the dark part of his own nature dominate."

"You're saying he may have *chosen* evil. Coldly, not out of a hot passion."

"Sometimes people make such choices." Vergere's tone was amused. "Usually these people are trivial or silly. Swearing a midnight oath, solemnly intoning, *'I choose evil!'*— what a ridiculous picture! But sometimes there may be a genius who chooses to free the dark side within him. Perhaps Palpatine was one such—I cannot say, I knew him only distantly, as a politician. But I can say this—the dark may enter through meditation as well as through anger."

Luke considered this. Certainly Palpatine and Vader's methods hadn't been to urge him to evil through meditation, but then—if he had joined them as their disciple— perhaps that would have come.

"Have I answered completely?" Vergere said. Luke nodded. "If so," Vergere went on, "I would ask another question. Do you think the Force *cares* what shade your thoughts may be?"

"The Force is all life. It embraces all options. But *I* care."

Vergere nodded. "A good answer, young Master. Because the shades, the dark and the light and all the colors of the rainbow—" She leaned forward and tapped Luke on the breast with one hand. "—they are *here*. Light and dark are not some great abstracts in the sky, but a part of you, and the Force reflects what it finds in *you*."

Later, when Luke spoke with Ayddar Nylykerka, he said, "You might as well let Vergere go. You're not going to get anything out of her that she doesn't want to give you."

Nylykerka was surprised. "You're no longer worried she might be a danger?"

"It still concerns me," Luke said, "but if Vergere is an enemy, we won't find out by keeping her here. We'll find out by watching what she does once she's been released."

The Tammarian looked thoughtful. "I'll give your recommendations serious thought, Master Skywalker."

"If you decide to release her," Luke said, "I'd be obliged if you'd let me know first. And you could let her know my address and comm code, in case she wants to speak with me."

"I'll do that."

Luke bowed. "Thank you, Commander Nylykerka."

"At your service, sir."

Luke made his way to the planet's surface, Vergere's words spinning through his mind.

What has changed?

Perhaps everything.

"We know that there must be many refugees from Vortex on Mon Calamari," Lando Calrissian said. "And we're sure that they're in touch with your office."

"A great many of them, yes," said Fyg Boras, the Senator from Vortex. He and Lando were seated comfortably, with drinks, in the hotel suite Lando had rented.

"We sympathize," Lando said. "And as you know, we've brought sixteen ships' worth of relief supplies to Mon Calamari to help settle the refugees here."

Ice tinkled in Boras's drink. The discreet scent of his minty cologne wafted through the air. "I'm grateful on my constituents' behalf."

"We have a problem, though, and perhaps you can help."

"How may I assist you?"

"We have the supplies, but no way to distribute them. What we thought we'd do is present you with twenty-five metric tons of supplies. You can distribute them to your constituents as you think best."

Boras's eyes grew wide. "That's certainly . . . very generous," he managed. "Twenty-five tons?" He was almost visibly calculating how much twenty-five tons of relief supplies was worth in the current market, with the planet's few surface areas swarming with refugees from dozens of worlds, all desperate for the most basic necessities. Boras no longer had a homeworld to return to, and without a homeworld to vote him in he was obviously never going to be returned to the Senate: he had to think about his future.

"Twenty-five tons," Lando repeated. "Though there *is* a catch."

Boras's wide eyes narrowed to slits. "And what might the catch be?"

"We hope to be able to sell our YVH droids to the military," Lando said. "If you can use your best efforts to vote an amendment onto the upcoming military appropriations bill, you'll find us extremely appreciative."

Boras sipped his drink carefully. "You'd best tell me about these droids."

"I have a full array of literature," Lando said, "and of course a demonstration holo . . ."

After Boras left with an armful of datapads to distribute to his peers, Talon Karrde stepped from the next room. "It's all recorded," he said.

"Boras's bribe weighs twenty-five *tons*." Lando smiled. "It's going to be hard for him to claim it doesn't exist."

Unlike the distinguished Senator from Bilbringi, who, on being offered the relief supplies, simply demanded their equivalent in cash. *That* holo was particularly entertaining.

"Who's our next guest?" Lando asked.

Karrde glanced at his datapad. "Chau Feswin, from the Elrood sector."

"The Elrood sector isn't threatened by the Yuuzhan Vong. Do you think he'd have any use for relief supplies?"

"Make the offer," Karrde shrugged. "We can always turn it into cash later." He looked up. "We've also got some calls from other Senators who must have heard about us from, ah, our other clients. They're *very* interested in the military acquiring our droids. Practically begging us to bribe them."

Lando looked at him with a growing smile. "I think we should oblige."

Karrde shrugged. "I can't think of any reason not to." He looked thoughtful. "But I wonder—if these people are on *our* payroll, who *else's* payroll are they on?"

"That answer would be interesting, wouldn't it?" Lando said. "By the way, have you heard how Mara's doing?"

"Not yet. But I hope to hear from her soon."

Mara was in fact doing well. She had taken YVH-M-1 out for its maiden Yuuzhan Vong hunt, wandering government buildings and large public concourses. She lunched at a kiosk set up in a shopping concourse and then sat down to digest and to watch the passersby. She told the droid to search on its own.

She was distracted by the sight of a pair of children, children Ben's age, taking their first hesitant steps in the open-air crèche the concourse provided as a convenience to its customers. Sadness rose in Mara and took her by the throat. For a moment she missed Ben so much that it was almost a physical pain.

And then the mouse droid signaled her portable comm. Mara looked up from the crèche, startled. The mouse droid signaled again.

The droid had located a Yuuzhan Vong infiltrator—or at least someone the mouse droid *claimed* was a Yuuzhan Vong. Mara asked the droid for a homing signal, and followed it until she saw the person in question: a tall, rather broad female human, inconspicuously dressed, who wandered seemingly at random along the shopping galleries. Mara called the Force into her mind, letting the lives of all the thousands of living beings in the concourse flood into her awareness.

All the beings save one. Her target was a cold void in the Force, an emptiness that Mara had learned to associate with the Yuuzhan Vong.

"Good work, mousie," Mara said.

Mara was plainly dressed, in worn robes such as a refugee might wear, with a hood that she could wear over her overly conspicuous red hair. She alternated the hood with a floppy-brimmed hat in order to change her silhouette, and she carried a datapad through which she could issue commands to the mouse droid, and also view what the droid was seeing.

She followed the target at a distance and let the droid do most of the spying for her. The target wandered through the shopping concourse for twenty minutes or so, and then sat on a bench as if to take a rest. At this point Mara managed to get the droid close and behind the bench, just in time to observe the target reach beneath the seat and peel off something that had been stuck there.

Aha! Mara thought delightedly. This was better than getting an idiot's array at sabacc.

The target lumbered to her feet and strolled down the concourse. Mara drifted after. The target paused a moment by a vending machine, then continued on. When Mara purchased a snack from the machine and looked behind it, she saw something stuck there with an adhesive. It was just the size of a bundle of credits.

Mara decided to let the mouse droid follow the Yuuzhan Vong and to wait near the vending machine for whoever was scheduled to pick up his payment. She perched on a store windowsill and ate her snack, which was some kind of fried, salted seaweed that tasted of iodine and was obviously intended for a Mon Calamari palate. Within an hour the money was picked up by a Sullustan male, who used part of the cash immediately on a flashy new jacket purchased in one of the most exclusive boutiques in the arcade. The Sullustan then returned to work, which turned out to be in the building the Senate had requisitioned for its offices. Mara discovered that the Sullustan worked in the office of Senator Krall Praget, a member of the Security and Intelligence Council.

Most interesting, Mara thought.

She then caught up with the mouse droid, which had followed the suspected Yuuzhan Vong infiltrator to an apartment building. Mara made a note of the address, and then called Ayddar Nylykerka on her comm, and told him to buy as many of the mouse droids as Lando and Talon Karrde had available.

YVH-M-1 had proved its worth on its very first day.

Cola Quis dropped out of the race for Chief of State following a ringing endorsement for Cal Omas, who had quietly promised him chairmanship of the Commerce Council, midlevel ministry jobs to several of his friends, and a branch office of the Kellmer Institute for Ryloth. On the next vote, Cal added enough votes to raise his percentage to 35. Not all of Quis's supporters followed his lead, however, and Fyor Rodan picked up another couple of percentage points and stayed in the lead, with 37. Pwoe held steady with three votes total. Tal'aam Ranth added enough to his total to raise his percentage to 22, which meant that the soft-spoken, exquisitely polite Gotal chairman of the Justice Council now controlled enough votes in the Senate to deliver the election either to Cal Omas or to Fyor Rodan.

Ranth was now being courted in earnest.

Tons of refugee supplies were shipped to the planet's surface from the smuggler fleet overhead. The new military appropriations bill, with riders attached involving the purchase of thousands of YVH droids, passed out of the Defense Council and onto the Senate floor. The Senate, urged by all three candidates to act quickly, passed the bill with only a few token attempts at adding amendments to earmark funds for a particularly worthy planet or cause or brother-in-law.

Mara found a second Yuuzhan Vong infiltrator. She and a squad of mouse droids and Nylykerka's agents began mapping the two infiltrators' contacts and associates. Primary residences and safe houses were located, and eavesdropping devices quietly inserted.

Considering the alarming implications of everything she was discovering, Mara was having a strangely pleasant time.

"Every morning, I want every person in my command to ask himself the same question. And that question is: *how can I hurt the Yuuzhan Vong today?*"

Admiral Traest Kre'fey was visiting every ship in his command, first to conduct an inspection and then to address ship personnel. He was speaking from the enlisted mess of *Starsider*, a room large enough to contain all the fleet personnel who were stationed or passing through or barracked on the old Dreadnaught. Jaina, flanked by Kyp and Lowbacca, sat at a table on one edge of the room, watching the white-furred Bothan bound up and down on his speaker's platform.

Kre'fey was in good spirits today, and his body language showed it. He bounced on the balls of his feet as he repeatedly punched the air to emphasize his points, and his fur continually peaked and smoothed with surges of emotion.

"And if you *can't* find a way to hurt the Vong," the admiral continued, "I want you to ask yourself *this* question: *how can I help my own side grow stronger?*"

"At least it's leadership," Kyp said, his murmur pitched to carry only to the ears of his fellow Jedi. "It's not like we've seen a lot of leadership in this war."

"Maybe it's a little more leadership than we need," Jaina murmured in answer.

Lowie knew better than to say anything himself—his translator droid lacked discretion, and would probably shout the translation out at full volume—but he allowed himself a small moan of agreement.

"We're going to win the war of production!" Kre'fey proclaimed. "Our factories are building more starfighters, more capital ships, and more weapons than ever before! Our schools are turning out more pilots and other personnel! Within months we'll have replaced all the terrible losses we've suffered so far in this war!"

Jaina thought of Anakin and Chewbacca, and Anni Capstan and others, the millions who'd lived on Sernpidal and Ithor. Unique, individual beings, alive and responsive to the other lives around them. *Replaced?* No one could replace any of them.

"That trip to Bothawui has changed the admiral," Kyp said. "He used to be a lot less bouncy."

"The Bothans declared ar'krai and removed any necessity for moral responsibility," Jaina said. "I imagine that could cheer a person up."

"We're going to *smash* the Vong!" Kre'fey proclaimed. "We're going to *smash them every day!* We're going to smash them *until there are no more Yuuzhan Vong!*"

The room erupted in applause. Jaina and the other Jedi remained silent.

After Kre'fey's speech had worked its way to a rousing conclusion, Jaina was stopped at the exit by one of the admiral's aides.

"Major Solo?" he said. "The admiral would like to see you."

Kre'fey met Jaina in an office loaned him for the purpose by *Starsider*'s captain. Kre'fey was still clearly exhilarated from his speech, still bouncing energetically on the balls of his feet. His vicinity smelled very strongly of excited Bothan.

"I saw you in the audience and I thought I'd have Snayd pull you in for a chat."

"Very good, sir." Which seemed a proper sort of thing for a bewildered officer to say. Chats with admirals were a rarity in her experience.

Kre'fey's whiskered face beamed. "Did you like the speech?"

Jaina answered truthfully. "I thought it was the strongest speech I've heard in this war, sir." At least it said *most* of the right things.

Kre'fey was impressed. "Coming from Leia Organa's daughter, I'll take that as a very special compliment indeed."

"My mother hasn't had many chances to make speeches lately, sir," Jaina said.

"Regrettably true." Kre'fey paused, his furred hand brushing the polished tabletop. "I thought," he began, "that I would send you to see your brother."

"Sir?" Jaina was almost speechless with delight. *She could see Jacen! Touch him! Feel his mind floating toward her in the twin bond . . .*

"Colonel Darklighter tells me that you've been in continuous action against the enemy for many months. You deserve a rest, but the war hasn't been able to spare you. But things have grown quiet with both sides reorganizing after Coruscant, and we can spare you *now*. So I'm going to send you on a furlough to Mon Calamari, for two weeks . . ." He drawled out the last words, then raised a finger and pointed at Jaina. "But you're going on a special mission for me, understand?"

Jaina tried her best not to stare at him. "No, sir," she said. "I *don't* understand."

"You said that you needed more Jedi for your experiment in Force-meld to work. I want you to talk to your mother, to your uncle Luke, and I want you to *get me those Jedi*. I want to put those Jedi in my ships and have them link through the Force in combat." He grinned. "What do you think?"

"I'll do my best, sir. But—" Protests rose reluctantly into her mind. "My squadron's been completely reorganized in the last month, sir. I have two brand-new pilots fresh out of flight school. Another four who have only been with us a few weeks. We haven't flown together long enough to—I need time, sir—I'm afraid my squadron can't spare me."

"Your number two can take over for a few weeks," Kre'fey said. "He's another Jedi, isn't he? The Wookiee?"

"Yes, but he's busy with his team investigating *Trickster*."

"His team can do without him for a few hours every day. I want you on Mon Calamari finding Jedi for me." He smiled kindly. "And getting some rest, of course. You've been working too hard, like all of us."

He rose, and Jaina realized the audience was over. She stood and saluted.

"I'll have Snayd draw up your orders," Kre'fey said. "You're to leave tomorrow."

"Very good, sir." Soon she could *see Jacen!*

The next day, as she set out in her X-wing for Mon Calamari, Twin Suns Squadron soared past her, brilliant in the light of Kashyyyk's sun, and tipped their wings in salute before cutting in their engines and flashing away, out of sight.

She felt like a traitor for leaving them behind. The rookies needed much more training before they'd have a chance of surviving against the Yuuzhan Vong, and she wouldn't be there to supervise it. What if one of them died because of something she hadn't been present to teach them? What if the whole squadron was led to disaster because of something she could have prevented?

Jaina had every faith that Lowie would do a good job as squadron commander. But it wasn't Lowie's squadron, it was *hers*. Whatever happened to it, it was she who was responsible.

Jaina sighed, settled into her molded seat, and began plotting the first of the long series of jumps that were calculated to avoid the dangerous parts of the wide Yuuzhan Vong–occupied swath of worlds between Kashyyyk and Mon Calamari.

She thought about seeing Jacen again, and all her doubts faded.

"Welcome, Senator." Lando, smiling broadly, shook Fyg Boras's hand and escorted him to an armchair. "I'd like to express my admiration on the rapidity with which your committee dealt with the YVH amendment."

"A surprising number of my colleagues were in favor of the amendment," Boras said. "An unsubtle number, perhaps."

"These days," Lando said, "a person with tons of relief supplies can't help but make a lot of friends."

"You're giving away enough. The price of basic commodities has dropped enormously in the last few days."

"But surely that's a *good* thing, Senator!" Lando said.

"No doubt," Boras gloomed. Lando and Karrde had so flooded the market with relief supplies that the Senator's illicit profits were barely keeping ahead of the costs of warehousing everything he was secretly offering for sale.

Cheaters never prosper, Lando thought virtuously.

"I thought we might discuss the future of our relationship," Lando said, and seated himself adjacent to the Senator.

"I hope you're not going to offer me more relief supplies."

Lando steepled his fingertips and tried to ignore Boras's nose-tickling minty cologne. "What I hoped," he said, "was to discuss the next Chief of State."

"I'm committed to Fyor Rodan, as you know."

"I was hoping to change your mind."

"That's not possible," Boras said shortly. "I've made a definite commitment."

"I regret that extremely. Because it's then possible that people may see this holovid."

He touched the control of the room's holoprojector, and Boras watched with increasing petulance at the sight of himself in his first meeting with Lando.

"You can't release that!" he snapped finally. "If I'm guilty of taking a bribe—which I'm not—then you're guilty of offering one! To release that holo would be to put your own head into the noose!"

"I would *never* claim that I bribed you," Lando said with indignation. "I've never bribed anyone in my life!"

"Then what's all this about?" Boras snarled.

"I gave you the supplies to be given free to refugees," Lando said. "That's very clear in the holo. If it could be demonstrated that you were *selling* the supplies, instead of giving them away, then that would be—why it would be *illegal*, wouldn't it?"

Boras stared at Lando with burning hatred in his eyes.

"Now," Lando said with a perfect white smile, "about the next Chief of State."

The next three days saw an extraordinary number of defections from the camp of Fyor Rodan. Not just those who had allowed themselves to be bribed, but others whose activities had been revealed by a little of Talon Karrde's research. Those who stole fleet elements in order to make their escape from Coruscant, or who called for the fleet to escort them to safety while other naval units, deprived of support, stayed and died. There were those who had sprung criminals from custody on condition that the criminals help them escape the Yuuzhan Vong. Others had taken massive bribes in order to take world-class criminals offplanet. There was one Senator who had left his whole family behind in order to provide transport to a well-fed Coruscant plutocrat and his harem of mistresses.

Some of these—the supporters Fyor Rodan most counted on—were persuaded to announce publicly that they had changed their minds and intended to vote for Cal Omas.

The following morning Mara—now operating with a pair of YVH-M mouse droids—picked up a Yuuzhan Vong infiltrator at her place of residence and followed her through refugee-packed streets toward the edge of Heurkea Floating City, where gracefully curved seawalls kept the green ocean rollers from sweeping right up the streets. The Yuuzhan Vong wasn't interested in the view, but walked along the base of the seawall to a bubble-topped structure that projected out over the water.

When the target entered, Mara remained outside and sent one of the mouse droids through the broad, open doorway. The structure proved to be a private marina, with boats and submersibles of various sizes moored in long rows of slips. The Yuuzhan Vong spoke to a Quarren who sat behind a desk near the entrance, and the Quarren handed her what might have been a set of keys. The infiltrator then walked out onto one of the jetties.

Mara left her second droid near the entrance and entered the marina herself. The salt-and-iodine scent of the sea was strong in the confined space. The Yuuzhan Vong, she saw, was inspecting a submersible. Drawing the hood of her robe forward to partly mask her face from the Vong, Mara approached the Quarren.

"Do you rent submersibles here?" she asked.

"No," the Quarren said. "We rent berths to private vehicles only." One of its facial tentacles pointed politely toward the door. "If you want to rent submersibles, you can turn right at the entrance, then walk along the seawall to—"

Mara's comm unit chittered at her. "Excuse me," she said, and stepped away from the desk just as a large human male walked into the building. The new arrival blinked as his eyes adjusted to the relative darkness inside the covered marina, and during that time Mara read the information that her mouse droid was trying to tell her.

The new arrival was another Yuuzhan Vong.

Mara's heart leapt. She turned her head away from the new arrival and tried to shrug into her hood—it wasn't as if Mara Jade Skywalker wasn't someone an enemy infiltrator might recognize at close range. But the infiltrator wasn't interested in her, or in the Quarren. Without looking left or right, the Yuuzhan Vong marched into the building, walked down the long jetty, and joined the first Vong.

Frantically Mara considered her options. For years she had been the Emperor's Hand. She had lived as a spy, infiltrator, and assassin, and she understood spy work well. Two Yuuzhan Vong infiltrators meeting face to face violated *every single principle* of tradecraft—if the two needed to speak, they could do so by villip with complete privacy; if villips weren't available, they could use dead-letter drops or, with precautions, simple comm units.

There were three possible reasons why the two Yuuzhan Vong were meeting face to face.

They could be stupid.

They could be overconfident.

Or, third, something was happening that was of such overwhelming importance that the Yuuzhan Vong were forced to throw all caution to the winds and conduct the operation together.

Mara knew which way she wanted to bet.

The Yuuzhan Vong had opened the cockpit of their submersible and were descending into it. Mara returned to the Quarren at the desk.

"Are you *sure* you don't have any submersibles for rent?" she asked, and made a gesture with one hand.

"Yes," the Quarren said. "We have submersibles for rent."

"I want a fast one, and I need it immediately."

The Quarren reached beneath the desk and produced a set of keys. "Berth Five-B, ma'am," it said.

"Thanks," Mara said, snatching the keys.

The face-tentacles waved good-bye. "Have a nice voyage."

The Yuuzhan ·Vong were swinging their cockpit closed. Mara tried to avoid a dead run as she headed for Berth 5B.

Her submersible was a slim sport model whose sleek lines showed the customary Mon Calamari attention to elegant design. The transparent cockpit seated two passengers, one behind the other, and the deep green paint job featured a scalloped pattern that suggested fish scales.

Mara cast off the two mooring lines, then put a foot on the submersible and felt it bob under her. She keyed the lock, and the bubble canopy rolled aside with a hydraulic hiss. Mara vaulted easily into the pilot's seat and found the main power switch. She pressed it and the instrument panel came to life.

The instrument panel was simple compared to that found in a starfighter. Mara pulled away a drape of her cloak that had caught on the cockpit coaming, then closed the canopy. Canopy locks clamped down to make the sub watertight. Ventilators whirred as they automatically switched on. Mara engaged the engine, and water jets hissed as Mara backed out of the slip.

The Yuuzhan Vong craft, she saw, was already moving through the seaward entrance of the marina and into the open sea. Mara kicked the rudder over and accelerated, shaving the stern of the nearest vessel by millimeters as she set out in pursuit.

She zigzagged around the piers and dashed through the exit to see the first ocean wave break over the Vong's canopy as it began to descend. Mara steered after the vanishing craft and looked for the ballast tank controls. Air sputtered from vents as she began her descent.

Piloting the submersible, she found, was like flying a starfighter, but in slow motion. It rolled and banked like any atmosphere craft, and like any atmosphere craft it flew better when it was in trim, the ballast tanks filled equally fore and aft, which meant she didn't have to be constantly fighting the dive planes to keep the boat at the right depth.

Visibility was quite good, but "good" visibility in the water only extended a hundred meters or so. Fortunately, her displays kept her informed of other craft in the water.

Radio-based detection systems were useless in the water, so submersibles featured a system based on sound. Rather than having every underwater craft pinging away all the time and confusing each other's sensors with overlapping noise, Heurkea Floating City itself issued regular low-frequency sonar pulses that highlighted every craft in the vicinity for thirty kilometers or more. In order to detect the vessels around them, all the submersibles had to do was set their own sonar sets to passively receive the city's pulses.

Mara had no trouble following her target and doing it without calling attention to herself, though she did speed up at one point in order to make certain that the craft she was following was the right one. She crept up on its tail until she recognized the configuration of the cabin, then allowed her boat to drift back. Compared to her own, the Yuuzhan Vong boat was a squat, broad, roomy vessel, with its two passengers sitting abreast of one another, and she reckoned her own tube-shaped craft was much speedier. This and the usefulness of Heurkea's city sonar allowed her to keep her distance from the Yuuzhan Vong vessel, even to join other traffic patterns in order to make it less obvious to the Vong they were being followed.

The target vessel plodded on at a deliberate speed, descending to thirty-five meters and circling the floating city until it was almost directly opposite the marina from which it had started. At this depth all color faded away to blue or gray, except for the occasional silver flash of a predator fish darting at the smaller fish attracted by the brightly lit windows of the residential areas. Below, the sea was a profound deep blue that seemed to stretch down forever, an azure vastness that seemed as limitless as empty space.

The Yuuzhan Vong boat checked its speed and began to hover. Mara slowed her own vessel, uncertain what she could do without giving herself away. If she began to hover herself, it might make the Yuuzhan Vong suspicious, but so might tracking back and forth in their vicinity.

Instead, she decided to pass within visual range of the target and see if she could make any sense of its actions. She dipped the dive planes to pass under the Vong craft, and set the throttle to a slow rate of speed to give herself as much time in visual range as possible. Then she almost jumped out of her skin as she passed in front of one of the city's sonar emitters and felt the deep low-frequency rumble as it shivered along her bones and caused her boat's small metal fittings to rattle.

The squat form of the target submersible loomed up, silhouetted against the bright blue and silver of the ocean surface thirty-five meters above. The Vong boat had its stern to the open ocean, its bow toward the floating city, and it was simply hovering in place. Mara peered up at the boat, unable to see much of anything along its dark underside—but then through the perfect acoustic medium of the water she heard the hum of an electric motor, and with it a brief scraping. The sounds repeated themselves.

This time, as she gazed up at the Yuuzhan Vong vessel, she caught a brief movement from the bows, a kind of dimple that appeared on its port bow, to match an identical dimple on the starboard side. And then her blood froze with horror at the realization of what she had just seen.

The Vong boat had opened a pair of torpedo tubes. It was about to open fire on Heurkea Floating City.

But why? she thought. Heurkea was *colossal*: a pair of torpedoes couldn't possibly sink it. Mara's head cranked to port, staring in consternation at the face of the city, at the series of clear windows that gave out onto the ocean deep, and there, silhouetted, she saw her answer: the tall, shaggy form of a Wookiee.

Triebakk.

Triebakk, gazing out of the sweating transparisteel wall of Cal Omas's apartment. Cal, the Chief of State candidate most likely to carry on the war against the Yuuzhan Vong. And Triebakk was soon joined by another, lanky figure that Mara recognized at once.

Cal Omas.

Cal and Triebakk continued to stand by the viewport. Mara realized they were holding drinks. Perhaps they had something to celebrate.

The Yuuzhan Vong boat swam into view dead ahead. Mara's boat had no weapons, no torpedoes of her own, but on the other hand her craft *was* a weapon. It weighed a metric ton or more, and it was moving fast, and if she couldn't sink her enemy by ramming, she might be able to disable it. Mara rolled her sub more or less upright and fed power to the water jets as she aimed her vessel at the enemy canopy, descending on the Yuuzhan Vong craft from above its starboard quarter. If she could smash in the canopy, the enemy would probably be killed outright, and at any rate would drown.

"Pull up! Pull up! Collision alert! Pull up!" Mara's nerves jumped as a roaring voice filled the cockpit, and her vessel's passive sonar went active with a series of high-pitched warning screeches aimed at alerting her target to its danger. The controls bucked in her hands as an autopilot seized control of the vessel. Grimly she fought the controls as she tried to keep her craft aimed at the enemy, while her eyes scanned the controls for a switch to turn off the autopilot.

"Pull up! Collision alert! Pull up!"

Things happened too fast for Mara to locate the autopilot override. There was an impact, then a scraping sound as her submersible rolled over the enemy craft. Her boat slewed violently to port as her aft port dive plane caught on the Vong's dorsal rudder. Locked together, the two subs whirled around each other, then parted with a grinding shudder. Mara looked over her shoulder to see the Vong sub inverted and pitched nose-down, cavitation bubbles spraying from its jets as it tried to right itself. One of the Yuuzhan Vong, thrown against the canopy by the impact, glared at her with his false human face distorted by a furious rage.

Mara sensed that Cal Omas and Triebakk weren't running away; they were peering out the viewport trying to make out what had just happened in the deep, distant blue of the water. Then the enemy faded into the darkness as Mara's boat sped away.

Mara fought the controls to pull her boat around for another pass. Her port dive plane had deformed with the impact; she could hear the hiss and squelch of water as it passed roughly over the distorted surface, and feel the sideways slewing motion that the distortion imparted to her craft.

Then suddenly she heard a whoosh and a frantic pinging, and her nerves keened with the knowledge that the Vong had just fired a torpedo. Her Force-sense told her that it was aimed at *her*, not at Cal Omas—she could sense the mass of the torpedo as it neared, and hear the increasingly fast, Doppler-shifted chirps of its active sonar as it sped closer.

Mara yanked the craft to port, hoping that the drag of the distorted port dive plane would assist her in making a tight turn. At the same time she pushed out with the Force, trying to shove a stream of water at the torpedo to push it off to the right.

The torpedo sizzled past Mara less than two meters beyond the sub's starboard dive plane, and Mara felt herself brace against the power of the explosion that would come with the detonation of a proximity fuse. But the torpedo must have had a contact fuse that ignited only on impact, because the underwater missile sped on, its frantic sonar pings Dopplering lower in pitch as it raced away.

Mara gazed at her displays and discovered the Vong craft lumbering in a turn, trying to bring its second and last weapon to bear on Cal Omas. Mara fought the damaged dive plane, lifted the sub's nose, and straightened once she'd gained five meters of altitude above the enemy boat. She could see no way to disable the autopilot that would try to interfere with her ramming maneuver—either it wasn't possible, or it required codes she didn't have. She would have to anticipate the autopilot's taking over this time, and take its interference into account as she held her course against the enemy.

As she pushed the throttles forward she realized that the fast pinging behind her had shifted, then began to pitch higher in volume. The torpedo had turned around and was coming at her again.

The Vong craft loomed ahead, still turning to bring its torpedo to bear on the floating city. The pings behind Mara grew more frequent and higher in pitch. She pushed her throttle to maximum speed and dived down onto the enemy boat, water hissing through her jets.

"Dive! Collision alert! Dive! Collision alert!" This time the autopilot was trying to pitch her downward to let her craft slip below the enemy. She fought the controls, trying to keep her machine on target.

"Dive! Dive!"

The pinging from astern beat faster than Mara's heart. Mara felt her sub shudder at the contradictory commands given the control surfaces, sensed the mass and speed of the torpedo approaching. And then she took her hands off the controls and let the autopilot take over.

The damaged dive plane screwed the sub around to port as it dived beneath the swollen shadow of the enemy craft. Mara saw the looming shadow of the Yuuzhan Vong sub's rudder dead ahead, cutting toward her cockpit like a huge knife, but the drag from the damaged dive plane pulled her out of the way with millimeters to spare. The torpedo was so close that Mara could hear its hiss as it shot through the water.

And then the torpedo hit the Yuuzhan Vong craft dead astern as Mara's boat slid beneath, and a great watery hand took Mara's sub and flung it spinning through the sea. Her hands and feet worked the controls as she tried to stabilize her craft, as she tried to gain her bearings in the giant white boil of the explosion.

Mara managed finally to bring her craft to a hover. She was hanging upside down in the cockpit, one of her legs clamped hard on her seat and the other braced under the instrument panel. With careful squirts of her maneuvering jets, she managed to roll her sub upright.

To one side, she could see the wreckage of the shattered Yuuzhan Vong craft spin downward into the blue depths below. The great mass of the floating city, on her other side, seemed intact. Triebakk and Cal were gone from the viewport, and through the roiling sea she could barely make out the apartment's front door, ajar—the two had fled.

Finally figured out what those fast pings meant, eh? she thought.

Well. Better late than never.

Luke, alerted once Mara got to the surface, stashed Cal Omas in their own apartment, which, with Jacen still there, was getting a little crowded, but was at least above water and in a part of the city with better security. Lando shipped down a pair of YVH droids for safety's sake—and, out of the presumed goodness of his heart, offered security droids to the other candidates as well.

Ayddar Nylykerka managed to get Mara out of the trouble she was in for stealing a submersible and getting it damaged during the course of an underwater dogfight.

Mara arrived at her apartment late in the evening to discover why Cal Omas and Triebakk had been celebrating. On a vote held earlier that day, Cal had jumped into the lead with 46 percent, followed by Fyor Rodan with 24 and Ta'laam Ranth with 20. Pwoe had actually gained a vote, for a total of four.

"Suddenly Ta'laam's twenty percent isn't worth as much to him," Cal told Mara. "I don't have to promise him much, because his supporters are going to defect in droves in the hope that I'll be grateful later." He looked puzzled. "What I can't work out is how Fyor's supporters turned out so wobbly." He glanced at Luke. "You didn't somehow arrange this, did you?"

"No," Luke said.

Cal grinned. "I didn't *think* Jedi mind control worked as well as that. I guess Fyor's supporters found out something about him that might be embarrassing if it got out, and decided to jump ship while they could."

"I didn't arrange it," Luke said, "but I think I know who did." Mara gave him a sharp look. *I'm not the only one who's been having adventures,* she thought.

Cal's grin faded. "Should I know about this?" he asked.

"Absolutely not," Luke said. "But I wouldn't count on Fyor's defectors for anything more than getting you into office. My guess is they're good for one vote only. If I were you, I'd court Ta'laam Ranth and as many of his people as you can, because you're going to need them later."

Cal rubbed his chin. "I'm not going to ask any more questions."

"You're an intelligent man," Luke said. "You'll work it out without *my* help."

By that point Mara had worked it out herself.

The next day Ta'laam Ranth released his followers to vote for Cal Omas, and Cal was elected with almost 85 percent of the vote. Fyor Rodan and a few diehards refused to make the vote unanimous, and three loyalists still voted for Pwoe. Cal moved off Mara's sofa and to the suite reserved for the new Chief of State at Heurkea's poshest hotel, where he was ably guarded by a platoon of YVH droids.

He began working on the acceptance speech he would have to give the Senate the next day. But before he began, he signed the order creating the new Jedi Council, with Luke at its head.

EIGHTEEN

"Your candidate has been elected," Vergere said over breakfast.

"Yes," Luke answered.

"Congratulations."

Luke looked toward Mara, who was busy with the apartment's comm unit. "It was more Mara's doing than mine. She kept Cal alive long enough to give his acceptance speech."

"Still," Vergere said, "you played a public role in his campaign."

"True."

"You realize that you and the Jedi will have to pay later for this political involvement."

Luke nodded. "I know."

"Just so you are prepared."

Luke tasted his glass of blue milk with a wistful yearning for the fresh, more richly flavored variety he'd enjoyed on his uncle Owen Lars's moisture farm. Mara rose from the comm unit, came to the table, and laid out several holos that had been transmitted from the hidden Jedi installation in the Maw.

"New images of Ben!"

Luke gazed at the holos with his usual mixture of delight and longing. Infants developed so rapidly at Ben's age that Luke could plainly see how the boy had grown and changed in the short time since he'd been sent to safety in the Maw. He was walking now, with greater and greater confidence. He was speaking, too, though at the moment his vocabulary seemed to consist mainly of the word *knee*.

At such moments Luke's misery at Ben's absence outweighed his thankfulness that Ben was in a place of safety.

Luke and Mara showed the holos to Vergere, who looked at them with quizzical eyes. "A handsome human child," she said. "As best as I understand these things."

"And strong in the Force," Mara said. "That's been clear from the beginning."

Vergere's crest sleeked back. "Perhaps that is misfortune," she said.

Luke stared at her in surprise. "Vergere?" he said.

"You permit Jedi to marry," Vergere said. "And permit not only marriage, but children. By *your* example, Luke Skywalker."

Luke tried to contain his surprise. "In your day," he said, "Jedi were chosen as infants. They were raised knowing they wouldn't marry. But I had to recruit Jedi who were already grown—who had already established relationships."

"It is very dangerous," Vergere said. "What if Jedi were forced to choose between their duty and their family?"

Luke had made that choice more than once and was comfortable with the necessity. "Family makes a Jedi more of a whole person," he said.

"It makes them less than Jedi!" Vergere said. Her head swung toward Mara on the end of its long neck. "And your child is strong in the Force—that is worse!"

Mara's green eyes glittered dangerously. "And how is that, Vergere?" she asked.

"Your Ben is heir to more than your husband's name—he is Darth Vader's grandchild," Vergere said. "Three generations now of Skywalkers, all strong in the Force! This is a Jedi dynasty!"

Vergere's head swung back toward Luke. "Can't you see

how governments will view this as a threat? Once it is possible for Jedi to *leave their power to their children*, the balance that exists between government and Jedi falls."

Luke held up one of the holos of Ben. "This is a threat? In a universe with the Yuuzhan Vong in it?"

Vergere's crest sleeked back again, and she made a hissing noise that raised the hairs on the back of Luke's neck. He almost wanted to snatch the holo of Ben from the danger.

The door chime sounded. Through a gentle Force projection coming from the other side Luke knew that the visitor was Cilghal, come to collect Vergere for another healing tutorial. When Vergere wasn't being debriefed by Fleet Intelligence—a process still ongoing—she had been perfectly amenable to spending time with Cilghal, teaching the Mon Calamari healer the art of *making herself small*. Perhaps Cilghal, too, would learn to heal with her tears, and then the two could pass the knowledge on to others.

At the sound of the chime, Vergere gazed stonily at Luke for a moment, then hopped off her chair. "I must go," she said. "But I beg you, young Master, to think of this."

She padded to the door and let herself out.

Luke looked at Mara. "What *do* we think?" he asked.

Mara reached for a knife. She began cutting up dried bofa fruit and adding it to a dried, crunchy form of Mon Calamari seaweed eaten by the locals.

"Maybe she's embittered over fifty years of loneliness," Mara said, "but I call that an overreaction."

"Yes."

"Vergere is too smart. Too perceptive. Too enigmatic." Her green eyes flashed. "Too willing to torture young humans to get what she wants. I don't want her ever to get near Ben."

"Agreed," Luke said. "I've checked the Jedi Holocron. There *was* a Jedi named Vergere fifty years ago, a former apprentice of a Master Thracia Cho Leem."

Mara's knife made neat little paring motions. "There *would* be, wouldn't there? If she was an infiltrator."

"It's awfully roundabout to infiltrate the Jedi by way of the Yuuzhan Vong."

Mara put down her knife. "Maybe she *was* a Jedi. The question is, after fifty years with the Vong, what is she *now*?"

Luke had no answer. "She doesn't feel dark," he said.

"She doesn't feel *anything*. She's practically invisible. We only sense what she wants us to sense."

"Are you going to play spy today?"

"Nylykerka can handle the enemy networks on his own today if you have another idea. Do you?"

"I have a Jedi Council to put together," Luke said. "I thought you might help me."

Mara smiled. "We get to spend the day gossiping about our colleagues and calling it work? I'm willing."

He leaned over and kissed her cheek. "I knew I could count on you," he said.

Ruined. Ruined.

Warmaster Tsavong Lah gazed in revulsion over the Square of Sacrifice, where the great formations of Yuuzhan Vong, each in formal robes, had been assembled to witness the painful, extended death of more than a hundred captives, all for the glory of Yun-Yuuzhan, whose great temple was being dedicated on this day.

Many of the captives were of high rank, military officers or Senators captured in the battle for Yuuzhan'tar. Their lives had been carefully preserved just for this moment. They had been strapped to their execution beds, and the priests stood by with their flesh-eating beetles, and their flaying knives. The symphony of the captives' screams would have risen for many hours to the delighted ears of the god.

But instead it was ruined. While Supreme Overlord Shimrra

stood on the steps of the temple, the high priest of Yun-Yuuzhan had gone into his extended blessing, hands raised over the thousands assembled to watch the work. And then a pestilential odor swept over the assembly, and the squares of formed Yuuzhan Vong began to eddy as something crept among them.

The square was being flooded by a noxious liquid, something spewed up from beneath ground level. The muck spread through the crowd, but the Yuuzhan Vong were disciplined, and remained in their ranks, plucking up the hems of their cloaks to keep them out of the ooze.

The rank fluid was composed of every kind of waste. Below ground level lived the maw luur who digested the sewage produced by the growing city, but apparently something had upset their omnivorous stomachs, and they were regurgitating onto the square.

The high priest's voice hesitated, resumed, hesitated again. He wheezed as a gust of wind brought a wave of stench to his nostrils. The high priest managed to renew his prayers, but Shimrra's booming voice cut him short.

"The sacrifice is spoiled! Dismiss the onlookers, and kill the captives!"

The high priest turned to face the Supreme Overlord. "Are you certain, Dread One?"

Shimrra gave a savage laugh. "Unless you think that sewage is deep enough to drown our victims in."

The high priest looked out over the flooded square. "I don't believe so, Supreme One."

"Then order your people to kill the captives." Shimrra turned on his heel to enter the temple. "The rest of you, follow me."

Tsavong Lah followed his Overlord into the shadowed green-and-purple depths of the temple, where the air smelled properly of heavy organics. Shimrra seemed more thoughtful than angry, which Tsavong Lah thought was not a good sign—it might mean the rage would burst out later, and in an unpredictable direction. At least the Dread One wasn't accompanied today by his shadow Onimi, as the presence of a Shamed One at a sacrifice this grand would have been an insult to the gods.

"Another failure," Shimrra growled. "Another *public* failure, witnessed *again* by thousands of our people—and by our chief god."

"Treachery, Supreme One!" someone called. "Sabotage by this so-called underground!"

"Or by heretics!" said a priest, loyal to his leader Jakan.

"I have six remaining voxyn, Dread Lord," Tsavong Lah said. "Let me take one or two out, and if there are *Jeedai* involved in this business, the voxyn will find them and tear them!"

Shimrra looked left and right. His burning eyes turned yellow, then red as they settled on Nom Anor. "You have received no reports of underground activity?" he demanded.

Tsavong Lah rejoiced at Shimrra turning to Nom Anor with this question. After Nom Anor's attempt to brand him with the catastrophe of Vergere, any discomfort in Nom Anor could only be to Tsavong Lah's delight.

"No reports, Supreme One," Nom Anor said.

Nom Anor almost wilted beneath the fierce glare of Shimrra's mqaaq'it implants. But Shimrra again chose to withhold his anger, and his savage look again turned thoughtful.

"We know the World Brain has been contaminated by that fool Ch'Gang Hool," Shimrra said. "Could this be another manifestation of the shapers' incompetence?"

No one dared to either confirm or deny this supposition. "It's almost as if the World Brain has developed a nasty sense of humor," Shimrra said thoughtfully. "Onimi won't care for that—he much prefers being the only one permitted to make jokes."

No one commented on that, either.

The Supreme Overlord turned to one of his assistants. "Find a shaper to die for this."

"I will, Supreme One."

Nom Anor seemed to sag with relief once he realized that the shaper class was going to get the blame for the botched sacrifice. Tsavong Lah snarled at him. *Next time, filth,* he thought.

Shimrra's glowing, restless eyes swept again over the company, then settled on Tsavong Lah. The warmaster straightened, then bowed from the waist, keeping his back rigid.

"Dread Lord?" he said.

"Your forces eliminated an enemy cruiser at small cost to themselves. Vengeance for Komm Karsh, though a small one."

Tsavong Lah took a grip on his courage. "With your permission, Supreme One, I will exact vengeance in full. Give me permission to take the fleet and—"

"No, Warmaster."

"Give me a decisive battle, Supreme One! Let the infidels' blood fill the spaces between the stars!" The words sprayed from the warmaster's slashed lips.

"Be silent!"

Tsavong Lah threw himself to the ground before the Supreme Overlord's feet. "I obey," he said.

There was a moment of awful emptiness in which Tsavong Lah contemplated his own immediate death.

Then the silence was broken by an unexpected voice. "With respect, Supreme One," Nom Anor said, "I agree that a decisive battle must be fought, and soon."

Astonishment filled Tsavong Lah's soul, followed immediately by suspicion. Nom Anor couldn't be agreeing with Tsavong Lah out of sympathy for his position. This had to be some plot, some devious scheme by the executor to discredit him.

To Tsavong Lah's surprise, Shimrra restrained his anger. "Your reasons, Executor?" he asked.

"We aren't growing any stronger, Supreme One," Nom Anor said. "As soon as our auxiliaries are in place and the fleet is at full strength, we must seek to bring about a decisive engagement that will win the war."

Mockery entered Shimrra's tones. "I thought the Battle of Yuuzhan'tar was supposed to be 'the decisive engagement that would win the war.' "

Nom Anor hesitated. "The infidels have proved more adaptable than we suspected."

Tsavong Lah stepped in. "We shouldn't waste our strength on an offensive for its own sake. If we choose the right moment, however, the right target ... if we can catch their forces at a disadvantage, then we can smash them beyond recovery."

The mockery continued. "How can we choose such a time, such a target?"

"We must depend on accurate intelligence of the enemy, Supreme One," Nom Anor said.

Shimrra laughed. "On *you*, then. All hail Nom Anor! This victory depends on *you*, who has just lost a pair of valuable agents in a bungled assassination."

Nom Anor wisely chose not to rise to the mockery. "Assassination is always a risky business, Supreme One. Agents may be risked in this way, but no chances should be taken with the fleet."

"Very well then." Shimrra hesitated. "Rise, Warmaster."

Tsavong Lah got to his feet, his clawed vua'sa foot scrabbling for traction on the chitinous temple floor. He looked at Nom Anor and tried to mask his resentment.

Shimrra looked from one to the other. "Warmaster, you will have your decisive battle, after the fleet is ready. But you will not launch the battle blindly; you will wait for Nom Anor's spies to report that the time is ripe. And my own permission will be required. Do you understand?"

"Completely, Supreme One." Tsavong Lah bowed in submission.

A smile twisted across Shimrra's features. "It seems that the two of you are bound together once again. The fate of one will depend entirely on the fate of the other. If success comes to one, it will come to both. But if one fails . . ." He left the thought unfinished.

Tsavong Lah straightened and looked at the executor, who he found looking back at him. Tsavong Lah let a smile spread across his slashed lips.

At least if I fall, he thought at him, *I may rejoice in the thought that you will not long survive me.*

Though it was not comfortable to think that Nom Anor was probably thinking the very same thing.

"I want Cilghal," Luke said. "I want a healer. The fact that she's an ambassador is a bonus."

He and Mara were in their apartment, trying to choose five Jedi to serve with Luke on the new Jedi Council. In the background, a live holo of Cal Omas was giving his acceptance speech before the Senate.

"With sorrow for our countless dead, but with hope for the future," Cal was saying. "With sadness for the many who have fallen, but with confidence in the many who have taken their place . . ."

"Cilghal," Mara said. "Very well."

Luke looked at her. "Who I really want," he said, "is you."

Mara's green eyes sparkled. "I'm always flattered to hear that."

"For the council, I mean," Luke said, "as of course in

every other way. But a Jedi Master can't appoint his wife to government jobs without people disapproving."

"You'll get my advice anyway," Mara said. "You won't be able to avoid it." She looked at the list they'd compiled. "Who's next?"

"How about Kenth Hamner? He has the contacts, and the knowledge."

Mara nodded, and entered the name on her datapad. "Hamner's in, then." She looked up. "Kam Solusar? Or Tionne? It would be good to have someone representing the Jedi academy."

"Put them down as maybes. If we weren't at war, I'd put one of them on the council for certain, but right now we may need a council oriented more toward action."

"Then why Cilghal?"

Luke looked at her. "Healing is important."

Mara held his gaze, then nodded. "Of course."

"Saba Sebatyne. She commands an all-Jedi squadron, and brings all the Barabels on board. She's proved herself many times over, and it's time she had a higher profile."

Saba hadn't been trained at the Jedi academy, but on Barab I by the Jedi Master Eelysa. Saba in turn had recruited and trained a whole pack of her fellow Barabels, most of whom formed her Wild Knights Squadron.

"You've thought about this pretty thoroughly, haven't you?" Mara said.

"I do my best."

She gave a sly smile. "Maybe Cal is right—you *are* turning into a politician."

Luke affected horror and made a warding gesture.

Mara laughed. "My only objection is that Saba is a Knight," she said, "not a Master."

"Knights should have some representation on the council, too."

Mara looked at her datapad. "Saba's representing a lot of people—Knights, Barabels, and an all-Jedi squadron."

"Then it's all the more important that she have a seat."

"With compassion for the millions of our dispossessed," Cal's holo was saying, "with firmness in the rightness of our cause . . ."

Mara shrugged and made a mark by Saba's name. "Streen?" she suggested.

"A maybe. Tresina Lobi?"

"She'd be good."

From the holo came Cal's voice. ". . . I accept the Senate's nomination to be Chief of State of the New Republic." Roars followed, and applause.

"That was a good speech," Mara said.

"It was." Luke glanced thoughtfully at the holo Cal listening respectfully to the Senate's applause. "You know, I'm beginning to have a lot of sympathy for Cal. He's got to fill seats not only on the Jedi Council, but in all the government departments as well."

"He has more practice at this sort of thing than we do."

"Let's hope so." Luke glanced at Mara's datapad and the list of names. "Let's add one more. My most controversial nominee."

Mara turned her eyes to him in rising horror. "Not Kyp Durron!"

Luke returned her gaze, then gave a deliberate nod. "For what it's worth," he said, "I think that Kyp's actions at Hapes and Borleias show that he's a much more stable person than he was. He seems to have made peace with himself. Remember, he renounced pride on Ithor, and since then he voluntarily put himself under Jaina's command. He's always supported the idea of a Jedi Council."

"You're setting yourself up for a lot of grief."

"Wouldn't it be more grievous to have a Kyp running around loose, where the council can't control him?" Luke said. "Remember, he's only one vote. If he takes an independent line, he'll be outvoted by the rest, and then he'll be obliged to support the majority."

"I think you have a very generous idea of Kyp's sense of obligation. Plus," Mara considered, "how do you know he'll be outvoted? There are going to be six non-Jedi on the council now. What if Kyp's arguments make sense to them?"

"If Kyp's arguments make sense to half a dozen political appointees, then I'd better pay more attention to those arguments than I have been."

Mara gave him a skeptical look. "I think you're going to regret this."

Luke shrugged. "I may. I probably will. But if a person in authority talks only to those who agree with him, he soon finds himself *out* of authority."

Mara sighed. "You *are* a politician," she said.

Luke presented his nominees for the Jedi Council to Cal Omas the next morning. Cal leaned back in his office chair—the office smelled of fresh paint and newly laid carpet—looked at the list, and gave Luke a skeptical look.

"Kyp Durron?" he said.

"Kyp has changed," Luke said.

"He hasn't blown up any planets in a few years, that's true."

"That wasn't precisely Kyp who did that," Luke said. "He was possessed by the spirit of a long-dead Sith Lord named Exar Kun."

Cal shook his head, and when he spoke his voice had a mournful air. "That's *exactly* the sort of thing I hope *never* to have to explain to a Senatorial committee," he said.

Luke looked at Cal in concern. "Should I withdraw the nomination? I don't want to wreck our chances of reestablishing the Jedi Council."

Cal considered, then shook his head. "No," he said. "I understand why you did it. It's best to have the opposition inside the tent, where you can keep an eye on them. That's why I'm putting some of Fey'lya's old faction on the Advisory Council. And Fyor Rodan, if he'll agree." He looked at Luke. "And you."

Surprise rose in Luke. "Are you sure?" he asked. "Don't you think Leia would be better?"

"Maybe. But Leia hasn't returned from Bastion, and you're here."

Luke smiled. "You're going to keep me so busy running to meetings that I'm not going to have time for anything else."

"Would that be a bad thing?" Cal asked. "Does the head of the Jedi order *need* to be blowing up Death Stars and engaging in lightsaber fights at *his* age?"

Luke smiled. "I haven't blown up a Death Star in ages."

"That's what your young folks are for," Cal said. "If you put me back in a starfighter, I'd feel like an idiot."

"I doubt that very much," Luke said.

"Maybe I exaggerate." Cal smiled. "I'm appointing myself to the Jedi Council, by the way."

"I had hoped you would."

"And Triebakk, as Senatorial representative—the Senate will need to confirm that, but I don't think we'll have any trouble. Dif Scaur, the chief of Intelligence. Someone from the Justice Council—I haven't worked out just who as yet. Releqy A'Kla, who will also head the Ministry of State."

"Her uncle was a Jedi."

"I know."

"You don't have any of Fey'lya's people. Or Fyor Rodan's."

"I know." Cal smiled. "They'll have to be satisfied with seats on the Advisory Council, won't they?"

"You haven't mentioned the sixth."

"Sien Sovv, as head of the military." He looked troubled.

"If I decide to retain him. He offered me his resignation practically the second I finished my acceptance speech."

Luke gave Cal a serious look. "You need to call on Ackbar."

Cal looked curious. "To be Supreme Commander?"

"No, but you need to talk to him. He has a plan to deal with the Yuuzhan Vong."

"I'll talk to him."

"Very soon, Cal," Luke warned. "You know how good he is."

Cal nodded again. "Fine. Soon."

The voice of Cal's comm droid came from the speakers on his desk. "Senator Rodan is here for his appointment."

Cal rose. "I shouldn't keep Fyor waiting."

He escorted Luke to the door, allowing the Jedi Master to precede him into the outer office.

Fyor Rodan stood there, wearing a stainless gray suit and a cold demeanor. Luke gave him a polite nod, but Rodan only returned a glare.

"I see you have the compliant Chief of State required by your plans," he said.

"I don't believe you ever asked me my plans," Luke said. "You only assumed you knew them."

"You interfered," Rodan said. "You and your wife did something to my supporters."

"We did nothing of the sort," Luke said.

"Then it was your pirate friends. Do you deny that?"

"I deny that I have pirate friends," Luke said mildly. "And I have no idea what my other friends may have done, if anything."

"Jedi virtue!" Rodan said. "You remain stainless, while your friends do the dirty work. I couldn't help but notice that your friends' droids are guarding the Chief of State whom they created."

"The YVH droids in the corridor belong to the government," Cal Omas said. "You voted for the appropriation yourself, Fyor."

Fyor Rodan turned his scornful eye toward Cal. "I thought you had more pride than to sell yourself to a bunch of renegades and their witch-doctor accomplices!" he said. "I refuse to have anything to do with supporting the illusion that your government is anything but illegitimate. I'll thank you to keep my name off any list of appointees."

He turned, stiff-spined, and marched out. Luke and Cal looked at each other.

"Stickier than I thought," Cal said.

NINETEEN

Jacen spent his first day of freedom in the apartment, marveling at its strange solidity. The scratch of the carpet against his bare feet, air that didn't taste like a rich stew of organics, walls that were vertical and a ceiling that was a flat plane above his head. Holos on shelves. Popular music that bounced its rhythms from hidden speakers. A kitchen full of wondrous, gleaming appliances. A refrigeration unit full of food designed for the human palate.

Furniture. The Yuuzhan Vong didn't have furniture the same way that people did. It wasn't crafted or assembled, it was *sprouted*. And their sense of scale was different, the way they placed it in one of their rooms with its resinous floors and walls of coral or stabilized protein.

Jacen had said farewell to furniture, to holos and kitchen equipment and refrigeration units and to everything else that was human. Finding it again was a rediscovery.

Messages appeared on the comm unit. WAY TO GO, SPROUT. And ONCE AGAIN, JACEN, YOU HAVE ANSWERED A MOTHER'S PRAYERS. The messages gave him a singing joy that stayed with him for the rest of the day.

That evening his aunt Mara tactfully hinted that he might buy some clothes, so the next morning he set off to do some shopping. He borrowed some of Uncle Luke's clothes and threw a cloak over everything, but people recognized him anyway. His face had been everywhere in the holocasts.

Many were friendly, many curious, and only a few turned away with angry glares or muttered asides. The Jedi, it seemed, were more popular than they had been.

He bought clothing from a Quarren tailor who assured him that the drape was perfect and in the mode, at least for humans. Afterward he wandered the city, enjoying the elegant architecture beneath the vivid blue sky, and tried to ignore the fact that wherever he went he was the center of attention.

Later, from the apartment, he tried to contact Vergere, but was told she wasn't allowed calls. He spoke to Luke about it, but Luke only said, "You're on vacation. And that includes being on vacation from Vergere."

Then Luke invited Jacen to sit by him. "I'd like to hear your ideas on the Yuuzhan Vong," he said.

"Vergere would be the one to ask," Jacen said.

"I *have* asked her. But I'd like to ask you. Their immunity to the Force aside, are the Yuuzhan Vong so very different from us?"

Jacen considered. "No. They have a tyrannical government, and their religion is absolute poison. But they're no better or worse than humans would be if we were raised in their system."

Luke looked at him. "Do you hate them?" he asked.

"No." Jacen's answer was swift and very certain.

"Why not?"

This time Jacen had to think. "Because," he said finally, "it would be like hating a child for being raised badly. It's not the child's fault, it's the parents'. I could hate the leaders who made the Yuuzhan Vong what they are, but they're long dead, so why waste energy in hatred?"

Luke rose and put a hand on Jacen's shoulder. "Thank you, Jacen," he said.

"I . . . understand them," Jacen said.

Luke seemed startled, his mind inward. "You do not hate, because you understand," he murmured.

"Sorry?"

Luke's attention snapped back to Jacen. "No. Go on."

"I was implanted with a slave seed, remember, and it interfaced with my nervous system. It was supposed to be a one-way communication link, to enslave me and give me my orders, but I discovered that it worked the other way. It's produced a kind of . . . telepathy. I can extend my mind into the Yuuzhan Vong and into their creatures, and sometimes I can influence them."

Luke looked at him in surprise. "You can touch the Yuuzhan Vong with the Force?"

"No. It's different. I can't use the Force and my—my 'Vongsense' at the same time."

Luke's eyes narrowed in thought. "Can you teach this?"

Jacen had been wondering this himself. "I don't know," he said. "I don't think so. I think perhaps you need to be implanted with a slave seed, or some other form of Yuuzhan Vong control that can interface with your nervous system." A thought struck him. "I might be able to teach Tahiri. After what they put her through, it's possible that she . . . might still be attuned enough to the Yuuzhan Vong to learn to do as I've done."

Luke frowned. "Tahiri found her experience at the hands of the Vong to be highly traumatic. And she's—had some traumatic experiences since. I wouldn't want to force her to revisit an experience that damaged her."

"Nor would I."

Jacen didn't tell Luke about one of the consequences of what he'd just called his "Vongsense"—the fact that he was still in occasional mental contact with the entity whom the Yuuzhan Vong called the World Brain, the dhuryam who controlled the environment of Coruscant. He and the dhuryam were conspiring against the planet's worldshaping, sabotaging it in minor but annoying ways: through the creation of an itching plague, for instance. Jacen had just inspired the World Brain to cause a sickness in the maw luur, the creatures who recycled Yuuzhan Vong waste, during what the dhuryam sensed was an important occasion or ceremony.

Though Jacen could theoretically inspire the World Brain to more deadly action, from poisoning Yuuzhan Vong food to causing an ecological catastrophe, he had refrained. His empathy with the Yuuzhan Vong had grown along with his Vongsense: he would not be a mass murderer, not even of a deadly enemy.

In part, that was why he hadn't told Luke of this particular ability. He didn't want his ability known for fear that someone would want him to use it as a weapon. Though he realized that Luke would never ask such a thing of him, he felt that the more private he kept this secret, the better.

The conversation with Luke was interrupted when a holojournalist commed, asking for an interview. Jacen told the comm unit to refuse anyone it didn't already know was a friend.

The following morning Jacen felt delicate, ate a bland breakfast, and returned to his bed. Luke left to do political things, and Mara went off to play counterspy with her mouse droids. He was awakened by a call on the comm, which meant that the comm's artificial intelligence recognized the caller as family or a friend.

He answered and stared into a pair of green eyes framed by curling blond hair. Danni Quee.

"Hello, Danni."

"Jacen. I hope it's all right to call."

"I'm not sick or in quarantine or anything. I'm allowed to talk to people."

"That's good. Would you like to see a bit of the city? Or are you being besieged by friends?"

"I'm not besieged by friends," Jacen said, "I guess because they're as tactful as you are. But I'd just as soon not go anywhere public, because I seem to attract crowds."

She grinned, teeth white against her tanned face. "I saw you on the holonews yesterday. Was that cloak supposed to be a disguise?"

"Not exactly."

"If you're not ready to face your public, then, why don't I get a hovercraft and take you out to Mester Reef?"

"Sure."

Twenty minutes later, Jacen met Danni at a public pier. "Nice clothes," she remarked, and gave him a hug. Soon they were on a craft racing west on its repulsorlifts ten meters above the water. Danni had provided diving equipment for two, as well as a light lunch.

"Fast work," Jacen said.

"I was going to go anyway. If I hadn't reached you, I would have gone with another friend."

He looked at her. "Anyone I know?"

"Thespar Trode. She's another unemployed astrophysicist."

"You're not employed these days?"

Danni gave a wry grin. "We'll talk about that later."

Mester Reef was in such tropical waters that no insulation suits were necessary, but Jacen and Danni wore them anyway to minimize abrasions. The air supply was a light unit worn on the back that silently extracted air from the water and fed it to the diver, and was limited only by its power supply, which was good for about fifty years. There was a vest that could be inflated or deflated to adjust for buoyancy, with pockets for weights to make sure the diver didn't pop back to the surface.

Danni held up a pair of swim fins. "Old-fashioned transportation," she said. "I could have brought some drive units to speed us along under the water, but I think they're a distraction—it's better if it's just you and the reef and the ocean."

"Fine with me," Jacen said. "It's not like we're in a hurry to go anywhere."

The water was like a warm salt bath. Adjusting to the breathing apparatus felt natural and was easier than using a pressure suit. The inflatable vest was a little more difficult, and Jacen found himself sinking or bobbing toward the surface until he managed to equalize his buoyancy properly. Once he adjusted to the experience, he found he could *think* himself higher or lower—and he didn't need the Force for it either, just a kind of relaxation.

A current ran along the reef here, and he and Danni simply drifted along. The water that leaked past the mouthpiece tasted of salt and iodine and a thousand living things. Above was the rippled sunlight of the ocean surface; to one side the vivid colors of the reef; on the other side the boundless ocean; and below the profound blue of the ocean deeps, clear and seeming to go down forever.

They didn't dive below twenty meters or so, because below that depth the light faded away badly, and they wanted to see the brightness of the coral. The coral formations, the anemones, and the sponges were ablaze with brilliant color, and the fish and other animals were as incandescent as the coral through which they swam.

There were hierarchies here. The coral rose like great ramparts of a castle, occasionally breaking toward the surface in towers. Living things attached themselves to the coral, or sheltered inside its convolutions, or imitated the coral with its colors, its seeming quiescence, and its stinging spines. Reef fish hunted these, searching among the coral for their dinners and sometimes being engulfed and digested by a cunningly camouflaged predator, while torpedo-shaped pelagic fish from the deep water ate the reef fish, darting in from the open ocean to strike, kill, and devour, coming from a place far beyond the comprehension of the reef fish, like pirates from another world.

And everything on the reef was alive! The coral, the sponges, the fish, the crustaceans, and anemones—all were *living* things. Even the seemingly empty ocean was filled with microscopic life. That was the true wonder of it. Jacen summoned his Force-sense and let the song of the reef enter him, all the tiny creatures living together in a complex, interconnected pattern, basking for a moment in the sheer glory of it.

This was such a glorious change from the Yuuzhan Vong environment. There everything lived as well, but all was alien, strange, and full of sinister purpose. It was like living in a void. Here, the reef and its life practically shouted at him through the Force.

Jacen extended his Force-sense toward Danni. She was Force-sensitive, but her training had been unsystematic, scattered into spare moments between battles and obsessive research. He sensed her startled surprise at the first touch of his mind, but she then relaxed, and he let the reef's existence flow into her, the great vital accumulation of all the tiny lives, and the two floated along the reef in silent communion, absorbed in the reef's complexity and abundance.

Eventually they grew chilled even through their insulation suits, so he and Danni rose to the surface, and Danni triggered the transponder that would bring her hovercraft flying toward them. It settled into the water five meters away and lowered its ladders so they could climb aboard. They took off their dive suits and let the sun warm them as they ate their lunch. And then, while digesting, they simply relaxed, stretched out side by side on the foredeck.

"You said you weren't working?" Jacen asked.

"No. I was working for the Jedi until my unit began to achieve results, and then we were co-opted by the government. And then, after we reached a certain stage, we were—

well, we weren't disbanded, but some of my team was taken away. I'm taking some training in communications and infiltration, so that I can help set up Resistance cells, and then I'll get back in the war."

Jacen rolled on his side to look at her. "But you've done such crucial work!" he said. "You discovered how to jam the yammosk signal. That's the single critical discovery that's enabled our ships to survive battle with the Yuuzhan Vong. Why would they disband your group now?"

She turned her green eyes to his. "Astrophysicists aren't important for war work," she said. "I made the initial discovery about how yammosks communicate, yes. But now that the discovery's been made, it isn't a theoretical problem anymore, it's an engineering one. Now it's up to the engineers to build jammers and spoofers and try to work out more and more ingenious ways to foul up enemy communications. All the theoretical work has been quietly shunted aside." She sighed. "I was working so hard and for so long—nothing has ever been so thoroughly studied in such a short time as the Yuuzhan Vong. What Cilghal and I did alone could have won us half a dozen major scientific prizes. But our work is secret, so the prize committees will never find out, and as far as anyone knows, I'm just a twenty-three-year-old stargazer without a job and with no hope of finding one." She stretched languidly and looked at the brilliant sky.

A strange look came onto her face, and she sat up, crossing her legs and leaning toward Jacen. "Not *all* the theoretical work has been pushed aside. Did I mention that? There's some still going on, and it's kind of strange."

Jacen blinked up at her. "Tell me."

"We had some people in our group who were working on the details of Yuuzhan Vong bioscience. They made a discovery, and right away were pulled away into a new unit in the Intelligence division. They're working directly under a group of Chiss, who report directly to Dif Scaur."

"Scaur's working with Chiss?" Jacen was surprised.

"They're all offplanet now. None of my messages to my friends get through, I just get messages saying they're temporarily off the HoloNet."

"All at the proverbial secret laboratory off in deep space," Jacen muttered.

"And why the *Chiss*?"

"And you say they're working on Yuuzhan Vong bioscience." Jacen pondered for a moment, then shook his head. "The problem is, we don't know enough about the Chiss to know why they'd be valuable. We don't even know where their home planet is. Maybe their bioscience is ahead of ours. Maybe they know something about the Yuuzhan Vong that we don't. Maybe their own weird metabolism gives them an insight into what the Yuuzhan Vong can do."

"Weird metabolism?"

"They're *blue*. That's a clue right there."

Danni laughed.

Jacen looked at her. "Do you know the nature of the discovery the bioscientists made?"

She nodded. "It had to do with Yuuzhan Vong genetics—which are generally like ours, by the way."

Jacen blinked. "That's pretty odd, considering they're from another galaxy."

"There's one bit of their genetics that *isn't* like us," Danni said. "There's a sequence that seems completely unique, and it's common to all Yuuzhan Vong life. Yorik coral, yam-mosks, plant life, the Yuuzhan Vong themselves. All of it."

"Is that what makes us unable to see them in the Force?"

Danni shrugged. "Maybe. The geneticists didn't know—or anyway they didn't when I last saw them."

Silence fell. Jacen gave a reluctant grin. "We probably shouldn't even be talking like this," he said. "Whatever

Scaur's doing with the Chiss, it's probably so deeply secret and off the map that our speculations are going to both be wrong and get us in trouble."

"Even speculating *here*?"

"It wouldn't surprise me if I'm under some kind of casual observation," Jacen said. "I just came back from weeks of imprisonment at the hands of the Yuuzhan Vong. Intelligence can't be sure I haven't switched sides." He looked up at the sky and gave a wave. "Say hi to the satellites!"

Danni laughed and waved at any invisible observers, then turned back to Jacen. "That's enough danger for today," she said. "I think I feel safer underwater."

"Me, too."

Danni and Jacen flew in their craft a few kilometers farther down the reef and put on their equipment again. As soon as they descended to the reef Jacen drew again on his Force-awareness and let the life of the reef fill his spirit. He reached out again to Danni, and the two shared the swarming, intricate existence of the reef until it was time to return to Heurkea.

The next day Jacen went to the reef again with Danni, this time with her friend Thespar Trode, a female Ishi Tib, whose dive gear had been adapted to her giant head and eyes that thrust out on stalks. The two astrophysicists' conversation tended to be technical, but Jacen didn't mind: he enjoyed the display of agile intelligence even though he didn't understand it, and while he listened he let his Force-sense descend to the reef and fill his mind with living glory.

After the dive he invited Thespar and Danni to the apartment for snacks, but when he opened the door he saw Jaina standing in the front room, still in her pilot's coveralls, her military duffel partly opened on the floor. He and Jaina stared at each other for a long moment of exquisitely painful joy, and then their twin bond flared with a thousand shared emotions and memories, the rich harvest of lives shared since their first day in their mother's womb, and they rushed into an embrace. They pounded each other on the back and laughed until the tears came.

Family was another thing that Jacen had surrendered to the Yuuzhan Vong. The sensation of finding his twin again took his breath away.

When he found it he looked at the insignia on Jaina's coveralls. "You're a major now?"

"I'm better than that, I'm a holovid star. Not to mention a goddess." Her eyes shifted to the two visitors standing near the door. She knew Danni Quee, of course, but had to be introduced to Danni's friend Thespar.

"I have to change now, and run," Jaina said. "I've got dispatches to deliver to headquarters." She gave Jacen a look. "And I've got a personal message from Admiral Kre'fey to Uncle Luke. He wants Jedi."

Jacen was pleasantly surprised. "At least *someone* wants us."

She took a more formal uniform out of her duffel, disappeared into a bedroom to change, and then returned only to head for the door.

"We'll talk later, right?" she said as she paused on the threshold. "I want to hear everything." And then she was gone.

Jacen gazed at the closing door in surprise as his mind tingled with the sensation of the fading twin bond. He had expected more from his first meeting with his sister, much more.

She wasn't avoiding him, Jacen thought. Not exactly. But she definitely needed some time to get her thoughts together before she could face him.

He thought he knew why.

Jacen shared with his guests some jewel-fruit he found in

the refrigeration unit, and then the two astrophysicists said their good-byes.

Luke and Mara returned before Jaina did. When Jaina finally arrived, she was taut and high-strung, her neck and shoulder muscles rigid with tension. First she delivered Kre'fey's request for more Jedi pilots to Luke, who was pleased to hear that someone in the military was willing to take Jedi. He asked about Jaina's action at Obroa-skai, and from there gently drew her into a discussion of her activities since the fall of Coruscant. Particularly the battles at Hapes, and the way she'd used the Yuuzhan Vong's own dovin basals against them, to sow confusion and destroy the invaders.

And her state of mind at the time. The obsession. The fury. The darkness.

Jaina looked at Jacen with bleak eyes and said, "I thought you were dead. You and Anakin both. It didn't matter to me how many others were sent to join you. I was ready to go myself."

It was easier, Jacen thought, for Jaina to speak to Luke and Mara than it would have been to speak to him alone. Luke had known that.

"More than through anger or lust for power," Luke said, "the dark enters through despair. Through the belief that, in the end, there is nothing but pain and sorrow and death, and that nothing we do truly matters." He gave Jaina a look. "I'm here to tell you that we *do* matter. And that despair is an illusion that the dark casts before our eyes."

Jaina lowered her eyes. "Thank you, Uncle Luke," she said.

Jaina and her duffel moved in to share Jacen's room. He wanted to talk to her before sleep, but she said she was exhausted from her long journey from Kashyyyk; she'd talk to him in the morning.

Jacen fell asleep at once and dreamed of the coral reef. He

was awakened two hours before dawn, with the arrival of his parents. Half awake, he stood in the door while his father howled his happiness like a Wookiee, picked Jacen off the floor, and whirled him around as if he were a two-year-old.

Leia's emotion was less demonstrative but no less powerful, and Jacen felt it through the Force even as his father twirled him through the air. When Jacen found his feet again he embraced his mother, and he sensed the force of Leia's profound thankfulness.

It was she whose faith had never faltered, he knew. Her husband had deserted her and returned a changed man; the New Republic she had created had betrayed itself; one of her three children had been killed, another torn away into captivity, and she had watched the third slide toward the dark side.

Leia alone held firm. Leia alone insisted that Jacen was alive. And now Jacen stood within the circle of his mother's arms, and let her know that her faith had not been in vain.

The hours that followed were exuberant and very emotional. Han was almost bouncing off the walls in his joy, at least when he wasn't trying to conceal a tear in his eye.

C-3PO moved Han and Leia's belongings into their bedroom, and Jaina and Jacen's gear out. The twins sacked out on the floor of the front room. C-3PO, with nowhere to go, propped himself against a wall and shut himself down. No sooner had Jacen closed his eyes than he heard a respectful tap at the door—Leia's Noghri bodyguards, who hadn't been taken to Bastion, were now reporting for duty.

They were placed outside in the corridor, and an hour later knocked again, this time because Vergere had been released from detention and had nowhere else to go.

Jacen was delighted to see her, but clearly the apartment was too crowded, even after Jaina volunteered to shift to bachelor officers' quarters. But fortunately Jacen had a mother who was a Princess and had connections.

The Solo family, with C-3PO, moved to another apartment along with the Noghri. Jacen hoped Vergere might come along, but Luke rather firmly stated that she would remain as his guest.

It was probably a good idea, Jacen reflected later. When his parents found out what Vergere had actually done to him when he was a prisoner, they wouldn't have looked at the little alien kindly. Jacen would hate to have to get between Vergere and Han's blaster.

The move took much of the day, and as soon as it was over Jaina had to report to Fleet Command to see if any decision had been made about Kre'fey's request for Jedi. She wasn't back until very late.

The next morning, Jacen rose, seated himself at the foot of his bed, and began to do his Jedi meditations and exercises. Calling the Force, using it to help modify his bodily state, slowing or speeding his heartbeat; shifting blood flow to his muscles, as if for combat; to his internal organs, as if wounded or short on air; or to his skin, to help radiate excess heat and cool the body.

He sensed Jaina waking as the Force radiated from him, and likewise sensed her resentment. With a sigh, she climbed out of the bed, joined him on the floor, and merged her meditations with his.

They synchronized breathing and heartbeat, lifted small objects, and then engaged in a mental lightsaber fight, sharing a mutual mental image of themselves in battle with one another, visualizing every move, every parry, the shuffle of their feet on the ground, the *thrumm* of the lightsabers, the impact as the blades grated against each other. Jaina's fight was methodical and cool, utilizing minimal energy, content to back away until she saw an opening for an absolutely ruthless riposte. Jacen permitted himself more freedom, making wild attacks and lunges, spinning in and out of range, striving to do the unexpected. As a result he got nailed more often than not, and in the moment of his "death," he sensed his sister's steely resolve.

Afterward, as a calming exercise, Jacen sent his Force-sense radiating outward, sensing his sleeping parents in their bed, the two Noghri (one on guard, the other asleep), the sparks of life in the adjacent apartments. Seeking the wondrous, dynamic complexity he'd found on the reef, Jacen sent his Force-sense floating even farther, down into the deeps surrounding Heurkea Floating City, sensing the masses of microscopic life, the swarms of fish that had adopted the city as their home, the deepwater pelagic fish that darted into the city's shadow to prey on the smaller fish . . .

Jaina pulled away. Jacen opened his eyes in surprise and saw her getting to her feet.

"Sorry," she said. "I can't go there right now."

He blinked at her. "Why not?"

She reached into the closet and took out her uniform. "I've got to stay focused on my job. I can't let my mind go floating around in the ocean, I've got to stick with what I can use."

"It's life, Jaina," Jacen said. "The Force is life."

Jaina looked down at him. Anger smoldered in her eyes. "Life isn't what I *do* anymore," she said. "What I *do* is death. I kill, and I try not to get killed myself. Anything else—" She waved her hand. "—is a luxury."

"Jaina—" Jacen began.

"Every second I spend floating around the ocean," Jaina said, "I'm getting weaker and the Vong are getting stronger. So what I'm going to do—" She opened the door. "—is take a shower, get into my uniform, and go to headquarters to see if Admiral Sovv has a message for me. And if he doesn't, I'm going to find some pilots and talk tactics, so that maybe I can learn a trick or two that will keep my squadron alive through another fight. I'll see you later, maybe."

"It's all about balance, Jaina," Jacen said, but she was gone, and the refresher door shut behind her.

Jacen rose and sadly began to change into his clothes. Later, after breakfast, he told his mother what Jaina had said. Leia sighed.

"Jaina and I already had this argument at Hapes," she said. "I *begged* her to get some leave, get away, get some perspective. But she wouldn't, and I know how far I'd get if I repeated my arguments now."

"Uncle Luke said that despair was access for the dark," Jacen said.

Leia shook her head. "Jaina's learned about the dark now," she said. "She's been there, and I can't believe she'd go again. What I fear now is that she'll set herself one impossible task after another until she breaks."

Jacen looked at his mother. "No one in the family's like *that*, I'm sure."

She laughed. "Of all the things Jaina could have inherited from me, she had to pick my work ethic." She reached out and took Jacen's hand. "Jaina's tough, you know. She'll get through this—and it will help that she has one less brother to mourn."

Jacen tried to smile. "At least I've given her that," he said.

Four days into his term of office, Cal Omas summoned Admiral Ackbar and Winter to the former resort hotel that now housed the executive branch of government. The meeting was small; the only other guests were Luke, Ayddar Nylykerka of Fleet Intelligence, New Republic Intelligence chief Dif Scaur, and Supreme Commander Sien Sovv.

YVH droids patrolled the corridor outside. Scaur's people had thoroughly swept the room for listening devices, and so had Nylykerka's, who sneaked in later without Scaur's knowledge. The room was small, with no viewports; a small white marble table, scalloped like a seashell, held indentations for each of the guests. On one wall, a little fountain tinkled and chimed, emitting a mild scent of brine.

Ackbar wore his old uniform. His skin was gray and his hands trembled, and Winter had to help him to his feet as Cal entered the room. But his voice was firm as he congratulated Cal on his appointment, with none of the slurring that Luke had heard before.

"I would like to thank you all for agreeing to meet with me," Ackbar said. "I know that you're all very busy trying to put the new government together."

"We're never too busy to meet with one of the greatest heroes of the Rebellion," Cal Omas said. "You were my commander for many years, so please don't think I'm going to start pulling rank on you now."

"It was Borsk Fey'lya who insisted on your retirement," Sien Sovv said. "Please understand that no one in the Defense Force wished you to go—and least of all myself."

"That's very kind," Ackbar said. His trembling hands keyed a datapad on the table before him. "Though the retirement was welcome in one sense. I now possess a great deal of time to think. And I have been thinking a great deal about the Yuuzhan Vong, the greatest menace to the security of the galaxy since Palpatine." He splayed his huge hands on the marble table. "My speculations aren't completely uninformed because I have . . . friends . . . within the government who have provided data." He looked up at the others. "Nothing secret has come my way, but some analyses have found their way to me."

Luke glanced into the polished tabletop and viewed the reflections of Nylykerka and Dif Scaur, both of whom were being careful to maintain innocent expressions. Admiral Sovv's jowled face was likewise bland.

"And of course I've been in the service a great many years, all at the highest level," Ackbar continued. "And I understand how the service works. Even the service under

Borsk Fey'lya." He nodded his huge head. "So let's open the survey with our military.

"We are growing stronger," he began. "When the war started, contracts were awarded in order to increase in our force strength. More capital ships, more fighters, more transports, larger ground forces. The shipyards at Kuat, Talaan, Corellia, and here at Mon Calamari have been disrupted by the war but not fatally injured, and now they are delivering new capital ships, while many contractors dispersed throughout friendly space are delivering large numbers of smaller craft."

It took a while, Luke knew. First you built droids. And then the droids built a factory—not for warships, but for more droids. Then the first set of droids, plus the new droids built by the factory, built *another* factory, and that built ships, while the *first* factory continued to build new droids to build new factories to build new droids to build new factories to build ships. You could keep going forever building new factories, new droids, and new ships, provided supplies weren't interrupted and someone was willing to pay for it all. Once the cascade started, it just kept growing, and the only way to stop it was to destroy *all* the factories, ships, and droids, because if *just one droid* survived, that droid could start the cascade all over again, by building another droid.

What this meant was that new ships were coming into service, and they'd *keep* coming, in geometrically increasing numbers as the largely droid workforce brought new factories on-line.

"We also have many new recruits," Ackbar went on. "Despite the efforts of the Peace Brigade and others favoring surrender to the Yuuzhan Vong, many idealistic citizens have volunteered for the military. Many of these have been drawn from refugee populations who prefer the hazards of battle to the tedium of refugee camps—and the refugees, who have seen their homeworlds destroyed or occupied, provide a highly motivated brand of recruit, who wish to win back their homes and take vengeance on the enemy. The bottleneck in making use of their volunteers hasn't so much been their numbers, but the necessity of building training camps in safe areas and staffing them with qualified instructors. But this has now been done."

Luke knew that building training camps and training recruits ran along the same lines as building ships and droids, except that military instructors couldn't be built as easily as droids, or turned out in a factory. Still, in addition to the instructors the military possessed at the beginning of the war, there were a great many veterans of the Rebellion who had returned to the colors, and were busy training the next generation in every tactic they knew.

"The drawback to so many new ships and personnel is that they are untried," Ackbar continued. "Successful actions against the Yuuzhan Vong have been few, so there is no standard fleet doctrine based on consistent success in battle. Now that New Republic research groups have succeeded in at least temporarily canceling the advantages given the Yuuzhan Vong by their—" He glanced at the datapad. "—their 'yammosks,' " his pink-whiskered lips working delicately at the alien word, "we may take greater risks with our new forces, but still we will be putting raw recruits up against seasoned enemy veterans, and in the normal course of events may expect to take heavy casualties.

"Our problems have been compounded by failures in intelligence," Ackbar continued. The two intelligence directors, Luke saw, received this judgment without surprise. "We were invaded by an unknown enemy of unknown force, of a species unknown to us, and impelled by unknown motives. We could not infiltrate them, we could not scout their homeworlds, we could not even speak their language. Even the famous and highly regarded Bothan secret services were able to accomplish nothing. Small wonder that we could not predict their actions. That lack has, to a degree, been remedied, with better knowledge of the enemy and with agents now in place on enemy worlds.

"So much for our capabilities." Ackbar paused, and one large hand loosened his collar. "I should like to continue with an analysis of the enemy."

He paused, perhaps waiting for a question, then went on. "The Yuuzhan Vong invasion of our galaxy has a religious justification," he said. "Perhaps the leadership cynically uses religion to camouflage other, less noble reasons for the assault, but there is no doubt that most Yuuzhan Vong sincerely believe that their gods have given our worlds to them. Because they have no doubts on this score, they form a highly motivated, dedicated, tenacious, and ideologically unified corps of invaders. While the experience of Jacen and Anakin Solo suggests that the Yuuzhan Vong have divisions among themselves, and disagreements among their leadership, they nevertheless present a united front to all outsiders. Our attempts to divide or corrupt them have been fruitless. As far as I know—and my knowledge on this score is necessarily incomplete—we have been unable to turn a single Yuuzhan Vong into an informer or spy. While it is possible that Yuuzhan Vong religious faith and ideology may weaken as a result of contact with us, with occasional defeats, and with a galaxy more complex than their ideas can sustain, we can't count on being able to divide one group of Yuuzhan Vong from another as a means to our victory."

While Ackbar spoke, Winter quietly rose from her place, walked to the tinkling fountain set in the wall, and soaked a handkerchief in seawater. She returned to Ackbar and efficiently swept moisture onto Ackbar's graying skin.

Dif Scaur gave a ferocious sneeze. Ackbar paused for a moment, then continued. "The enemy's greatest successes have been in the realm of intelligence. The galaxy was thoroughly scouted before the first attack. Spies and informers were placed or recruited throughout all target areas. Our government was penetrated at its highest levels. Agents such as Nom Anor had stirred civil conflict that distracted us from the real threat of invasion. Enemy agents, puppets, and collaborators were able to keep us thoroughly off balance throughout the critical early months of the assault. Even now we have no certain knowledge that our most closely guarded secrets are not in the possession of the enemy. The knowledge that the Yuuzhan Vong may be fully aware of our movements has paralyzed our leadership, and tended to make them overly cautious."

Luke glanced at Sien Sovv. His heavy-jowled face was expressionless, but Luke sensed no resentment of this analysis in the Sullustan.

"Material losses are irrelevant to the Yuuzhan Vong," Ackbar continued. "Apparently their ships are grown and harvested like interstellar fruit. They can have as many warships as they can find Vong, and Vong collaborators, to crew them.

"And as for crews," Ackbar said, "I have on my datapad some estimates of initial Yuuzhan Vong strength, and their casualties thus far in the war. These are approximations, since we really don't know the strength of any extragalactic reserves, nor do we have anything but estimates of Yuuzhan Vong casualties, and these may be exaggerated." He cleared his throat. "They often are. You may view these figures, if you like, on your own datapads—I am prepared to send them to you."

Luke took out his datapad and set it to receive. Figures shimmered across its screens. Estimated total population, percentage of population estimated to consist of the warrior caste, an estimate of the number of casualties inflicted by New Republic forces—almost all members of the warrior caste—casualties reflected as percentage of total warrior caste.

Luke looked at Ackbar in astonishment. "We've killed almost a third of their warriors?" he asked.

"So these figures imply," Ackbar said.

"They're very approximate," Cal Omas pointed out.

"They're the best we have," Ackbar said. "I don't think they're far wrong."

"Our figures at New Republic Intelligence imply much the same thing," Dif Scaur said. Luke was always surprised that someone as pale and thin as Scaur had such a strong voice.

"The Vong lost an entire battle group at Obroa-skai," Nylykerka put in. "They failed at Hapes. And Yuuzhan Vong casualties at Fondor and Coruscant were heavy, even though both were victories for the Vong."

"They cannot afford many more such victories," Scaur said.

"*If* these figures are correct," Cal said. "I don't want to throw our fleets at the enemy on the basis of guesswork."

"There are ways of testing whether the figures are correct," Ackbar said. "If the Yuuzhan Vong stage another large offensive against a major target in the next two months, we'll know that they have warriors to spare. If instead they consolidate their gains, we'll know that their losses have taught them caution."

Ayddar Nylykerka and Sien Sovv looked at each other uneasily. The thought of a massive attack on Corellia, Mon Calamari, or other important targets was never far from their thoughts.

"The Yuuzhan Vong warriors are brave," Ackbar went on. "They are aggressive, they obey orders without hesitation, fight to the death, retreat reluctantly or never, and never surrender." He drew a long breath, and sighed it out.

"Considering their other advantages, it is lucky for us that they possess these weaknesses."

Luke stared at Ackbar. *Of course.* Why hadn't he realized this before?

"Weaknesses!" Scaur's astonished cry filled the air. "You call these *weaknesses*?"

"Of course," Ackbar said simply. "We can *count* on the enemy to have these traits. That means they are predictable. And while each of these traits may be admirable in itself, together they add up to *massive and systematic weaknesses*!"

He held up one giant hand. "Consider," he said. "Bravery and aggression result in foolhardy courage, and in any case are useful only with adequate direction. Unthinking obedience means a lack of flexibility. To fight to the death, and never to surrender, is to deny oneself useful alternatives. Together, we can use these Yuuzhan Vong traits to draw the enemy into a trap from which he will never escape."

Ackbar extended a single finger as far as the hand's webbing would permit. "Foolhardy courage will bring the Yuuzhan Vong into the trap." He held out a second finger. "Unthinking obedience means that Vong subordinates won't dare to question their superiors even if they have doubts." A third finger. "Unthinking obedience also means that warriors can't exercise initiative and will continue to follow their superiors' plans even after a fluid combat situation has made them irrelevant. They won't change their plans without their superiors' permission, even if their superiors are out of touch or have an unrealistic idea of the situation."

Ackbar held up a fourth finger. "Because the Yuuzhan Vong consider death inevitable and never seek to prolong their lives, they will continue to fight on even in a hopeless cause. Their superiors' courage and belief in their cause will make them reluctant to order a retreat until it's too late. These facts together, my friends, form a weapon with which we will *destroy the Vong!*" He closed his hand into a fist and smashed it on the table. Cal Omas jumped.

"A trap," Luke said, "implies bait."

Ackbar gasped agreement as Winter moistened his forehead. "And the bait must be real. It must be something for which the Yuuzhan Vong will commit all their available strength."

"And what is that?" Cal asked.

"*Us*, I suppose," Dif Scaur said, looking about the table. "The government." His eyes, in their hollow sockets, turned to Ackbar. "What sort of timing are you considering? When should this trap be set?"

"At the moment we have a great advantage," Ackbar said. "We can defeat their—their 'yammosks'; we can confuse their communications and cause them to fire at one another. We don't know if these advantages will last for long, so we should seek a decisive battle very soon."

"But most of our forces are inexperienced," Sien Sovv said quickly. "You have said this yourself. Dare we fight a decisive battle with so many raw troops?"

"No," Ackbar said. "We daren't. Our forces must be seasoned in battle before we attempt a major engagement."

"How do we season them *without* a major engagement?" Dif Scaur asked.

"Through many *small* engagements," Ackbar said. "The Yuuzhan Vong now have the same disadvantage that we had at the beginning—they have too many worlds to defend. Too many trade lanes. Too many resources. We should let the fleet loose on these targets—on *all* of them." He held up a hand. "But we should never attack where we know the Yuuzhan Vong to be strong. Never engage where we do not possess an advantage. Our military must be seasoned, but seasoned only in victory. Through one success after another, they will learn to trust their commanders, and will grow in confidence to the point where they expect *only* victory." His huge pop eyes turned toward Admiral Sovv. "You must give your commanders a great deal of initiative in choosing their targets. You must give them permission to take risks, and occasionally to fail. Raid, skirmish, pounce on isolated detachments. Disrupt lines of communication, isolate enemy worlds from one another, establish hidden bases from which you can mount raids. But you must never engage the enemy where he is strong. Only where he is weak."

"The Rebellion all over again," Cal Omas said. "That's how we fought the Empire for the first years."

"That's correct."

"But when we fought the Empire," Cal continued, "we didn't have so many places to defend. Our government was small and able to move to places like Yavin or Hoth. We didn't have millions of refugees to feed and resettle, or hundreds of Senators demanding special protection for their worlds."

"We must defend only those places that are vital to the war," Ackbar said. "They must be defended, as we defended Coruscant and Borleias, to the point where even a victory would cost the enemy too much."

"And what places are those?" Cal asked.

"Places where the new fleet elements are coming into being. Mon Calamari. Kuat. Corellia." Ackbar sighed again. "That's all."

"That's *all*?" Cal said.

"Anything else"—Ackbar waved a hand—"give away when the enemy attacks. It will stretch Yuuzhan Vong resources and make them weaker everywhere else."

"And the refugees?" Luke asked. "Those huge convoys that we've tried to protect? Those millions of people we've had to resettle?"

Ackbar turned to Luke. His eyes were cold. "We must not defend these huge targets. Tying our forces to them only makes us weak."

Luke felt a chill settle into his spine. "I've sworn to defend the weak," he said.

"Who is weak?" Ackbar asked. "*We* are weak. The government. The military. While *we* are weak, the enemy thrives and the refugees are doomed no matter what we do. Once *we* are strong, the enemy will have more important things to do than to attack convoys."

Luke turned away. "I understand," he said, but all his instincts warred against Ackbar's bitter logic.

Dif Scaur put his thin, knobby-jointed hands on the table. His skin was so pale that the hands seemed to fade into the white marble.

"I ask again for your timetable," he said. "You propose to put our untried forces into a kind of live-fire exercise against a real enemy in order to season them. How long before you think the fleet will be ready for a major action, or for this decisive battle your plan calls for?"

Ackbar's response was swift. "Three months," he said. "Three months of continuous low-level engagement with the enemy should give us a battle-tested force able to hold their own against the Yuuzhan Vong."

"Three months . . ." A cold smile played about Scaur's cadaverous face. "The timing is expedient."

The timing for *what*? Luke wondered. There was something highly significant about that three months, but Luke and Ackbar were two, at least, who weren't meant to know what it was.

Ackbar slumped into his chair. Presenting the plan had exhausted him, and now that he was finished he permitted himself to show that exhaustion. Winter stroked more brine onto his head. "I only regret that my health doesn't permit me to serve the New Republic in a more active way," Ackbar said.

"Your contribution has always been fundamental," Cal said. "I can only wish myself and these others as useful a retirement as yours has been." He turned to Sien Sovv. "Admiral, do you have any comments on Admiral Ackbar's plan?"

"Other than to admire it, no," Sovv said. "I'm ready to put the plan into action immediately, or I can resign in favor of Admiral Ackbar and he can carry out his proposals without any interference from me."

Ackbar waved a weary hand. "No, my friend. I'm not in condition to command the Defense Force, and everyone here knows it."

Cal gave Ackbar a thoughtful look. "Can you take a consultative role?" he asked. "We can invent a title for you—'Fleet Director of Strategy' or some such."

The glabrous head nodded. "I'm willing to perform this task to the best of my powers."

"His powers are very limited at present," Winter said. These were the first words she'd spoken since the meeting had begun, and they were in tones of quiet admonishment, like a governess bringing her charge under control. She looked at Cal Omas. "It won't be possible for the admiral to be kept on a schedule, running to meetings and inspecting fleet units."

Ackbar waved a hand in protest, but Winter was firm. "No. None of that. And no parades of visitors asking for advice or campaigning for promotion, either." She looked at Admiral Sovv. "Some reliable staff officers would be useful, to do the paperwork and take care of communications. But we can't have meetings like this all the time."

"We won't." Cal's voice was firm. "If I need to speak to the admiral again, I'll call for an appointment, and I'll visit him myself." He looked at Sovv. "You'll make the other arrangements?"

The Sullustan nodded. "I will."

Cal turned to Luke. "Is there any way the Jedi can aid this plan?"

Luke hesitated. "I'd like to suggest that we place the matter on the agenda of the first Jedi Council meeting."

"Very well." Cal looked at the two intelligence directors, Scaur in his civilian suit and Nylykerka in his military uniform. "Any other comments?"

"I work for Admiral Sovv," Nylykerka said. "At his direction, we can assist in formulating assessments of enemy strength and suggest possible targets."

Dif Scaur nodded his long head at Cal. "We can do much the same, of course, at the direction of the Chief of State."

Luke detected the very slightest degree of condescension in Scaur's tone, as if he were humoring the others in the room with a show of cooperation, and again he wondered what it was that Scaur knew that he didn't. It was almost as though Scaur thought that Ackbar's plan was irrelevant somehow, but he was willing to pretend it mattered. He had been very careful to question Ackbar concerning exactly when his plan for trapping and destroying the Yuuzhan Vong would become operational, and had been satisfied when he'd learned it would take three months.

What was going to happen within three months that would change Ackbar's plans? Did Scaur have some other plan that would win the war? Or—a chill wafted up Luke's neck—did Scaur know that the *enemy* would render Ackbar's plan ineffective, perhaps by staging a unstoppable offensive within the three-month period?

Luke would have to watch Dif Scaur very carefully, he thought. Perhaps, very quietly, Mara should watch him, too.

Two hours after the end of the meeting, the signal ACK-BAR IS BACK was broadcast to all New Republic military units.

In some of the larger ships, the cheering went on for an hour.

TWENTY

"I would like to welcome everyone," Luke said, "to this first meeting of the—" He hesitated, then looked to Cal Omas. "What is it, anyway? We're not the Jedi Council, with half of us not being Jedi."

Cal hesitated, too. "Let's just call it the High Council, for now," he said.

It wasn't the most auspicious of beginnings. The hotel room that had been given to the council was oddly shaped and, like many of the rooms requisitioned by the hastily formed government, smelled of fresh paint. The oval table, shiny mother-of-pearl from a huge seashell, was too large for the room, and there was crowding at either end of the table.

At the table's thick waist, Luke faced Cal Omas. It would have seemed too suggestive of division to have all the Jedi at one side of the table facing the non-Jedi, almost as if he were asking the council to split into two parties right from the beginning, so he'd alternated Jedi with others along the table's circumference.

To Luke's right was the Wookiee Senator Triebakk, large and hairy and snarling with vigor. To the right of Triebakk sat the Jedi healer Cilghal, her protuberant Mon Calamari eyes able to scan the entire room. At the end of the table was Intelligence Director Dif Scaur, whose thin human frame withstood the crowding at the table better than most.

To Scaur's right sat Kenth Hamner, a human Jedi retired from the military, who sat rigidly upright and wore his well-tailored civilian suit as if it were a uniform. To Hamner's right was the soft-spoken Ta'laam Ranth, the Gotal Senator whose support had given Cal his majority in the Senate, and who had demanded a seat on the council as a reward for his loyalty.

To Ta'laam's right was Cal, and to Cal's right was Kyp Durron. At the moment Kyp looked uncomfortable: he and his squadron had been ordered to Mon Calamari on very short notice, and no sooner had he arrived than he'd been told he'd become a council member and taken to the first meeting. He had been on the planet for less than three hours, and his disorientation showed.

To Kyp's right was the golden-furred Minister of State, Releqy A'Kla, daughter of the late Elegos A'Kla, the Caamasi Senator who had been ritually sacrificed by the Yuuzhan Vong on Dubrillion. Releqy had absorbed many of her father's memories through the Caamasi memnii and possessed the knowledge, demeanor, and political skill of someone years older than her chronological age.

To Releqy's right, at the cramped far end of the table, sat the erect figure of Saba Sebatyne, who regarded the others with bright, intent reptilian eyes. She was used to hunting Yuuzhan Vong with packs of other Barabels, and Luke hoped she would come to regard the Jedi Council as a pack of a different order.

To Saba's right was Sien Sovv, the Supreme Commander, and between Sovv and Luke bulked the wrinkled gray frame of the Chev Jedi Knight Tresina Lobi, whose long snout was partly unrolled on the surface of the table.

To these was added C-3PO, whom Luke had borrowed from Leia in order to act as secretary, transcriber of the minutes, and (if necessary) translator. The droid stood out of the way in the corner and regarded the meeting with his glowing gold eyes.

Luke looked at the datapad and the notes he'd made to himself about the meeting. "I'd like to start the meeting by finding out if any committee members have anything to bring before the council."

Cal Omas cleared his throat. "This is a momentous occasion, Master Skywalker. And you're not going to make a speech?"

"I hadn't been planning one," Luke said. "But if I know Jedi, I think I can promise you speeches in plenty as the meeting goes on." And then he looked at Cal and said, "Would *you* like to make a speech?"

"My throat's a bit tired from the speeches I *have* been making," Cal said. "But I can give you some of the applause lines from my acceptance speech—some of them were real corkers."

"I think we all heard that speech the first time." Luke smiled.

"I'd like to think so," Cal said. He waved a hand. "Never mind, then—sorry for the interruption."

Luke looked at the others. "Does anyone wish to offer a report?"

"Master Skywalker." Kyp raised a hand.

"Master Durron?"

Kyp's discomfort showed plainly on his face. "Can you explain to me why I'm here?"

Saba Sebatyne gave a brief hiss of amusement.

"What do you mean?" Luke replied.

Kyp twisted in his seat. "I'm not sure that I belong on the council. Not really. I've been a lot of trouble to you, and I hardly think I've earned a place here."

"While that may be true," Luke said, "that doesn't mean you haven't earned a seat. You're one of our most experienced Jedi, particularly in fighting the Yuuzhan Vong. No one questions your dedication or your talent or your mastery of the Force. You've always supported the formation of a Jedi Council."

"I surrendered pride on Ithor," Kyp said. "And while I haven't always lived up to that vow, I've tried my best. I disbanded the Dozen and placed myself under Jaina Solo's command, and though I ended up re-forming the Dozen at Admiral Kre'fey's request, I've been trying to keep my head down and do my job and keep out of the kind of trouble I seem to get into. And now——" He struggled for words. "—now you've put me on the governing body of the Jedi. That's a temptation to the pride I've renounced. I think I might be happier flying at the head of my squadron."

"The happiness of one iz not the issue," Saba hissed. "The issue iz where one may best zerve."

"I think your voice on the council is necessary, and welcome," Luke told Kyp. "Though I won't keep you here if you insist on resigning."

Kyp was exasperated. "I don't want to go against your wishes yet *again*, Master Skywalker."

"In that case, stay."

"Besides," Cal Omas said, "if you're worried about your overweening pride, I think everyone here can work out ways to keep you humble."

Even Kyp laughed at this. He waved a hand. "As you wish, Master Skywalker. But I hope I won't make you regret this."

So do we all, Luke thought.

"Since you asked for news," Kyp went on, "I have information from Kashyyyk, from Lowbacca and the team of Wookiees who are investigating Yuuzhan Vong biotechnology."

"Go ahead," Luke said, and was aware of Triebakk, on his right, leaning forward with great interest.

"They've been working with the dovin basals from the captured frigate *Trickster*," Kyp said. "They're now able to use our own interdiction technology to duplicate the effects of dovin basal space mines. Since the war began, the Vong have used their mines to yank our ships out of hyperspace and ambush them with fighter craft, and now it looks as if we'll be able to do the same to them."

"Wonderful!" C-3PO said, translating for Triebakk. "Well done!"

Sien Sovv was pleased. "Splendid. That will fit in well with Admiral Ackbar's plan."

"Perhaps Admiral Sovv should explain Ackbar's plan for those of us who haven't heard it," Cal said.

"Perhaps only the *first* part," Dif Scaur cautioned. "The plan's ... ultimate objective ... is perhaps beyond the scope of this meeting."

In other words, Luke thought, *let's not tell too many people that Ackbar hopes to lure the Yuuzhan Vong into a trap. If only a few people knew, maybe the Vong could actually be surprised.*

Luke had been watching Dif Scaur with care, through the Force as well as visually. He still wasn't certain how much he trusted Scaur. In this case, however, he sensed only a genuine concern for keeping Ackbar's ultimate goals secret.

Sovv obliged Scaur by explaining Ackbar's plan to season the Republic's raw recruits through a series of skirmishes and small engagements rather than risking a large battle. "Admiral Kre'fey," he finished, "has requested as many Jedi pilots as possible. He hopes to merge many elements of his fleet into what he calls the 'Jedi meld,' so that all may maneuver together as one. He reports that he's had limited success with this tactic at Obroa-skai, but needs more Jedi to make it more effective."

"I've also received a message from Kre'fey requesting Jedi," Luke said. "I have no objection to sending any who wish to go."

"I hope the council can see its way to helping Kre'fey,"

Cal said. "The military's reeling and needs all the help we can give. They're on their heels with one defeat after another, they rightly blame the political leadership, and some are on the verge of mutiny. I'd really hate to have to give an order to Garm Bel Iblis right now—who knows what kind of answer I'd get? If the Defense Forces don't think we're going to stand behind them, I'd hate to think what might happen."

Kyp cleared his throat and half-heartedly raised a hand. "Yes?" Luke said.

"I'm sorry to have to say this after everything the president has just said, but we may have a potential problem with Admiral Kre'fey. He's a good commander, I guess. But the Bothan clans have—well, they've declared genocide against the Vong, and Kre'fey's taken it to heart. It's called ar'krai. I don't think I want the council to declare its support for mass murder, even the mass murder of Yuuzhan Vong."

Luke turned to Cal Omas. "Cal, have you heard of this?"

Cal shook his head. "If the Bothan government has made any such declaration, they certainly haven't informed *me*."

"Speak to Admiral Kre'fey," Kyp said. "He's a happy warrior these days—I'm sure he'd be glad to explain it to you."

Dif Scaur's pale, skeletal fingers fingered his jaw. Cold intelligence worked behind his deep-set eyes, and Luke sensed that he found this development highly intriguing. "Bothans are rather secretive," he said. "It's possible that they consider this a private decision."

"A private decision with galactic consequences," Cal said. He seemed unsettled and angry. "It's not the Bothans' decision, anyway, blast it."

"What do we do with Admiral Kre'fey's request?" Kenth Hamner asked.

"He already has Jedi serving under him," Tresina Lobi said. "Including Master Durron. What is his opinion?"

Kyp hesitated, then shrugged. "He's an effective commander—not a genius like Ackbar or a master of tactics like Wedge Antilles, but a problem solver and dedicated to victory. Ar'krai is a new policy. I don't know what he plans to do, but I know that I'm worried."

From the Gotal Senator Ta'laam Ranth, Luke sensed a wave of wry amusement. Gotals were thought unemotional and hyperlogical by those who could not detect the emotions radiating from the twin cones on their heads. Though Luke wasn't as good at reading Ta'laam as another Gotal would be, he nevertheless received an indication of the Senator's disposition through the Force.

"Kre'fey may wish to eliminate the Vong," Ta'laam said. "I may wish to eliminate the Vong. Most of the people in this galaxy doubtless wish to eliminate the Vong. But may I remind the council that neither Kre'fey nor anyone else can do it. We are losing the war. The issue isn't whether we destroy the Yuuzhan Vong, the issue is whether *they* destroy *us*." His scarlet eyes glimmered in their deep sockets. "Moral conundrums make an entertaining mental exercise, but I suggest we keep this discussion within the realm of the possible."

"I agree," Scaur said. He had been watching Ta'laam narrowly, and Luke sensed that he was agreeing, not because he cared about the Senator's position, but for secret reasons of his own.

Luke wished he knew what these reasons were.

Releqy nodded her golden head in agreement with Scaur and Ta'laam. "Perhaps that is best," she said.

"Very well," Luke said. "The issue is whether we should send Jedi to Admiral Kre'fey."

Saba Sebatyne put an elegant, scaled hand onto the table. "I and my kindred are highly experienced in the kind of

Force-melding that Admiral Kre'fey desirez for hiz Jedi. Perhapz I should point out something that otherz may not have realized. If Kre'fey succeedz in building this meld in his forcez, it will not be Kre'fey who commandz his fleet, it will be *ussss*."

The last sibilant hiss floated down the table to Saba's startled audience. Triebakk, vastly amused, gave an untranslatable roar.

"The fleet will be conditioned to obey the orderz of the Jedi," Saba went on. "They will fight at our direction and under our leadership. Should Kre'fey attempt any sort of—shall we call them illegal actionz?—he will need both our permission and cooperation. It would be within our power to withhold them."

The others watched the Barabel for a long, silent moment. Then Luke said, "I think we should send Jedi."

Kyp raised a hand in halfhearted protest, then dropped it. "Very well. But they should be warned about the Bothans' declaring ar'krai."

"Agreed. And while training with this meld, they should consider what to do if the meld is ever misused."

"Master Skywalker," Cilghal said. "You have throughout the war warned us of the dangers of aggression. But now you send Jedi to war under a commander who will use them aggressively. Have you changed your mind?"

Cilghal had been watching him with those bulging eyes, Luke thought, and had sensed his mind within the Force. She was never less than acute. "I have changed my policy, yes," he answered.

At once he had Kyp Durron's full attention. "How?" Kyp asked.

"I'm willing to give my blessing to those Jedi who wish to act offensively against the Yuuzhan Vong, provided that they confine their objectives to military ones."

Kyp's eyes flashed. "You could have saved us both a lot of grief if you'd told us that a couple of years ago!" He waved his arms. "For *years* you've been warning me about aggression leading to the dark side! I didn't listen, and over and over and over again *reality whacked me on the side of the head!* Finally I decided you were *right!* I watched someone else go to the dark and it was *worse than I could have imagined!*" He pointed a finger at Luke. "You finally convinced me! I've been a *good little Jedi* for—for *months* now! I've been telling everyone who would listen that Master Skywalker's been right all along! And now you tell me that you've *changed your mind?*"

Now *this* was the Kyp that Luke knew.

"How dare you?" Kyp demanded. *"How dare you?"*

It was all Luke could do to keep from laughing out loud.

"At the beginning of the war I didn't have the same information that I have now," Luke said. "Perhaps you did, however."

"What information?" Kyp crossed his arms and glared at Luke with grudging patience.

"At the beginning I was deeply disturbed by the fact the Yuuzhan Vong couldn't be found in the Force. It seemed to me that they might be a mockery of the Force, a deliberate profanation of life, and that I would be destined to lead a dark crusade against them." He looked along the table, meeting every pair of eyes. "It would have been a dreadful thing," he said. "So many Jedi would have turned against the light in a war like that. I might not have been able to resist the darkness myself."

"What changed your mind?" Kyp's gaze was wary.

"New information." Luke looked up. "From Jacen Solo, and from Vergere. It's now possible to understand that the Yuuzhan Vong aren't some exception to the rules of creation. If we can't see them in the Force, it's our fault, not theirs. We can fight them without wanting to wipe them from existence. We can fight them without hate, and without darkness."

Luke looked across the table at Kyp. "If you knew this two years ago, I apologize for doubting you. But in the meantime I'm not sorry that I was cautious."

"I couldn't have known any of that," Kyp said. "You *know* I couldn't have known it."

"There was so much at stake. I didn't want anyone to turn to the dark side because I misread the situation."

"*You* . . ." Kyp accused, pointing. "*You* . . ." He banged his hand on the table in frustration and looked at the others. "Am I the only one here who simply wants to punch Master Skywalker in the nose?"

Again Luke concealed laughter, and he sensed that he wasn't the only one. Cal Omas looked from Luke to Kyp and grinned. "I won't throw any punches," he said, "but I'm willing to be entertained."

Kyp threw up his hands in frustration. "I think Skywalker does this for his own entertainment!"

"If you want the practical argument, Kyp," Luke said, "the Chief of State has now given us his full support and made a place for the Jedi in the government. It seems only polite to support the government that is supporting us."

"That's all very well," Kyp said. "But your warnings about aggression weren't without foundation. It's still possible for the darkness to take our people. I know. I've been there." He looked at Luke, pain in his eyes. "And very recently I've watched it happen to someone else."

Now you know what it's like, Luke thought. He had watched Kyp fall into darkness without being able to stop him. Now Kyp understood, when Jaina let the dark take her, what it was to feel that helplessness.

"The Jedi Code is made confusing by the fact that *aggression* is never defined," Luke said. "So I'm going to define it right now. Aggression is making an unprovoked attack, or taking something that doesn't belong to you, or aiding someone else in doing one of these things."

Kyp nodded thoughtfully. "That definition could have prevented a lot of misunderstanding between the two of us."

"It could have," Luke said. "I'm sorry for that."

"The dangers are still very real," Kyp said. "They'll become even more real when we start sending our people into combat."

Luke shook his head. "We have to trust them. They're Jedi. We trained them."

Let them all go, he thought. Vergere had shown him what he knew: he needed to trust that his training and his example would bring the Jedi through this crisis. *Let them all go.*

"There iz no great danger with the meld," Saba said. The others were startled by her complete certainty. "All Jedi together, and of one mind? Should one fall into darknessss, otherz would draw her back to the light."

Luke hoped this was true. "We have to trust the Jedi and their training," he said. "We've given all the warnings we can. The meld is another tool we can try to use."

"What about the Great River?" Cilghal asked. She seemed in genuine distress. "We have painfully set up this conduit for refugees, agents, and information. Are we all to engage in warfare now, and let the Great River dry up at its source?"

"Of course not," Luke said. "Each Jedi must decide how he or she wishes to help defeat the Yuuzhan Vong. And unless there's some pressing need, I intend myself to continue my work with the Great River."

Cilghal seemed reassured. Luke turned to Cal. "Have you had enough speeches for today?"

"It's been enlightening." Cal looked around the table. "Somehow I expected that Jedi would have more certainty and less discussion."

"I always hope for that," Luke said. "I hardly ever get it."

Other members of the council made reports concerning the Great River or other projects. Dif Scaur made a brief presentation concerning what he understood of current Yuuzhan Vong goals, and Triebakk spoke about the Senate, which seemed alarmed with itself at its boldness in electing Cal as Chief of State, but was otherwise fairly quiet.

"Is that all, then?" Luke asked.

Tresina rolled up her snout to allow herself to speak without being muffled. "I'd like to ask about the Jedi apprentices just arrived, with a refugee convoy, here on Mon Calamari," she said. "They have no Masters or current duties. What are we to do with them? Send them to—" She hesitated, on the verge of letting a secret slip. "—to join the other apprentices at the hidden academy?"

"Who are we talking about?" asked Cilghal.

"Zekk and Tahiri Veila."

"All were with my son Tesar on the strike at Myrkr," Saba said.

All watched Anakin die, Luke thought.

"They're being looked after by Alema Rar," Tresina said. "But Alema doesn't feel ready to take an apprentice, let alone two of them, so she's asked me to query the council."

Alema was right, Luke thought. Alema had lost her sister Jedi Knight horribly to a voxyn, and was very vulnerable even before the Myrkr strike, probably too vulnerable to spend her days looking after apprentices who had problems of their own.

"They're all warriors, then," Kenth Hamner said. "Veterans. They'll all be needed." He turned to Luke. "Perhaps we should promote them to Jedi Knight? Then they can decide for themselves where they'll be most useful."

Luke hesitated, then spoke. "Tahiri is very young, not even sixteen. And she was a . . . special friend . . . to Anakin. I don't know if she's gotten over his death." He shook his head. "Knighting her and sending her against the Yu-uzhan Vong might be sending her straight to the dark side."

"Send them to Kashyyyk," Saba said. "Send them to Tesar, and to the meld. Send Alema Rar az well. The Force-meld will save them from the dark side." Her yellow eyes flicked over the group. "Just az melding with the Barabelz saved me, when Tesar's hatchmatez Krasov and Bela were lost."

Saba's sincerity was convincing. Luke nodded. "Very well."

"There are other apprentices who were with Anakin's strike force," Kenth reminded. "Jaina, Jacen, and Low-bacca, and of course Cilghal's apprentice Tekli. Shouldn't we promote them as well?"

Luke felt embarrassment that he hadn't realized this him-self. "Of course."

"Don't forget Tenel Ka," Kyp added.

Cal's eyes lit up. "They'll be the first Jedi Knights of the new order," he said. "Shouldn't you do something special when you knight them? A ceremony, or—?"

"The Jedi have never engaged much in ceremony," Kyp said. "Jedi *do*. Jedi don't playact."

Luke laughed. "Do you want to make a speech so badly, Cal? There's never been any ceremony in the past."

Cal flushed a little, but said, "Why not have one? They're heroes, and people should know it. Bring them all here and I'll pin medals on them and talk until their ears turn blue."

"Tesar and Lowbacca are on Kashyyyk," Tresina reminded.

"They're in the military, aren't they?" Cal said. "Jaina's squadron? Reassign the squadron to Mon Calamari."

"Sir." Sien Sovv spoke tactfully. "Admiral Kre'fey will hardly appreciate losing three Jedi just when he's asked us to send more."

"Then tell him he'll get more!" Cal said. "Tell him that he'll send us apprentices, but he'll get Jedi Knights in return!"

"Tenel Ka has *already* been promoted," Releqy pointed

out. "To Queen Mother, in fact. I don't know if we can persuade the Hapans to let her go just because we want to hold a ceremony."

Cal's enthusiasm was undimmed. "Why should the Hapans object if we want to honor their queen? Besides, I'm sure she'll want to be present when her friends are knighted."

Luke found himself grinning at Cal's zeal. Perhaps a ceremony *was* in order, just to show everyone—the Jedi not least of all—that things had changed. That the Jedi now had a place in the galaxy, and were in the forefront of the struggle against the Yuuzhan Vong.

Champions again of the New Republic, and of the billions of lives for which it fought.

". . . the brilliant leadership of Anakin Solo." Cal's voice, unusually formal and ringing and solemn, filled the darkened auditorium. "As we honor these young warriors, let us never forget the others who shared their mission but never returned. Ulaha Kore. Eryl Besa. Jovan Drark. Raynar Thul. Bela and Krasov Hara. Ganner Rhysode, who returned from Myrkr only to die later, in defense of a comrade . . ."

As each name was called, an image of each Jedi was projected above the stage, floating as a kind of ghostly presence. In the orchestra pit before the stage, drums thudded out slowly, like a heart beating its last.

". . . and their leader, Anakin Solo."

Anakin's image appeared. Luke, standing at stage right with the rest of the High Council, looked up at the grinning, boyish face and felt a lump rising in his throat.

It had been Cal who had planned the whole knighting ceremony. Luke had objected to its theatrics but had been overruled. "Most people will never see a Jedi Knight in their whole lives," Cal had said. "I want them to see Jedi Knights *now*, and I want them to see the Jedi Knights doing something *meaningful*."

Cal had been right. The slow invocation of the dead was affective and moving.

Cal turned toward Luke. "Master Skywalker will now take the podium."

Cal left the podium and rejoined the High Council at stage right, his feet falling into the solemn rhythm of the drums. Luke, dressed simply in his Jedi robes, marched in the opposite direction and passed Cal along the way. Myrkr's dead floated overhead like stars in a lost constellation.

Luke reached the podium. The drums fell silent. Luke could sense the crowd before him—the auditorium was filled—but he couldn't hear them. The silence was profound.

Then a lone trumpet sounded three rising notes, the last held just an instant longer than the others. The notes were played again, in a different order, again the last held for the slightest bit longer than the others. And then the three notes repeated, again in a different order, again with the last drawn out. The sound was heartbreakingly pure, and somehow heartbreakingly sad.

The drums rattled once, then stilled. The trumpet repeated the three basic notes in varying order, then built on them and took flight, rising high and swooping low, but overall climbing higher and higher until the instrument finally sang out one last, high note that rang high and perfect and seemed to sing in the mind forever.

The images of the dead faded with the last echo of the trumpet.

Luke looked at the invisible audience. He wanted to be anonymous. He didn't want to be Luke Skywalker, hero and Jedi Master. He wanted it to seem as if any Jedi could be speaking these words.

"The roll call of the Jedi goes back for many millennia," he said.

Luke spoke of the first who had realized the existence of the Force, and who had discovered and used its vitality, and who—realizing their power and its dangers—had devised a code for its use. The first Jedi Knights, sworn to serve, not to rule. He spoke of those who had driven the menace of the Sith from the galaxy, and then guarded the Republic against all dangers until betrayed from within. He spoke of those new Jedi who had risen with the New Republic, and who even now were standing against the invading Yuuzhan Vong, a thin bright line of fiery lightsabers directed against the enemy.

"We are here to welcome nine new members into the order," Luke said. "Each has felt the Force grow within him or her. Each has felt the sting of combat and the pain of a comrade's loss. Each has searched his or her heart, and now stands ready to make the commitment to serve the New Republic for as long as life lasts."

Luke turned to the apprentices standing in their line at stage left. Each was dressed simply in a jacket, trousers, and boots.

"As I name you," Luke said, "may you step forward and be garbed in the robes of a Jedi Knight.

"Tenel Ka!"

The Queen of Sixty-Three Worlds, for good or ill, took formal precedence over the others. As the drums began a solemn march, she stepped from the line of apprentices and came to stand by the podium.

"Remove your lightsaber, please," Luke said. Two Jedi Masters, Kenth Hamner and Kyp Durron, stepped forward from the group of the Jedi Council carrying Tenel's new robe. They pulled the robe around her, then buckled her lightsaber over it.

Luke stepped away from the microphone. He hadn't told Cal that he was going to do this, but he wanted a part of the ceremony to be a private thing, for the Jedi alone.

He put his hands on Tenel's shoulders and looked at her closely.

"Yours is perhaps the most difficult task of all," he said. "The path of a queen is different from that of a Jedi. Your duty as queen of Hapes will inevitably come into conflict with the simpler values of the Jedi."

He looked into her shadowed gray eyes. "I don't tell you to choose one path over another. I only hope that you choose with your heart, and choose wisely."

Luke reached over Tenel's shoulders, took her cowl, and drew it over her head. Tenel Ka returned to her place. Luke stepped back to the podium.

"Tesar Sebatyne!"

The Barabel came forward, and it was his mother, Saba, assisted by Kenth Hamner, who clothed him in his robes.

Luke once again stepped away from the microphone. To Tesar he said, "The flame of a warrior burns bright in you, Tesar. You have shown that you will never falter or abandon a stricken comrade. May the Force guide you in all you do." Tesar, yellow eyes burning with pride, returned to his place in the line.

"Alema Rar!" Alema stepped from the rank of her comrades. Through the Force Luke could perceive her aura of sadness. While she was garbed by Tresina and Kyp, Luke considered the Twi'lek, what he knew of her savage childhood in the ryll dens and of the sister who had died in her arms, her flesh afire with the acid of a voxyn. Alema had also loved Anakin, and suffered at his loss. Luke touched her gently, careful not to contact the sensitive head-tails.

"Fate robbed you of your childhood, and your only family," he said. "Though the Jedi can't replace either, I hope you will look to us for the love and friendship we can give you, and the strength we can lend you in times of need. Now go to Kashyyyk, join your mind with the others, and heal."

As he raised Alema's cowl over her head, he saw tears glimmer in the Twi'lek's eyes.

"Lowbacca!"

The ginger-haired Wookiee towered over Luke and looked down at him with a fanged grin. Luke couldn't help but grin back.

"You're the one I've never doubted," he said. "Your path has never veered from the right, and you've shown that it never will."

Lowbacca had to bow deeply in order for Luke to reach high enough to draw the cowl over his head. A murmur of laughter ran through the audience.

"Jacen Solo!"

Jacen stepped out in silence, and Luke could sense his readiness in the Force. He took Jacen by the shoulders. The young man looked at him from his startlingly bearded face—he had trimmed the whiskers that had grown in captivity, but not gotten rid of them entirely. Luke could sense his utter openness. His honesty. All the Jedi virtues he had maintained despite the trials and terrors of the last few years.

"Jacen," Luke said. "Never stop asking questions."

Jacen seemed stunned. "I never thought I'd hear you say that!"

"I never thought I'd say it, either," Luke said, and hugged him.

Jacen returned to the line, radiating bemusement.

"Zekk!"

Zekk was robed by Kyp and by Luke himself. All were Jedi who knew darkness firsthand.

"Zekk," Luke said. "You are a Jedi who created himself in the image of the Jedi Knight you wanted to be. Once the Shadow Academy called you its Darkest Knight, but all the forces of darkness couldn't keep you from seeking the light. Now that you have found it, may you live always in its radiance."

Zekk returned to the line, his pride a brilliant fire in the Force.

"*Tahiri Veila!*"

On bare feet the little blond girl stepped forward, brave and pale in the darkness. She was another orphan whose childhood had been cut short. Another who had been captured and ill treated by the Yuuzhan Vong. Another who loved Anakin, and who had been loved in turn by him.

Cilghal and Saba robed her. Luke looked down into the small serious face, and touched her thin shoulders lightly.

"Life has torn much from you that you loved," he said, "but your courage has been equal to everything. Never forget that the Jedi will always be here for you. Never forget that the Force begets life as well as death." He touched her cheek. "And never forget that here you are loved. Go to Kashyyyk, join your mind to that of others, and heal."

Tahiri's chin trembled, and she swallowed tears as Luke drew the hood over her bright hair.

"*Tekli!*"

Cilghal and Tresina robed her. Luke thought it was too ridiculous for him to tower over the one-meter-high Chandra-Fan as he spoke, so he hitched up his robes and sat cross-legged on the ground in front of her.

"Your mastery of the Force is not as strong as some of us," Luke said, "but your devotion is second to none. You've taken upon yourself the role of healer. While others may garner more fame and glory, remember that yours is the noblest art, and that the preservation of life is the greatest gift a Jedi can bestow upon another."

Luke drew the hood over her snouted face and rose easily to his feet from his cross-legged position. Without, he was pleased to note, using either the Force or his hands.

"*Jaina Solo!*"

Jaina stepped forward, and Luke could feel her cool presence in the Force, the precise way her footsteps matched the drumbeat that still thudded up from the orchestra pit. She wore her military uniform—Cal Omas had asked her to, in order to show her commitment to the New Republic. Kyp and Kenth Hamner, the two pilots, robed her.

Luke put his hands on her shoulders and looked into her dark eyes, and a chill suddenly seized him, flooding his nerves with cold fire.

"I name you the Sword of the Jedi," he said. "You are like tempered steel, purposeful and razor-keen. Always you shall be in the front rank, a burning brand to your enemies, a brilliant fire to your friends. Yours is a restless life, and never shall you know peace, though you shall be blessed for the peace that you bring to others. Take comfort in the fact that, though you stand tall and alone, others take shelter in the shadow that you cast."

Luke fell silent, and for a long horrified moment he stared into Jaina's wide-eyed face.

He hadn't meant to say that. He hadn't meant to say anything like it. Yet the words had poured forth from him like the ringing sound of a giant bell, a bell that was being tolled, not by Luke, but by someone else.

He sensed the other Jedi staring at him. Had he actually spoken loudly enough for them to hear?

Luke's hands trembled as he drew the cowl over Jaina's head. When he returned to the podium he had to fumble for the microphone switch.

"Draw your lightsabers," he said, "for the first time as Jedi Knights!"

The *click-swoosh* of nine igniting lightsabers hissed through the air. He turned to the newly minted Jedi Knights and drew his own lightsaber, as the Jedi members of the council drew theirs.

"We salute you for the first time as colleagues," he said, and he and the council members performed a ritual salute with their lightsabers.

"Face front," he said, turning toward the audience, "and recite with me the Jedi Code."

"There is no emotion; there is peace," they all said. *"There is no ignorance; there is knowledge. There is no passion; there is serenity. There is no death; there is the Force."*

As they chanted the words, the lone trumpet rose again, the three rising notes calling them to their destiny. Illuminated by their lightsabers, the Jedi Knights stood erect and silent in the darkness.

The trumpet rose again to its last, high note and died. As its echo faded, the lights died away.

The audience burst into applause. But when the lights came up again, the stage was empty.

TWENTY-ONE

"Technically speaking," Jacen said, "I'm still on vacation."

"For how long?" Zekk asked.

"For as long as Master Skywalker *tells* me I'm on vacation."

Zekk shrugged. "Enjoy it while it lasts."

"I plan to. I just feel a little . . . odd, seeing the rest of you shipping out to Kashyyyk while I'm getting bronzed out on the reef."

"You've earned your leave," Zekk said. "You earned your leave in ways I don't even want to *think* about. Don't worry about it."

Jacen, Zekk, and the other newly made Jedi Knights were at the reception thrown in their honor by Cal Omas. The room was huge and marble-lined and featured a pair of tinkling fountains ornamented by frolicking bronze fish. The freshly minted Jedi Knights still wore their Jedi robes, and lightsabers, and carried drinks in their hands. Older Jedi and politicians and military stood about and made polite conversation.

Zekk looked around the gathering. "This is really strange," he said. "What are all these people *doing* here?"

Jacen smiled. "I was the son of the Chief of State," he said. "For me, this is an ordinary night at home."

Zekk shook his head. "Diplomacy wasn't something the Shadow Academy cared much about."

"I guess not."

Han loomed up at Jacen's shoulder, a broad grin spread across his face. He put an arm around Jacen's shoulders. "Now let me tell you about *my* graduation night . . ." he began.

"It was lovely," Leia said. "I had tears in my eyes."

"The ceremony was mostly Cal's work," Luke said. "He's got a flair for dramatics that I didn't know existed."

"My children," Leia sighed. "All grown up. And the Jedi have them now."

Luke looked at her. "Does that bother you?"

"A little. Sometimes I wish they'd grown up to be something other than Jedi. Something safe. But—" She sighed again. "—that's not going to happen in *our* family, is it?"

Luke tried to picture Ben grown up, sitting at a desk cluttered with actuarial tables. "I guess not."

Leia looked at him narrowly. "What happened when you talked to Jaina? I could feel it in the Force, but I don't know what it was I felt."

Luke hesitated. "I'd rather not say. It's for Jaina to tell you."

"Hm." Leia looked at him suspiciously, then decided not to pursue it. She gave a sidelong glance toward Lando Calrissian, who stood nearby chatting with Triebakk. She leaned close to Luke and lowered her voice. "How did Lando and Talon Karrde get Cal elected?" she asked. "Do you know?"

"I don't. But we can make a highly educated guess."

Leia bit her lip. "I hate to just *ask*. But we should know. We're going to have to try to protect Cal when it all comes out."

"You think it'll become public knowledge?"

"I *know* it will." Her eyes hardened. "Right now we've got smugglers controlling a swing vote in the Senate. That's *not* a good thing, and the New Republic is going to pay for it."

Luke looked at Lando appraisingly. "We should have a talk with Captain Calrissian."

Leia nodded. "Yes. And soon."

Jacen patiently listened to his father's reminiscences until Han was approached by Kenth Hamner, who wanted to find out about what fighter pilots were already calling the "Solo Slingshot," the dive toward a dovin basal that could be used to loop a combat craft in an unexpected direction to take the enemy by surprise. While Han was describing his encounter with the Yuuzhan Vong battle group, Jacen—who had already heard the story—slipped away to find his sister.

Jaina stood with her back against one of the room's side columns, a plate of food held out in front of her like a shield. She gave Jacen a dark look as he approached.

"If this is about what Uncle Luke said, I don't want to talk about it."

"Then let's not." He took a fruit-filled pastry from her plate. "I thought we should congratulate each other."

She gave a skeptical tilt to her head. "Congratulations."

"Congratulations, sis." Jacen popped the pastry into his mouth. The filling oozed onto his tongue as he bit down. It tasted like the product of an extractive industry specializing in fossilized hydrocarbons, and he coughed.

Jaina grinned as she pounded him on the back. "Vile, aren't they? I think the caterer must be a Vratix."

"He's in the pay of the Yuuzhan Vong," Jacen coughed. "He's trying to poison all the Jedi along with the high command." He took a swig of Gizer ale to wash the foul-tasting pastry down. "That's better." He looked at her again. The inadvertent comedy had broken the tension between them.

"Can we do this congratulations thing again?" he asked. "I have a feeling we wrong-footed it the first time."

She smiled. "Sure. My fault." She put the tray on a nearby table, then embraced him and kissed his cheek. "Congratulations."

"Congratulations." He held Jaina against him for a moment, feeling in the Force the twin bond that united them, and then stepped back. "You've always been my best friend, you know."

"And you've been mine." She looked over his shoulder at someone in the crowd. "I see Danni Quee is here. Have you talked to her yet tonight?"

"Not yet."

She gave a little smile. "Are you and Danni seeing each other?"

He blinked in surprise. "No, not that way. Or anyway, I don't think so."

Jaina laughed. "You don't *think* so. Don't you think you'd know?"

"We don't see each other that way. I don't think. I mean, she's five years older than I am."

"Dad's older than Mom. What does that matter?"

"And Danni's so accomplished. She's brilliant. She's got all these science degrees. I don't see why she'd be interested in me—all I know how to do is be a Jedi."

Jaina found this hilarious. She tried to strangle her laughter, but all that did was turn her red and send tears popping from her eyes.

" 'She's so accomplished!' 'I'm just a Jedi!' " Laughter choked the words. "And from *Jacen Solo*—!"

Jacen tried to gather the shreds of his dignity. "I don't see what's so funny."

She patted him on the shoulder and wiped the tears from her eyes. "That's fine, brother. I'm hardly the one to advise anybody on romance."

Suddenly Jacen was very interested. "Oh yes? And what does *that* mean?"

She looked at him in the dawning knowledge that she'd just made a mistake. "It means what it means," she said.

"*Who* does it mean?" Jacen asked.

She looked away, then sighed. "Jagged Fel," she said.

Jacen was astonished. "You must be joking. That stuck-up fighter pilot?"

Jaina scowled. "You don't know anything about him. He's not really like that."

"If you say so." There was a moment of silence. Jacen thought it might be an apt time to move off this topic. "What are you doing tomorrow?" he asked. "I don't know how much of this planet you've seen, but we could go—"

She shook her head. "I'm shipping out with the rest. Back to Kashyyyk."

He looked at her in surprise. "Why are you leaving now?"

Her defiant look was back. "I was on a special mission from Kre'fey. It's over. I'm bringing his Jedi back, and I'm going back with them."

"You're on a two-week furlough. I've seen the datapads. They're on the table in the room we're sharing."

Jaina sighed. "I've learned some new tactics since I've been here—one of them Dad's slingshot maneuver. We've got a bunch of new Jedi to integrate into the command system. I'm needed back on Kashyyyk, drilling all this new material into the fleet."

"Every moment you're here, the Yuuzhan Vong are getting stronger," Jacen half quoted.

"That's right. Besides," she added, "you heard Uncle Luke. I'm the Sword of the Jedi. I'm always in the front rank. Peace is *not* my job."

Jacen tried to navigate through the thorns he sensed springing up around his sister. "The Yuuzhan Vong may be getting stronger while you're here. But if you don't get some time to relax, I don't see *you* getting stronger at all."

"It's not just me. I've got eleven other pilots in my squadron to look after, and half of them are rookies, and if I don't beat them to pieces in training, the Vong are going to blow them to pieces in combat." She shook her head, then looked at him. "It's all right, you know," she said. "I've accepted my own death."

Jacen looked at her in surprise and horror. "You haven't—" he stammered. "You haven't felt your death in the Force?"

"No." Her eyes were strangely without animation, as if these were words she'd spoken a thousand times before. "But I can count. I can count the enemy, and I can count the number of friends who have been killed, and I can count the number of battles before we can hope to end the war *and* the number of shots that are going to be fired in my direction in those battles. I don't have to do anything *wrong* to be killed. I don't have to make a *mistake*. All that I need to do is *be there* long enough, and it'll happen." She looked at him, and with a half-smile reached out to touch his shoulder. "But it's all right. It's what I've sworn to do. All that will happen is that I'll join the Force, and I'm part of the Force already, so with luck I'll hardly even notice the change."

"All life is precious," Jacen urged. "All life is unique. You shouldn't just throw yours away."

"Anni Capstan was precious and unique," Jaina said. "So was Ulaha Kore. So was Anakin. Uniqueness isn't a protection." She looked at him. "And I'm not throwing *anything* away. I'm just looking at the odds, and I'm not arrogant enough to believe that I'm an exception when so many of our friends aren't." She looked at him. "*There is no death, there is the Force.* Didn't we all just say that? I'm not just saying it, I'm living it."

"Don't cut us off from you," Jacen said. "We need you, too."

Jaina's look softened. "When you need me, I'll do my best to be there. That's a promise. That's being a Jedi, too."

She walked away quickly, leaving Jacen looking after her. Then he turned and gazed blindly into the crowd. It was only then that he saw, amid taller figures, the small figure of Vergere.

At any other time he would have been delighted to see her, but now he felt too troubled to talk to anyone. But she saw him and came toward him, and he tried to put a smile on his face as she arrived.

"You are now a Jedi Knight," she said. "Felicitations."

"Did you see the ceremony?"

"I did not." Her wide mouth drew down in disapproval. "The ceremony was a piece of political theater. Jedi should have nothing to do with such things. When I was made a Jedi Knight, it was simple—'*A Jedi Knight you are,*' Yoda said, and that was that. What more should we need?"

"But you're here." Jacen looked at the assembled dignitaries. "This gathering is political as well."

"I came for personal reasons—to see you and wish you well."

Jacen looked at her. "Thank you."

"I wonder, now that you are a Jedi Knight, if you have made any plans."

Jacen shrugged. "I'm on vacation until Uncle Luke says I'm not. And then, unless Uncle Luke has other ideas, I'll join the fleet like the rest."

Vergere made a *chrr*-ing noise. "Why? Your nature is not that of a military man."

Jacen nodded. "No, it's not. But the Yuuzhan Vong have to be defeated, and I can help. And I'll be with my friends."

"And your sister." Vergere's eyes were almost accusing.

"And my sister." Jacen nodded.

Her expression grew severe. "A Jedi Knight must not decide as a child decides."

Jacen looked at the avian in surprise. "Are you trying to tell me something?"

"I cannot speak to those whose ears are blocked!"

Jacen took a sip of his drink and glanced around the room. "Then let's talk about the weather."

"Sunny. Light clouds. Small chance of rain." Vergere's tone was acid.

Jacen smiled. "Sounds like a good day to visit the reef."

Vergere huffed again.

Jacen glanced again over the room and saw Luke talking seriously to Cal Omas and Releqy A'Kla.

"You can't tell me that in the old days, your Jedi Masters didn't consult with politicians. You served the Supreme Chancellor, after all."

"Chancellors came and went," Vergere said. "We served the *Republic*."

"Master Skywalker," Jacen said, "is on his fourth Chief of State."

"That is as it should be." For once, Jacen sensed grudging respect in Vergere's words.

Jacen's eyes traveled the room, and he saw the gaunt figure of Dif Scaur speaking with Cilghal. He remembered Danni's telling him about Scaur's project, the one involving Yuuzhan Vong bioscience.

"Some of our biogeneticists may have found the genes that keep the Yuuzhan Vong isolated from the Force," he said.

He could sense Vergere's hyperalertness through the Force. "Tell me," she said.

Jacen told the little avian about the Yuuzhan Vongs' genetics, which had proven to be largely compatible with the human, the exception being a unique strand that seemed common to all Vongformed life.

"I suppose that could be responsible for the Yuuzhan Vong not being discernible in the Force," Jacen said, but he fell silent when he became aware that Vergere had ceased to pay attention. Her crest had fluffed forward, as had her antennae, and she radiated intense concentration. When she finally spoke, it was as if she was speaking to herself.

"It is as I feared," she said. Urgency rang in Vergere's voice. "Who else knows this? Who?"

"It's been kept very secret," Jacen said. "You and I and Danni know. And the scientists themselves, but they've been placed in seclusion."

"Who has them?"

Jacen nodded his head toward Dif Scaur. "New Republic Intelligence," he said.

Vergere looked at Scaur's cadaverous figure. Jacen could feel the intensity of Vergere's gaze through the Force, and was glad she wasn't turning this scrutiny on him. Vergere's crest swept back, and she gave a little, ominous hiss.

"I can imagine what happens next," she judged. "And there is *another* evil."

"What?" Jacen was bewildered. "What evil?"

Vergere swung back to him. "You cannot guess, young Jedi?" she asked. She gave a dry little laugh. "Despite all your adventures, I fear that you possess insufficient experience of depravity."

TWENTY-TWO

Jaina came out of her roll right onto the tail of an enemy TIE fighter. She launched a missile by pure reflex, and the fighter blossomed into a brief, scarlet flower. In another two seconds she'd vaped the first TIE's wingmate, and the rest of her squadron accounted for three more.

Through the Force she could sense enemy pilots engaged with Kyp's Dozen and completely unaware of her existence.

"Starboard sixty degrees, Twin Squadron," she said. "Three, two, mark."

Her three four-fighter flights rolled over and through one another in a perfect crossover turn. "Accelerating now," Jaina warned, and pushed the throttles forward. She had already marked out a target, and she pushed her mind into the Force-meld to tell Kyp she was coming.

Kyp sent a series of thoughts and impressions that translated to something like, *You're welcome to a piece of this sorry bunch if you want one*. The Force-meld was powerful here, with so many Jedi present: it was almost like being a party to a large, private conversation. Though Kyp's squadron was tangled up with superior numbers, he didn't seem terribly threatened.

It was strange to feel the enemy in the Force again. The Yuuzhan Vong were defending their convoys and rear areas in part with mercenary and Peace Brigade forces. These enemy pilots defending Duro were still present in the Force, and often Jaina knew what the enemy pilots were going to do before they knew themselves.

Jaina hadn't felt the enemy in the Force since the fleet had raided Ylesia, a few weeks before. The Peace Brigade headquarters had also been defended by natives of the galaxy, which made them easy to fight, but the raid had gone wrong for other reasons. Bad intelligence, inadequate operational plan, bad luck.

This raid was going to go right, if Jaina had anything to do with it.

Jaina's targets were Howlrunners, which partly explained Kyp's lack of urgency. Jaina told each of her pilots to pick a target, slam it, then rendezvous on the other side of the furball in order to regroup for another slash.

Her attack left a Howlrunner trailing flame and the panic of its pilot a distant shriek in the Force. Her other pilots succeeded in damaging or destroying their targets, and as Jaina told her fighters to regroup, she heard Kyp's laconic voice in the Force suggesting that she go find someone else to shoot at.

At that instant Jacen's presence blossomed in the Force, and somehow Jaina knew exactly where he wanted her to go, and that he wanted her to use her shadow bombs.

"On my way," Jaina said.

Jacen was on the bridge of Admiral Kre'fey's flagship, the Bothan Assault Cruiser *Ralroost*. His vacation on Mon Calamari had lasted three weeks—after that, Luke had told him he had the choice of working with the Great River or of joining Jaina and the fleet at Kashyyyk.

Perhaps Luke had been a little surprised by Jacen's choice.

He left his life on Mon Calamari with small regret. He had enjoyed his brief respite from the war, enjoyed the company of his parents, of Luke and Mara and Danni Quee, but he as well as Luke knew that it was time to move on.

Once he'd joined Kre'fey, Jacen's experience with the Jedi meld on Myrkr had helped him rise above the weeks of training that he'd missed. And in time it had become obvious that his talents were less tactical than spatial and holistic. Through the Force, and through the combined minds and perceptions of the Jedi, he seemed to gain a sense of the entire battlefield. He could sense where to move tactical elements and when to press an attack and when to hold back or withdraw. With the other Jedi as his eyes and ears, he felt the necessity of moving a squadron *here*, of pulling back the main body *there*, of maintaining a hovering threat *elsewhere*. He couldn't have said why he knew this, he only knew that he knew.

If he narrowed his focus to the individuals who made up the meld, he could sense their distinct personalities: Corran Horn with his stubborn resolve; Kyp Durron flying with controlled fury; Jaina with her machinelike tactics, brain abuzz with calculation.

Everything was calculation with Jaina these days. She had fashioned herself into a weapon—the Sword of the Jedi—and there was room for nothing else. If he tried to talk to her about anything but her job, anything but the daily necessities of fighting and survival, she simply would not respond. It was as if much of her personality had simply ceased to exist.

It was painful to watch. Jacen might have been hurt by Jaina's attitude if he weren't so concerned over the damage that she must be doing to her own spirit.

Now. He almost heard the Force speaking in his ear, and he ordered Saba Sebatyne and the Wild Knights into a slashing run on an enemy cruiser.

Two months of constant raids and skirmishing had demonstrated that Jacen's chief value wasn't in the cockpit of a starfighter, but on the bridge of a flagship, where he could help direct an entire armada. Kre'fey had happily taken him aboard the *Ralroost*.

And now, as turbolasers flared and missiles erupted against shields, he sensed a place for Jaina and her squadron.

And then, in the whirling movement of the squadrons that blazed in the night, Jacen sensed something else hovering in the darkness, weapons ready.

"Scimitar Squadron," he said in response to this sudden knowledge. "Please stand by."

"Twin Squadron," Jaina said, "turn toward Duro on my mark. Three, two, mark."

Twin Suns Squadron performed another perfect crossover turn, placing the disk of Duro directly ahead. It was the first time Jaina had seen the planet since its loss to the enemy. She had been in a field hospital here after being wounded— she'd been blind, dependent on others, embroiled in conspiracy, and with a major Vong offensive in the offing. Her memories of the planet weren't happy ones.

But Duro was now a different world. She remembered Duro as a gray-brown waste of desert and slag, but the disk was green now, bright with vegetation. The Yuuzhan Vong had converted the poisoned planet to their own purposes, but in so doing so had taken a near-dead world and made it thrive.

As Jaina neared Duro, she could see the fires of deadly energies flashing across the green disk of the planet. Three Yuuzhan Vong cruisers were fighting to hold Kre'fey's main body from a cluster of huge transport craft, and though outnumbered two to one the enemy cruisers were fighting hard. Their starfighter pilots weren't Peace Brigade draftees in motley craft, either, but first-rank Yuuzhan Vong warriors in coralskippers. That was obvious enough from the way they fought, using a high degree of tactical intelligence even though their yammosk had been jammed.

As Jaina watched, one of the enemy cruisers broke apart in flame and ruin, and she sensed the satisfaction of Saba Sebatyne with the part her Wild Knights had played in the attack. *Go for the next cruiser,* Jacen sent, and Jaina pulsed a silent acknowledgment.

"First flight goes in now," she said. "Second flight follows. Third flight watches our tails until we're clear, and then you can make your run."

Lowbacca and Tesar acknowledged.

"Dropping shadow bombs now," Jaina said. The missiles, packed with explosives instead of propellent, dropped from her X-wing's racks. With the Force Jaina shoved them on ahead, braking her own X-wing slightly so as to increase their separation. She set them on a trajectory for the aftmost enemy cruiser, then concentrated on leading her flight's run with standard missiles and laserfire, bringing them to the target at a slightly different angle so as to fool the enemy dovin basals, which might snatch her concussion missiles without noticing the less visible shadow bombs as they approached.

Space lit up ahead, a brilliant display of turbolaser fire, plasma cannon projectiles, magma missiles, concussion missiles, and burning craft. This was the most dangerous part of her approach, Jaina knew, flying in between the big capital ships pounding each other at point-blank range. She could be flamed by her own side without their even noticing her presence.

Yet she knew, somehow, that she was in no real danger. More tangible than the missile and turbolaser fire she could sense the Force, and this time the Force wouldn't let her fail.

Her laserfire raked the enemy hull. Dovin basals sucked down her concussion missiles and one of the shadow bombs, but she saw a geyser of brilliant fire as the two other shadow bombs struck the enemy, and she pulled up and away as more bombs dropped into the inferno.

Lowbacca's second flight, six seconds behind, scored another series of hits. Though the cruiser wasn't destroyed, it was no longer able to defend itself effectively, and the New Republic cruisers began to strike home with one attack after another. The Yuuzhan Vong ship was doomed.

"First flight! Second flight! Skips on your tail!" Tesar's voice called, not through the Force, but over Jaina's headphones.

"Scissors, Lowie!" Jaina called. "I'll break right!" One flight would go right, the other left, and then they would interweave to shoot the enemy off each other's tails.

"Negative, Twin One!" another stern voice called. It was a voice that Jaina had learned to trust.

Behind her burning coralskippers lit the night. "Thank you, Colonel Harona," she called as Scimitar Squadron flashed past her cockpit, their colossal ion engines speeding them past.

"Don't thank me," Harona said. "Jacen told us you might need help about now."

Sometimes, Jaina thought, her brother was positively eerie.

The second enemy cruiser was a burning wreck, unable to fire and unable to defend itself, leaving only one functional enemy cruiser against six of Kre'fey's. Three concentrated on the lone enemy while the others and most of the smaller ships dived after the transports. About a third of the transports tried to land on Duro, but were blown out of the atmosphere before they could put down. The rest scattered and were picked off one by one by the New Republic forces.

After the transports and the single cruiser were destroyed, Kre'fey's cruisers settled into low orbit over Duro and pounded anything on the ground that looked like a warrior damutek, warehouse, command center, factory, or spaceport.

Jaina didn't know if she liked the idea of bombardment from orbit, and she could sense Jacen's stern disapproval through the Force. Though she could understand the advantage of hitting an enemy from a position of safety, a bombardment was contrary to her Jedi instincts and training, which focused on actions that were more precise and far less random.

Despite the Jedi's attitude, bombardment of the enemy was part of Admiral Kre'fey's standard orders. Kre'fey's Question Number One, *How can I hurt the Vong today?*, was best answered by blowing up things.

"Remember," Kre'fey had said, "they destroyed entire worlds by seeding alien life-forms from orbit. Just think what they did to Ithor. What we're doing is merciful by comparison."

True, Jaina supposed. As far as it went.

"Regroup, Twin Squadron," she called. "Prepare for recall."

Her fighters slotted neatly into their assigned formations. Through the Force she could feel their pride, their sense of accomplishment. Her relentless insistence on drills and practice sessions had paid off. In the nearly three months since her visit to Mon Calamari, months filled with raids and skirmishes and alarms, she hadn't lost a single pilot. Three X-wings had been destroyed or so badly damaged they were scrapped, but the pilots had always ejected before their craft were wrecked and were recovered afterward.

Her six rookies were now proud veterans, all with kills to their credit. A few weeks ago Jaina had astonished her Neimoidian wingmate, Vale, by sitting with her at the breakfast table and engaging in a conversation that had nothing to do with tactics or with Vale's deficiencies as a pilot.

Vale and the other rookies had proved themselves. They were worth knowing.

But though Jaina was friendlier than she'd been, she was careful to avoid actual friendship. Her determination hadn't lessened over the months. She knew that the raids on Yuuzhan Vong territory had been carefully planned to take advantage of temporary enemy weaknesses. The attacks had been made only against outnumbered or ambushed forces, and were aborted if the enemy proved stronger than anticipated. Often the enemy were second-rate troops, Peace Brigade or mercenaries or Yuuzhan Vong workers with scant warrior training who fell apart into a confused muddle once their yammosks were jammed. Jaina's own rookies had been blooded, but they'd been blooded in battles where great pains had been taken to assure only victory.

Jaina knew that Twin Suns Squadron couldn't expect battle on such favorable terms forever. Sooner or later the enemy would launch another offensive, and then her squadron would be up against first-line Vong warriors attacking from a position of overwhelming strength. It would make every fight her new pilots had experienced look like a playground skirmish between children.

The knowledge that the enemy offensive would inevitably come kept Jaina on edge. Just because things had been going well was no reason to relax. In fact, she had to be harder than ever in order to keep her pilots from slacking off due to overconfidence.

Fortunately, a few things kept Jaina from exploding with tension. Kyp's powerful and strangely stabilizing presence. Jacen's otherworldly calm. Regular messages from her parents, from Luke and Mara . . . and from Jag Fel.

His squadron was still hunting Yuuzhan Vong on the Hydian Way, and with her he shared the frustrations of a veteran pilot training a large number of rookies.

She was confused about what she should allow Jag to mean to her. She feared he was a distraction; that if she let him into her life, she'd lose her edge. But then moments would come in which she yearned for his embrace, felt the press of his phantom lips on hers . . .

It was lucky they were apart, she decided. If they were together, the turmoil of her own thoughts and desires might overwhelm her.

But a part of her very much wanted to be overwhelmed.

Her heart lurched as her cockpit displays flashed. A Yuuzhan Vong task force had just left hyperspace. Seven capital ships of varying sizes, all of them now venting squadrons of coralskippers. The Yuuzhan Vong defending Duro had called for help, but it had arrived too late.

For a moment Jaina waited in suspense. The two forces were nearly evenly matched. Kre'fey's cruisers had taken little damage in their lopsided fight, and few fighters had been lost. The Jedi Force-meld was an advantage the enemy couldn't match. A nearly bloodless victory had been won, and the New Republic forces were exultant. Morale was as high as it was ever going to get. If Kre'fey gave the word, his task force would fling itself on the enemy in absolute confidence of victory.

Kre'fey could *win* this, win two battles in a single day. He had to know that.

"Cruisers regroup," came the order on the command channel. "Starfighters stand by for recovery and transit to hyperspace."

Jaina felt the tension drain out of her, and the exultation, too. Kre'fey was playing it safe.

He was probably right, she thought. This might not be the only enemy force on its way to help Duro.

But Jaina felt disappointment. She knew the Force was with her today, and might not be on the day of the next battle.

"I believe I've found the trap I've been looking for," Ackbar said. "The trap that will spell doom for the Yuuzhan Vong." He floated in his pool at home, with Luke, Cal Omas, and Admiral Sovv sitting in plush chairs on the rim. The room smelled pleasantly of the sea. Winter stood by with a holoprojector.

She switched on the projector, and a star map floated in the air over Ackbar's head. Luke knew from the star density that it had to be somewhere in the Core, but otherwise the configurations of the stars were unfamiliar to him.

"This is Treskov One-Fifteen-W," Ackbar said, as one of the stars blinked against the background. "It's an old main-sequence star on the outermost fringe of the Deep Core, completely unexceptional. As you can see from the overlay of our official hyperspace route charts"—a narrow golden ribbon appeared on the display, a hyperspace route leading to the blinking star—"Treskov is a dead end. But if we add the secret Imperial Core routes that Princess Leia brought back from Bastion . . ." Four other routes appeared on the display, marked in red and radiating from Treskov. "You see that unmarked routes from Treskov lead farther into the Core. One of these"—another blinking light—"leads to an Imperial star base code-named Tarkin's Fang. The base was sealed and evacuated at the end of the Galactic Civil War, but otherwise remains intact and usable. There is also a large cache of supplies stored at Tarkin's Fang that the Empire intended to use in the event of renewed hostilities."

"Even Tarkin's Fang is a dead end," Admiral Sovv pointed out. "If we put forces there, they could be blockaded by any enemy who sealed the route to Treskov."

"I agree," Ackbar said. "And I intend the enemy to agree as well."

Perspective shifted on the holo, the display zooming to display Treskov and its system. The fifth planet out, a gas giant striped in white and several shades of green, began to wink.

"This is Ebaq, a gas giant with eleven moons. Of these,

Ebaq Nine was once exploited by the Deep Core Mining Corporation for its deposits of bronzium. The moon was opened up shortly after the rise of Palpatine. During the war years the Empire maintained an observation post there, and used Ebaq Nine as an emergency resupply point, but the moon is now empty."

Ackbar ducked his head beneath the water, refreshing himself, then shook stray drops from his massive head. "I propose we reoccupy the moon and use it as bait in a trap. We must make it an irresistible target for the Yuuzhan Vong. And then, once the enemy begin their assault, we seal off the end and turn the Treskov system into a killing ground in which the enemy forces are hunted down and destroyed."

Ackbar turned to Sien Sovv. "Admiral, it is you who must commit the forces necessary to destroy the Yuuzhan Vong."

And then Ackbar turned to Luke, and Luke felt a chill run down his spine. "Master Skywalker," the admiral said, "it is for you and the Jedi to provide the bait."

"I'm calling this meeting of the High Council for two reasons," Cal Omas said. "First, we must discuss Admiral Ackbar's plan for a renewed attack against the Yuuzhan Vong. Second, Intelligence Director Dif Scaur has an announcement of critical importance."

Cal looked abnormally grim. He was usually relaxed at meetings, joking as he slouched his lanky body into its seat. Today he was erect and businesslike. Clearly something important was at hand.

The council members weren't as crowded as they had been at their first meeting, even though they met in the same room, with the same overlarge table. The crowding had eased because fewer were present: Kyp Durron and Saba Sebatyne were at Kashyyyk, fighting with their squadrons, and had given their proxy votes to Cilghal and to Luke, respectively.

"I have no intention of communicating the details of Admiral Ackbar's plan to this council," Cal said. "Its usefulness depends on secrecy, and in any case it's irrelevant to the case I wish to put. Ackbar's plan requires detaching large forces from their current deployments and using them against the Yuuzhan Vong. This will mean that many of our squadrons now engaged in the defense of our worlds won't be available in case the Yuuzhan Vong choose to attack."

[If our fleets are on the offensive,] Triebakk proclaimed, [the Vong will have more urgent things to do than to attack our planets.]

"Sir, our briefings have indicated that many more ships will be available in six standard months or so," said the soft voice of Ta'laam Ranth. "Would it not be possible to delay our offensive until we can both defend our planets and attack the enemy?"

"My Gotal colleague has a point," Releqy A'Kla said. "It may be possible to delay any offensive until we have greater numbers."

"There's a time limit on the admiral's plan," Luke said. "We currently have a technological advantage over the enemy. We don't know how long this advantage will last, so the admiral wants to move now."

"Delaying six months," Sien Sovv said, "means the war goes on six months longer than it would otherwise. Six more months of killing and uncertainty and expense." He looked at Ta'laam Ranth. "Thousands of worlds are under threat. The fleet can't defend them all, even with six months' worth of reinforcements."

"My colleague's arguments are logical," the Gotal said. "I concede that an attack is logical."

"If I may interrupt," Dif Scaur said, "I'd like to bring my own business before the council. It may have a direct bearing on whether the New Republic wishes to go on the offensive or not."

Luke looked at the thin man with care. When Ackbar had first presented his plan, Scaur had been meticulous about discovering Ackbar's timing. This had made Luke suspicious, and Luke's suspicions had been confirmed at Council meetings. Scaur clearly had an agenda of his own, and it was an agenda with a timetable.

Scaur looked from one council member to the next. "I am now able to reveal the existence of a secret unit in New Republic Intelligence called 'Alpha Red.' It is headed by Joi Eicroth, a xenobiologist formerly belonging to Alpha Blue, another secret unit charged with Yuuzhan Vong affairs. Since the beginning of the war, Alpha Red has undertaken covert research on Yuuzhan Vong biology with the assistance of a team of scientists supplied by the Chiss."

Here it is, Luke thought. Something big, something very quiet that had gone on for at least two years without a breath of it getting out. In a government as porous as Borsk Fey'lya's, that was a major accomplishment.

Unless Fey'lya himself didn't know, Luke thought.

"Why Chiss?" Sien Sovv asked, bewildered.

"The Chiss come from a hidden, remote section of the galaxy far from the Yuuzhan Vong invasion routes," Scaur said. "It was highly unlikely that the enemy would have infiltrated them."

Which means, Luke thought, *that Scaur's had contact with the Chiss for some time. He knew in advance that he could count on them to deliver.*

"Our xenobiologists and geneticists have investigated Yuuzhan Vong genetics," Scaur continued. He placed his pale, thin hands on the table before him. "They have located a unique genetic signature in Yuuzhan Vong DNA, something common to all Yuuzhan Vong species—the plants, the living buildings and ships, the animals, the Vong themselves. This genetic signature is unknown in any plant, animal, bacterial, or viral life within our own galaxy."

"You've developed a weapon," Ta'laam Ranth said. Luke could feel surprise among the other council members, followed by apprehension and dread.

"Yes." Cal's face was grim. "We have a weapon."

"A biological weapon," Dif Scaur said. "An airborne weapon that will attack only those plants or animals that possess the genetic signature of the extragalactic Vong. If the weapon is dispersed efficiently on enemy worlds, we calculate that the menace of the Yuuzhan Vong will be ended within four weeks at the most—probably three."

"What do you mean, *ended?*" asked Cilghal.

"I mean the Vong will be dead," Scaur said. "And everything the Yuuzhan Vong brought with them—all the plants, all the buildings, all the ships." He shrugged. "There may be some survivors in remote areas. But they'll be infected if they travel to Vong worlds, and if they don't, they can be hunted down." He glanced briefly at each of the council members.

"Biological weapons are notoriously capricious," he continued. "Normally I would never recommend their use on a dispersed population like the Vong, but this weapon will be so effective that I consider it an exception to my usual rule. The Vong can't escape it. It will attach to their genetics. There is a latency period of four or five days in which they will feel no effects, but will be infectious and contaminate everyone and everything they contact. After that they will begin to break down on the cellular level—their living tissue will dissolve into a fluid, and even that fluid will be infectious. They will be infected by their ships. Their weapons. Their armor. Their *homes.* Their *food.* Everything in their environment will carry the disease. Once the breakdown starts, the Vong will be dead within three or four days."

Luke let the horror sink in. The horror was followed by

anger—*anger is a* useful *emotion,* he remembered Vergere telling him—and he turned to Cal Omas.

"How long have you known about this?" he asked.

"Since I was sworn in," Cal said.

"Almost three months."

Cal turned his own eyes to Luke. "Master Skywalker, I'm extremely sorry. But you understand that the secrecy of this project was paramount."

"I understand your reasoning," Luke said. *And I disagree,* he thought coldly. *Because if I'd known in advance, I could have prepared arguments against this. As it is, I can only make the arguments that occur to me, and hope the Force will be with me.*

He looked at Dif Scaur. "You want to use the Great River to distribute this weapon, don't you?" he said.

Scaur nodded. "That would be convenient."

Luke shook his head. "Jedi won't touch this. I ask you not to require it of us."

Scaur seemed unsurprised. "The Great River isn't vital to the project. Our own intelligence networks now extend into Vong space. The fleet can deliver the weapon on missiles to enemy fleet targets, to space facilities, or to planets. And the Bothans made Alpha Red much more convenient when they declared ar'krai on the Vong—the Bothan spynet is famously efficient, and Alpha Red will settle all their goals for this war." He shrugged his thin shoulders. "The Yuuzhan Vong themselves will do most of the distribution on our behalf, as their infected personnel and ships travel from world to world."

Ta'laam Ranth turned his red eyes to Luke. "Master Skywalker obviously objects to this plan," he said. "I wish he'd explain his protests."

Luke looked at the others. "The Jedi exist to preserve life. This slaughter of entire species runs contrary to our principles." He took a breath and summoned the Force and hoped that it would make his arguments as brilliant as they needed to be.

"Let me point out that the Yuuzhan Vong are not so completely unlike us," he said. "They are intelligent and educable. If you took one of their young and raised it, the child wouldn't be unlike one of ours—their evil isn't innate to the species. It's their government and their religion that have made them aggressive, and it should be our task to defeat that government and religion, not to wipe out the common people who have had no choice but to follow their leaders."

"The Yuuzhan Vong have done this to *our* worlds," Ayddar Nylykerka pointed out. "They've sown our worlds with life-forms that have killed everyone on the planet."

"Which is simply another point against the use of this weapon." Ta'laam Ranth's declaration surprised everyone at the table. "If we unleash this weapon against them, they could retaliate against us. We could lose worlds to Vong biologicals."

"Alpha Red is a defense *against* such an attack," Scaur said. "Alpha Red would destroy any biological assault the Vong could launch."

Triebakk gave a roar that brought silence to the table. [I know something of science,] he said finally through translation. [I know the word *blowback*.] He glanced at the others. [For those who don't know this term, it describes a weapon's unanticipated side effects turning on the user.] He looked at Dif Scaur. [You're planning to distribute Alpha Red throughout Vong space. Billions upon billions upon billions of live bacteria—or viruses, or whatever Alpha Red is—cast loose on viable ecosystems.] He shook his shaggy head. [You can't tell me that Alpha Red won't mutate, not in all those replications. And you can't assure me that one of those mutations won't be harmful to *us*. Blowback could *kill all of us*.]

"The Chiss assure me this is highly unlikely," Scaur said.

"Unlikely," Luke said. "Not impossible."

Scaur shrugged. "If this is a worry, we could quarantine Vong worlds until we can assure they're safe. Refugees will be upset at not being able to move home immediately, but once victory is achieved, we should be able to pacify them."

Scaur had anticipated every argument. He'd had months to prepare this. Luke had only this moment.

"You haven't spoken of Yuuzhan Vong biological capabilities," Luke said.

Scaur raised an eyebrow. "I don't understand, Master Skywalker."

"The Yuuzhan Vong have formidable biological knowledge," Luke said. "They do *everything* through biotech. Can you tell me they haven't anticipated this form of attack? How do you know they aren't ready for it? How do you know that once they see we're ready to commit genocide and ecocide both, they won't retaliate in kind?"

For the first time, Scaur seemed at a loss. "We see no sign of it."

[You don't understand everything about the Vong,] Triebakk said. [My guess is that you have at best a cursory knowledge of their immune systems. *What if they're ready for you?*]

Scaur hesitated. A corner of his eye twitched. "We have no evidence to show anything of the sort."

"Have you looked?" Luke asked.

Scaur seemed nettled. "Of course. We've captured and examined shaper facilities. We have a decent knowledge of the weapons they've used against us. We've captured their ships and examined them."

"Our knowledge of the enemy is deficient," Ta'laam Ranth said. His double-horned head turned slowly left and right, scanning the table. "Clearly it would be illogical to proceed with this plan."

Dif Scaur's face tautened, only increasing the death-mask

effect. "The weapon is fully tested," he said. "And that includes on live subjects." He raised a hand to cut off Luke's explosion of protest. "Warrior prisoners," he said. "We have to keep the warriors unconscious after we capture them, because the second they wake they try to commit suicide. We infected a small number of these with the weapon. The weapon . . ." He took a breath. "The weapon works. I regretted extremely the necessity of having to do this, but a test was required, and their deaths were as painless and humane as we could make them." He put his hands on the table before him. "I assure everyone here that Alpha Red will work, and will do everything that is promised."

"This is unconscionable," Luke said. Never had he felt such cold rage. "This is something Palpatine might have done."

Dif Scaur gave him a furious glance. "No, this is *not* what Palpatine would have done," he said. "Palpatine would have tested the weapon on the population of an entire world, and used it as a terror weapon to keep other worlds in subjugation. I ask Master Skywalker to avoid such odious comparisons."

There was a long moment of silence, broken by Cal.

"Perhaps we should vote, then," Cal said. "Those in favor?"

Dif Scaur's hand went up first. Then Nylykerka's. Then, with hesitation, the hand of Sien Sovv.

Luke kept his hands on the table. So did all the Jedi. "I cast Saba Sebatyne's proxy against the motion," he said.

"And I cast Kyp Durron's," Cilghal echoed.

"The motion fails," Releqy A'Kla said.

Then Cal Omas turned to Luke. There was regret in his eyes. "I'm sorry, Luke," he said, "but in a war that we're losing, we can't afford to throw away any weapons. Particularly one that will end so much suffering and heartache for our people." He turned to Dif Scaur. "This council is advisory, not legislative. As Chief of State, I order Dif Scaur to continue the Alpha Red project."

Luke sat stunned. Dif Scaur looked at his hands in order to hide the cold triumph in his eyes.

Sorrow dug deep furrows into Cal's brows. "This is a tragedy in every way," he said. "But our only choice is between one tragedy and another, and I prefer to make the Vong's story a tragedy and not ours." He looked at Dif Scaur. "When can you have your weapon ready?"

"There is only a small sample of the material at present," Scaur said. "We'll need to produce much more—tons at least. The secure Alpha Red facility is unsuited for producing such quantities." He turned to Cal. "There's an old Nebulon-B frigate in orbit above Mon Calamari, used as a hospital ship. If we could shift the patients to the surface, Alpha Red could take advantage of the ship's isolation and sterile environment. Once we get there, I anticipate enough product can be made to begin distribution within two weeks."

Cal turned to the others. "In that case," he said, "we'll postpone implementation of Admiral Ackbar's offensive plans. We may as well stay on the defensive until Alpha Red wins the war." He looked at the others. "Of course, no one is to speak of this matter until the end of the war. If then."

He brought the council meeting to a swift end. He cast one regretful glance at Luke, then stood and made his rapid way out, followed with equal rapidity by Dif Scaur.

Feeling a hundred years old, Luke rose slowly from the table. Triebakk and the Jedi came to stand beside him.

"What can we do?" Cilghal asked.

Luke forced a casual shrug. "Try to change Cal's mind. We have a couple of weeks at least."

[If there is more that you wish to do . . .] Triebakk left the thought unfinished.

Luke shook his head. "Thank you for the offer, but no."

If Luke did anything, he would do it himself, and take the responsibility on himself alone.

But he knew that if he did, he would throw away everything he'd worked for in the course of his long, exacting life.

Luke returned home after the meeting of the High Council with dread and anger warring in his mind. Nothing could be done as long as he was in this state, so he sat on the floor and began to apply relaxing techniques to get his thoughts and emotions under control.

He felt Mara in the Force before she entered the apartment. She paused for a moment in the doorway, her own Force-awareness gently enfolding him, and then she closed the door, put down the briefcase she was carrying, and joined him on the floor. She sat behind him, her hands on his shoulders, and began working at the taut shoulder and neck muscles. Luke surrendered to the touch, let her fingers turn his muscles to liquid. His breath fell into rhythm with hers. Mara worked herself closer until she was pressed against his back. Her arms went around him, and she rested her chin on his shoulder.

"What's the bad news?" she said.

Luke hesitated, but he knew Mara could be trusted, and besides the horror was too vast to keep to himself. He told her about Alpha Red.

Mara drew back slightly as she considered the problem. "What can we do?"

"Try to change Cal's mind."

Her chin dropped onto his shoulder again. Her voice was a breath on his ear. "And if his mind doesn't change?"

Luke took a long breath. "I don't know. We could try to wreck the project, but unless we killed the scientists they'd be able to duplicate their work. And even if we killed the scientists, or managed to kidnap them and hold them somewhere, other scientists would be able to duplicate the project.

The problem is that once this weapon is known to be possible, anyone with the proper facilities can create it."

He shook his head. "I've worked all my life to rebuild the Jedi. Now we have a government that's willing to work with us, that we've helped into office, that's reestablished the council, and which we've sworn to uphold. How can I turn on the New Republic at the *very first crisis*?" He took Mara's hand in his own. "That would finish the Jedi. We'd be outlaws. We'd be everything that people like Fyor Rodan said we were."

She looked at him with sad concern. "What you're saying is that we really can't stop Alpha Red; at best we can only delay. But can we really stand by and let this thing happen?"

"We can protest. We can refuse to have anything to do with it. That's all I can think of."

"Protest, yes. But how publicly?"

Again Luke shook his head. "Too public and the Yuuzhan Vong find out. Then they could hit us with bioweapons first, and it would be catastrophe."

"You say that Triebakk knows. And that Ta'laam Ranth voted with you."

"Yes."

"You need to contact them. See if they can change the minds of others on the High Council."

Luke nodded. "A quiet lobbying campaign, then. Dif Scaur caught me by surprise, and I didn't have my arguments in order." He nodded, and kissed Mara's cheek. "Thank you."

"You're welcome." She rose to her feet and helped him to rise. "Kam Solusar sent new holos of Ben. Would you like to see them?"

"Of course."

Seeing Ben speeding over the carpet on hands and knees gave Luke the usual mixture of sadness and joy, but served to shift his mood. He walked to the back of the apartment to change and wash before helping with dinner, and then froze as he saw a bundle of feathers in the spare room.

Vergere. She had been in the apartment all along. She was crouched in a meditation posture, her knees high, her head tucked in.

Horrified, Luke returned to Mara. "Vergere's in her room. I didn't sense her when I came in."

Mara's green eyes widened. "I didn't either. She was making herself invisible again."

"Do you think she heard us?"

Mara considered. "It isn't as if we were shouting. We were centimeters from each other, practically whispering. How could she have heard?"

"I wouldn't put anything past her."

Mara's look hardened. "Neither would I."

"We're going to have to watch her carefully. Unless—do you think we should have Nylykerka put her in detention again?"

"And give her a chance to stage a spectacular escape? And what if she doesn't want to go—do we fight her?"

"Watch, then," Luke decided. "And watch very carefully."

TWENTY-THREE

Vergere was a model of innocence for the next eight days, during which time Luke and Mara kept track of her when she wasn't with Cilghal or other Jedi. During that time Luke's lobbying efforts were nothing but frustration. Cal listened politely to his arguments, but didn't change his mind.

On the morning of the ninth day, New Republic security burst down the door and swept through the apartment. Dif Scaur had come in person, flinty eyes hard in his gaunt face. "The Chief of State wants to see you," he told Luke. His eyes flicked to Mara. "And Mara may come as well."

Cal Omas was in his office. He was unshaven and disheveled and had clearly just risen from bed. As Dif Scaur marched Luke and Mara into the office, Cal stared for a moment at a fragrant fruit-filled pastry that had been provided for his breakfast, and then with a look of disgust swept it from his desk. He looked at Luke with eyes of stone.

"Where's Vergere?"

"We saw her tonight, in her room," Luke said. "Just before bed."

"She's not in her room now," Cal said. "We don't know where she is."

Luke took a deep breath. "What has she done?"

"As if you didn't know," Dif Scaur breathed from behind Luke's shoulder.

"Vergere has sabotaged Alpha Red," Cal said.

Luke's mouth went dry. "Sabotaged it how?"

"The Alpha Red team was in the process of moving to the Nebulon-B cruiser in orbit. Somehow Vergere got on board in the confusion. She's wiped the records, and somehow she's . . . altered . . . the weapon."

"Altered?" Luke echoed.

"Rendered it ineffective. We don't know how."

Through her tears, Luke thought. She could modify the weapon at the molecular level.

"And she's rendered three of my security guards unconscious," Dif Scaur added.

Mara turned to him. "They're all right?"

"They will be."

Cal's eyes bored into Luke. "So where is she?"

"I don't know." Truthfully.

"Where would she run to?"

"Back to the Vong, of course," Dif Scaur said. "She's been working for them all along."

"I—I don't think so," Luke said. "I think Vergere is entirely on her own."

"She doesn't owe the Yuuzhan Vong her allegiance any more than we do," Mara added. "She's a servant of the Old Republic, not the New."

"So tell us why the Old Republic wants the Yuuzhan Vong to win the war!" Dif Scaur shouted.

"She doesn't," Luke said. "She just doesn't want an atrocity like Alpha Red to be unleashed."

"And who told her about the atrocity, then?" Cal's voice was cold. "Who broke security?"

Luke gathered himself for the admission, but Mara forestalled him.

"We didn't tell her," she said. "If she found out, she found out on her own."

True enough, Luke decided.

"But how?" Scaur demanded. "You had no documents to take home, no recordings . . . unless," his voice turned suspicious, "you surreptitiously *made* one."

"I didn't," Luke said.

Cal looked at him for a long moment, then looked down at his desk. "That's what Vergere herself confirmed." He scratched his bristly chin. "She left a note saying that something a scientist said made her suspicious and that she followed up her suspicions. She specifically exonerated you."

"But then she would," Scaur said. "Especially if she did this under your orders."

"I gave no orders," Luke said. He felt helpless under this kind of suspicion; there was no way to prove himself innocent. He looked at Cal. "I hadn't given up trying to talk you out of it."

"Sir." Dif Scaur spoke to Cal. "If she goes back to the Vong with Alpha Red, then the New Republic is in jeopardy. The enemy will know our capabilities, and they'll have to do whatever they can to destroy us before we can revive the Alpha Red project."

"The Skywalkers think she won't go to the Yuuzhan Vong," Cal said.

"They've been wrong up until now," Scaur said. "And in any case we can't afford to take the chance."

"True." Cal's eyes moved restlessly over his desk. "All right then." He looked at Scaur. "You need to reestablish Alpha Red at . . . a safer location . . . and have the team duplicate their original work. That will take how long?"

"At least three months. Probably four."

Cal nodded. He turned to Luke. "We'll move on Ackbar's plan immediately. If the Vong are responding to Ackbar's moves, then maybe they won't have time to kill the rest of us."

"Yes, sir," Luke said. His mind buzzed with calculation.

It would be three or four months before Alpha Red was unleashed.

That meant Luke had three months to win the war.

If the enemy were on the edge of defeat, then perhaps Cal wouldn't feel it necessary to wipe the Yuuzhan Vong from existence.

The Jedi were his eyes and ears. Formations hovered in Jacen's mind: lumbering transports, weapon-studded capital ships, racing squadrons of starfighters.

It was a fleet exercise, featuring a force aided by the Jedi meld against a superior force unaided by the Jedi. The Force glowed in Jacen like a flame, and he maneuvered the friendly squadrons like elements in a gigantic puzzle, trying to sense what would happen many moves in advance . . .

The opposing fleet made its move. As the fleets clashed, powered-down lasers flashing as computers launched simulated missiles, the picture in Jacen's head seemed to expand, information arriving in larger and larger bundles until he strained to keep up with it all. He felt sweat trickle down the bridge of his nose. The picture deteriorated into frantic, busy hash, punctuated only rarely by moments of clarity.

The meld always broke down when the situation grew too complex. Jacen could contain and control a large number of Jedi, like those engaged on the raid at Duro, but beyond that his abilities faded. This was frustrating, because he always sensed that comprehension was possible, if just beyond his reach. If only there were more Jedi in the link. If only he were more clever.

Still, his preliminary maneuvering had put the fleet in good shape, and as the battle went on he was able to achieve some flashes of insight that made sense out of the chaos. When the exercise ended, the opposition's advantage in numbers had been annulled, and the exchange of simulated "casualties" had favored Jacen's force.

"Try not to get me killed next time, Solo." Corran Horn, whose commitment to the fight had been mistimed, sent a dour message over the comlink.

Jacen sent an apology. He had to get better at this. Next time the missiles wouldn't be simulated.

"Splendid work, Jacen!" Out of the Force and on *Ralroost*'s tactical command center, Admiral Kre'fey's cream-colored body bounced on the balls of its feet. "Next battle, we're going to hammer them!" The Bothan punched his palm by way of emphasis.

"I hope so," Jacen said.

He had to get better at this. Too many people were counting on him.

It had become a custom for the Jedi to dine together after the exercise. They reviewed the maneuvers, the way the meld had worked or failed to work, and suggested improvements. After the group broke up, Jacen sought out Tahiri Veila.

"You're doing well?" he asked.

She frowned. "I'm working hard."

It was the truth. Since Anakin's death she had grown serious, almost grim in the way that she pursued her goals, a considerable change from the impetuous, fiery girl Jacen remembered from the Jedi academy.

"I wonder if I might ask you a question," Jacen said.

"Of course."

"I wonder if—since you came back from capture—whether you've ever felt the ability to, ah, sense the Yuuzhan Vong."

Tahiri was startled. "No. Why do you ask?" She brushed the blond hair from her face.

Jacen explained about his own capture, and how the implanted slave seed had given him the ability to connect telepathically with the Yuuzhan Vong.

Tahiri shivered. "No, I've never experienced that, and I'm glad. That must be *awful*."

"It's . . . all right. It's helped me understand them." He looked at her. "And it can be useful in detecting the enemy, and in controlling their bioweapons." Jacen hesitated. "The truth is, I was wondering if it might be possible to teach the Vongsense to someone else."

Tahiri took a step back, her eyes widening. "And you want to see if I can contact the Yuuzhan Vong through the Force?"

"No, *not* through the Force. It's a different sort of bond."

"Through their—" Her face twisted. "—slave implants."

"Yes."

"You know that I hate them." Her eyes burned fiercely into Jacen's. "I *hate* them. I know I'm a Jedi and I'm not supposed to hate anyone, but I can't help it. Not after what they've done."

Jacen nodded. "I understand. I don't want to put you through anything that will make you uncomfortable, or that will bring back bad memories."

"All right, then." She nodded. "I'm sorry, Jacen."

"That's fine."

Tahiri began to walk away, and then she hesitated, and turned. "Is it important?" she asked.

"I can't say," Jacen said. "But it will help you understand the Yuuzhan Vong. And perhaps when you understand them you won't hate them so much."

"I *want* to hate them." Her lips pressed together in a firm, defiant line.

"It takes a lot of energy to hate," Jacen said. "You might have other uses for that energy, Tahiri."

Again she hesitated. "All right," she said finally. "I'll give it a try."

They went to Jacen's small cabin, sat in meditation posture on the floor, and touched hands. He sensed Tahiri's expanding Force-awareness, and he said, "No, not the Force. This power comes from somewhere else."

Tahiri's mouth curled in annoyance. "What do I do, then?"

"Try to look into—into an empty place where the slave implants were. I'll try to guide you."

Jacen could find the empty place himself, and he could feel, at the edge of his awareness, the World Brain he had left behind on Coruscant. He tried to build a bridge between Tahiri and the dhuryam, but he couldn't seem to bring the two closer together, and he could sense Tahiri's growing frustration.

The problem was that there weren't any Yuuzhan Vong nearby. If there were, perhaps Tahiri wouldn't have such a hard time.

"I'm sort of glad it didn't work," Tahiri said afterward.

"Would you mind trying again later?"

She grimaced. "I suppose we could try. But I'm not looking forward to it."

After she'd left, Jacen had begun to record a holovid letter to his parents when he realized he wasn't alone. Not even in his own mind.

Vergere? he probed.

In return Jacen received impressions, pictures of a green treetop landscape that he recognized as Kashyyyk, and a strong, nonverbal command to come to the planet.

And this was followed by an equally powerful compulsion to silence.

A secret meeting? Jacen sent. There was no reply.

Jacen received permission to leave *Ralroost* from the officer of the deck and took his X-wing to the surface, homing on Vergere's presence in the Force.

She had chosen a small, remote island for the meeting place. No Wookiees lived there, but the lower depths of the wroshyr forest was filled with the usual deadly native life-forms.

The meeting place was marked by an old four-passenger Trilon shuttle perched at a dangerous angle in the uppermost branches of one of the wroshyr trees. Jacen floated the X-wing toward it on his repulsorlifts and carefully dropped the starfighter onto an interwoven net of branches. As he shut off the repulsorlifts and let the branches take the fighter's weight, he was surprised by the sight of a four-meter-long, many-toothed serpent flying past his canopy.

"Their instinct is to eat birds," Vergere explained as Jacen climbed out of the cockpit and lowered himself to one of the massive wroshyr limbs. "I try to discourage them, but they are unintelligent and thus persistent."

As Vergere spoke, another, larger snake was torn free, in a shower of green foliage, from an overhanging limb and went whipping through the air and over the green horizon. "If I throw them into the sea," Vergere said, "it delays their return, but they *do* come back."

The branch swayed under Jacen's feet. It was wide as a highway, but the motion was unsettling. "Can't you make yourself small?" he asked.

"They don't detect me in the Force. I think they smell me."

"I'm good with animals. Let me try." He expanded his awareness of the Force to include the fauna of the treetops and detected the primitive, purposeful minds of several of the snakes, all of them stalking through the foliage toward Vergere. Jacen tried turning off the instinct to hunt, but the compulsion was hardwired into them, and he failed. Then he suggested to them that better, more appetizing food was to be found elsewhere, and they turned away in search of it.

"Nicely done," Vergere said. "And it is a tactic that can be applied to species other than snakes."

Jacen looked at her. "Why are you here?"

Vergere's feathery antennae crooked forward and back, as if scanning the air for invaders. "I sense no other presence," she said.

"Did you run away? Is Nylykerka after you?"

"Nylykerka and many others. Your Master Skywalker among them, I think."

Jacen took a deep breath. He squatted on his heels on the wide branch, and said, "You'd better tell me."

Vergere told her story. Jacen was horrified. Not simply because Alpha Red was a weapon for mass murder, but because, thanks to the slave seed tendrils coiled about his nerves, he now possessed an empathy for the Yuuzhan Vong. It was not only the human part of his mind that quailed at this revelation, but the part that understood the enemy.

Vergere looked at him. "I have given the Jedi only a few months to respond to this horror," she said.

"They can rebuild the weapon?"

"Of course."

He shrugged helplessly. "What should I do?"

"I can't advise you."

"Should I tell people? We could put pressure on the government, but that would tell the Yuuzhan Vong, and—" He shrank before the consequences of that decision, the Yuuzhan Vong realizing that they were in a war of extinction rather than a war of conquest.

Her dark, tilted eyes gazed into his. "Since I first met you, I have had an intuition that you were in some way bound up with the fate of the Yuuzhan Vong. Perhaps this is the moment I've been anticipating."

Jacen looked at her in surprise. "The fate of the Yuuzhan Vong? Is that why you've taken such an interest in me?"

Her eyes narrowed. "Beyond any other interest I would have taken in a Jedi in distress, yes."

He rose to his feet. The huge branch swayed beneath him

as a breeze ruffled the leaves. "What are you going to do?" he asked.

Her wide mouth twisted in thought. "There isn't a general search for me, or you'd have heard. That means that only the Intelligence people will be looking for me, which will make it easier to evade them." She craned her long neck to look at her shuttle. "My craft came to Mon Calamari with a family of refugees who sold it to buy food. Sooner or later the dealer to whom they sold it will notice that it's missing from its orbit, and then there'll be a search, but that won't matter—the hyperdrive engines are ready to give up the ghost, and I'll be lucky to get out of the Kashyyyk system." She turned to Jacen. "Can you give me a ride in your fighter?"

"Certainly. But to where?"

"To your ship, perhaps?"

He blinked at her. "It's an assault cruiser," he said. "It's got over a thousand crew."

"It's easy to pass as one among thousands, yes?" Vergere smiled. "And I would be less conspicuous in a uniform, no?"

"No," Jacen said. He decided to pass over the unlikely chance that he'd find a uniform that would fit Vergere. "Most of the crew are Bothans. The starfighter pilots are from all over, but there aren't that many of them, and—"

"No doubt there are supply vessels coming on and off the ship all the time," Vergere said. "Cargo coming on and off, and being placed in storage. And dispatch boats, and shuttles to other ships. Hundreds of escape pods. With all that confusion, surely one single individual could find a way off the ship and to safety." She smiled. "I am very good at being invisible."

Jacen sighed. He sensed an inevitability in the offing. "Let's hope there aren't any big snakes aboard," he said.

*   *   *

"I'm glad to know that creepy little bird is gone," Han said. "It was all I could do not to wring her neck for what she did to Jacen." He looked around. "Where did Vergere go to, anyway?"

"I'm not sure," Luke said. He quelled the uneasiness in his mind and asked Han and Leia to sit. The pair took the seats offered and then the drinks that Mara brought into the room. Mara took her own drink and sat on the sofa next to Luke. He put his arm around her.

"I wanted to tell you that I'll be leaving for a while," Luke said. "I'm going across the galaxy to Fondor, and I'm not sure when I'll be back."

Leia looked at him. "Is it something you can talk about?"

"I'm going to Garm Bel Iblis," Luke said. "He commands at Fondor, and since the fall of Coruscant he's been operating independently of Sien Sovv and the military."

"Just like he did in the Rebellion," Han said. "Bel Iblis likes running his own show."

"When he was given orders, at first he responded that the situation in his sector was different than the Supreme Commander thought, and therefore he declined to carry them out. Lately he hasn't been responding to orders at all."

"You brought him into the fold once before," Leia said. "I guess Cal thinks you can do it again."

"It hasn't been important until now," Luke said. "Bel Iblis has been doing more or less what he should have been doing anyway, defending his sector and harassing the enemy. But now Ackbar has a plan to win the war, and we need to know whether Bel Iblis will be in at the finish."

Leia considered the question. "He'll be in. He's headstrong and independent, but he'll be on the right side when it counts."

"I hope so," Mara said. "I'd hate for Luke to make that long trip for nothing."

Leia gave Luke a curious look. "This mission is taking you away from the Jedi—I mean, the High Council. Can you be absent for such a long time?"

"I'll give my proxy to Cilghal," Luke said. "She'll speak and vote for me, and for Saba, who gave me her proxy when she joined."

The strain between Luke and Cal hadn't affected the running of the High Council. Cal seemed perfectly friendly, if a bit reserved. But he no longer shared confidential information with Luke—if there were military or political secrets that Luke wasn't already a part of, then they were never mentioned in Luke's presence.

The trust was gone. Luke didn't know whether he would ever win it back.

Luke, for his part, still had hopes of convincing Cal not to use Alpha Red at all.

But if necessary, Luke would poll the other Jedi members privately. The influence of the council as a whole might tip the balance against Dif Scaur and his plan. Together, they might be able to take a principled stand against the use of the weapon.

But that was for the future. For now, Luke was dedicated to making sure that Ackbar's plan was carried out. If the Yuuzhan Vong were defeated, then the arguments against Alpha Red would bear all that much more weight.

Luke turned to Han. "Speaking of Ackbar," he said, "he asked me if you'd do him a favor."

Ice rang in Han's glass as he drained it. "Anything," he said.

"He'd like you to resume your military rank and take command of a squadron."

Han placed his glass firmly on the table next to his seat. "You know, I never did take to the military," he said. "And the military never took to me. If Ackbar just wants to make both me *and* the fleet miserable . . ."

"He'd like you to take command of the squadron contributed by the Smugglers' Alliance," Luke said. "Talon Karrde, Booster Terrik, and the *Errant Venture* . . . They're a hard bunch, anarchic and rebellious and undisciplined. The ships are a heterogeneous jumble, and any tactics would have to be improvised by the squadron commander."

Leia, a little grim, turned to her husband. "I'd use the word *never* if I were you."

"Lando's part of it, too," Luke added. "You know he'd make mincemeat out of a regular fleet officer. Anyone who could control that bunch would have to be as rough as they are, and as experienced. The commander would have to be able to fly the pants off any of them, and—"

"And whip fifty times his weight in angry krayt dragons," Leia finished. She looked at Han. "You see what my brother's trying to do, don't you?" she said. "He's trying to *flatter* you into taking this job. He's trying to tell you that *only Han Solo* could *possibly* be tough enough for this assignment."

Han smiled. "He's right of course," he said. "But the word *never* is still on the tip of my tongue."

Luke sighed. "You're going to force me to fight dirty," he said. "I really didn't want to do this."

Han laughed. "Hit me with your best shot."

Luke made an apologetic gesture. "During the upcoming operation, the Smugglers' Alliance squadron will be in support of Admiral Kre'fey's fleet. Which includes your children. Sorry."

Han looked stricken. Leia narrowed her eyes and glared at her brother. "That is really underhanded, Luke," she said.

"I know," Luke said.

"We had both gotten out. We were going to have time together. We were going to be *happy*."

"Sorry."

"And now . . ." She clenched her fists. "Now it's all up to us again, isn't it?"

Luke smiled. "The fate of the galaxy may well rest in your hands. Yes. It's unfair, but that's the way it is."

Leia raised a fist. "When this is over," she said, "remind me to hit you."

Luke raised his hands peaceably. "Kyp's first in line," he said, "but when this is over, take all the shots you want."

Jacen was returning from Kashyyyk to the *Ralroost* when he was commed by Kyp Durron.

"I need all Jedi on *Mon Adapyne* for a meeting. It's urgent."

"Can I wash and change first?" Jacen asked. "I've been down on Kashyyyk, and I'm kind of a mess."

"I said *urgent*," Kyp snapped. "We need you now."

Jacen considered the small figure of Vergere, who was crammed into the cockpit on his lap. *Better make yourself very small*, he thought.

"Acknowledged," he said.

Vergere managed to avoid discovery when Jacen landed his X-wing in the cruiser's capacious docking bays. She remained in the cockpit, ducking down out of sight as he dropped to the deck and went in search of his fellow Jedi.

Kyp, seated at the end of one of the mess tables, had assembled the other Jedi in a corner of the officers' mess. Jacen entered cautiously and saw Corran Horn along with Jaina, Tesar, Lowbacca, and the other newly made Jedi. As he entered, Saba and her squadron of Wild Knights turned to stare at him with glittering reptilian eyes. Jacen tried to calm the panic that fluttered in his rib cage, and said, "What's going on?"

Kyp looked at him. "I have an urgent message from Master Skywalker. He said that Vergere has run away from Mon Calamari, and if we see her we're to detain her and take her to Mon Calamari or to New Republic Intelligence."

Even though he'd known approximately what the message would contain, still Jacen felt an unpleasant surge of emotion at Kyp's words.

In the last few months, Jacen had become an expert at deception. He'd lied to the Yuuzhan Vong, and he'd lied to Ganner Rhysode in order to capture him for the enemy. But lying to an entire room of Jedi—Jedi alongside of whom he'd been fighting for the last months—was a new ordeal.

"Vergere?" he said, calming himself. "What's she done?"

"Master Skywalker didn't say. But it has to be important, because Vergere is now our number one priority. If we have *any* notion where she might be, we're to drop everything and go in search of her. But we're not to search alone—Vergere is to be considered dangerous and should be apprehended by Jedi working as teams."

Saba Sebatyne raised a hand. "We are not to break into packz and search the galaxy *now*, are we?"

"No. We're to stay with the fleet until we hear from Vergere or until we hear of her. And then we're to get her secured and back where she belongs." He turned his eyes to Jacen, and Jacen felt a cold hand brush his spine.

"You're closer to her than anyone here," Kyp said. "Master Skywalker thought she might try to contact you."

"She'd have to be out of her mind to come to Kashyyyk," Jacen said, with perfect truth. "There are too many Jedi here."

"Right," Kyp said, though Jacen still sensed his suspicion. Kyp rose from the table. "It's unlikely that we'll see her—we're all moving out, anyway."

Jacen stood quietly motionless on the deck. "Moving out?"

"Right, brother," Jaina said. "We're on continual alert. Something big's happening—the whole fleet's getting ready to move."

"Rumor says it's the Core," Corran Horn said. "But we know how accurate rumor's been in this war."

Jaina, on her way out of the meeting, slapped Jacen on the shoulder. "See you when we get there," she said.

Wherever there *is*, Jacen thought.

And wondered, now that the whole fleet was on alert, how he was going to get Vergere off his ship.

TWENTY-FOUR

"We're installing blastproof doors here," the engineer said. "Once you get your people inside, you can drop the doors and be perfectly safe for, oh, several hours at least."

"Several hours at least," Jaina repeated. In the frigid air, her breath misted out in front of her as she spoke. She looked at the busy droids, which were lifting huge, clattering pneumatic hammers to widen the old mineshaft.

What no one had yet explained to her was *why* she would have to seek safety from the enemy in the tunnels of Ebaq 9, which seemed to be a perfectly useless moonlet at the end of a twisty hyperspace passage into the Deep Core.

But that seemed a part of the plan. Whatever the plan was.

Ebaq 9 was abuzz with military engineers, modifying the docking bays that once held mining shuttles, installing shields and a modern communications system, bringing the old life-support and artificial gravity systems up to current specs. The engineers were protected by a reinforced squadron under General Farlander, forty capital ships in all, far larger than the force he'd led at Obroa-skai.

Farlander, with Jaina under his command, was supposed to defend this useless moon. But the moon was also being turned into a giant bunker, and Jaina and the others were being given instruction in how to hide there.

Why hide? Why defend Ebaq 9 in the first place? The plan didn't make any sense.

Nor did Jaina know where the rest of Traest Kre'fey's fleet had gone. Kre'fey, Jacen, and most of the other Jedi hadn't come to Ebaq 9 with Jaina and Farlander; they were off on some other mission. Jaina didn't know where.

All she knew were the drills. Maneuvers aimed at readying Farlander's squadron for defending the mined-out moon, then more maneuvers aimed at breaking off combat, landing on the moon, and hiding deep underground.

"We'll have power packs, lifesuits, blasters, and ammunition stored here," the engineer went on. "We'll also have dried rations and water."

"Blasters," Jaina repeated. "Ammunition." She shivered in her heavy jacket, and the movement almost lifted her from the deck in the moonlet's light gravity. Her inner ear trembled on the edge of vertigo.

According to rumor, this plan was Ackbar's work.

Jaina hoped not. Because that meant that Ackbar, as well as his plan, was insane.

"Time to give them their first hint," Mara said. "The first hint of the final redoubt in the Deep Core."

Nylykerka's eyes brightened. "How much should we tell them?"

"Just give them a hint at first," Mara advised. "We don't want to hand them the whole thing. If they put the pieces together themselves, they'll believe even more in what they're learning."

"Very well," Nylykerka said.

"Perhaps the office of Senator Krall Praget could hear about an emergency appropriation for a base in the Deep Core. And you could combine that with a leak concerning an evacuation drill for the Chief of State and the Advisory Council."

Nylykerka's air sac throbbed thoughtfully. "Yes," he said. "Yes, I think that might do the job."

Stars blossomed around Jacen as *Ralroost* fell out of hyperspace. He sat in front of Admiral Kre'fey on the assault cruiser's bridge, with tactical displays laid out around him.

They were as deep in the Deep Core as he'd ever ventured, the stars packed so tightly around them that it was never quite night.

"Ebaq Nine," Kre'fey said meditatively, as the moon and its giant primary appeared on the navigation arrays. He turned to the communications officer. "Send my compliments to General Farlander, and request that he report aboard at his earliest convenience." He turned to Jacen. "If you wish to see your sister," he said, "you have my permission."

"Thank you, sir."

Jacen rose from his seat and withdrew from *Ralroost*'s bridge. Kre'fey's fleet had reached the end of their long, erratic journey.

While Farlander's squadron had flown directly to Ebaq, *Ralroost* and the rest of Kre'fey's fleet had been engaged in a series of raids against the enemy. On every occasion the Jedi wove their Force-meld to coordinate the attacking forces. Wayland, Bimmisaari, Gyndine, and even Nal Hutta had been hit. Gyndine had been defended by a larger force than Kre'fey wanted to tackle, but elsewhere the defenders, fighting bravely but at hopeless odds, had been destroyed.

Diversionary raids, Kre'fey had explained after they were over. They were designed to show the enemy that Kre'fey and his fleet were anywhere but where they were going—Ebaq 9, and the Deep Core.

Being continually in action meant that Jacen had been unable to smuggle Vergere off the flagship. After two days of hiding her in the cockpit of his X-wing, he'd managed to smuggle her to his quarters. There, she'd taken up residence in the storage area under his bunk. He'd told the droid that cleaned his quarters to keep out.

Fortunately, he was in officers' quarters and had a room to himself. The worst part was getting food to her, especially as she had a more-than-healthy appetite.

Another problem concerned Tahiri, who gamely continued with Jacen to try to find out if she could discover in herself a Vongsense. Jacen couldn't have her in his cabin while Vergere was there, and produced various excuses why their practice had to be somewhere else less convenient. Not all of the excuses were convincing, but Tahiri seemed to accept them.

They failed in their attempt to develop any Vongsense in Tahiri, though Jacen privately thought this might be because there were no Yuuzhan Vong in the vicinity. And if there *were* Yuuzhan Vong around, the Jedi would be fighting them and have no time for meditations.

The only compensation for the perilous situation was that he and Vergere, in the privacy of his cabin, were able to share their meditations.

Leaving *Ralroost*, Jacen took his X-wing to the moonlet and met Jaina in the docking bay that had been modified to fly and arm military craft. Twin Suns Squadron's X-wings were neatly parked there, ready to launch on a moment's notice.

Jaina looked tired. Her skin was pasty, her hair limp, and she looked as if she hadn't been out of her jumpsuit in days. Jacen didn't need the Force to sense her discouragement.

"I don't know what we're *doing* here," she said, after giving him a weary embrace. "Half the time we're drilling on launching to defend the system, and the rest of the exercises have us running for bunkers."

"We've got dozens of capital ships here," Jacen said. "We have all the Jedi we need to form a meld. We can start joint exercises."

"You *all* can't run for bunkers," Jaina said. She shook her head. "This is worse than anything I've ever seen. I *hate* this—I'm just *nailed* to this rock. It's like we have a huge target sign pasted on us. I'm best if I'm given freedom of action—freedom to be the Trickster. That's the role that works for me."

The Trickster, Jacen thought.

I must inform you that you possess insufficient experience of depravity. Vergere's words floated to the front of Jacen's mind. He stared at Jaina in horror.

"I just realized what's happening," he said.

Jaina looked at him, and apprehension dawned in her brown eyes.

"You're the bait," Jacen told her. "You're the bait that will bring the Yuuzhan Vong here." He paused, and then nodded as he followed the thought to its inevitable conclusion. "And I'm the bait, too."

"The bait must be real," Ackbar said. "And the bait must be seen by the enemy."

"If necessary," Mara said, "we'll have one of our Senators ask whether it's true that the Chief of State has hidden himself in a redoubt along with his twin Jedi bodyguards. But I think we can do it more subtly than that."

The tinkling of fountains and the scent of brine filled the air. Mara and Winter sat by the edge of Ackbar's pool, swirling their legs in the water. Ayddar Nylykerka had unbent to the point of taking off his boots and dipping his hairy toes.

Mara reviewed her mental checklist. "The plans for the Final Redoubt," she said. "Who's going to glimpse them?"

"We've already used the Sullustan in Senator Praget's office," Nylykerka said. "Perhaps this time we should try the Peace Brigade contractor working in the shipyards. He can be given a moment alone with the plans in his supervisor's office."

"We know the Vong gave him a holocam."

Mara, Nylykerka, and the mouse droids had located a third Yuuzhan Vong spy network operating in the new capital. She and Fleet Intelligence were keeping all three happy by feeding them information that was perfectly accurate, but either out of date, irrelevant, or useless. The Yuuzhan Vong wouldn't suspect a spy who delivered no false information, even if the information wasn't completely useful.

"The government needs to disappear," Winter said.

"Cal will say he's on a tour of military facilities with the heads of the Senate councils," Mara said. "And then no one will hear from him for a while."

"And the Solo twins need to disappear as well."

"Perhaps Senator Praget can be indignant about it," Nylykerka suggested. "He was an opponent of Leia Organa Solo—there's no reason why he can't dislike her children as well."

Mara laughed. "That's right! He can complain that Jacen and Jaina are hiding in some secret fortress just when the New Republic needs them most!"

"Bait," Ackbar said. He lifted one hand and let a stream of seawater pour from his palm into the pool. "The bait must be real. And it must be seen to be real."

The Sword of the Jedi, Jaina thought. *A sword that's about to be beaten into iron filings between the hammer of the Vong and the anvil of Ebaq.*

"Twin Squadron, prepare to withdraw on my mark. Three, two, mark."

Jaina rotated her fighter's nose and triggered the ion engines. Deep in her gut she absorbed the tug of shifting momentum.

Now that she understood Ackbar's plan better, she had to admit it made sense. Lure the enemy into an attack on a supposedly hidden base guarded by Jedi elites, trap them in a starry dead end, annihilate them.

The problem was, the Yuuzhan Vong would have every chance to annihilate Jaina and her squadron first.

"Request a shield drop on Sector Seventeen," Jaina called to Ebaq Control.

"Shields dropping in five seconds. Four. Three . . ."

The shields dropped as Twin Suns Squadron raced through the gap. Jaina triggered the starfighter's repulsorlifts and maneuvered into the docking bay space.

"Twin Suns Squadron, abandon fighters and rendezvous at the entrance to Tunnel Twelve-C."

Jaina popped the canopy before the X-wing quite touched down, cleared her webbing, and used the Force to lift herself clear of the cockpit and drop onto the docking bay deck. She led the squadron in sprinting for the head of the giant main shaft that ran clean through the moonlet.

As she ran she kept thinking how tired she was. Tired of the war, of the constant drills, tired of having so many others who depended on her.

She was losing her edge.

"I'm worried," Jacen told Vergere. "She's exhausted, she has too many responsibilities. She's on the edge."

"Of darkness?" Vergere asked.

Jacen shook his head. "No. Of despair." He hesitated, then spoke. "She doesn't think she'll survive the war."

They spoke in hushed tones in Jacen's cabin, Jacen on his bunk, Vergere perched on his desk chair. Most of the warship's crews were asleep. After two days of joint exercises, *Ralroost* and most of Kre'fey's fleet hung motionless around the old Imperial star base called Tarkin's Fang, just a few minutes' hyperspace jump from Ebaq 9.

"To despair of life is to despair of the Force," Vergere said.

"How do I help her?"

Vergere's head thrust forward on its angular neck, peculiarly insistent. The chair creaked at the shift in weight. "You are responsible for your own choices alone."

"But if I *choose* to help my sister?"

"She rejects your help, does she not?"

"Maybe I haven't gone about it right. If I can find the right way to get to her . . ."

"From here you can do nothing." Vergere's tone was unusually harsh. "Think of your own choices only."

Jacen looked at her as a warning sang in his nerves. "What do you know?" he asked.

Vergere's eyes were opaque. "Of your sister? Nothing."

"And of me?"

"I know, young Jedi, that you must choose wisely." She turned away from him, toward the wall. "I will meditate now."

"You're hiding something."

She looked at him over her shoulder. "Always," she said.

And that was all he got out of her.

The door shivered open, and Nom Anor's heart lurched at the sight of a grotesque face grinning at him like some demon's parody of a Yuuzhan Vong. He controlled himself as he realized it was only Onimi, who broke into a slash-mouthed grin and ushered him into the room with a bow. The Shamed One sat in the shadows before Shimrra's feet and declaimed.

"What one-eyed lurker skulks outside my door?
Behold the furtive agent, Nom Anor."

Nom Anor imagined kicking Onimi out of his way as he stepped into the shadowed room. In the dim light he made out the huge form of Supreme Overlord Shimrra reclining on a dais of pulsing red hau polyps. Nom Anor prostrated himself, all too aware of the relentless scrutiny of Shimrra's rainbow eyes.

He tried not to think of what he knew about the eighth cortex project, about Shimrra's cynical manipulation of religion, about the dreadful hollowness of all the Supreme Overlord stood for.

The Overlord's deep voice rolled out of the darkness. "You have news of the infidels?"

"I have, Supreme One." He rose to his feet and tried to control the excitement in his voice. "I believe that I have the information that will bring about the decisive battle."

The battle that *you* need, he thought. The victory that will give the eighth cortex project time to succeed.

Shimrra's voice was deadly calm. "Very well, Executor. We shall await the warmaster."

"As you wish, Dread One."

Nom Anor repressed a shiver of fear as he stood alone before the Supreme Overlord. This was Shimrra's private audience chamber, not the great reception hall, and Nom Anor was without support here, unable to hide behind Yoog Skell and a deputation of intendants. He remembered the way the Supreme Overlord's mind had overborne his own, the way his thoughts had been squeezed as if between two giant fingers.

Onimi opened the door before Tsavong Lah could touch its membrane.

"Behold the great soldier, commander of corps,
Great Tsavong Lah, the master of war."

Tsavong Lah padded balefully into the room on his clawed vua'sa foot, his eyes glaring hatred at Nom Anor.

The warmaster lowered himself to the floor before the Supreme Overlord.

"At your command, Supreme One."

"Stand, Warmaster."

Tsavong Lah rose heavily to his feet, the vua'sa claws scrabbling for traction. Even though he was large for a Yuuzhan Vong, the massive form of Shimrra outweighed him by at least half.

"May I congratulate the warmaster on his mating?" Nom Anor said.

"You may," Tsavong Lah said, looking at Nom Anor with more than his usual suspicion.

Tsavong Lah, in obedience to Shimrra's order that all warriors mate, had been seen with a subaltern. A beauty, too, known for the sublime blue of the pouches beneath her eyes.

"I hope that Domain Lah will soon have another addition to its ranks," Nom Anor said.

"That," Tsavong Lah said, "is none of your business."

Shimrra vented a basso chuckle. "To business," he said. "Report, Warmaster."

"The fleets are ready, Dread Lord. Our auxiliaries have been trained and stand ready to guard our conquests. We continue to recruit mercenaries."

"None of these elements have distinguished themselves thus far," Shimrra pointed out.

"The enemy raid us, that is true," Tsavong Lah said. "But they flee whenever we face them with anything approaching equal numbers. And in any case the raids will cease once we resume the offensive." He formed a fist on the end of the radank leg he had in place of an arm. "We are ready for conquest, Supreme One! With your permission, I am ready to take Corellia—five planets in the system, Lord, shipyards and the Centerpoint weapon! They are isolated, and I believe I can take them at small cost. They will try to defend all five planets, but that will stretch them too thin, and I will defeat them in detail." Eagerness contorted his scarred face. "May I have your permission to advance, Supreme One?"

A giggle escaped Onimi's slash of a mouth. "I believe Nom Anor has another suggestion."

Nom Anor felt the warmaster's anger as Tsavong Lah glowered at him. "*This* one?" the warmaster said. "I have followed his advice before—to my cost."

The Supreme Overlord's eyes shimmered from a bloody red to a sulfurous yellow. The hau polyps, shifting beneath his weight, gave a squelching sound and an acid stench. "Speak, Executor," Shimrra said.

Nom Anor ignored Tsavong Lah and turned to face Shimrra. "My spies inform me that the New Republic government has fled Mon Calamari and is hiding in the Deep Core. The warmaster and his forces may trap them there and crush them. Without a central government, the enemy will fall apart." He deigned to glance at Tsavong Lah. "The warmaster may then be able to take Corellia without fighting."

Tsavong Lah's expression hesitated between triumph and scorn. "What spies?" he demanded finally. "What evidence? How do we know this isn't a trap?"

Nom Anor turned once again to Shimrra. "I have correlated the evidence from different independent networks operating on Mon Calamari. The plans for what the enemy calls the 'Final Redoubt' came from one source. Its location came from another agent. News of an emergency appropriation to pay for it came from a third. The government's absence from Mon Calamari is public knowledge, though it is presented as a kind of tour of the military." He smiled. "And the fact that the Final Redoubt is guarded by Jedi—in fact by the Solo twins—came from my most reliable agent."

He sensed Tsavong Lah straightening at the mention of the Solo twins. Nom Anor swept one hand triumphantly across his chest. "After this one battle, the warmaster may sacrifice Cal Omas, the heads of the Senate councils, the Solo twins, and many other Jedi. My life in payment if I am wrong, Supreme One."

"As you say, Executor," Shimrra rumbled. "If you are wrong, it *shall* be your life in payment."

Nom Anor heard the words without fear. He knew that he was right, that the victory was within their grasp.

Shimrra leaned forward on the trembling bed of polyps. "Now let us examine this evidence, and make our plans . . ."

TWENTY-FIVE

Alarms blasted Jaina from sleep. She slept in her pilot's coveralls because it was warmer that way—the techs had never quite got the heating system to work in the pilots' quarters, though strangely enough the engineers' own heaters seemed to work perfectly well. So frequent had been the drills that she drew on her boots and grabbed her pilot's helmet without even opening her eyes.

She managed to pry open her gummed lids as she sprinted down the corridor that led to the docking bays. Five strides later the artificial gravity snapped off as the moonlet's defense shields went on—power supply problems had been continuous, and judging by present evidence were unresolved. There had been a rumor that someone had dropped a decimal point in a requisition, and that Ebaq 9's power supply was one-tenth the size it was supposed to be.

Jaina used the Force to push herself forward, snagging Vale on the way as her wingmate floundered in the reduced gravity, unable to get traction for her boots. In the docking bay, Jaina flung Vale toward her starfighter, then jumped for her own X-wing. R2-B3, which had never left the bay, was already in the second seat and had the electronics switched on, the repulsorlifts glowing, and the quad ion engines warming.

The astromech tweedled a greeting as Jaina buckled herself into her seat and watched the last of her squadron's pilots race, float, or flop their way through the reduced gravity to their craft. When the last one had checked in over the comlink, Jaina opened a channel to Ebaq Control.

"This is Twin One. Twin Suns Squadron ready for launch."

"Launch immediately, Twin One! The shield in Sector Twelve is down for you!"

Ebaq Control seemed a little overexcited this morning. "Acknowledged." She switched to her intership channel. "We have clearance, people. Let's go."

Jaina's X-wing swung aloft on its repulsorlifts and floated toward the docking bay doors. As the massive doors parted for her, she triggered the ion engines and launched herself into the star-strewn half night beyond.

In space, as she waited for the others to launch and form on her starfighter, she looked at her displays and saw Farlander's capital ships hovering eight light-minutes out, all of them launching starfighters. And beyond Farlander, bright starbursts blossomed onto the displays, squadrons of enemy ships in their hundreds and thousands.

Sudden electricity snarled through her nerves, and the sleep that clung to her was burned away.

This was not a drill. This was a force of a size that hadn't been seen since the attack on Coruscant.

And then Jaina felt a surge through the Force, a sense that a powerful mind had just focused on her, like a searchlight on a helpless insect. Horror shivered through her bones as she recognized the sensation.

Voxyn . . .

The howls of the voxyn rose around Tsavong Lah, and he felt triumph rise in him like a glorious wind. He raised his arms, hands clawed as if to tear the sky asunder.

Jeedai. The *Jeedai* were here. That skulking coward, Nom Anor, had been right.

Above him, blaze bugs rose into the air, hovering in place

to form a three-dimensional representation of the battle, the pitch of their wings and the flashing of their scarlet abdomens identifying the size and status of all ships in the area, friend and enemy alike.

The voxyn howled again. Wild joy rose in Tsavong Lah. "By Yun-Yuuzhan!" he shouted. "The stinking intendant was *right*!"

The New Republic forces were completely outnumbered. No doubt if it were possible to flee, the enemy would be doing so. But Ebaq was in a dead end, and no retreat was possible. They *had* to fight.

And should the *Jeedai* attempt to hide on Ebaq 9 or any other body in this system, Tsavong Lah had the voxyn. Six of the Jedi-hunting beasts had been off Myrkr when the rest of their species was destroyed. The voxyn had very short life spans, and these were near the end of theirs, their green scales yellowed, their eyes filmed and weary. But as soon as they'd sensed Jedi in the system they'd thrown off their lethargy, and their tails lashed eagerly back and forth.

The embracing tendrils of the cognition throne writhed atop his head, feeding him tactical data and keeping him in contact with *Blood Sacrifice*'s yammosk, which wordlessly directed the thousands of ships, coralskippers, and transports at the warmaster's command. In a circle around the cognition throne were a group of subalterns, apprentices, and readers, the former with villips that kept Tsavong Lah in touch with his squadrons.

Tsavong Lah felt sudden confusion from the yammosk. The enemy were jamming its signals.

This hardly mattered, the odds were so great. Tsavong Lah called out orders that would be transmitted by the subalterns around him with their villips. "The Battle Group of Yun-Yammka will advance and engage the enemy! The Battle Groups of Yun-Txiin and Yun-Q'aah will advance on the flanks of the enemy and envelop him. The Battle Groups of Yun-Yuuzhan and Yun-Harla will remain in reserve."

The battle group named for the Slayer would engage the enemy. And then the battle groups named for the Lovers would converge on the enemy, in a true lovers' embrace, and destroy them.

Two more battle groups would remain in reserve, including the warmaster's own, to follow the enemy through hyperspace should they manage to escape. Though it was unlikely that the infidels would manage an escape, pinned as they were against the gravity well of a huge gas giant.

Acknowledgments poured in from the commanders of the different battle groups. The blaze bugs overhead swarmed and flashed as dispositions shifted.

The enemy were maneuvering cautiously, trying to keep between the advancing Battle Group of Yun-Yammka and Ebaq 9. This suited the warmaster perfectly—the defenders were a slow, easy target against which he could hurl his overwhelming strength.

Tsavong Lah's satisfaction grew as he watched the enemy plod toward destruction. The Battle Group of Yun-Yammka began to maneuver into extended order to lay itself alongside the enemy, two capital ships to the enemy's one. And then Tsavong Lah sensed a shift in the infidels' dispositions—the blaze bugs began to move, their whirrs and patterns swinging subtly to a new configuration.

The warmaster watched in growing unease as the enemy squadron shifted swiftly from a long, extended line into a compact, pointed blade, a spearhead pointed into the Yuuzhan Vong battle group. In a flare of intense fire, the New Republic squadron pierced the Yuuzhan Vong extended line, shattering the invaders' formation. Eight of the largest Yuuzhan Vong ships, hit by the combined power of the entire enemy squadron, were left disabled or dead.

The claws of the vu'asa at the end of Tsavong Lah's leg

clutched at the frame of his throne in anger. But his words, as he gave his next order, were calm. "The Battle Group of Yun-Yammka will engage the infidels as closely as possible." The Yuuzhan Vong would take more losses as the dispersed ships closed with the compact enemy, but then superior numbers would begin to tell, and so would the Battle Groups of Yun-Txiin and Yun-Q'aah, which would soon be in a position to envelop the enemy and finish them off.

The battle was still his. It would take a little more time, that was all.

And time the warmaster had in plenty.

In a room that smelled of protein and blood deep within the Damutek of the Intendants, Nom Anor stood before his superior Yoog Skell, a villip in his hands. The villip had formed into the face of an executor on Tsavong Lah's flagship, one of the few members of the intendant class on the expeditionary force.

"The enemy is maneuvering well," the executor said. "But still we will crush him. Our numbers are overwhelming."

Yoog Skell growled as he paced back and forth.

"We've been surprised," he muttered. "I don't like surprises. And neither does Supreme Overlord Shimrra."

When the call came, Mara was alone in the Skywalker apartment looking at holos of Ben. She went to the comm, and saw Winter gazing calmly back at her.

"It's begun," Winter said. "Ackbar and I are going up to Fleet Command. You may join us if you wish."

Mara felt a sudden dryness in her mouth. "Of course," she said. "I'll be right there."

It's not working. The faint thought floated toward Jaina from Madurrin, in position on General Farlander's bridge. *What's not working?*

The Trickster jammers. The ones that would identify enemy ships as belonging to the wrong side and cause their friends to shoot at them.

Another piece of bad luck, but Jaina was too frantic to feel badly about it now. Her own target was coming up.

"Shadow bomb away." Jaina shoved the dumb weapon ahead with a push of the Force and drew back on the stick to bring her X-wing to a slightly different trajectory. Ahead, the target enemy cruiser lay in a blaze of fire as Keyan Farlander's entire squadron swept past it, turbolasers churning out fire while missiles corkscrewed through the void between ships.

"Bomb away," came Tesar's hissing voice, followed by Lowbacca's howl as he, too, flung a shadow bomb at the enemy.

General Farlander hadn't been content to punch through the enemy formation only once—he had spun his entire squadron around and done it a second time, before the enemy could concentrate against him.

Jaina felt Tesar and Lowie through the Force, as well as the dumb shadow bombs they were all shoving at the enemy, while Madurrin was a presence from her place on General Farlander's flagship. As the only Jedi in the system they were too few to create a proper Force-meld, but the three Jedi who led the flights of Twin Suns Squadron were so close, and by now so experienced in their work, that the meld was hardly necessary.

"Skips at point two, Major." Vale's voice was calm. "Getting set to bounce us."

"Turn to engage . . . *now*." Jaina rotated and fired the X-wing's quad engines. Engaging the enemy head-on was a lot safer than letting them jump on Twin Suns' tails.

Ahead, flashes marked oncoming enemy fire, a steady pulse of projectiles.

"Leapfrog, even and odd," Jaina said, and extended her

forward shields as she was aware of Twin Three pulling up even with her, the overlapping shields of the two X-wings covering her entire four-fighter flight. She began stuttering laserfire at the enemy, though she doubted it would have much effect. Doubtless the enemy would have their dovin basals deployed forward against her fire.

Enemy fire began to hammer her shields. Flying by instinct and the Force, she blinked against the brilliant flashes and tried to read her instruments to know when the shields' power situation grew critical.

In the event, it was R2-B3 who chittered the warning at her.

"Leapfrog *now*," she called, and throttled back.

Twins One and Three fell back while Twins Two and Four surged into their place, their fresh shields covering the entire flight. It was a precision maneuver, all four starfighters maneuvering within a tolerance of mere centimeters.

Thanks to endless drills and practice in battle, Twin Suns Squadron had come a long way since the battle over *Far Thunder*, when all Jaina could do was arrange them in a long line and have them play follow the leader.

The coralskippers flashed by, no more than blurs on their converging course. Normally she'd call for the squadron to split and drop on them, but maneuvering and combat took too much time. She needed to stick with Farlander and his compact group, not get caught away from support.

"Turning left sixty degrees," Jaina said, a course that would bring them toward Farlander and the main body.

As her flight performed a perfect crossover turn, the maneuver turned her cockpit toward the enemy cruiser just in time to see the brilliant explosions of three shadow bombs planting themselves along its flank. She could see the ship tremble with each hit.

Over her comm she could hear the hissing of Barabel

amusement. She was glad Tesar could find something funny in all this.

Then Tesar's tone turned serious. "Skips astern, Twin Leader."

"Maximum acceleration," Jaina said, and punched throttles.

Her displays showed more enemy than she could properly comprehend, but her sense of the battle suggested the enemy were finally coordinating a response to General Farlander's maneuver. He had cut twice through the enemy squadron, wrecking ships both times, but it was clear the Yuuzhan Vong weren't going to let him do it again. Those ships nearby were keeping their distance, while those farther away were scrambling to catch up. Swarms of coralskippers were pouring in from all directions. Soon Farlander would find himself swamped by superior numbers and held in place for destruction, like a bantamweight fighter grappled by a 160-kilo wrestler.

Not to mention the two huge squadrons looming on his flanks. Or the other two squadrons hanging in the rear.

Enemy fire boomed on Jaina's aft shields as she fled, a surprising number of shots. The pursuing coralskippers were throwing everything they had. Jaina did a little jinking, but it didn't seem to help. The sheer volume of fire was disturbing.

The pursuers broke off when Jaina's squadron entered the overlapping fields of fire of Farlander's capital ships, but by that point it hardly seemed to matter. So much fire was coming from so many directions that Jaina still found her shields getting slammed, even though it didn't seem as if anyone was taking the trouble to aim specifically at her.

"Friendly cruiser on our left," she said. "Let's take some of the pressure off it." She led Twin Suns on a high-speed slash against the coralskippers that had just made their attack runs on the cruiser and were now perfect targets as they maneuvered in preparation for another attack. One burst into flame at the touch of her quad lasers, and she thought she killed another with a missile.

"Rolling right," she began to call, and then there was a brilliant flash on her canopy matched by a wail in the Force, a mental keen that brought tears to Jaina's dazzled eyes.

"What was *that*?" she demanded.

"Twin Two," said Twin Three. "She's gone."

"What do you mean, *gone*?" Jaina demanded.

"She didn't get out." Twin Three sounded stunned. "A huge projectile hit her fighter—it was vaporized."

"Who hit her?" Jaina's hands suddenly got busy on the controls, ready to jink if the squadron was under attack.

"No one. Just random fire. There's a lot of it out here."

"No kidding," someone said.

Vale, Jaina thought. Another wingmate had gone, like Anni Capstan. The first casualty since the battle over *Far Thunder*, the first since she'd built Twin Suns Squadron into its highly drilled, perfected form.

The first casualty, she thought with a sick certainty, but not the last.

She fought away the tears and the grief. She had to be in control now. "Twin Three, Twin Four, keep close to me," she said. "Rolling right."

The rolling maneuver put her in an inverted position with regard to the New Republic squadron, able to view the fight through her canopy. She saw a *Republic*-class cruiser hit with a lance of fire, saw compartments venting ice crystals that had once been air. The space between the heavy ships was thick with fighters, both friendly and enemy.

A furball, she saw, was now forming around the damaged *Republic*-class cruiser, a horde of arriving coralskippers tangling with a couple of squadrons of E-wings. "Starfighter battle at zero-three-zero," she said. "Each flight form echelon. Each pilot pick your target. Re-form on the other side, look for your wingmate first and then for me. Understood?"

They understood. She had drilled them well.

"This is for Vale," she said, and had to blink back tears again as she punched the throttle. She felt Lowie, Tesar, and Madurrin sending her strength through the Force, and she radiated her thanks.

For her first target she picked a coralskipper that was lining up for a shot at an E-wing. Hers was a deflection shot, but she synced perfectly with her ship, slewed the nose of the X-wing around just slightly, and touched the quad triggers. The coralskipper blew with the second shot and then she whipped past the debris, triggering a missile onto the tail of another skip that presented itself. She had the satisfaction of seeing the coralskipper shatter before she was through the furball and pulling into the clear.

Clear being a relative term. The void was still filled with beams and missiles and cannonades, all of it once aimed at *something* but now possessed by a dreadful randomness.

"Re-form on me!" Jaina called, frantically scanning her displays.

Tesar's hissing voice came over the comm. "We're being bounced, Twin Leader! This one requestz assistance!"

"You got it!" She cast a glance at her displays, saw Tesar's blip behind her. "Twins Three and Four, with me! Streak, take your flight and—" A roar from Lowbacca confirmed Jaina's order before she finished giving it.

Jaina hauled back on the stick, hoping she wouldn't get smacked out of space while her maneuvering killed her velocity. She half rolled through the turn to keep herself out of enemy sights.

When she'd completed her maneuver the sight took her breath away.

An enemy frigate had laid itself along the *Republic*-class cruiser, the space between them a blaze of furious energies as the two huge vessels slammed each other at point-blank range. Around both capital ships were at least two hundred smaller craft, darting and weaving and blasting each other. She could see at least a dozen craft on fire.

Most of the smaller craft were Yuuzhan Vong. More enemy were appearing every second. General Farlander was getting swamped by the enemy.

"Stay with me, Three and Four," she told her remaining flight. "Now let's go."

As she shoved the throttles forward she felt Tesar's predatory presence through the Force, and she sent him a burst of strength. And then she sent, through the Force, a simple message to Madurrin.

We need help!

Madurrin sent a breeze of calm through the Force, and with it the knowledge of help already on the way. The sending was followed immediately by bright splashes on Jaina's cockpit displays as more ships appeared out of hyperspace. Jaina's heart leapt as she felt her mental horizons expand. Personalities crowded into her mind: Kyp Durron, Saba and the Wild Knights, Zekk, Corran Horn, Alema Rar, and Jacen. Jacen, in his place on the bridge of the Bothan Assault Cruiser *Ralroost*.

We're here! The Force message was a massed shout.

Glad to hear it, Jaina sent as she got a coralskipper in her sights, but right now she had to get some Vong off Tesar's tail.

She triggered her lasers.

A new howl chorused from the voxyn, and Tsavong Lah watched in amazement and rising anger as more blaze bugs rose from the floor to form a new enemy squadron in the overhead display. A large force, he saw, a match for any of his five.

Perhaps not so large. He saw now that a number of the enemy ships were big transports, which promptly vanished into hyperspace, leaving the rest behind to fight.

Apparently the new enemy were a supply convoy and its escort. It wasn't so inexplicable they should be here, then.

The new arrivals had appeared just as he was about to order the Battle Groups of Yun-Txiin and Yun-Q'aah to complete their envelopment of the enemy, the lovers' embrace that would destroy the infidels. But the new enemy force hung off to one flank, near the Battle Group of Yun-Txiin, and if he ordered the enveloping movement now, the new arrivals could pounce on Yun-Txiin's rear.

"The Battle Group of Yun-Txiin will engage the newcomers," he said. "The Battle Group of Yun-Harla will move to support, but will not engage without my command. The Battle Group of Yun-Q'aah will reinforce the Battle Group of Yun-Yammka and destroy the original defenders."

That left his own Battle Group of Yun-Yuuzhan still in reserve against any further surprises. With his group were the troopships that would be used to secure Ebaq 9 once the enemy fleet was dealt with.

He still had overwhelming numbers.

And since the voxyn had howled again, there were more Jedi among the newcomers.

More sacrifices for the gods, he thought with satisfaction, and sat back in the cognition throne to watch his forces complete his victory.

Through the Jedi Force-meld Jacen could feel Jaina in her cockpit—feel her determination, her cool analysis, and the edges of panic that sometimes broke through her composure. "Skip on my six! Breaking right . . ."

"This one has destroyed it." This from Tesar.

Thanks! They weren't words, really, these bursts of image and intensity from the Force, but that's how they translated.

Jaina, Twin Suns, and all of Farlander's force were heavily engaged at great odds. His own new arrivals, with most of the fleet's Jedi, were moving against one of the huge battle groups that loomed like an overhanging cliff on Farlander's flank.

The Jedi meld was skating on the edge of Jacen's ability to comprehend. There were too many ships in the picture for him to absorb. Fortunately, three-fifths of the enemy were unengaged, and he could safely leave them out of his mental picture.

He called out coordinates, maneuvering Kre'fey's force so as to provide maximum effectiveness at the moment of collision.

"Fire dovin missile!" Admiral Kre'fey ordered. He was too excited to sit in the grand chair reserved for a full admiral, and instead paced back and forth just behind Jacen. Jacen was going to find this annoying if Kre'fey kept it up for long.

"Dovin missile fired, sir."

"Transmit coordinates of the space mine to General Farlander."

"Coordinates transmitted, Admiral."

"Wonderful!" Jacen heard Kre'fey clap his hands. "This is working well, don't you think?"

But Jacen's mind really wasn't on what was occurring on the admiral's bridge. Instead he kept his focus on Twin Suns Squadron and the desperate battle Jaina was fighting.

Missed!

Lowie, look out!

Jacen considered summoning his Vongsense, his ability to empathize with and sometimes influence the enemy. But that would mean losing the Force, and the ability to help his comrades. He decided that remaining in the meld was his best option.

"I've lost my rear shields!"

"That was my last missile!"

Go with the Force, Jacen sent. He closed his eyes and pushed out as much care, strength, and support as he could.

And behind him, dim in the Force, he felt another presence, powerful but cloaked, that radiated strength, but to Jacen alone.

Vergere.

Thirty light-years from the battle, at a narrow point of the long hyperspace route that led to Ebaq and its moons, a small New Republic task force dropped out of hyperspace. Most of the ships were unarmed. This was not a fighting force, but even so its mission was vital.

The squadron commander first fired a single missile, one containing an interdictor, modeled after a Yuuzhan Vong dovin basal. The interdictor would serve as a space mine.

Once the mine had been set in the center of the hyperspace lane, the other ships began to drop more conventional mines, mines with detection gear, explosive cores, and maneuvering thrusters. The mines immediately took up station around the dovin basal mine.

The unarmed ships continued to lay mines. Dozens of mines.

Hundreds.

Thousands.

Tens of thousands.

"Got it!" Twin Six shouted. She'd just shot a skip off Lowie's tail, and the Wookiee gave a roar of thanks.

Jaina blinked sweat from her eyes and hauled her X-wing right, away from a stream of plasma cannon fire. That enabled her to get a deflection shot at a coralskipper speeding by, but the Vong's dovin basal sucked the laser bolts and suddenly Jaina was dancing away from more fire coming at her from her starboard quarter. It was friendly fire, laser bolts from a B-wing, but it was deadly for all that and Jaina didn't want any part of it.

"All ships," came an announcement on the command comm, "this is General Farlander. All ships to alter course simultaneously on the following coordinates . . ."

Jaina tried to absorb the coordinates and failed. She'd have to just get a visual and follow, that is if she could ever get free of this furball composed of friendly and enemy craft, debris, and random deadly fire.

"What was that coordinate?" From Twin Nine.

"I didn't get it either." Twin Four.

"Course change on my mark," Farlander continued. "Five. Four. Three. Two. Mark."

Jaina saw the capital ships around her suddenly swing massively to a new heading and ignite their engines. The Yuuzhan Vong took a moment to respond, but soon they, too, were matching Farlander's maneuver.

Except for the ships that couldn't. Trailing behind were the casualties, the dead ships, the wounded, and the out-of-control, both friendly and enemy.

And Jaina, who was too tangled up with the Yuuzhan Vong to follow. If she straightened her course to pursue Farlander, she'd be blasted by a dozen enemy.

"Squadron to form into single line ahead," came the order from Farlander.

"Slagged him!" From Twin Three.

Enemy fire banged on Jaina's rear shields, and she jerked the fighter into a roll as her astromech chittered angrily at the attackers. "Rolling left," she said, as if anyone were keeping track of her movements. As far as she could tell the members of Twin Suns Squadron were all on their own, so separated in the melee they could no longer guard one another's backs.

There was a flash. Debris thundered on Jaina's shields.

"Who was that?" Twin Seven's voice.

"Twin Nine." Tesar's voice was calm, but Jaina could feel his anger in the Force.

"Did she get out?"

"Negative."

Anger ripped into Jaina. She'd lost another pilot, and she hadn't even known Twin Nine was in danger.

Time to kill some Vong, she decided. It was what she was here for.

She looked for a coralskipper, and put it in her sights.

Tsavong Lah watched with pleasure as Farlander's squadron fled the battle. The sudden maneuver had caught the Yuuzhan Vong by surprise, but the Battle Group of Yun-Yammka had corrected quickly and were now hanging tenaciously on to the enemy. The Battle Group of Yun-Q'aah had altered course to intercept and would soon join the fight and finish the infidels.

The warmaster's pleasure was increased as the Battle Group of Yun-Txiin slammed into the newly arrived squadron with proper headlong Yuuzhan Vong spirit. The blaze bugs overhead began to moderate their pitch as missiles and projectile weapons began to inflict damage.

A sudden whine from the blaze bugs caught his attention, and his eyes widened in surprise.

Farlander's squadron was in the process of another course change, a radical one this time. Tsavong Lah couldn't believe how rapidly the New Republic capital ships were turning—they were whipping around a full 270 degrees, and without losing velocity!

It was a clear impossibility. Yet they were doing it, and leaving the Battle Group of Yun-Yammka behind.

And then his nerves turned chill as he realized that the infidels' new course was sending them straight into the battle between the Battle Group of Yun-Txiin and the newly arrived force. The Battle Group of Yun-Txiin would be caught between the two forces and hammered.

"The Battle Group of Yun-Harla will engage the enemy immediately," he ordered. That would reinforce the Battle Group of Yun-Txiin and repair some of the damage the enemy maneuver had created. "The Battle Group of Yun-Yammka will regroup and prepare to reenter combat. The Battle Group of Yun-Q'aah will—"

He paused as more blaze bugs began to whine, a whole host of them rising from the floor to hover in the air and form something new.

What now? he thought.

Jacen watched as Keyan Farlander's entire squadron of capital ships performed the Solo Slingshot around the dovin basal space mine analog, the modified interdictor missile that Kre'fey's *Ralroost* had fired on its arrival on the field of battle. The enemy fighting them continued on their previous course, unable to claw their way after Farlander without performing a conventional turn and losing most of their speed. A few of the enemy, by guesswork or luck, managed to work out what was happening and make the turn along with Farlander, but these were outnumbered and quickly blasted out of existence.

The rest would be out of the battle for some time as the capital ships lumbered into their turns and tried to maneuver into some kind of appropriate formation.

Nice work, Jacen sent to Madurrin.

Thanks.

Ralroost shuddered to a hit, and Jacen was reminded that a Bothan Assault Cruiser was so named because it concentrated most of its power on attack, not to shields or defense.

"Breach between frames M and N," someone said. "Frame seals are holding. Damage control is responding."

"Hammer them! Hammer them!" Admiral Kre'fey, shouting, swung his fists dangerously in the air over Jacen's head.

Kre'fey's ships were engaged in a furious close-range action with the enemy. Jacen could feel Kyp and his Dozen, Corran Horn and Rogue Squadron, and the all-Jedi Wild Knights flying in frantic combat. The Knights in particular were tearing through the enemy, their predatory reflexes in perfect synchronization with the Force. An all-Jedi squadron was a terrible thing indeed.

Then Jacen felt another surge in the Force, and he felt a new mind enter the Jedi meld, a mind uncertain and only half trained.

Hello, Mom, he sent.

The full power of the Force-meld took Leia by surprise. She was in the copilot's chair of the *Millennium Falcon*, which was echeloned with the rest of the Smugglers' Alliance ships around the bright red Star Destroyer *Errant Venture*. No sooner had she fallen out of hyperspace than the meld reached for her, and part of her mind was viewing a burning enemy frigate with Corran Horn, fighting a jaw-clenching combat with Kyp Durron, or engaging in vicious, efficient pack behavior with the Barabel Wild Knights. The intensity of it took her breath away.

Hello, Mom. Jacen's presence was clear in the Force.

Hello, Jacen, she sent uncertainly. Unlike the others in the fight, her Force training had been haphazard, and she hadn't had the opportunity to practice the meld with others. But the power of the meld was so strong that she felt her uncertainty fade as soon as she received her first order from Jacen.

She received another message from Jacen, *felt* the coordinates burning in her mind. She looked at the *Falcon*'s navigation displays and saw the point indicated. She translated the coordinates and keyed them in.

"Han, Jacen wants us *here*."

"What Jacen wants, Jacen gets," Han said, and switched his comm unit to the command channel.

Han—Captain Solo, again, with his insignia pinned to his otherwise civilian vest—commanded the Smugglers' Alliance squadron from the *Millennium Falcon*. "I'm happier in a smaller ship," he said when Booster Terrik offered *Errant Venture*. "And besides, a Star Destroyer is too big a target."

The motley Smugglers' Alliance squadron began its change of course.

Leia's Noghri bodyguards, in the turbolaser turrets, chuckled in their whispery voices and fired practice shots into the void.

And then Leia felt a shard of terror clear through the Force-meld, and she knew Jaina was in trouble.

"This is the critical moment," Ackbar said. He, Winter, and Mara sat in a gallery above the Fleet Command operations room, where Sien Sovv stood amid a bustle of aides, screens, and constantly flowing data. A holo of the battle at Ebaq 9 floated in the air above the busy room. The Smugglers' Alliance squadron under Han Solo had just appeared in the display, the ships picked out in brilliant orange.

It was a massive contrast to the last time Mara had watched Sien Sovv in action. Then the Supreme Commander had been forced to conduct his defense of Coruscant in front of a full session of the Senate, with the Senators shouting advice and hurling threats, and Chief of State Borsk Fey'lya countermanding Sovv's orders from the speaker's podium.

The Supreme Commander seemed a lot more comfortable in his current situation. And no wonder.

"It is at this point that the enemy might begin to suspect a trap," Ackbar said. He slumped in his chair, and his voice was slurred with weariness. Being on dry land again was taking its toll. "Alas that we needed to send this squadron to prevent Farlander and Kre'fey from being overwhelmed . . . fortunately it is small and innocuous . . ." He sighed heavily. "Perhaps they will not take alarm. Perhaps not."

"Rolling left!" Jaina shouted. But a stream of plasma cannon projectiles met her as she rolled, one stunning impact after another on her shields, and she knew there was a second enemy behind her. If she broke right she'd run into the first enemy.

Fortunately, space is three-dimensional. She went *up*.

An enemy missile shot past her canopy, and then she was free. She rolled again and went after her pursuers.

She found one and was on the verge of attempting a deflection shot when R2-B3 chittered a warning and she jerked the stick away from the flaming projectiles that soared past her.

"Twin Three and Four, I'm in a crossfire here—where are you?" she demanded.

"Three's hit!" Four's voice. "I saw him eject!"

"Where are *you*?" Jaina demanded.

"I don't know!"

Jaina jinked away from a line of fire only to have her shields slammed by a missile. Her astromech droid squealed at the state of the shields, which were near collapse. Jaina blinked sweat from her eyes and jinked again, and by chance found a coralskipper floating across her sights. She fired the quad lasers and felt satisfaction at the sight of fire burning along the enemy hull. If she hadn't killed it, she'd at least hurt it.

A howl came over the comm, and Jaina's Force-impelled reflexes jerked at the controls.

The howl was followed by another, this one of satisfaction, as Lowie scragged the coralskipper that had been on Jaina's tail. Between the two of them, Jaina and Lowie hunted down and blew apart a third coralskipper, and then she found a moment to raise her faceplate and mop sweat from her face with a gloved hand. They were on the edge of the fur-ball that had originally surrounded Farlander's squadron, but which had now become a separate fight, starfighters and coralskippers circling and hunting each other in a remark-ably small area.

She felt Tesar's urgency through the Force. "This one has losst shieldz and an engine!" he called.

The Force told her where Tesar was before her displays did.

"Streak," she told Lowie, "stay on my wing!"

And she dived back into the fight.

Tsavong Lah gazed in furious concentration at the small squadron that had appeared on the flank of the Battle Group of Yun-Q'aah. It was built around a single very large wedge-shaped ship, with a modest number of medium-sized vessels and a lot of small ones. By itself it wasn't very men-acing, except that it could attack the rear of the Yun-Q'aah battle group if he committed it to battle.

Better to squash this small group first, he decided. Even though this little squadron wasn't large enough to turn the tide of battle, it was better to be safe than not.

"The Battle Group of Yun-Q'aah is to engage the small squadron on its flank and destroy it."

A subaltern relayed the order. There was a moment in which the subaltern communed with his villip, after which he turned and saluted with crossed arms. "Commander Droog'an begs to ask whether we have been led into an am-bush, Warmaster."

For a moment Tsavong Lah's lip curled at the insolence of Droog'an, but then he stopped to consider the question.

Had all the information of the Final Redoubt been nothing but an attempt to lure him here into the Deep Core? Had that schemer Nom Anor been outschemed?

The appearance of two enemy squadrons *was* suspicious. But one of them seemed to be a convoy escort, and the other was understrength and composed of such a heterogeneous array of vessels that it was barely military at all.

If he, Tsavong Lah, had planned an ambush, he would have used overwhelming force and pounced from all directions. He wouldn't have fed in two squadrons piecemeal, neither of them large enough to do anything more than delay the outcome.

No, it had to be a coincidence that a convoy arrived at just this moment. The second squadron was probably a scratch force summoned by a distress call.

"Tell Commander Droog'an there is no ambush," Tsavong Lah said. "Order him to engage immediately."

"At once, Warmaster!"

Leia could see that Han was impressed by the size and strength of the enemy battle group that suddenly swerved to engage him. He blew a long breath, then cast a glance over his shoulder at Leia and said, "I don't suppose the United Jedi Cluster-Mind has any suggestions about how to handle this one?"

"I'm afraid not," Leia said. The meld knew an engagement had to occur, but its tactical advice was a little unclear.

"Well then," Han breathed. He looked at the displays again, then flicked on the comm. "This is Captain Solo," he told the squadron. "We can't hope to match the enemy with numbers or firepower, so we'll have to make use of speed, flexibility, and—" His brow creased in worry. "—tactical brilliance," he finished hopefully.

Leia reached out and squeezed his shoulder. "Go get 'em, Slick," she said.

*   *   *

Ralroost shuddered to another hit, but Jacen's mind was in the Force, seeing through the eyes of the Jedi meld. His mind strained to keep up with all the information flowing through the Force. Through Leia's eyes he saw Han's slashing attack on the larger enemy battle group, a hit-and-run assault that the enemy was too large and slow to counter. Through Madurrin's perceptions he felt Farlander's battered squadron slam into the enemy, taking Kre'fey's enemies in the rear and inflicting damage beyond their numbers. Through the eyes of Kyp and Corran and Saba he saw the flash of fire, coralskippers burning, enemy frigates and cruisers trembling to the force of shadow bombs.

And he felt Jaina's desperation and Lowbacca's ferocity as they aided Tesar's grim fight for survival. Jacen's fingers twitched with the impulse to run to *Ralroost*'s fighter bays, to jump into his X-wing and fly to Jaina's assistance. But he knew he served the cause better on *Ralroost*, where he was able to keep the other Jedi focused, help them sense each other's locations and coordinate their actions with one another.

Jacen jumped as Kre'fey's white-furred hand dropped onto his shoulder. "Now, Jacen!" the admiral said. "Our minefield is complete! Now you'll see the destruction of the enemy!"

Kre'fey gave an order on the comm.

And then, mere minutes later, as the squadrons leapt from their hiding places in the Deep Core hyperspace lanes, more New Republic ships began to appear, one squadron after another. A host of Jedi minds rose into the meld: Tahiri, Zekk, Alema, and the burning power of Luke Skywalker.

All here at the finish.

The voxyn cried again as they detected one new Jedi after another, their weary howls now more akin to whimpers.

The blaze bugs that flew into the air to mark the new infidel squadrons provided a strange dissonance in Tsavong Lah, for the picture that rose to Tsavong Lah's brain, fed by the tendrils of the cognition throne, showed the enemy in even greater numbers, vast numbers of infidels all around him.

It took a moment for him to realize why he was receiving two different impressions. So many were the infidels that the warmaster had run out of blaze bugs to represent them in the display.

Fury possessed him. What did it matter that he was now outnumbered? That his forces had been drawn out of position and were about to be engulfed? The Yuuzhan Vong were conquerors! The gods had promised them victory!

Swiftly he reordered his forces. The Battle Groups of Yun-Harla and Yun-Txiin were heavily engaged against the original enemy squadron and the first set of reinforcements. They had local superiority in numbers, though both sides had lost all formation and the battle had dissolved into a general melee. Tsavong Lah ordered these forces to redouble their efforts and destroy their foes before more infidel battle groups could intervene.

The Battle Group of Yun-Yammka, which had opened the battle and been left on its own since the original enemy squadron had made its unexpected turning maneuver, had regrouped. Tsavong Lah decided to sacrifice it. He ordered the battle group to hurl itself against the enemy reinforcements in order to keep them occupied while he tried to win the fight with his other forces.

"*Do-ro'ik vong pratte!*" the group commander replied when he heard the order, the battle cry of the warrior caste. Tsavong Lah swelled with pride at the unquestioning spirit of the doomed commander. He knew he, his ships, and his warriors were going to their deaths, but still he gladly accepted the clash of battle.

The Battle Group of Yun-Q'aah, which had been in pursuit of the small, agile force that had appeared as the second group of reinforcements, was ordered to break off its pursuit and maneuver against several of the infidel squadrons. If Commander Droog'an maneuvered cleverly enough, he could occupy a large group of the enemy without committing himself against overwhelming numbers, thus buying time for the rest.

That left the reserve Battle Group of Yun-Yuuzhan, under Tsavong Lah's personal command. It was the only force that hadn't been engaged with the enemy, that hadn't suffered casualties, and that still had complete freedom of maneuver.

Tsavong Lah hesitated for a moment, then decided to take his battle group straight into battle alongside the Battle Groups of Yun-Harla and Yun-Txiin. If he could force a victory there, it might create other opportunities.

He gave the orders, and his forces screamed toward the battle.

Tsavong Lah had been led into a trap—by Nom Anor's information.

"You have betrayed us," Yoog Skell said. "You must pay with your life."

Nom Anor calmly reached into his pocket for the blorash jelly that he then flung at Yoog Skell's feet.

The high prefect waved his arms, trying not to topple, as the jelly pinned his feet to the floor. He gave Nom Anor a wild look. *"What are you doing, Executor?"* he demanded.

"Giving Shimrra an itch." Nom Anor surprised himself with how calmly he was behaving.

He slashed his amphistaff down on Yoog Skell's head. The high prefect folded into unconsciousness, his feet still pinned by the semisentient jelly tendrils.

Nom Anor looked at the sprawled body of his superior

and hoped he wasn't dead. He'd always rather liked Yoog Skell.

Nom Anor knew, of course, what had happened. His spies had been identified and fed false information designed to lead the Yuuzhan Vong fleet into this trap. Whoever had done this had been brilliant, setting out a series of clues and letting Nom Anor himself draw the conclusions.

But there would be little use explaining to his superiors how brilliantly he had been played by the enemy—not in the wake of a military disaster of this magnitude. They would want Nom Anor's head, not his explanations.

It was time for Nom Anor to vanish, to don an ooglith masquer to disguise his appearance and then to disappear among the anonymous worker caste. After the search died down, he could create further identities and credentials that would get him off the planet.

But where would he go? He would be hunted throughout Yuuzhan Vong–controlled territory. And if he escaped into the New Republic, he would have to live forever in disguise, an object of suspicion wherever he went.

He decided to think about all that later.

Right now, he needed to concentrate on escape.

Twin Suns Squadron was down to eight starfighters, and of these only Lowbacca's was intact. Tesar had lost an engine and half his shields. Jaina had lost her rear shields and her upper right foil along with its laser, and her cockpit smelled of fear and sour sweat. Others suffered light to heavy damage. They had expended all their missiles and bombs.

Fortunately, they were no longer engaged with the enemy. The larger battles had passed them by, and the fighter-versus-fighter battle seemed to be over. The coralskippers had either been killed or gone somewhere else, and only scattered B- and E-wings were near them.

Through the Jedi meld Jaina could still feel others experiencing the shock of combat. Wearily she turned the nose of her craft toward the huge battle nearby, where Jacen and Kyp and the Wild Knights were engaged, but from Jacen she felt a cool touch of the mind, followed by his voice on the comm.

"Don't. You're too shot up."

"I can feel the others fighting. I can't stand by."

"You must. The others would only endanger themselves protecting you."

The meld was in agreement with Jacen. She felt their unanimity, but still she felt the urge not to abandon her friends.

"You have acquitted yourself honorably, Jaina Solo." This was Saba's voice. "It is now your task to preserve your own life."

"Twin Suns has permission to withdraw to Ebaq Nine." This came from Ebaq 9, from her own controller.

Jaina felt her tension drain away. *Preserve your own life.* How long had it been since anyone told her to do that? Her battle was over, and the annihilation that she had feared— that she had expected—had not come.

"Acknowledged," she told the flag, and then spoke to her pilots. "Streak, I want you to cover Tesar. The rest of you, form on me."

Wearily, Jaina turned her craft toward safety.

Jaina, Tesar, and Lowbacca had landed on Ebaq 9. Luke could sense their weariness in the Force, but still he felt them trying to send strength and clarity to the others in the Jedi meld.

Luke sat on the bridge of the Mon Calamari cruiser *Harbinger*, flagship of Garm Bel Iblis, and played a game of holochess in his mind with the enemy commander. Luke's mission to the old hero of the Rebellion had succeeded: Bel Iblis had brought into the Deep Core half the fleet with which he had been guarding Talaan, divided into three battle groups.

Maneuvering against that fleet was a single Yuuzhan Vong squadron, the one that had earlier been pursuing Han's squadron of Smugglers' Alliance ships. Its commander was clever and had managed to keep all three of Bel Iblis's battle groups occupied without quite engaging any of them.

But it was an unfair contest. The Yuuzhan Vong had only a single piece on the holo board, the New Republic three— four, if Han's small squadron counted. Luke, maneuvering with the aid of the Jedi meld, slowly reduced the enemy's options to two: fight and die, or flee.

And he knew the Yuuzhan Vong did not run away.

He ordered the three battle groups to converge.

No good, Tsavong Lah realized. His plan wasn't working.

He clenched his teeth in rage. *May Nom Anor's flayed skin be trampled by* rakamats.

The Battle Groups of Yun-Harla and Yun-Txiin were fighting bravely but being overwhelmed by the enemy. Two new enemy battle groups had joined the fight, fresh and formed and well organized, while the Yuuzhan Vong were scattered and locked in combat with their old enemies.

The Battle Group of Yun-Q'aah was in the process of being trapped by three enemy battle groups.

The Battle Group of Yum-Yammka, as instructed, was immolating itself against the enemy, but such bravery was useless because nothing else was going well.

Only the Battle Group of Yun-Yuuzhan, under Tsavong Lah himself, still had options. He had planned to join the Battle Groups of Yun-Harla and Yun-Txiin and help them win at least a local victory, but he saw now that this plan, too, would fail, that all he could do was reinforce a battle that was already lost, offering himself to the enemy like a sacrifice upon the altar.

Like a sacrifice . . .

Despair gripped his heart in iron talons. He should die in battle. After a defeat of this magnitude, Shimrra could scarcely be expected to let him live. Tsavong Lah would be lucky not to be cut down like an animal, like Ch'Gang Hool, and instead die a sacrifice to the gods.

Sacrifice . . .

Tsavong Lah jerked bolt upright on the cognition throne. A smile drew his slashed lips tight.

A sacrifice. *Of course.*

"Alter course at once for Ebaq Nine!" he commanded. "Order the Battle Group of Yun-Q'aah to head for the moon at maximum acceleration!"

Jeedai, he thought. The voxyn had howled when he had first brought his fleet to the system. There had been *Jeedai* in the system then. Some of them were probably with the fleet, but Tsavong Lah believed some, at least, would be on the ninth moon of Ebaq.

A sacrifice.

Luke watched in surprise as the enemy battle group, the one he had been carefully maneuvering against, suddenly bolted, its formations dissolving, every ship for itself. The Yuuzhan Vong had never before fled from a fight in such disorder, and the New Republic battle groups were unprepared for what looked like a panicked withdrawal. There was a little skirmish across the front of one of the battle groups—a few ships flared in the night, and died—and then the enemy were away, with the entire fleet in pursuit.

Luke didn't understand where the enemy intended to go. They weren't running directly away from him; it was almost as if they were running *toward* something.

And then, with a dreadful certainty, he knew where they were headed.

And he thought, *Jaina*.

*   *   *

"I did not foresee this!" Ackbar beat with one huge hand on the arm of his chair. "What a fool I have been!"

Countless ships whirled in Jacen's mind. He struggled madly with his expanded senses to understand what the new enemy maneuver meant, and suddenly he understood. At his realization an electric shock rang through the Jedi meld.

He struggled to find an answer. *Calm*. He sensed Vergere's thoughts in his mind. *Calm. The Force will tell you what to do*.

Suddenly Jacen understood, and he was shouting orders to Admiral Kre'fey while he sent an urgent message through the Force.

"Mom! You've got to intercept that squadron! Use everything you've got!"

That would keep one of the enemy squadrons away from Ebaq, at least for a while.

It was only after he'd sent his instructions that he realized he might have just sent his parents to their deaths.

Jacen rose from his chair and turned to Admiral Kre'fey. "I need my X-wing now!" he shouted, and without waiting for permission ran for the turbolift.

"Jacen?" Kre'fey seemed more astonished than anything else. "We need you on the flagship!"

The turbolift wasn't parked at this level. In an agony of frustration Jacen slammed the control buttons. "You've already won the battle!" he said. "Now I have to save Jaina!"

Kre'fey's white fur rippled as he stared at Jacen. Distant rumbles echoed through the room as *Ralroost*'s inadequate shielding absorbed hits.

"Very well," Kre'fey said, waving a hand. "Very well."

And Kre'fey turned back to hammering the enemy.

*   *   *

"Han, we need to stop them."

Han cast a bewildered look over his shoulder. "Stop *who*?"

Leia jabbed an urgent finger at the displays. "The enemy squadron!"

Han shrugged. "They're fleeing, but they still outnumber us. Let 'em go."

Anger flared in Leia's voice. "They're not running! They're heading straight for Jaina!"

There was a moment of stunned comprehension, and then the lines in Han's face turned grim. "Right." He faced front and snapped on the comm. "This is Solo," he said. "It's up to us to hold the Vong until our people can catch up and finish them off. Everyone pick your targets carefully—this will *not* be fun."

He rolled the *Millennium Falcon* toward the enemy and throttled up.

The enemy ships—hundreds of them—got nearer and nearer.

"Keep an eye on the displays, sweetheart," Han told Leia. "When this gets hairy, I don't want anyone sneaking up on us."

Han brought the Smugglers' Alliance squadron right across the front of the Yuuzhan Vong formation, which meant that every weapon on his squadron bore on the enemy, while the enemy could only reply with bow weapons. Han was either going to blow the Vong noses off or force them from their course.

The Vong didn't turn.

Errant Venture fired first, its enormous turbolasers hurling neon-colored destruction at the enemy, and then one by one the rest of the squadron opened fire. Leia could hear the rhythmic crashing of the Noghri firing the *Falcon*'s turbolasers.

And then return fire began smashing at the shields.

* * *

Jaina felt cold sweat breaking out on her nape. "Back to the fighters!" she told her squadron. "We'll launch and get out of the enemy's sight."

"That's a negative, Twin Leader." It was General Farlander himself on the comm, which spoke to the importance of the message. In the background she could hear the shouts, murmurs, and crashes of a big ship in combat.

"Just get into the mineshafts and slam the blast doors behind you," Farlander said. "Stick to the plan. You can hold out for hours in there, and we'll come get you before you know it."

"The general iz wise, Jaina," Tesar hissed. His heavy tail lashed left and right. "Our starfighterz are too damaged to make a clean escape. Several of us would be losst."

Jaina hesitated as she looked at the expectant pilots around her, then nodded. *Lost.* Tesar was right.

"Understood, General," she said.

Around her, Ebaq 9's command center braced itself for the oncoming blow. Two huge Yuuzhan Vong squadrons were headed their way.

Stick to the plan, Farlander had said, but this *wasn't* the plan. The plan assumed that when the New Republic fleets arrived the Yuuzhan Vong would realize they were ambushed, and either run or fight to the death. The plan never considered that the Yuuzhan Vong would continue their assault on Ebaq's ninth moon, which had no real military value at all.

"Right," Jaina said. "This way."

The weary pilots limped out of the command center. The gravity was still erratic: sometimes they walked normally, and sometimes an ordinary step would catapult them to the ceiling. They took a hovercar down the great central shaft that drove through the moonlet's core. From here mineshafts branched off into the old diggings. Several of these had been equipped with the massive durasteel blast doors designed to keep the enemy out for hours.

Jaina stopped the car by the bunker that had been converted to an armory. "I'm going to assume that everything *else* is going to go wrong," she said.

"Voxyn," Lowbacca howled. "How can things go *right*?"

Jaina nodded. "That's why I want everyone here to have blasters, body armor, grenades, grenade launchers, and command-detonated mines. And vac suits—we're pressurized here, but what can be pressurized can be depressurized."

Tesar gave a hiss of Barabel amusement.

"The major speakz wisdom," he said.

The turbolift seemed to take an eternity in its glide toward the fighter docking bays. Jacen used his private comm to call his astromech droid and have the fighter ready for him.

The Jedi meld sang in his mind. He was aware of his own anxiety eddying out to the others, reflecting back toward him. He remembered how the Force-meld had kept dissolving on Myrkr, as Jedi were hurt or died, or fought one another over strategy, and he tried to keep his worries from feeding out into the others.

The turbolift jolted to a stop. It had come to a bulkhead, and all bulkheads were sealed during combat.

Jacen flung the lift doors open with the Force and sprinted for one of the internal air locks that communicated between bulkheads. There was another eternity while the lock recycled, and then a narrow, spiral stair—Jacen used the Force to fly down it—and then another bulkhead that communicated to the docking bay deck.

He wasn't surprised to find Vergere waiting for him. She held up a hand.

"Where are you going?"

Jacen didn't break stride. "To help Jaina."

"You cannot help. Ebaq is being attacked by a squadron of capital ships. Your single starfighter will make no difference."

"I have to try." Jacen sprinted on. His X-wing was alone in the docking bay next to a partially dismantled A-wing, its weapons and sensor system scavenged to repair other starfighters.

"Stop. This is not your destiny."

"Maybe not, but it's my *family*."

Vergere followed Jacen, flying on pulses of the Force to match Jacen's running pace. "What can you hope to accomplish besides your own destruction?" she demanded.

Anger flamed through his mind. Jacen turned to the little alien and put a hand on his lightsaber. "Are you proposing to stop me?" he demanded.

Vergere settled onto the deck and slowly, sadly bowed her head. "I will not stop you, Jacen Solo. You have chosen your destiny." Her eyes glittered. "It is the consequences you must deal with now."

Jacen turned and vaulted into the cockpit. He closed the canopy and put on his helmet.

Through the Force, he could feel the cold fear that ran through Jaina's nerves.

He opened the comm and asked *Ralroost*'s docking control for permission to launch.

The *Millennium Falcon* skimmed along the hull of the enemy cruiser, quad lasers pumping shots into the hull as well as toward the coralskippers that danced astern. The coralskipper pilots were having a problem trying to nail the agile *Falcon* without hitting their own ship, and Han was trying to make the solution to that problem as difficult as he could. The Yuuzhan Vong had already put several shots into their own vessel, and Han didn't want them to stop now.

The problem was that *Millennium Falcon* hadn't been built as a bomber. Proton torpedoes and shadow bombs had the punch to knock out a capital ship, but *Falcon* didn't carry either. Neither did Lando's *Lady Luck* nor Talon Karrde's *Wild Karrde*—they'd been built with the intention of keeping patrol craft off their backs, not with having to knock out large targets.

They all had to improvise. Han figured the best way to splatter a big Yuuzhan Vong ship was to trick the Vong into doing it for him.

And that's just what happened. One of the pursuing Yuuzhan Vong tried to duck closer to the cruiser than *Falcon*, in order to shoot *up* at Han without danger of hitting his own vessel, but unfortunately he forgot about Leia's bodyguard Meewalh in the belly turret. Meewalh gave a yowl of pleasure at the appearance of the target and hurled an array of laser bolts at the Vong. The enemy pilot was either hit or dazzled by the flares, because the coralskipper splashed into the enemy cruiser, its store of weapons erupting in fire as it slashed a brilliant flaming scar across the giant hull.

Han shot off the bow of the cruiser and performed another frantic series of evasive maneuvers before the skips on his tail were dispersed or discouraged. Behind, the cruiser shivered as secondary explosions blasted outward through its coral skin. The cruiser arced into a wide turn as dovin basals used for propulsion along one side were destroyed, while those on the other side continued to drive the ship forward, like a rowboat with one oar pulling while the other trailed in the water.

Another ship turned away from Jaina. He could leave it to Bel Iblis's fleet to finish the cruiser off.

He cast a glance at Leia, who was sitting white-knuckled in the copilot's seat. "How are we doing?"

She shook her head. "Bel Iblis has caught up to the rearmost enemy. But we're still the only force between the Yuu-zhan Vong and Ebaq Nine."

"Better find us another target, then," Han said.

The Smugglers' Alliance squadron was doing a lot of bril-liant flying, but it was outnumbered and many of its ships, like *Millennium Falcon*, were unsuited for fleet combat. Fortunately the enemy seemed largely at a loss as to how to cope with the attack—the Alliance had no uniform ships, therefore no uniform tactics, and that meant that both sides were improvising, and the smugglers had a lot more experi-ence at improvising than the Yuuzhan Vong.

"Look out!" At the yelp from Leia, Han jerked at the sweat-slick controls and managed to avoid being swatted by the huge *Errant Venture*, the only real capital ship under his command. The Star Destroyer was pumping fire in all directions, from every weapon on the ship, and as the largest New Republic target was receiving a lot of attention in re-turn. Booster Terrik was driving straight at one enemy ship after another, trying to force them away from their course—a tactic fraught with hazard, but thus far he seemed to be doing well enough. Perhaps the Vong remembered the way *Lusankya* had rammed their worldship at Borleias.

Han found a pair of smuggler ships in the melee, and these had proton missile launchers. "Follow me," he told them, "I'll carve a path for you."

And he led them in another slash at the Yuuzhan Vong.

And later, after more slashes than he could remember, he saw the enemy battle group turn away from its objective.

Tsavong Lah howled in triumph as the Battle Group of Yun-Yuuzhan, completely unmolested, drew near to Ebaq 9. He had caught the infidels utterly by surprise.

"Open fire on the shields!" he commanded. "*Kusurrun*, you will dive onto the shield over the enemy command center at maximum thrust! Victory Section, you will follow *Kusurrun* to the shields and try to destroy them."

As the other ships hammered away at the defenders, *Kusurrun* made its death-dive toward the moon. The frigate made a colossal impact on the shields, debris rising amid a roil of brilliant plasma jets. Other ships dived close, their dovin basals reaching out to snatch at the shields, trying to overload them.

No success, but the warmaster wasn't distressed. He had plenty of time before the nearest enemy could reach him.

Tsavong Lah ordered another frigate to immolate itself, and then paused to consider the rest of the battle. Blaze bugs, their lights and voices extinguished, represented the hundreds of craft that had been destroyed. His forces were being overwhelmed, even the Battle Group of Yun-Q'aah that he'd ordered to join him. The little motley squadron that stood in its way was, it appeared, too troublesome.

"Attention all other battle groups!" he commanded. "Once our troops are down on Ebaq, you are commanded to withdraw into hyperspace and make your way to Yuuzhan'tar. This battle is lost, but you are ordered to preserve your lives and ships for the victorious battles that will follow.

"The Battle Group of Yun-Yuuzhan will cover your withdrawal." He drew his slashed lips back for his final message, which he shouted in a tone of angry defiance that filled the huge room. "Praise to the gods! Long live Shimrra, the Supreme One! *Do-ro'ik vong pratte!*"

The group commanders—those who still lived—returned the warrior salute.

Ebaq 9's shields shuddered as another frigate thundered down.

Tsavong Lah sat back in his chair and ordered another capital ship to its death. "Prepare the oggzil," he said, and as one of his subalterns attached the grasping appendages of the creature to one of the villips used for communication,

Tsavong Lah detached himself from the cognition throne and lumbered from the dais.

He wanted to deliver this particular message himself.

The oggzil had enfolded the villip by the time he arrived, its long antenna-tail dangling. Tsavong Lah took the creature in one hand, gazed at it, and forced his face into a smile.

Knowing that the oggzil was broadcasting his words and his image on New Republic frequencies, he said in his crude Basic, "This is Warmaster Tsavong Lah. We are having a *Jeedai* hunt on Ebaq Nine! Although anyone else coming near will be destroyed, all *Jeedai* are welcome to participate!"

TWENTY-SIX

The commander's voice hissed with interference as he spoke, through the comm, from his armored communications center in the old mine headquarters. "They've brought down our shields. We're evacuating into the bunkers."

"Thanks for letting us know," Jaina said. She shivered from cold as she signed to Lowbacca to seal the blast doors.

"We're setting the mines," the commander said. "We're going to nail a lot of them as they come in."

"Good luck," Jaina said, but hydraulics began hissing and the doors boomed shut, and she doubted the signal ever reached the commander in his communications center just below the surface of the moonlet.

Jaina turned off the comm and looked at her group of pilots. "Put on your vac suits. And your body armor *over* the vac suits."

At that moment the artificial gravity switched off. And so did the lights.

How many Yuuzhan Vong warriors to capture a moon? Tsavong Lah wondered. He had twenty thousand in the troopships under his command, but surely that was excessive.

Ten thousand, then. The rest could escape to fight another day.

Nor did he need the entirety of the Battle Group of Yun-Yuuzhan. One-third should be sufficient to repel the New

Republic forces long enough to assure the success of his sacrifice.

"Come, *Jeedai!*" he shouted to the oggzil. "Come to the hunt! Where is your courage?"

Then, turning to the subalterns around the cognition throne, he told them to order the other battle groups to withdraw from the fight. He ordered two of the three divisions of his own squadron to flee as well, and half the troopships.

"But not those containing grutchyna!" he called. "These we shall need once we land on the moon!"

The rock-eating grutchyna would be a surprise, he thought. The *Jeedai* would be forced to move through the tunnels that already existed, but the grutchyna could dig their own.

But before the grutchyna landed, the soldiers would have to secure the area. He ordered the first transports to the surface, covered by the fire of the ships above.

"Warmaster!" came the call from one of his subalterns. "A report from the Battle Group of Yun-Harla. They succeeded in withdrawing into hyperspace, but their jump has failed. They report *mines . . .*"

Mines . . .

The Battle Group of Yun-Harla and the Battle Group of Yun-Txiin leapt into hyperspace together, racing to safety down the narrow corridor that snaked through the Deep Core. But both were yanked out of hyperspace by the interdictor mine that had been set up in the lane's choke point, and all then found themselves in the middle of the enormous minefield that had been laid clean across the narrow corridor.

Every second the enemy remained in the minefield, thousands of mines detected the intruders, swung toward their new targets, and fired themselves at the Yuuzhan Vong.

Many of the Yuuzhan Vong ships were damaged and unable to defend themselves properly. Overwhelmed by the mines, many of these were destroyed in a blizzard of explosions. The few with undamaged defenses fared better, though few escaped without any damage at all.

The Battle Group of Yun-Q'aah, which had been engaged by the fleet of Garm Bel Iblis and the small Smugglers' Alliance squadron, managed a clean jump into hyperspace and arrived in the minefield more or less together. Fewer of their ships had suffered critical damage, and most were able to fight their way out.

The two-thirds of Tsavong Lah's Battle Group of Yun-Yuuzhan were warned of the minefield's existence before they jumped, prepared themselves beforehand, and fared best of all. But the lightly armed troop transports were unable to defend themselves effectively, and within a few minutes in the minefields ten thousand Yuuzhan Vong warriors met their deaths.

As for the Battle Group of Yun-Yammka, it was too far into Ebaq's gravity field to jump, pinned by overwhelming New Republic forces, and wiped out.

More than a third of the Yuuzhan Vong fleet had been destroyed, and that did not count the remainder of Tsavong Lah's battle group, gathered about Ebaq 9 to defend their commander and his ground forces.

There, the first Yuuzhan Vong warriors to charge into the New Republic command centers were met by automatic mines that shredded them through their vonduun crab armor. The warriors charged over their own dead and encountered even more mines.

"You are *already* dead!" Tsavong Lah told them by villip. "The only question is whether you will die honorably as Yuuzhan Vong, or as a cowardly disgrace to the gods who made you!"

None of the warriors were cowards. More than a thousand gave their lives to the mines, and the rest trampled their dead brethren and found only an abandoned facility. There, they wrecked enough of the equipment to finish off the power supply and drop all of Ebaq's shields.

"Bring *Blood Sacrifice* to the surface!" Tsavong Lah commanded. "We will release the grutchyna—and the voxyn!"

The huge flagship was brought to the moon's surface. Before Tsavong Lah left for the moon, he seized the oggzil again and shouted again in Basic.

"Are you not coming, *Jeedai*? Won't you join the hunt? Where is your courage?"

To his surprise, the answering voice was one he recognized.

"This is Jacen Solo," the villip reported. "*I'll* play your game, Warmaster."

Tsavong Lah's answer was filled with grim satisfaction. "Welcome, traitor! I shall look forward to seeing you again."

"And I you, Warmaster."

Menace rang in the warmaster's words. "Once I swore to sacrifice you, Jacen Solo. Perhaps we shall have the sacrifice after all."

"Perhaps I'll manage to delay it again," Jacen said. "Will you let me land, Warmaster?"

"Any *Jeedai* may land. I will so instruct the fleet."

"That's very courteous of you, Warmaster."

"Not at all. Would you come to Ebaq if I order the fleet to blast you out of existence the second you arrived?"

Jacen would, but there was no point in telling the warmaster that.

"I'll see you soon, Warmaster," Jacen said, and keyed off.

His astromech droid bleated at him to let him know he had another incoming call. Jacen switched frequencies.

"Jacen," Luke said. "What are you doing?"

"Helping my sister." Jacen couldn't quite keep defiance

out of his voice. Jacen felt a surge of Luke's presence through the Jedi meld, a forceful effort by Luke to contact him emotionally as well as by words.

"You can't help her by sacrificing yourself," Luke said.

"I'm not planning on getting sacrificed."

"Jaina and the others are in a hardened bunker. All she has to do is wait there until the fleet comes to get her. And we *are* coming, all of us. Kre'fey, Farlander, Bel Iblis. And your parents."

Jacen felt the Force-meld urging him to listen to Luke, to surrender to his reasonable argument. He fought the compulsion and tried to sound as calm and reasonable as he could.

"I don't trust Tsavong Lah to do what people expect him to," he said. "I felt *your* surprise when he moved on Ebaq Nine."

Luke didn't have an answer for that.

"I have a plan," Jacen continued. "I'm not going to run right into his arms, I'm going to distract him and keep him off Jaina's neck."

A stab of fear ran through the Jedi meld, and the taste of it was Jaina's.

"Jaina's being hunted," Jacen said. "I've got to go now."

He snapped off the comm. Luke and others continued to try to contact him through the meld, but Jacen withdrew, and tried instead to concentrate on his Vongsense. He was out of practice—there had been no Yuuzhan Vong to practice *on*—but as he slowed his respiration and entered a meditative state, he felt the enemy out ahead of him, grim determined flecks of consciousness, all ready to sacrifice themselves for their leaders.

Yuuzhan Vong bravery and determination weren't surprising. What did surprise him was the *numbers*.

On Ebaq alone, there must have been *thousands*.

* * *

Jaina waited in the dark. The Jedi were perfectly at home in the dark, strengthened by the Force and able to sense the walls around them, but she felt anxiety grow in her non-Jedi companions, so she had them all switch on helmet lights and belt lights.

Through the Jedi meld she felt the growing certainty of victory, and then the growing triumph as one Yuuzhan Vong squadron after another fled the battle. She sensed that Jacen was doing *something* completely out of the box, but she didn't know what, and she sensed the others trying to do something about it. Distress trickled into her at this knowledge, but she didn't have a comm unit that could reach Jacen, and she couldn't talk to him. She had made up her mind to try to reach him through the meld when something else drew her attention.

Or perhaps, something *not* else.

Through the enhanced perceptions of the Force-meld she felt an emptiness, a void. Something that was not in the Force.

The Yuuzhan Vong.

And then she felt a surge through the Force, a purposeful sensation as malevolent and certain as the sound of a blaster being cocked next to her ear. Voxyn.

Voxyn hunting *her*.

Lowbacca snarled.

"Remind me to tell the high command how much I hate their battle plan," Jaina said. There were hundreds of mineshafts in the old diggings, and a dozen or so that had been shielded by blast doors to delay the enemy. Some had been booby-trapped to make the Vong cautious. The battle plan assumed that the odds of the Yuuzhan Vong finding *her* particular blast doors and committing their forces to breaking through were very low.

The battle plan hadn't assumed the presence of voxyn that could sense any Force-user and lead the enemy straight to Jaina, whether she was anonymous behind blast doors or not.

"Too bad we don't have any of those YVH droids," one of her pilots said.

"There aren't enough of them," Jaina said. "The ones they've got are guarding the government." She considered. "Stand well away from the doors," Jaina decided. "I don't know what they're going to use to bring them down, but I know I don't want to be anywhere near the blast."

"Perhaps it iz time to deploy the minez," Tesar said. His vac-suited tail lashed left and right.

"Yes. But away from the entrance. I don't want our mines wrecked by whatever they use to knock the door down."

And then, on cue, they felt as well as heard a crash. The floor trembled, and the still air of the shaft reverberated to the sudden thunder that came from the other side of the blast door.

The eight pilots of Twin Suns Squadron fell back down the tunnel without a word. They busied themselves in the dark setting up antipersonnel mines while the crash repeated itself again and again.

It was through the Force as much as by eyesight that Jaina sensed part of the wall cracking, parts of it flaking off and coming down.

"They're not coming through the door!" she said. "They're coming *around* it!"

Something else the plan had not foreseen.

The Yuuzhan Vong filled the long tunnel that ran the length of the moon, a thousand in the advance guard followed by baying voxyn and a pair of massive grutchyna, surprisingly light and agile in the low gravity. Then came the main body, with Tsavong Lah and half the communications staff from the *Blood Sacrifice*.

Explosions ripped the air ahead, and two score of the advance guard went down in their own blood—another trap laid by the cowardly infidels, who would not fight hand to hand but instead with these machine snares. The rest marched over them, past one set of durasteel blast doors after another.

The Yuuzhan Vong would not halt until the voxyn did.

The voxyn, their sensory bristles erect, stopped before a blast door indistinguishable from the others. One of them was so close to death that it could barely drag itself along, even in the low gravity. They tasted the door with their forked tongues, and then their howling filled the huge tunnel and sang like a melody in Tsavong Lah's nerves.

"Voxyn back!" Tsavong Lah told the trainers. "Bring the grutchyna forward!"

The grutchyna were sleek black armor-plated beasts six meters long, much larger cousins of the metal-eating grutchins that Yuuzhan Vong fighter craft used as weapons. The grutchyna lacked the grutchins' flight capability, but also their mindlessness: these were trainable and semi-intelligent, and Tsavong Lah had brought them on this expedition knowing he might have to dig the infidels out of their hiding places.

The huge beasts snarled forward, steel-sharp mandibles deployed. Tsavong Lah looked for a moment at the blast doors, then shouted at the trainers.

"Have them dig through the tunnel walls! The walls are softer, and the doors may be mined!"

The tunnel shivered as the grutchyna hurled themselves at the rock walls. Tsavong Lah, thinking of mines, prudently retreated into the main body. He had no fear of death—and in any case he knew he would die today—but dying foolishly as the victim of a mine would be to trivialize his own end.

"*Blood Sacrifice* reports that Jacen Solo has landed," one of his subalterns reported.

"Very good," Tsavong Lah said. "Did *Blood Sacrifice* say where?"

The subaltern communed with his villip for a moment. "Not at the main entrance. Somewhere on the far side."

Tsavong Lah drew his slashed lips into a smile. "We shall find him soon enough." He turned to the voxyn handlers. "Two voxyn to join the advance guard!" he ordered. "All of them to find Jacen Solo!"

"At your command, Warmaster!"

"Capture him for sacrifice if possible. But if not, call the gods to witness and kill him where he stands!"

Tsavong Lah had to shout over the noise the grutchyna made disassembling the tunnel wall. Two of the voxyn snorted on to the head of the advance guard, and the whole body of a thousand set off at a purposeful trot.

Jacen Solo. At the thought of Jacen the warmaster's vua'sa foot clenched, the claws scoring the stone floor. Jacen had thwarted him at their every encounter—had smashed his foot in personal combat, requiring its replacement, and when captured had humiliated him with his sham defection. Now Jacen dared to thwart him again.

It was only now that he wondered why. Why would Jacen Solo fly alone to Ebaq 9 so that he could be hunted by Tsavong Lah and ten thousand Yuuzhan Vong warriors?

At once the answer came to him. *The twin sister!*

Jaina Solo—she who mocked Yun-Harla the Trickster with her devious ploys—must be among the Jedi trapped on Ebaq 9.

Joy raged in Tsavong Lah's breast. The twin sacrifice! Once he had planned to sacrifice the Solo twins, an ambition that had been thwarted by the treasons of Jacen and Vergere. But now the sacrifice would come to pass! And once the two were dead, Tsavong Lah himself could go to his gods with a smile on his slashed lips.

The tunnel wall crashed in as the grutchyna broke through to the mineshaft beyond. "Onward, soldiers!" Tsavong Lah cried. "The *Jeedai* are to be sacrificed! Forward!"

Jaina heard the tunnel wall come down, and then she heard the massed baying of Yuuzhan Vong warriors from the corridor beyond. It sounded like *thousands* of them. "Back!" she said. "Fall back to the next intersection."

They left antipersonnel mines behind, set to go off when they detected the body heat of the enemy. The mine galleries branched here, and Jaina consulted the map of the diggings she'd stored on her datapad and chose the branch that gave her the most options. They moved down the tunnel, and the Jedi used the Force to keep everyone from bumping into each other in the low gravity.

Then came a shriek, a screech with an ultrasonic component that froze Jaina's blood and raised the hairs on the back of her neck.

"What was *that*?" one of her pilots demanded.

"Voxyn," Tesar said. "They hunt uss."

"We can kill them, right?" Anxiously.

She heard one mine go off, followed by a shriek and a roar of anger from a hundred warrior throats.

"I hope we just did," Jaina said.

Jacen sped down the corridor, flying easily with the Force in the moonlet's light gravity, his flashlight picking out the details of the tunnels ahead of him. He, too, had a map of Ebaq 9 on his datapad, and he figured the Yuuzhan Vong were in occupation of the command areas and the central corridor. He planned to materialize in the central corridor, strike the Yuuzhan Vong, then retreat. He would do his best to sow confusion and lead the enemy away from Jaina.

At least he could lead the voxyn on a chase, and with any luck trap them in the narrow passages and kill them.

His expanded Vongsense filled the moon. The sheer number of enemy warriors was intimidating, but he still hoped that, with luck, his plan would succeed.

Unfortunately his equipment was sparse. He had just his lightsaber, plus the blaster pistol and the two grenades that were in the X-wing's survival kit. But he could fight with Yuuzhan Vong weapons if he needed to, and if he got the jump on some enemy warriors he could equip himself with their gear.

And then he felt the mental surge of a voxyn looking for him, and he pushed out with his Vongsense, tried to convince the voxyn not to see him. But he wasn't expert enough—there was a mental *click* of the voxyn locking on to him, and he heard a distant howl that echoed down the shaft, followed by a surge of glee and determination from hundreds of Yuuzhan Vong warriors, and he knew he was being hunted.

He reversed direction—there was no possibility now of catching the Yuuzhan Vong by surprise. It was time to find one of those narrow corridors he'd been thinking about.

Jacen found a right-angle bend in the corridor and decided to make a stand while he still had options for retreat. He stationed himself behind a curve in the tunnel and ignited his lightsaber, then primed one of his two grenades and held it in his left hand. Objectively he considered the use of the Vongsense in combat—he could influence some of the enemy weapons, render them useless—but decided against it. There were simply too many enemy coming for him. He could convince a few of their amphistaffs to bite their owners or go limp, he could convince a few thud bugs to go off prematurely—but he couldn't influence them *all*.

The Force was better for this situation. He let his Vongsense ebb and called the Force to him.

He heard the enemy rush toward him, shouts and the

rush of feet. A horde packed into the corridor, skimming along under the light gravity.

The ultrasonic screech of the voxyn caught Jacen by surprise and almost paralyzed him—he had forgotten how numbing and terrifying the sound was. He wrenched himself free of the shock and hurled the grenade around the corner, exposing his head just enough to use the Force to guide the grenade down the open mouth of the voxyn. The voxyn, in its turn, was spitting toxic sludge at Jacen, but Jacen used the Force to catch the acid stuff and flung it back in the direction of the enemy warriors.

What shocked him was the number of those same warriors. It was one thing to sense them coming; it was another to actually *see* them, and at close range. They seemed to go on forever down the tunnel. There were *hundreds* . . .

He ducked back around the corner as the grenade took off most of the voxyn's head. Jacen knew that even this was unlikely to kill the creature, so he drew his blaster pistol with his left hand and began firing around the corner again, at the voxyn and at any enemy warriors behind it.

The voxyn, blinded or mad with pain, thrashed in the corridor with amazing energy and incredible speed. Its flogging tail had already brought down a number of warriors, but as Jacen began firing, again exposing only his hand and head, the Yuuzhan Vong gave a shout and surged forward, right over the thrashing voxyn, some even shoving the creature ahead of them as they impaled themselves on its poisoned spikes. From the warriors' hands came a rain of thud bugs.

Jacen leapt back from the corner, parrying wildly with his lightsaber as the thud bugs soared toward him, either making the sharp turn or bouncing off a wall and then coming on. One bug hit him on the thigh and spun him around, and he used the Force to maintain the spin, his lightsaber a green blur as he batted the missiles away. He made a complete turn and then used the Force to hurl himself backward down the tunnel while he parried with his lightsaber and fired the pistol left-handed to discourage the Vong from rounding the corner.

He didn't discourage them. The first half dozen went down in a sprawl alongside the wounded voxyn, but then the rest came on, a long column of them, shouting their battle cry.

"Do-ro'ik vong pratte!"

From behind them somewhere came the cry of another voxyn.

Jacen fired round after round from the blaster, though he knew it would do no good. And somewhere in the Force, he felt Jaina's anguish.

"Bring the roof down," Jaina said. "Right here."

"How?" one of her pilots asked. "We've got mines, not explosives."

Jaina reached out with the Force and sought out cracks and flaws in the structure of the stone overhead. Tesar and Lowbacca joined their power to hers.

"Stand back," Jaina said. A half-ton overhead boulder came down with a sudden crash, followed by debris and rubble. She widened the hole overhead, gouging at the rock, bringing more of it down.

Then a shriek seemed to steal the breath from her throat, and a voxyn was there, somehow managing to writhe through the storm of falling rock and leap into the midst of Jaina's party. She had forgotten how fast they were.

She managed to get a Force shield up in time to deflect a hail of toxic spit, and leapt over the first lash of the tail while she drew her lightsaber and ignited the violet blade. There was a thud and a cry behind her. Blasters flamed in the dark, confined space, and concussions slapped her ears. Lowbacca was slashing at the thing's head, the brilliance of his lightsaber reflecting off the voxyn's glittering eyes.

The tunnel reeked of the voxyn's acid spit. The tail lashed a second time and Jaina leapt again, then came down slashing at the tail. The tail parted near its root, and acrid blood spattered Jaina's vac suit.

And then the three Jedi were fighting side by side, light-sabers swinging in a frenzy of close combat against teeth and claws and poison and sheer single-minded viciousness. Whenever one of the other pilots could get a clear shot he let fly with a blaster. Blood and acid spattered and hissed on the tunnel walls.

The voxyn didn't stop fighting until it was literally cut to pieces, and the fight left Jaina exhausted, gasping for breath and leaning against the wall of the shaft. She had taken only a few breaths when she heard the howl of Vong warriors, and looked up to see them filling the tunnel just beyond her rock barrier.

A barrage of thud bugs came over the obstruction, fol-lowed by a mob of warriors scrabbling over the fallen stone. Jaina fired her blaster rifle left-handed at point-blank range while using her lightsaber to slice the thud bugs that came at her.

"The roof!" she gasped. "Let's get the roof down!"

She and Tesar and Lowbacca united their Force talents once more and clawed at the roof, bringing down rubble and stones at first, then boulders. Blaster bolts ricocheted among the rocks, reflecting in all directions—Jaina parried one with her violet blade. And then the roof was down with the sound of thunder, a billowing cloud wall of dust rolling down the mineshaft toward Jaina. She had seen at least half a dozen Yuuzhan Vong warriors buried.

"That won't hold them long," one of her pilots said. "Those rocks won't weigh much in this gravity. And look how they got around the blast doors."

Maybe it'll hold them long enough for me to get another idea, Jaina thought.

"Pull back," she gasped. She wiped dust and sweat from her face and felt a faint surprise that she had any sweat left.

It was only then that she found she had casualties. Her stomach queased as she saw Twin Four sprawled against the wall where the voxyn's tail had thrown him, his vac suit punctured by a score of poison spines. Twin Seven had been hit in the chest by a thud bug and knocked sprawling. He claimed he'd just had the wind knocked out of him, but Jaina didn't like the way his face shivered with pain when the others stood him on his feet.

Two carried Twin Four's body to the rear, and another two supported Twin Seven. The Jedi stayed behind as rear guard until they reached a three-way intersection. The pilots ahead halted, and one of them looked over his shoulder.

"Which way, Major?"

Jaina pulled her datapad from the pocket on her sleeve and looked at it. The map seemed to swirl before her eyes. She was too tired to think properly, she realized. She forced her mind to work on the problem.

"You go left," she said. "Streak and Tesar and I are going straight ahead."

"Wait a minute!" Twin Ten, with Twin Seven's arm around his shoulders, was indignant. "What do you mean by splitting us up?"

"The Vong are hunting Jedi," Jaina said. "You'll be safe if you take a detour. And we'll be safer if we don't have to worry about protecting you."

And you won't die with us, she thought.

"We can fight, Major!" Twin Ten insisted. "We can help you!"

"I appreciate it, but—"

"We haven't come this far with you just to let you go off and fight the Vong on your own. You made us a team, and we're sticking together."

Jaina fought back the tears that suddenly stung her eyes. This was the fighting spirit that *she* had created, created with the drills and painstaking labor and blood. But all this admirable resolution could do right now was get the others killed unnecessarily.

She straightened and took a breath and looked at Twin Ten. "Do I have to make this an order, Lieutenant?" she asked.

Anger and frustration twitched across Twin Ten's face. Then he shook his head. "I guess not, Major," he said.

"Then get moving. I'll see you when this is over."

Jaina watched for a moment as her weary pilots limped away, then dragged herself down the tunnel she'd chosen. Her mind swam with weariness.

"Gather strength from the Force," Tesar said. It was more an order than a suggestion.

Jaina was too tired to agree verbally; she just expanded her Force awareness and let its power drain into her. There was a limit as to how long she could keep this up—ultimately there was no substitute for nutrition and bedrest—but as the Force swam through her body, flushing every cell with energy, she found herself standing straighter. Her step was more firm, her breathing less labored. She consulted the map in her datapad and made a decision.

"We turn here."

Tesar and Lowie looked at the blank tunnel walls in surprise. Lowie growled a question.

In answer, Jaina pointed above their heads.

An air shaft went up, connecting the tunnel to another gallery above their heads. The other two used the Force to help Jaina rise into the shaft, and then by bracing her arms and feet against the rough sides of the shaft she was able to chimney up six or seven meters to the gallery above, where she turned and aided the others. The maneuver was made very easy by the light gravity. Even Lowbacca didn't weigh any more than fifteen kilos.

Tesar turned on his belt light and looked each way down the corridor. Frost glittered on the rough stone walls. "Where now?" he asked.

"We wait right here. We can hold this shaft forever, or at least until they find another way into this gallery. And then when they come, we run the other way."

Tesar seemed to find this plan acceptable and switched off his belt light. The three stood in the frigid tunnel and waited, knowing they wouldn't wait long.

Jaina closed her eyes and opened herself to the Jedi meld. *Uncle Luke*, she sent, *where are you?*

Luke was wondering how to retake the moon when the New Republic didn't have any troops on hand. They hadn't anticipated ground combat, so the only forces available were the lightly armed military police on the large capital ships.

These, and the Jedi. Whom Warmaster Tsavong Lah *hoped* would land on the little moonlet. Whom he had *invited* to land.

The New Republic forces were on the verge of engaging the small squadron the Yuuzhan Vong had left behind to guard their ground forces. The Yuuzhan Vong would fight bravely but wouldn't last long against the New Republic's numbers.

Luke wondered how long it had been since the odds were on his side. It was then that he felt the query from Jaina.

The reply he sent was nonverbal, just a basic mental impression that meant, *Where are you?*

Jaina's response was equally nonverbal, pictures as well as anything else. *Tunnel. Voxyn. Troops.*

How many troops? Picturing numerals and enemy warriors.

Lots. Coming soon. With mental pictures of Vong packed shoulder to shoulder in the narrow mineshafts.

Luke verbalized his next sending. *Can you get to the surface from where you are?*

Negative.

He clenched his teeth. His next message was complicated, and it took him a moment to arrange his thoughts. *Would it be possible to get a starfighter down Ebaq's central shaft?*

In Jaina's reply, Luke sensed a weary amusement at the sheer audacity of the idea, flying an X-wing down the shaft and blasting hosts of Yuuzhan Vong from their perches.

In response was a picture of the shaft, which showed it wide enough; but then Jaina sent another picture of the shaft head, with its heavy ore-hoisting equipment that would have to be gotten out of the way.

Still, it was the best plan Luke had come up with.

We're coming for you, he sent. *Just wait.*

Again Luke sensed amusement, tinged this time with bitterness. As if Jaina had said, *Like I have a choice.*

Through the meld, Luke told the other Jedi to prepare for a landing on Ebaq 9, and a fight against overwhelming numbers.

The first voxyn that Tsavong Lah sent up the vertical shaft came down in pieces, and was followed by a grenade. A dozen brave warriors who tried to chimney up the shaft were killed by blaster fire before they got more than a few meters, and another grenade dropped down and killed a dozen more.

This would delay things only a little. "Send for the grutchyna," the warmaster ordered.

He wouldn't send any more brave warriors up that shaft. Instead he'd dig away the floor from beneath the infidels' feet.

"*Blood Sacrifice* reports they have engaged the enemy," one of his subalterns reported. "They will delay the infidels' arrival as long as possible."

"Tell the fleet that the gods will salute their courage." He turned to another subaltern. "How is the search for Jacen Solo?"

"No change, Warmaster. He flees, but our forces are keeping him in sight. He—"

"Warmaster!" The subaltern with the oggzil interrupted. "A communication for you!"

Tsavong Lah took the oggzil from the subaltern. "Who wishes to speak to me?" he demanded.

"Can you not guess, Warmaster?"

At the sound of the voice Tsavong Lah's heart began to rage within his chest. "Vergere!" he said in surprise, and then he forced amusement into his voice. "Have you called to beg for the lives of the Solo twins?"

"No. I have come to join your Jedi hunt, if you'll let me."

The warmaster laughed. "You're a miserable traitor, and very clever, but you are not a *Jeedai*."

"But I *am* a Jedi. A *real* Jedi, not one of these imitations you've been fighting. Haven't you worked that out by now?" Smug pleasure oozed from Vergere's words. "I lived alongside you for fifty years without detection, and then I betrayed you. I'm surprised the Supreme Overlord allowed you to live after I made you look so ridiculous."

Fury gripped Tsavong Lah by the throat. "Come to Ebaq Nine!" he shouted. "Come to the sacrifice of the Solo twins!"

"If you'll let me."

"I'll instruct the ships to let you by." He threw the oggzil back to his subordinate. "See to it!"

"Immediately, Warmaster."

The packed warriors surged aside as the first of the two grutchyna arrived, half floating in the low gravity. "Ah," he

said to the trainers, and pointed at the roof. "Begin there!"
Then he turned to the nearest group of Yuuzhan Vong. "Up
the shaft, warriors!" he ordered. "Keep the *Jeedai* busy
while we dig."

The three Jedi stood in the dark, illuminated only by their
lightsabers. Jaina had just begun to think that the Yuuzhan
Vong had been too inactive for too long, when the floor reverberated to an impact, and from below there was a crash
of falling rock.

"Vong!" Tesar said, and leaned out to fire into the shaft
as warriors began to scramble up. Razor bugs shot up in a
useless attempt at providing a covering attack, and Lowbacca and Jaina sliced them effortlessly with their lightsabers.

The floor rocked to another shattering blow. Jaina could
hear rock cracking.

Drop a grenade, she thought, and run.

Run until they caught her. And then fight until she couldn't
fight any longer.

Jacen had decided he might as well make his stand. The
mineshafts branched and narrowed, branched and narrowed, and when the roof got less than two meters high he
realized he was out of choices. When the tunnels were so
small he could only crouch, then the voxyn would have too
great an advantage.

He made a turn into a branching tunnel and readied his
lightsaber and blaster. He'd save his last grenade for the
next voxyn.

The enemy warriors hurled themselves down the tunnel
and Jacen fired on them. Thud bugs and blorash jelly flew at
him; he ducked some and cut at others. He was strangely
calm.

This wasn't the first time he had made a mistake. And
dying was nothing new, either.

It was the thought of Jaina that brought despair. He had failed to help her; and through the Force and their twin bond he felt her own hopelessness.

The Yuuzhan Vong kept coming, dozens of them lunging, charging, hurling thud bugs, spitting poison from the heads of their amphistaffs. Jacen's blaster was running out of charges. His lightsaber was a brilliant green blur as it parried and slashed. Pace by pace, he stepped back into the narrowing shaft.

Jacen felt rage building in him, a red fury that was his response to his own despair. The blaster hummed empty and he threw it at the warrior. And then he remembered the power he could call upon, the power fueled by the kind of despair and anger he felt now and had felt before, and he hurled it at the warrior, the brilliant emerald fire that lanced from his fingertips.

The Force lightning threw the first rank of Yuuzhan Vong back into their comrades, and in the confusion Jacen launched another blaze of fire. He hadn't killed them—the murderous form of lightning was a dark side weapon—but they wouldn't be waking for a long time.

"Young Jedi."

Jacen looked around, and somehow wasn't surprised to find Vergere standing there. "Hello," he said, and fired another sizzling blast at the Yuuzhan Vong.

Vergere looked up at him, her tilted eyes glittering and wise. "You're about to lose your air," she said.

"Vergere!" the subaltern cried, his voice ringing high above the sound of the grutchyna bringing down stone.

Tsavong Lah swung at the subaltern. "What of her?" Impatiently. "Isn't she coming?"

"She comes! *But she isn't slowing down!*"

* * *

The A-wing that Vergere stole from *Ralroost*'s fighter bays impacted Ebaq 9's main shaft head traveling at thirty-five thousand kilometers per hour. The starfighter's weapons had been scavenged for use elsewhere, but weapons were scarcely necessary. The impact vaporized the heavy girders and machinery at the shaft head, and the starfighter's power plant and the two huge Novaldex engines turned into a fast-moving ball of plasma that swept the length of Ebaq 9's central shaft and blew out the other side, a brilliant volcanic eruption that blinded any holocams that happened to be turned in that direction.

As the superheated ion storm rampaged through the moonlet it flashed into any open side corridors, and to a lesser degree any corridors branching off these, but Jaina and Jacen were too deep into the galleries to be directly affected.

What happened in their galleries was an enormous, eardrum-punishing buffet of pressure and heat, followed by a furious dust and windstorm that lasted mere seconds— after which the air was simply gone. The hurtling ball of plasma pushed a huge pressure wave ahead of it, and carried an underpressure behind, drawing air out of all the galleries. In addition, the storm of heat and pressure had set the moon on fire. Even metal will burn if it's hot enough and there's enough oxygen to keep the fires going. The fires set by the A-wing's ion fury were hot enough and powerful enough to suck every bit of oxygen out of the tunnels within seconds.

The Yuuzhan Vong had come prepared for decompression—it was an obvious defense strategy, after all. All of them carried ooglith cloakers that would enable them to survive without air.

But they had expected more warning. Even if the New Republic engineers had blown the shaft head and exposed it to the vacuum of space, it would have taken many minutes for all the great volume of air to evacuate the tunnels, and the warriors would have had all that time from the first decompression warning to safely don their cloakers.

Those who survived the great wave of heat and radiation experienced at first the brutal overpressure of the impact, followed by a dusty, disorienting, hurricanelike wind as the air was sucked behind the racing plasma ball and into the fires of the central core.

The oxygen was gone within two or three seconds of the impact. The few Yuuzhan Vong who realized what had just happened were caught in a pack of their cohorts, disoriented and unable to communicate in the sudden absence of air. Many experienced syncope and passed out at once. Any who tried to hold their breath died of embolism as their lungs frothed and exploded. In order to survive, any individual warrior would have had to claw his cloaker free and don it amid a scrambling, staggering, falling crowd of his fellows, many of whom would have tried to snatch the cloaker from him in order to don it themselves.

The three surviving voxyns and the grutchyna had no ooglith cloakers to wear, and they panicked in the absence of air and thrashed madly. Many Yuuzhan Vong were crushed or poisoned, slashed or bitten by the dying animals, including their handlers.

Within twenty seconds, all the Yuuzhan Vong had passed out. Within minutes, they were dead.

As deaths in battle go, these were comparatively merciful.

The first blast of heat and pressure knocked Jaina from the shaft, staggered with vertigo from the double slap to her ears. "Depressurization!" she called, her mind whirling.

With one quick movement she slapped her faceplate closed. The air around her howled, a screaming hurricane that threatened to drag her into the shaft, but within three seconds this was diminished to nothing.

By the time she had fully secured her pressure helmet the air was gone.

About time, she thought. She could have done with engineers blowing the shaft head a lot earlier.

Tesar stood closest to the shaft, able to use his tail to brace himself against the shaft walls and avoid being knocked about by the storm. Jaina gestured at him to take a glance down the shaft and see if the enemy were moving.

Tesar looked, then stepped back, one hand gesturing at Jaina to stay where she was.

Jaina understood. Whatever was happening in the lower gallery, it was something she didn't want to watch.

Jacen watched the Yuuzhan Vong die. He had no helmet, but thanks to Vergere's warning he was able to preserve the air in his immediate area with the Force, forming a seal across the tunnel opening ahead of him.

The Yuuzhan Vong fell in graceful silence, one by one, dropping slowly in the light gravity like the petals of some absurdly menacing flower.

"I wish I could help them," Jacen said.

"There is nothing more useless than an impossible wish." Vergere was severe.

He turned to her. "You did this, didn't you?"

Vergere's whiskers twitched with distaste. "It was necessary that you be liberated from your choices."

Jacen sighed. "My choices weren't very good, were they?"

"You chose with your heart. And you achieved your object, did you not? Your sister lives." She looked at him solemnly. "And I achieved my object as well. You are free to pursue your destiny."

Truth struck Jacen. He looked at Vergere in shock.

"I just realized," he said. "You're dead, aren't you?"

* * *

The *Blood Sacrifice* blew at the same moment the fireball blossomed from Ebaq's far side, and Luke was staggered by the double explosion.

He sought the Force-meld, searching for the Jedi trapped on the moon, but it was some time before their presence returned to the meld. They had been very busy.

What happened? he demanded.

Depressurization. A picture of wind whirling out of the tunnel, followed by another picture of enemy dead.

Jaina? Tesar? Sending pictures.

Luke received pictures in return—Jaina and Tesar, hale and well, beneath the blue skies of some green planet.

And Jacen?

Jaina's excited presence interrupted. *Jacen? He's here?*

Yes. Jacen's presence in the meld was calm. *With Vergere. She's saved us.*

Vergere, thought Luke. His reaction was strong enough to send his complex feelings into the Force-meld, and he felt the others react. Luke quickly dampened his contact with the meld. There were secrets he didn't want all Jedi to know.

Was Vergere with the Yuuzhan Vong? The complex idea took some time for Luke to formulate. If the answer to his question was yes, the Yuuzhan Vong knew of the Alpha Red weapon and this whole victory might be pointless.

No. Vergere's astringent personality flowed into the meld from wherever she had been concealing herself, and spoke with extraordinary clarity. *I have been hiding among the New Republic forces. I stole a fighter and dived it into the moon to destroy the enemy.*

Luke absorbed the implications of this. *You gave your life to save the others.*

Vergere's response was the answer she had given all along. *It was necessary.*

Luke hesitated. Battle was still raging, and people were still dying.

Hold on, he tried to send. *We'll get you out as soon as we can.* And to the rest of the Jedi, he sent a strong suggestion not to mention Vergere to anyone. *There are reasons.*

He shifted his mind to the battle. The Yuuzhan Vong had fought with their usual tremendous courage, but such courage hadn't served them well—it had become a trap, as Ackbar had foreseen. Their formation was broken, their ships afire, their crews dying. The New Republic forces were finishing them off.

Luke looked at Garm Bel Iblis, saw the man's knifelike profile gazing intently at the battle display.

"Can we call on them to surrender?" he asked.

Bel Iblis was surprised. "Why? They'll fight on. They always do."

"Because it will make us feel better to know that we offered. That we did all we could to preserve life."

Bel Iblis considered this for a moment as he tugged his long white mustache, then nodded. "Very well," he said.

The offer to accept the enemy's surrender was made repeatedly from that moment.

The Yuuzhan Vong did not answer, and died.

Jacen stood in the narrow mine gallery so that he wouldn't lose body heat by sitting or leaning on the cold stone. He was practic-ing Tapas, the art of keeping warm in a cold environment, but he was finding it difficult to concentrate on this and on maintaining the Force shield that retained his air, and so he was beginning to shiver.

"I got you killed," he said.

Vergere tilted her chin. "Dying was *my* decision, young Jedi. Not yours."

"But," Jacen reasoned, "I created the situation that led to your making that decision."

"In that case, you may rejoice in the fact that your sister is alive." Vergere shook her head. "Both of us could not live.

The situation would not permit that. The choice was between the young and promising, as against the wise and superannuated. And given that choice"—she sighed—"nature always chooses the young." She sighed again. "I chose to bow to the will of nature. My time ended forty years ago. Now at last I will join my Master, and my old comrades."

Tears stung Jacen's eyes. "I wish it had worked out differently."

Again Vergere looked severe. "What did I say about impossible wishes?"

Jacen hugged himself, and rubbed his upper arms for warmth. His teeth chattered.

"Can you help me stay warm?" he asked.

Amusement glittered in Vergere's eyes. "My abilities in this state are necessarily limited. I suggest you call upon your other friends."

Mara felt the tension go out of her as Sien Sovv delivered his report from Bel Iblis's flagship. "Master Skywalker reports that all the Jedi trapped on the moon have survived. In fact, no Jedi casualties have been reported at all."

Sovv looked as pleased as his heavy-jowled face permitted. His step was lighter, and his button eyes glittered. He turned to Ackbar.

"Your plan was brilliant, sir," he said. "It worked perfectly."

Ackbar made an agitated movement of his hands. "I should have foreseen the occupation of Ebaq." His words were slurred, and his skin had turned gray. "I should have insisted on ground troops defending that moon."

The Supreme Commander wasn't about to let second thoughts spoil his victory. "It all worked out for the best!" Sovv said. He gestured at the holo representation of Ebaq's system. "Look, sir! No surviving enemy craft—the board's nothing but blue!"

Ackbar's whiskered chin fell on his chest. "I should have foreseen it," he mumbled.

Winter looked at Mara. "We should get Ackbar home. Will you help me?"

Mara and Winter each took one of Ackbar's arms and helped him rise. As they made their way out of the command center, Ayddar Nylykerka ran up to Mara.

"Now we can roll up their spy networks!" he said. "The Vong will never believe any of these networks now."

"I've been thinking about that," Mara said. "Maybe we should let one of them stay in place."

Nylykerka cocked his head. "Really?" he said. "Can you explain your reasoning?"

"If we roll up two of the networks and leave the third alone, that will give the third more credence."

"Hmm. Very intriguing."

Mara and Nylykerka debated the matter all the way to the shuttle gate.

Luke was eager to mount a rescue mission immediately, but the central shaft of Ebaq 9 was too hot and too radioactive for living beings to enter. Droids were sent instead, bringing food, water, heaters, bedding, and vacuumproof tents in which the survivors could live while waiting for the moon to cool down. Cybot loadlifters were used, on the theory that their unsophisticated brains would be less subject to being scrambled by radiation. MD-series medical droids were sent in as well. One of them froze partway in, slagged by radiation, but the others got through intact.

Jacen was found keeping warm with energy sent to him by the Jedi meld. He set up the tent, ballooned it with air, set up the heater, and consumed several warm drinks. The medical droid pronounced him well.

The loadlifters found Jaina as well, but were unable to ascend the vertical shaft to her hiding place. She, Tesar, and

Lowbacca dropped easily through the shaft, and for the first time, in the loadlifters' powerful lights, Jaina saw the piles of Yuuzhan Vong corpses that choked the tunnel. She turned away and hoped she wouldn't be sick in her vac suit.

The MD droid's voice came through the headset of Jaina's vac suit. "I would like to examine you. And your companions."

"We're all right," Jaina answered. *If I don't throw up.* "I have a wounded pilot whom you should see first. Walk back the way you came, and take the first left facing out. Keep hailing on these frequencies and they should answer."

"Very well."

"Take one of the loadlifters with you. They'll need supplies as well. And there's a body that will have to be taken out." *Maybe thousands of bodies.*

The MD droid turned to go.

Then Jaina was surprised to see the droid's head fly off and strike the mineshaft wall.

Tsavong Lah passed out seconds after the tunnel was depressurized, and had survived only because his aides fought off the other Yuuzhan Vong who would have trampled him just long enough for one of them to deploy the gnullith that fed him air, and the ooglith cloaker that masked him against vacuum and cold.

When the warmaster woke, with the gnullith's tube down his throat, he was buried under an insulating pile of Yuuzhan Vong dead, mostly his own subalterns. At first despair consumed him, the knowledge that he had failed utterly, that his fleet had been broken and forced to flee, and even his personal revenge against the Jedi twins had come to nothing. He considered tearing the gnullith from his face and dying along with the brave warriors he had led to destruction.

But then he recalled that Jaina and her comrades were near. If they had moved while he was unconscious, then his revenge would still be thwarted, but there had been no *reason* for them to move—Jaina was still probably at the head of the vertical shaft just overhead. Animated by sudden hope, he clutched his baton of rank and worked his way to the top of the pile of corpses, where he gathered a stock of weapons. His baton and the amphistaffs were all dead, but had frozen into useful positions. Thud and razor bugs were no more than rocks. But the blorash jelly was in suspended animation and would live long enough when triggered to do what he intended. When Tsavong Lah had prepared his arsenal, he returned to the corpses, draping enough arms and legs over himself to remain inconspicuous.

It was a pity that it wouldn't be Jacen Solo he confronted at the end. But he comforted himself with the thought that to kill Jaina would be to hurt Jacen—to give him a lifelong sorrow that might be more damaging than if Jacen himself were killed.

Cold triumph sang through his nerves as he began to detect the powerful lights of the loadlifters approaching down the tunnel. He narrowed his eyes, keeping his focus on the vertical shaft just a few meters over his head.

Soon he would strike, and take his vengeance.

Jaina twisted as she drew her lightsaber, intending to spin away from any attacker, but her feet had somehow gotten stuck to the mineshaft floor, and instead of spinning she sprawled to one side—luckily, because at that moment Tsavong Lah hurled his baton of rank like a spear.

The baton missed Jaina entirely and impaled Lowbacca, piercing him clean through the shoulder. The Wookiee roared and wobbled—like Jaina, blorash jelly had pinned him to the floor—and he fell into Tesar, who was in the act of drawing his blaster.

Little jets of air began to spurt from Lowbacca's wounds, crystallizing immediately in the vacuum and drifting to the floor as glittering snow.

Half deafened by the Wookiee roar she heard over her headset, Jaina hauled herself upright, aided by muscle and low gravity, her lightsaber glowing a soft violet off the cavern walls. Tsavong Lah seized an amphistaff from the weapons he'd strewn nearby and slashed the weapon at Jaina's head.

Jaina was frozen to the floor by blorash jelly, and Tsavong Lah was behind her. Her helmet cut off her peripheral vision, and the only way she knew she was being attacked was that she saw Tsavong Lah's madly dancing shadow cast by the powerful lights of the loadlifters. She dropped the point of her lightsaber behind her back to guard against Tsavong Lah's swing, and the impact almost wrenched her arm out of its socket.

Her heart thundered in her ears. She twisted as far to her right as possible in order to see her attacker and managed to parry the next furious series of strikes. Tsavong Lah shifted to her left, and Jaina twisted toward him and swung her lightsaber in a sweeping parry from high to low to catch any possible strike. Again the impact was massive, and nearly tore the weapon from her grasp. The warrior kept chopping at her, the amphistaff held in both hands, and she parried furiously. She had no chance to counterattack, and the impacts were numbing her arm. If something didn't happen soon, her weapon would be knocked from her hand.

The fight in the vacuum was in utter silence. Jaina could hear only her own rasping breath and the throbbing of her heart, and then the silence was broken, over the comm, by Lowbacca's bellow as Tesar yanked the baton out of his shoulder.

"It'z Tsavong Lah!" Jaina was startled by Tesar's words

coming through her helmet phones. The warmaster's face was well known in the New Republic.

"Shoot him!" Jaina said. She didn't much care who he was; she only wanted him dead and her friends safe.

Tesar obliged by firing at the warmaster, the brilliant blaster bolts glancing off the rock walls, but the Yuuzhan Vong danced to Jaina's right again to put Jaina between himself and Tesar's blaster.

"This one must patch up Lowie!" Tesar said. "He'z losing air! You've got to hold off the Vong!"

"Thanks," Jaina muttered. She twisted to the right again, turning the movement into a cut. She chopped a chunk out of the frozen amphistaff, and Tsavong Lah stepped out of range to pick up another weapon. When he came on again he lunged rather than slashed, and Jaina was able to slide her blade into a circular parry and bind. But in her twisted position she lacked the leverage of wrist and arm to force the disarm that followed the bind; instead her blade grated on the amphistaff and locked.

Only a meter away she could see Tsavong Lah's silent snarl of triumph. He kicked and drove his heel into Jaina's thigh.

An overwhelming jolt of pain shot through her thigh and knee. With a cry she lost her grip on her lightsaber and pitched forward. In front of her Lowbacca crouched before Tesar, both nailed to the ground by blorash jelly. Lowie's hand pressed on his shoulder, trying to hold in his air, while Tesar worked frantically to apply a patch to the wound on the Wookiee's back.

Jaina snatched Lowie's lightsaber from his belt and triggered it as she pulled herself to her feet. Tsavong Lah had cleared Jaina's lightsaber from his weapon and lunged forward again, and his eyes widened in surprise as Jaina slashed two clawed toes from the radank leg he had implanted as an arm.

The warmaster stepped back as dark blood oozed from the wound and fell with a graceful lack of haste to the floor. Jaina kept the lightsaber on guard, pointed at his face. He glared at her, red murder glowing in his eyes.

"How's Streak?" she asked.

"He'z passed out. This one has patched the exit wound, but the wound at the front iz still venting."

Jaina watched Tsavong Lah take a grip on his weapon and dig his feet into the ground.

"Hurry," she said, "I think I just made him mad."

Tsavong Lah charged, the amphistaff a blur. He attacked to Jaina's right side, drawing her lightsaber out of line, then shifted to a vicious overhead cut coming in from the left. Jaina managed to block in time, but the impact bent her far over, the air going from her lungs in a *whuff*. Her head low, she could see the soft violet radiance of her own lightsaber lying on the floor past the warmaster's legs.

She sliced madly at the amphistaff as she straightened again, engaging the furious warrior in a long series of attacks and parries.

And then Jaina reached out with the Force, picked up her lightsaber from the ground behind Tsavong Lah, and drove the violet blade point-first through his throat.

The warmaster fell. Jaina didn't spare him another glance, but turned to Tesar and Lowbacca. Tesar was just finishing the patch on the front of Lowie's vac suit. She could see the suit begin to reinflate, the Wookiee's muzzle snarling open as he drew in a breath.

Tesar looked up at her. "The suit is patched. But the shoulder is not."

"Force-meld," Jaina gasped. "Tell Uncle Luke we need another MD droid. And blood to replace what Lowie's lost."

"That is wise."

Tesar straightened, then looked down at his feet. He tried to move one foot, and the blorash jelly shattered like fine glass.

Apparently it didn't deal with vacuum well.

"*Now* we can move," Jaina said. "Great timing, as usual."

TWENTY-SEVEN

Five days after the Battle of Ebaq, Luke Skywalker met with Cal Omas. Cal had spent the weeks prior to the battle in isolation on the Super Star Destroyer *Guardian*, cruising safely between the stars. Now *Guardian* had joined Kre'fey's fleet at Kashyyyk.

"My heart was in my mouth," Cal said. "I was sitting there watching the battle and—I wanted to *do* something. I wanted to give an order!"

"Thank you for your restraint." Luke smiled. "That's been one of our problems—too many voices giving orders."

"Don't I know it." Cal frowned. "Will you sit?"

The Star Destroyer possessed an admiral's lounge that seemed half the size of a hoverball field, filled with tasteful furniture and scented by the blossoms the ship's gardener cultivated and set in beautiful vases.

Cal and Luke sat in plush armchairs, and Cal rang for a steward to bring drinks.

"I've been thinking about the government and how to fix it," Cal said. "The war's sense of urgency has resulted in unity right now, but once the Senate decides we're going to win, they're going to want to figure out how to get their hands on the spoils."

Luke nodded. "What's your solution?"

"Persuade the worlds to elect more responsible Senators?" Cal suggested weakly, and then laughed at his own absurdity.

"You've got other ideas."

Cal nodded. "Confine the Senate to its proper sphere, for one thing. It should legislate and supervise, not try to run the administration from day to day. A truly independent judiciary would curb their more ambitious maneuvers. A new federalism that properly defines the boundaries between the Senate and the regimes on the various planets."

"You're talking a new constitution."

Cal gave a tight-lipped little smile. "I'm even thinking of names. Federal Galactic Republic. Galactic Federation of Free Alliances." He frowned. "Do you think it's possible?"

"I think a Chief of State who's just won a war against an implacable enemy might have a lot of currency with the Senate and the people."

Cal's smile faded. "Guess I'd better get busy and win it, then."

Which brought them to the point of the meeting. Luke looked at Cal and said, "Win it with Alpha Red?"

Cal's look turned grim. "No," he said. "Not now. It's a last resort only."

Luke nodded. "Thank you, sir."

Luke was able to assure Jacen that Alpha Red had been put on hold as soon as he and his nephew could find time to be alone. Jacen had been rescued mere hours after the end of the battle, but he had spent the intervening time with his parents, and Luke had been too busy to question him.

Now Jacen had returned to his quarters on *Ralroost*, a ship filled with the sound of clattering pneumatic cutters and hissing welders, all busy repairing battle damage. Jacen seemed rested and fit—he had put on weight since his escape from the Yuuzhan Vong, and his eyes were bright and his short beard neatly trimmed.

"But Alpha Red will still exist," Jacen said. He had courteously given Luke his only chair and sat cross-legged on his narrow bunk.

"We can't put the knowledge back in its box," Luke said.

Jacen shook his head, frowned down at the floor. "Insufficient experience of depravity," he murmured.

"Beg pardon?"

Jacen glanced up. "Something Vergere once said. Implying that I had much to learn."

"Vergere," Luke said, "thought knowledge was the answer to everything."

"Was she wrong?"

Luke considered the question. "I value compassion over knowledge," he said. "But I hope never to have to choose between the two."

"I chose compassion as well," Jacen said. "Compassion for Jaina over the knowledge that my attempt to rescue her was almost certainly useless."

Luke listened carefully to Jacen's tone for a hint of bitterness. He didn't hear it. Jacen seemed to have accepted what had happened, accepted it somehow and dealt with it.

He reflected that Jacen was remarkable in his capacity for acceptance.

"And then Vergere chose compassion as well," Jacen went on. "Compassion for me. And she gave her life for mine."

"She thought your life was worth saving," Luke said. "And so do I."

Jacen looked up sharply. "I hope you won't have to sacrifice yourself for me," he said.

Luke smiled. "Let's just say that's *another* choice I hope never to have to make."

Jacen looked away. "Vergere said the old must give way to the new."

"You're the future of the Jedi order," Luke said. "You

and Jaina and Tahiri and the others. In my time, I must make way for you as well."

Jacen looked thoughtful. "In your time . . ." he said. He scratched his brown beard, then looked in annoyance at his hand and returned it to his lap. He looked at Luke. "Do you think it's possible that the issues of this war are completely different from—from *your* war, from the war against the Empire?"

"How do you mean?"

A repair crew of droids clattered by outside the door, and Jacen waited for their sound to fade before continuing. "Your war was about light and dark. You and my mom versus Vader and the Emperor. But *this* war—" He hesitated. "For all the evil they do, the enemy aren't dark, exactly—the enemy are outside the Force entirely. So to fight them we need to . . . to *make the Force bigger*. Bigger than light and dark, bigger than human and Yuuzhan Vong . . ." He shook his head, then gave a laugh. "I'm talking nonsense, aren't I? *Make the Force bigger.* The Force is *already* all living things."

"Perhaps it's not the Force that needs to be bigger," Luke said. "Maybe what needs to be bigger are our *ideas* about the Force."

Jacen made as if to laugh again, then stopped. His face turned serious. "Bigger ideas about the Force. How do we manage that?"

Luke rose from the chair, and on his way out of the cabin put his hand on Jacen's shoulder. "If anyone can do it, Jacen," he said, "it would be you."

Jaina left Ebaq 9 eight days after the battle. The interior of the moon was still hot, but she was saved from the radiation by being carried by a loadlifter in a lead-lined container box.

She insisted on being the last one out. She had reunited after the battle with the pilots she'd sent away down the side passage, and they'd spent the week in their oxygen tents.

In the tents there had been nothing to do but talk, play sabacc, and sleep. Occasionally the MD droid changed Lowbacca's bacta patches. Jaina rebelled at first against this unstructured life—she was used to long days of drill, study, and instruction. She wanted to *do* something.

But no meaningful work was possible, and eventually the tension began to ebb and she began to relax. She joined the other Jedi in meditation, at first to help Lowie heal, and then because it became her only connection to the universe that lay beyond the tents. Through the Force and the Jedi meld, she bade farewell to her friends as they left Ebaq's system—Kre'fey's fleet had been recalled to the defense of Kashyyyk, and Bel Iblis returned to Fondor. Soon the only friendly force remaining in the system was the Smugglers' Alliance squadron led by her father, the squadron that had lost half its ships turning the enemy squadron from her.

From her. So many had died to keep her safe. Her father's friends, Vale and three other Twin Suns pilots, Vergere . . . She didn't know how to think about them now.

And so she meditated, and slowly relaxed, and opened herself to the universe. To its glories and pleasures, and its griefs and sorrows as well. Sometimes, when she was laughing with the others, she felt a wave of heartache strike her, and she had to turn away, gulping tears.

There were so many to mourn. A whole war's worth.

The final indignity came when she was carried out in the lead-lined box, like a package to be delivered to her friends. When she emerged, she was in the *Millennium Falcon*'s cargo bay, and the room was filled with applause.

The light dazzled her eyes. She stepped out of the box and wrestled the vac suit helmet off her head. Standing before her were her parents, Jacen, the eight surviving Twin Suns pilots, Kyp Durron, and old friends like Talon Karrde, Booster Terrik, and Lando Calrissian.

They all seemed inexpressibly dear to her. Jaina went along the room and embraced them one by one. As she touched Jacen she felt the twin bond roaring in her head, the memories and comradeship and love all singing in her heart like a chorus of concern.

Her father, himself blinking back tears, reached into a pocket and held out a pair of gleaming insignia. "Admiral Kre'fey's decided to promote you," he said. "Congratulations, Lieutenant Colonel!"

"Thank you." She focused on the insignia Han wore on his civilian vest, and snapped him a salute. "Thank you, General!"

Han returned the salute with a shamefaced grin. Then Jaina turned to her mother, who stood by Han's side with her arms open, and Jaina threw herself at Leia and buried her face in her mother's neck.

This is going to be really bad for discipline, she thought.

Leia stroked her hair. "Will you take a vacation *now*?" she demanded.

Jaina laughed, but the tears burned in her eyes. "You know what?" she mumbled. "Being the Sword of the Jedi really stinks."

His body twitched to remembered pain. Images of needles and knifelike claws floated through his mind. He remembered the shriek of severed nerves, the grind of bone against bone, the way blood oozed slowly from a wound.

He shivered. Why had this happened? Why? He had never harmed anyone.

He opened his eyes at a sound, and there before him was the withered one, a sneer drawn across his crooked slash of a mouth.

"Your guests have arrived, Supreme One."

At the words Shimrra felt his power flow into him, his majesty and command and presence. He sat on his spiked throne in the Hall of Confluence with its white bone pillars, and his subjects waited outside the huge doors—he could *detect* them there, feel the subdued fluttering of their busy minds.

Shimrra looked at the disfigured being before him. *Onimi*. "Let the doors open," he said.

The four doors trembled open, and the four castes and their leaders entered and filed in silence to their places. Onimi sat on the lowest step of Shimrra's dais and adopted a sullen expression.

Shimrra could sense the deep foreboding in his inferiors, the sense that the great defeat at Ebaq had been a disaster from which the Yuuzhan Vong might not recover. *Cowards*, he thought. These fools must be strengthened.

He rose massively from his throne, stood before them in the flayed skin of Steng. He sent his presence out among his listeners and began to work on their emotions, to drive them into a frenzy.

"The gods test their servants!" he shouted. "They have permitted enemy treachery to betray one of our fleets!"

One of the warriors flung himself to the ground. "Command us, Supreme One!"

"We must thank the gods for this chance to test our purity and resolve!" Shimrra roared. "Let the sacrifices be doubled! Let heretics be sought and punished! Let prayers rise to the gods from every temple!"

"So shall it be!" High Priest Jakan was on his feet, shaking a fist.

"Let the warriors redouble their vigilance! Any step backward is a betrayal! Let the commanders plan new offensives and new victories! Let them spill the blood of the infidels!"

The warriors bayed their approval, raising their amphistaffs.

"The traitor Nom Anor must be found!" Shimrra proclaimed. "Let him be slaughtered and his bones ground to powder!"

Afterward, after his audience filed out, Shimrra collapsed onto his throne. Onimi rose from his crouch and gave a sneering look at the far end of the hall.

"Fools," he said. "But what choice is there but to use them?"

Shimrra made no reply. His eyes were closed.

Onimi's voice was thoughtful. "We began this war, and now we must fight on and hope for the best." He gave a little shiver. "You've betrayed and used the gods—perhaps they now betray you in return."

Shimrra said nothing.

"Yet Nen Yim may yet fill the eighth cortex," Onimi mused. "She needs time. Perhaps her resources should be increased."

Shimrra remained silent, his torn nostrils flaring with each massive breath. Onimi cocked his swollen, misshapen head. "Do you not find it amusing, Supreme One?" he said. "We gambled and lost. And now we must double the stakes and gamble again, with the odds against us even greater than before. Is that not cause for laughter, Lord Shimrra?"

Onimi threw his head back and laughed, a full-throated shriek of amusement that rang from the room's high ceiling.

Shimrra drew in air and laughed, a huge deep booming that rattled his throne's coral spikes.

Their laughter redoubled, treble and bass, twining among the chitin walls, the bone pillars, the arching roof. The room built like the mouth of a great carnivorous beast, a beast that devours all who enter.

"Begun, this Clone War has!"
—MASTER YODA

Turn the page
for a sneak preview
of the very first Clone Wars novel,

STAR WARS: SHATTERPOINT

by Matthew Stover

an original Star Wars adventure
featuring Jedi Master Mace Windu.

ONE

CAPITAL CRIMES

The spaceport at Pelek Baw smelled clean. It wasn't. Typical backworld port: filthy, disorganized, half-choked with rusted remnants of disabled ships.

Mace stepped off the shuttle ramp and slung his kit bag by its strap. Smothering wet heat pricked sweat across his bare scalp. He raised his eyes from the ochre-scaled junk and discarded crumples of empty nutripacks scattered around the landing deck, up into the misty jade sky.

The white crown of Grandfather's Shoulder soared above the city: the tallest mountain on the Korunnal Highland, an active volcano with dozens of open calderae. Mace remembered the taste of the snow at the treeline, the thin cold air and the aromatic resins of the evergreen scrub below the summmit.

He had spent far too much of his life on Coruscant.

If only he could have come here for some other reason.

Any other reason.

A straw-colored shimmer in the air around him explained the clean smell: a surgical sterilization field. He'd expected it. The spaceport had always had a powered-up surgical field umbrella, to protect ships and equipment from the various native fungi that feed on metals and silicates; the field also wiped out the bacteria and molds that would otherwise have made the spaceport smell like an overloaded 'fresher.

Mace wore clothing appropriate to his cover: a stained

Corellian cat-leather vest over a loose shirt that used to be white, and skin-tight black pants with wear-patches of grey. His boots carried a hint of polish, but only above the ankle; the uppers were scuffed almost to suede. The only parts of his ensemble that were well-maintained were the supple holster belted to his right thigh, and the gleaming Merr-Sonn Power 5 it held. His lightsaber was stuffed into the kit bag, disguised as an old-fashioned glow rod. The kit bag also held what looked like a battered old datapad, most of which was actually a miniature subspace transmitter that was frequency-locked to the band monitored by the light cruiser *Halleck*, on station in the Ventran system.

The spaceport's probiotic showers were still in their long, low blockhouse of mold-stained duracrete, but their entrance had been expanded into a large temporary-looking office of injection-molded plastifoam, with a foam-slab door that hung askew on half-sprung hinges. The door was streaked with rusty stains that had dripped from the fungus-chewed dura-steel sign above. The sign said CUSTOMS. Mace went in.

Sunlight leaked green through mold-tracked windows. Climate control wheezed a body-temp breeze from ceiling vents, and the smell loudly advertised that this place was well beyond the reach of the surgical field. The other passengers who'd gotten off the shuttle were inside already: two Kubaz who'd spent the de-orbit fluting excitedly about the culinary possibilities of pinch beetles and buzzworms, and a mismatched couple who seemed to be some kind of itinerant comedy act, a Kitonak and a Pho'pheahian whose canned banter had made Mace long for earplugs. Or hard vacuum. Even incurable deafness. The comedians must have been far down on their luck; Haruun Kal's capital city is a place lounge acts go to die.

Inside the customs office, enough flybuzz hummed to get the two Kubaz chuckling and eagerly nudging each other.

Mace didn't quite manage to ignore the Pho Ph'eahian broadly explaining to a bored-looking human that he'd just jumped in from Kashyyyk and boy were his legs tired. The agent seemed to find this about as tolerable as Mace did; he hurriedly passed the comedians along after the pair of Kubaz, and they all disappeared into the shower blockhouse.

Mace found a different customs agent: a Neimoidian female with pink-slitted eyes, cold-bloodedly sleepy in the heat. The Neimoidian looked over his identikit incuriously. "Corellian, hnh? Purpose of your visit?"

"Business."

She sighed tiredly. "You'll need a better answer than that. Corellia's no friend of the Confederacy."

"Which would be why I'm doing business *here*."

"Hnh. I scan you. Open your bag for inspection."

Mace thought about the "old-fashioned glow rod" stashed in his bag. He wasn't sure how convincing its shell would be to Neimoidian eyes, which can see deep into the infrared.

"I'd rather not."

"Do I care? Open it." She squinted dark pink up at him. "Hey, nice skinjob. You could almost pass for a Korun."

"Almost?"

"You're too tall. And they mostly have hair. And anyway, Korunnai are all Force freaks, yes? They have powers and stuff."

"I have powers."

"Yeah?"

"Sure." Mace hooked his thumbs behind his belt. "I have the power to make ten credits appear in your hand."

The Neimoidian looked thoughtful. "That's a pretty good power. Let's see it."

He passed his hand over the customs agent's desk, and let fall a coin he'd palmed from his belt's slit pocket. The Neimoidian had powers of her own: she made the coin disappear. "Not bad." She turned up her empty hand. "Let's see it again."

"Let's see my identikit validated and my bag passed."

The Neimoidian shrugged and complied, and Mace did his trick again. "Power like yours, you'll get along fine in Pelek Baw," the Neimoidian said. "Pleasure doing business with you. Be sure to take your PB tabs. And see me on your way offworld. Ask for Pule."

"I'll do that."

Toward the back of the customs office, a large poster advised everyone entering Pelek Baw to use the probiotic showers before leaving the spaceport. The showers replaced beneficial skin flora that had been killed by the surgical field. This advice was supported with gruesomely graphic holos of the wide variety of fungal infections awaiting unshowered travellers. A dispenser beneath the poster offered half-credit doses of tablets guaranteed to restore intestinal flora as well. Mace bought a few, took one, then stepped into the shower blockhouse.

The blockhouse had a smell all its own: a dark musky funk, rich and organic. The showers themselves were simple auto-nozzles spraying bacteria-rich nutrient mist; they lined the walls of a thirty-meter walk-thru. He stripped off his clothes and stuffed them into his kit bag. There was a conveyor strip for possessions beside the walk-thru entrance, but he held onto the bag. A few germs wouldn't do it any harm.

At the far end of the showers, he walked into a situation.

The dressing station was loud with turbine-driven airjet dryers. The two Kubaz and the comedy team, still naked, milled uncertainly in one corner. A large surly-looking human in sunbleached khakis and a military cap stood facing them, impressive arms folded across his equally impressive chest. He stared at the naked travellers with cold unspecific threat.

A smaller human in identical clothing rummaged through their bags, which were piled behind the large man's legs. The smaller man had a bag of his own, into which he dropped anything small and valuable. Both men had stun batons dangling from belt loops, and blasters secured in snap-flap holsters.

Mace nodded thoughtfully. The situation was clear enough. Based on who he was supposed to be, he should just ignore this. But, cover or not, he was still a Jedi.

The big one looked Mace over. Head to toe and back again. His stare had the open insolence that comes of being clothed and armed and facing someone who's naked and dripping wet. "Here's another. Smart guy carried his own bag."

The other rose and unlooped his stun baton. "Sure, smart guy. Let's have the bag. Inspection. Come on."

Mace went still. Pro-bi mist condensed to rivulets and trickled down his bare skin. "I can read your mind," he said darkly. "You only have three ideas, and all of them are wrong."

"Huh?"

Mace flipped up a thumb. "You think being armed and ruthless means you can do whatever you want." He folded his thumb and flipped up his forefinger. "You think nobody will stand up to you when they're naked." He folded that one again and flipped up the next. "And you think you're going to look inside my bag."

"Oh, he's a funny one." The smaller man spun his stun baton and stepped toward him. "He's not just smart, he's funny."

The big man moved to his flank. "Yeah, regular comedian."

"The comedians are over there." Mace inclined his head toward the Pho Ph'eahian and his Kitonak partner, naked and shivering in the corner. "See the difference?"

"Yeah?" The big man flexed big hands. "What are you supposed to be, then?"

"I'm a prophet." Mace lowered his voice as though sharing a secret. "I can see the future . . ."

"Sure you can." He set his stubble-smeared jaw and showed jagged yellow teeth. "What do you see?"

"You," Mace said. "Bleeding."

His expression might have been a smile if there had been the faintest hint of warmth in his eyes.

The big man suddenly looked less confident.

In this he can perhaps be excused; like all successful predators, he was interested only in victims. Certainly not in *opponents*. Which was the purpose of his particular racket, after all: Members of any sapient species that are culturally accustomed to wearing clothes will feel hesitant, uncertain, and vulnerable when they're caught naked. Especially humans. Any normal man will stop to put on his pants before he throws a punch.

Mace Windu, by contrast, looked like he might know of uncertainty and vulnerability by reputation, but had never met either of them face to face.

One hundred and eighty-eight centimeters of muscle and bone. Absolutely still. Absolutely relaxed. From his attitude, the pro-bi mist that trickled down his naked skin might have been carbon fiber-reinforced ceramic body armor.

"Do you have a move to make?" Mace said. "I'm in a hurry."

The big man's gaze twitched sideways, and he said, "Uh—?" and Mace felt a pressure in the Force over his left kidney and heard the sizzle of a triggered stun baton. He spun and caught the wrist of the smaller man with both hands, shoving the baton's sparking corona well clear with a twist that levered his face into the path of Mace's rising foot. The impact made a smack wet and meaty as the snap of bone. The big man bellowed and lunged and Mace stepped to one side and whipcracked the smaller man's arm to spin his slackening body. Mace caught the small man's head in the palm of one hand and shoved it crisply into the big man's nose.

The two men skidded in a tangle on the slippery damp floor and went down. The baton spat lightning as it skittered into a corner. The smaller man lay limp. The big man's eyes spurted tears and he sat on the floor, trying with both hands to massage his smashed nose into shape. Blood leaked through his fingers.

Mace stood over him. "Told you."

The big man didn't seem impressed. Mace shrugged. A prophet, it is said, receives no honor on his own world.

Mace dressed silently while the other travellers reclaimed their belongings. The big man made no attempt to stop them, or even to rise. Presently the smaller man stirred, moaned, and opened his eyes. As soon as they focused well enough to see Mace still in the dressing station, he cursed and clawed at his holster flap, struggling to free his blaster.

Mace looked at him.

The man decided his blaster was better off where it was.

"You don't know how much trouble you're in," he muttered sullenly as he settled back down on the floor, words blurred by his smashed mouth. He drew his knees up and wrapped his arms around them. "People who butch up with capital militia don't live long around—"

The big man interrupted him with a cuff on the back of his head. "Shut it."

"Capital militia?" Mace understood now. His face settled into a grim mask, and he finished buckling down his holster. "You're the police."

The Pho Ph'eahian mimed a pratfall. "You'd think they'd hire cops who aren't so *clumsy*, eh?"

"Oh, I dunno, Phootie," the Kitonak said in a characteristically slow, terminally relaxed voice. "They bounced *real* nice."

Both Kubaz whirred something about slippery floors, inappropriate footwear and unfortunate accidents.

The cops scowled.

Mace squatted in front of them. His right hand rested on the Power 5's butt. "It'd be a shame if somebody had a blaster malfunction," he said. "A slip, a fall—sure, it's embarrassing. It hurts. But you'll get over it in a day or two. If somebody's blaster accidentally went off when you fell—?" He shrugged. "How long will it take you to get over being dead?"

The smaller cop started to spit back something venomous. The larger one interrupted him with another cuff. "We scan you," he growled. "Just go."

Mace stood. "I remember when this was a nice town."

He shouldered his kit bag and walked out into the blazing tropical afternoon. He passed under a dented, rusty sign without looking up.

The sign said: WELCOME TO PELEK BAW.

Faces—

Hard faces. Cold faces. Hungry, or drunk. Hopeful. Calculating. Desperate.

Street faces.

Mace walked a pace behind and to the right of the Republic Intelligence station boss, keeping his right hand near the Merr-Sonn's butt. Late at night, the streets were still crowded. Haruun Kal had no moon; the streets were lit with spill from taverns and outdoor cafes. Lightpoles—tall hexagonal pillars of duracrete with glowstrips running up each face—stood every twenty meters along both sides of the street. Their pools of yellow glow bordered black shadow; to pass into one of the alleymouths was to be wiped from existence.

The Intel station boss was a bulky, red-cheeked woman about Mace's age. She ran the Highland Green Washeteria, a thriving laundry and public refresher station on the capitol's north side. She never stopped talking. Mace hadn't started listening.

The Force nudged him with threat in all directions: from the rumble of wheeled groundcars that careened at random through crowded streets to the fan of death sticks in a teenager's fist. Uniformed militia swaggered or strutted or sometimes just posed, puffed up with the fake-dangerous attitude of armed amateurs. Holster flaps open. Blaster rifles propped against hipbones. He saw plenty of weapons waved, saw people shoved, saw lots of intimidation and threatening looks and crude street-gang horseplay; he didn't see much actual keeping of the peace. When a burst of blaster-fire sang out a few blocks away, none of them even looked around.

But nearly all of them looked at Mace.

Militia faces: Human, or too close to call. Looking at Mace, seeing nothing but a Korun in offworld clothes, their eyes went dead cold. Blank. Measuring. After a while, hostile eyes all look alike.

Mace kept alert, and concentrated on projecting a powerful aura of Don't Mess With Me.

He would have felt safer in the jungle.

Street faces: drink-bloated moons of bust-outs mooching spare change. A Wookiee gone grey from nose to chest, exhaustedly straining against his harness as he pulled a two-wheeled taxicart, fending off street kids with one hand while the other held onto his money belt. Jungle prospector faces: fungus scars on their cheeks, weapons at their sides. Young faces: children, younger than Depa had been on the day she became his Padawan, offering their services to Mace at "special discounts" because they "liked his face."

Many of them were Korun.

A later entry in his journal records his thoughts verbatim:

Sure. Come to the city. Life's easy in the city.
No vine cats. No drillmites. No brassvines or death hollows. No shovelling grasser manure, no hauling

water, no tending akk pups. Plenty of money in the
city. All you have to do is sell this, or endure that. What
you're really selling: your youth. Your hope. Your future.

Anyone with sympathy for the Separatist Cause
should spend a few days in Pelek Baw. Find out what
the Confederacy is really fighting for.

It's good that Jedi do not indulge in hate.

The station boss's chatter somehow wandered onto the
subject of the Intel front she managed. The station boss's
name was Phloremirlla Tenk, "but call me Flor, sweetie.
Everybody does." Mace picked up the thread of her ramble.

"Hey, everybody needs a shower once in a while. Why
not get your clothes spiffed at the same time? So everybody
comes there. I get jups, kornos, you name it. I get militia
and Seppie brass—well, used to, till the pullback. I get
everybody. I got a pool. I got six different saunas. I got private showers—you can get water, alcohol, pro-bi, sonics,
you name it—maybe a recorder or two to really get the dirt
we need. Some of these militia officers, you'd be amazed
what they fall to talking about, alone in a steam room.
Know what I mean?"

She was the chattiest spy he'd ever met. When she eventually stopped for breath, Mace told her so.

"Yeah, funny, huh? How do you think I've survived this
game for twenty-three years? Talk as much as I do, it takes
people longer to notice you never really *say* anything."

Maybe she was nervous. Maybe she could smell the threat
that smoked in those streets. Some people think they can
hold danger at bay by pretending to be safe.

"I got thirty-seven employees. Only five are Intel. Everybody else just works there. Hah: I make twice the money off
the Washeteria than I draw after twenty-three years in the
service. Not that it's all that hard to do, if you know what I
mean. You know what an RS-17 makes? Pathetic. Pathetic.

What's a Jedi make these days? Do they even pay you? Not enough, I'll bet. They love that 'Service is it's own reward' junk, don't they? Especially when it's *other* people's service. I'll just bet."

She'd already assembled a team to take him upcountry. Six men with heavy weapons and an almost-new steamcrawler. "They look a little rough, but they're good boys, all of them. Freelancers, but solid. Years in the bush. Two of them are full-blood korno. Good with the natives, you know?"

For security reasons, she explained, she was taking him to meet them herself. "Sooner you're on your way, happier we'll both be. Right? Am I right? Taxis are hopeless this time of day. Mind the gutter cookie—that stuff'll chew right through your boots. Hey, *watch* it, creepo! Ever hear that peds have the right-of-way? Yeah? Well, *your* mother eats *Hutt* slime!" She stumped along the street, arms swinging. "Um, you know this Jedi of yours is wanted, right? You got a way to get her offworld?"

What Mace had was the *Halleck* on station in the Ventran system with twenty armed landers and a regiment of clone troopers. What he said was, "Yes."

A new round of blasterfire sang perhaps a block or two away, salted with staccato pops crisper than blaster hits. Flor instantly turned left and dodged away up the street.

"Whoops! *This* way—you want to keep clear of those little rumbles, you know? Might just be a food riot, but you never know. Those handclaps? Slugthrowers, or I'm a Dug. Could be action by some of these guerillas as your Jedi runs—lots of the kornos carry slugthrowers, and slugs *bounce*. Slugthrowers. I hate 'em. But they're easy to maintain. Day or two in the jungle and your blaster'll never fire again. A good slug rifle, keep 'em wiped and oiled, they last forever. The guerillas have pretty good luck with them, even though they take a *lot* of practice—slugs are ballistic, you know. You have to plot the trajectory in your head. Shee, gimme a blaster *any* time."

A new note joined the blasterfire: a deeper, throatier *thrummthrummmthrummthrumm*. Mace scowled over his shoulder. That was some kind of repeater: a T-21, or maybe a Merr-Sonn Thunderbolt.

Military hardware.

"It would be good," he said, "if we could get off the street."

While she assured him, "No, no, no, don't worry, these scuffles never add up to much," he tried to calculate how fast he could dig his lightsaber out of his kit bag.

The firing intensified. Voices joined in: shouts and screams. Anger and pain. It started to sound less like a riot, and more like a firefight.

Just beyond the corner ahead, whitehot bolts flared past along the right-of-way. More blasterfire zinged behind them. The firefight was overflowing, becoming a flood that might surround them at any second. Mace looked back: along this street he still could see only crowds and groundcars, but the militia were starting to take an interest: checking weapons, trotting toward alleys and cross streets. Flor said behind him, "See? Look at that. They're not even really *aiming* at anything. Now, we just nip across—"

She was interrupted by a splattering *thwop*. Mace had heard that sound too often: steam, superheated by a high-energy plasma bolt, exploding through living flesh. A deep-tissue blaster hit. He turned back to Flor and found her staggering in a drunken circle, painting the pavement with her blood. Where her left arm should have been was only a fist-sized mass of ragged tissue. Where the rest of her arm was, he couldn't see.

She said: "What? What?"

He dropped his kit bag and dove into the street. He rolled, coming up to slam her her hip-joint with his shoulder. The impact folded her over him; he lifted her, turned, and sprang back for the corner. Bright flares of blaster bolts bracketed invisible sizzles and fingersnaps of hypersonic slugs. He reached the meager cover of the corner and lay her flat on the sidewalk, tucked close against the wall.

"This isn't supposed to happen." Her life was flooding out the shattered stump of her shoulder. Even dying, she kept talking. A blurry murmur: "This isn't *happening*. It *can't* be happening. My—my *arm*—"

In the Force, Mace could feel her shredded brachial artery; with the Force, he reached inside her shoulder to pinch it shut. The flood trickled to sluggish welling.

"Take it easy." He propped her legs on his kit bag to help maintain blood pressure to her brain. "Try to stay calm. You can live through this."

Boots clattered on permacrete behind him: a militia squad sprinting toward them. "Help is on the way." He leaned closer. "I need the meetpoint and the recognition code for the team."

"What? What are you talking about?"

"Listen to me. Try to focus. Before you go into shock. Tell me where I can find the upcountry team, and the recognition code so we'll know each other."

"You don't—you don't understand—this isn't *happening*—"

"Yes. It is. *Focus*. Lives depend on you. I need the meetpoint and the code."

"But—but—you don't *understand*—"

The militia behind him clattered to a stop. *"You! Korno! Stand away from that woman!"*

He glanced back. Six of them. Firing stance. The lightpole at their backs haloed black shadow across their faces. Plasma-charred muzzles stared at him. "This woman is wounded. Badly. Without medical attention, she will die."

"You're no doctor," one said, and shot him.